DELICIOUS FOODS

DELICIOUS FOODS

A NOVEL

James Hannaham

Little, Brown and Company
New York Boston London

The characters and events in this book are fictitious. Any similarity to real persons, living or dead, is coincidental and not intended by the author.

Little, Brown and Company
Hachette Book Group
1290 Avenue of the Americas, New York NY 10104
littlebrown.com

First Edition: March 2015

Excerpt from "Love Won't Let Me Wait," words and music by Vinnie Barrett and Bobby Eli © 1974 (renewed) Warner-Tamerlane Publishing Corp. and Zella Music. All rights administered by Warner-Tamerlane Publishing Corp. All rights reserved. Used by permission of Alfred Music.

Excerpt from "In the Bush," words and music by Patrick Adams and Sandra Cooper copyright © 1978 Universal Music Corp., P.A.P. Music, a division of Patrick Adams Productions, Inc., and Keep On Music. All rights for P.A.P. Music, a division of Patrick Adams Productions, Inc., controlled and administered by Universal Music Corp. All rights reserved. Used by permission. Reprinted by permission of Hal Leonard Corporation.

Little, Brown and Company is a division of Hachette Book Group, Inc. The Little, Brown name and logo are trademarks of Hachette Book Group, Inc.

The publisher is not responsible for websites (or their content) that are not owned by the publisher.

The Hachette Speakers Bureau provides a wide range of authors for speaking events. To find out more, go to hachettespeakersbureau.com or call (866) 376-6591.

ISBN 978-0-316-28494-3
LCCN 2014955137

10 9 8 7 6 5 4 3 2 1

RRD-C

Book design by Sean Ford

Printed in the United States of America

For Kara and Clarinda

The worm don't see nothing pretty in the robin's song.

—Black proverb

CONTENTS

CONTENTS

PROLOGUE

LITTLE MUDDY

After escaping from the farm, Eddie drove through the night. Sometimes he thought he could feel his phantom fingers brushing against his thighs, but above the wrists he now had nothing. Dark stains covered the terry cloth wrapped around the ends of his wrists; his mother had stanched the bleeding with rubber cables. For the first hour or so, the divot-riddled road jostled the car, increasing the young man's agony, and he clenched his teeth through the sickening pain. Steering the vehicle with his forearms stuck in two of the wheel's holes, Eddie couldn't keep the Subaru from wobbling and swerving, and he feared the police would notice, pull him over to find that he had no license, and arrest him for stealing the car.

When he came to smooth asphalt, he turned right for no good reason, and after a few miles he saw a sign that proved what he and his mother had believed all along. Louisiana, he breathed. Almost six years in that place. To finally see evidence of his whereabouts momentarily eased his mind, but he had to keep going. He had only a faint memory of where the farm ended, and he couldn't tell if he'd driven himself closer to the center, where someone might capture or kill him, or away toward freedom.

The gas-pump symbol on the dash turned red around the time he saw signs for Ruston. The owner of the Subaru had left his wallet by the gearshift, and Eddie found $184 in it, which to his seventeen-year-old mind meant he could pay for gas to almost anywhere.

First he went to Houston to look for Mrs. Vernon, but to his surprise, the windows and doors of her bakery had wooden boards nailed over them. That such a responsible woman had either failed or fled implied nothing good about the fate of the neighborhood these past six years. The only other safe place he could think to go was his aunt Bethella's house. He slithered into an oversize sweatshirt to hide his injuries from her, but when he got to the door, he could tell that someone else lived at her address—all the patio furniture had changed, toys lay jumbled on the cushions, and a wooden sign next to the mailbox said THE MacKENZIES. Since it was too early to knock, he left, but at the curb he spoke with a neighbor who remembered her. She told him Bethella lived in St. Cloud, Minnesota. His aunt had told him that she might move, but not that she had gone so far. Hadn't she said that she would call with the address? Was that before the phone got cut off?

In the abstract, Eddie knew that Minnesota was far away, but he couldn't fathom the distance. The name St. Cloud sounded to him like heaven. His confusion only rose when a sleepy Texan trucker in a Stetson made getting there sound easy. You take 45 North till you hit 35, the dude said. Then just keep on 35. That there's the ramp to 45 just yonder.

To save money, Eddie stopped only at Tiger Marts or On the Gos to get gas and snacks and use the john. If he saw a police car in the lot, he kept going. If a truck-stop bathroom needed a key, he'd go someplace else. After he got his zipper down the first time, he couldn't pull it up. He thought of sleeping, but whenever he pulled into the corner of a parking lot and lay down in the back-seat, fiery twinges of pain snaked up his arms into his neck. When he asked for help squeezing the gas pump, strangers would knit their eyebrows together, shocked eyes asking, *This kid can drive without hands?* He'd say nothing but bristle and think, *I got here, didn't I?*

On the third morning, feeling safer after reaching Minnesota, the pain now a dull throb, he sat nursing a Coke in a diner off I-94, the Hungry Haven, a cozy place decorated in beauty board, with citrus remnants cooked onto the silverware. In the smok-ing section, a lone waitress sat facing away from the counter, her body slack as any customer's. An urgent story resounded on the TV behind her. Some rock star in Seattle had shot himself dead. She stared at the highway as if it were God. It took Eddie a while to get her attention, but once he did, she snapped to and hopped over, spine straight, pen behind her ear.

Do you mind, miss? Can't light it myself, he said, his request muffled by the cigarette he'd wrangled from its box and picked up with his mouth. He grinned and raised his elbows, meeting the woman's eyes with his own.

Oh! Of course, right, she said, her wide eyes failing to mask her surprise. She struck a match and he inhaled the fire through the cigarette. Gonna be a nice day, she announced, like some-thing profound. Let me know if you need anything else.

Her name tag said SANDY, pinned onto a dingy pink dress with a gray apron wrapped around it. Under her nasal tone something cared so strongly that Eddie moved sideways down the bench a little, crablike, to avoid the power of her interest, fearing that she might get to know him against his will. Sandy turned away.

Actually, I'm looking for work, Eddie blurted out to her back. He wasn't looking yet, really, but suddenly he needed her kindness, superficial or not, craved it beyond his ability to stay distant. Near here, he went on. He didn't think Bethella would let him sponge for long. If at all. She might not even care that he'd lost his hands—she'd probably blame his mother.

Sandy turned and the glow left her face. Hmm, she said. What kind?

Of work can I do? You'd be surprised. Fixing stuff. Computers. I also do carpentry, wiring, odd jobs.

Doubt spread across her face, and Eddie thought he could almost read her mind: *Now how can this boy do that in his condition?*

He sat up. I can do just about anything I set my mind to, he said, pouring brightness over her hesitation. God makes three requests of His children: Do the best you can, where you at, with what you got now.

That's beautiful, Sandy said. I bet your mama told you that.

Eddie smiled because he knew his mother would never have said such a thing—he'd picked up the saying from Mrs. Vernon—but then it occurred to him that Sandy would think the smile meant *Yes, Mama sure did.* Confirming that her fantasy of his life was the truth would make her more likely to help. After a brief chat, he told her his full name and she wrote it down on a wet napkin. He figured he'd never hear from her again.

It took Eddie a day and a half to find Bethella. He asked one of the few black pedestrians where he could find a beauty shop, adding that he meant to find his aunt. The pedestrian asked his aunt's name, which she didn't recognize, and then recommended he try Marquita's Beauty Palace on St. Germain. To get there, Eddie had to drive across the Mississippi River—he read the sign aloud as he crossed. It astounded him to think that this was the same river as the one near his hometown, Ovis, Louisiana, and that it flowed as far as he had just driven. Seeing the same river here helped him adjust. The Great River wasn't wide or grand in Minnesota, but it didn't fill him with the same panic as it had back home—it had less to do with death. The past didn't slither through this shallower water; he didn't imagine any drowned ghosts staring up from the riverbed or bobbing out of culverts, their googly eyes asking *Why?*

St. Cloud pacified him—its evenly spaced suburban homes reminded him of a balsa-wood city he'd seen in a children's book. Even its housing complexes sat comfortably beyond tall, healthy trees and sprawling plots of grass, and though a hundred Day-Glo toys might lie upturned on one driveway, the next several lots would have neatly arranged yards already flashing a few green shoots, while here and there a crocus forecast a pleasant spring. It felt more like home than Ovis, a place he hadn't seen in almost a decade.

Eddie circled the area for nearly half an hour without getting out of the car, suddenly embarrassed not to have hands after what he took to be Sandy's condescension. But eventually, thinking of how his mother needed him back in Louisiana, he parked at a beauty shop and nudged the door open with his shoulder, holding his arms behind his back with calculated ease. The women at Marquita's did not know Bethella, but they did know a different beauty shop, the Clip Joint, on the west side. That place had closed for the day by the time Eddie arrived, so, finally exhausted, no longer in the kind of pain that prohibits sleep, he moved the car into the corner of a deserted parking lot, contorted his body into the hatchback, and took a long nap until it got too cold to sleep and he had to turn the engine on, twisting the key in the ignition with his teeth.

When he visited the Clip Joint the next morning, he kept his wrists shoved into his pockets. It was best to keep them raised, but self-consciousness had overtaken him. A beautiful fat woman in a skintight black-and-leopard outfit said she knew his aunt and told him exactly where to find her. She then began a long one-sided conversation, first about how much she admired Bethella, then about the situation in Rwanda and several other subjects. He walked backward out of the shop and she continued to talk, turning her attention toward her coworkers instead.

Still wearing the sweatshirt, now for warmth as well as sub-terfuge, he arrived at the address the woman had given him and stood on the stoop for a moment, fearing he had the wrong infor-mation, then ascended the remaining steps and rang the doorbell. When he swung his forearms, the fabric concealed his wounds and flopped over his wrists in a congenial way, almost like the ears of a friendly dog. He thought that this awkward solution, along with the baggy pants, might make him look enough like a normal seventeen-year-old to fool his aunt for a while. He stuck his wrists back into his pockets.

Presently, he heard movement inside the house, perhaps someone's feet descending a carpeted staircase, then he saw a finger move a bunched-up taffeta curtain at the side of the door, exposing one of his aunt's eyes, which registered instant shock. Eddie heard a muffled squeal of delight, and the air moved as she threw open the door in one wide swing. Bethella was a slight woman with a skeptical eyebrow and a high forehead. Grayer now, in chalk-mark streaks, her thin hair stuck to her skull under a pantyhose cap—she hadn't yet put on today's wig. A homemade dress with tiny daisies hung on her like it would on a wire hanger, her collarbones poking up, her angular fingers tipped with frag-mented nail polish.

The second-to-last time he'd seen her, the Thanksgiving of his tenth year, Bethella had shown up at the Houston apartment he shared with his mother carrying a sweet potato pie encased in tin-foil. Before crossing the threshold, Bethella had told his mother, You've got one last chance to be honest with me, Darlene. Have you been using? When his mother shouted, No! Bethella hurled the pie sideways onto the stoop, where it broke and stuck. Then she did an about-face and marched across the pavement to her car.

In her vestibule, she hugged Eddie, and he noticed she had on the same light gardenia perfume she had worn then. The scent returned Eddie to the time when he was eleven and had briefly stayed with Bethella and her husband, Fremont Smalls, in Houston. They had taken him in one night when Darlene had used heavily and gotten stabbed by someone the adults kept calling *a friend* or *her friend,* but even then he wondered what kind of friend could stab someone bad enough to require a hospital stay. Between her reluctance to return him to Darlene and his mother's unpredictability, Bethella ended up keeping him for a week. But she didn't like children much, and after Eddie accidentally toppled a vase from Thailand—which hadn't even broken—she decided, as he figured it, to wait long enough that she would not have to admit any causality and then deliver him back to his mother once she got home from the hospital. Or as Bethella put it, She needs you. Fremont worked long hours, he wasn't home often enough to weigh in on the matter. Two days later, Bethella returned Eddie to his apartment at dusk and locked him in hastily, not wanting to interact with his mother, but as soon as Eddie entered, he realized that Darlene had gone again already. He knelt on the couch, pulled the blinds apart, and watched Bethella drive away.

Bethella now taught social studies and French in the St. Cloud school system, she told him. She and Fremont had moved north from Houston to be closer to his family, and he had worked at Melrose Quarry almost five years.

From what his mother often said about Bethella, he expected to find empties piled in the closets and the backs of cabinets, but he saw none. Darlene felt that Bethella had her nerve judging Darlene when she had her own habits, but like many families, everyone wandered around like children in a funhouse—they could hardly see one another around the corners, and what they could see was completely distorted.

The sweatshirt trick did not fool Bethella. Almost immediately after standing back from his stiff hug, she stared at his right sleeve, lunged forward like someone trying to catch a falling plate, and seized his forearm. As she unsheathed his arm, her face took on an expression mixing compassion with horror.

Good God Almighty, Edward. What on earth! When did this happen?

Eddie supposed that she'd asked *When* because it was easier to answer than *How*. A few days ago, he said.

Bethella said, Lord have mercy, almost whispering, her lids narrowed, jaw low. Lord have mercy.

Everybody black knows how to react to a tragedy. Just bring out a wheelbarrow full of the Same Old Anger, dump it all over the Usual Frustration, and water it with Somebody Oughtas, all of which Bethella did. Then quietly set some globs of Genuine Awe in a circle around the mixture, but don't call too much attention to that. Mention the Holy Spirit whenever possible. Bethella shook her head and spoke hazily of the Lord's Plan.

We have to get you to a doctor, she said. Who did this? Why? Where have you been?

Too many questions to answer at once, Eddie thought. It's okay now, he told her, which seemed to pacify her momentarily, but it didn't take long for her to peer at him, her skeptical eyebrow rising like a drawbridge.

Okay in what sense? she said.

I have to go back for my mom.

Bethella pulled her chin back and shouted, Oh, Darlene! as if his mother were standing there. I am guessing this isn't the first time, she said. What the Sam Hill has that lady gotten you into now, that someone did this to you? Come in already, boy, let me close the door. Hands! My God!

Mostly Bethella's house smelled of mold, with hints of stale candy, mothballs, and something earthy, maybe manure from the garden or chitterlings boiled last night. Dust had settled on the plastic-covered furniture. Nobody had sat on it in a long time. Eddie decided not to be the first and took a seat in the kitchen. Bethella walked over to the kitchen phone, announcing that she was calling her doctor, but Eddie begged her not to, insisting that he did not need help, that the wounds did not even hurt much anymore. It took some doing to convince her, but she eventually relaxed and offered him tea in a chipped mug, and, wanting to placate her more than he wanted the beverage, he accepted.

You sip it out of that straw, she said.

The hot liquid was weird and bitter, something herbal you couldn't improve even with sugar.

Maté, she explained. From South America.

Having summers off allowed Bethella to travel and bring back bizarre cultural things. Eddie sipped, asking himself why exotic stuff always had to be disgusting. Bitter vegetables, fish heads. Trying not to taste, he commented on the odd flavor of the drink, knowing at once that this type of discomfort would color his whole visit. So much for freedom.

Bethella wrinkled her nose and said, And you won't be smoking in my house.

They moved into the dining room and he sat. How long you think you'll need to stay? Bethella asked. She probably hadn't meant for it to sound impatient, but a consistent quality in her voice telegraphed impatience no matter her intentions. A long pause clouded the space between them.

Eddie didn't know how long he would stay, maybe only until somebody from the farm discovered where he'd gone, or until he figured out how to get Darlene back. But he couldn't face that. He winced at Bethella's ability to reject—it was as if she had brought him back to his drug-addict mother again. The pressure she put on him to explain and the memory of her previous rejection rising up a second time made him feel like someone had taken hold of his gut and twisted until it emptied out at both ends. He projected his agony through his face and let out a strange sound, a sigh blended with a growl, burnished with a whimper. Then he put his wrists in front of his face and curled into his own lap.

Bethella pulled her shoulders back slightly and remained silent for a while in the face of his animal response. She swallowed. Oh no, dear! she said. I meant how long do you *need* to stay before you go get your mother. I'm sorry. She patted his shoulder and stroked it. It's fine, everything's fine, she soothed. And though it wasn't—and might never be—the words painted over everything. I mean, I hope you're not expecting me to go with you. I'll help you to the amount that I can, but it's probably best if you don't bring her up here and—

Eddie scowled and his aunt closed her mouth. After a pause, she sighed and turned on the television, which she kept in the dining room for some reason. Afternoon-news trumpets blared.

Stay awhile, she said to the television. I understand. It's okay.

She lied, he figured, because the truth was always a tiger, and the past, with its ugliness and struggle, was a ditch so deep with bodies it could pass for a starless night.

After the news, she showed him to what she called the guest room—actually the attic—by pulling down the staircase from the ceiling with a rope and urging him up without going in herself.

A former student in need of sanctuary was my last guest, she told him. About a year ago. A few months before Fremont passed.

Eddie flinched.

Right, I guess you didn't hear that Fremont passed. She sighed. Since your mother dragged you off to God knows where.

Eddie shook his head and stared at her dumbly. I reckoned he was working, he said.

You know he had a bad heart. I mean a good heart, but it didn't work so well. Plus the hypertension. And hard as I tried, I could not get that man to eat right. It happened at work. Bethella paused, her eyes glistening. February seventeenth last year, she whispered.

He was a good man, Eddie managed to say as he turned to climb the stairs. He loved music.

Lit by a single bulb, a twin-size mattress, neatly dressed with striped bedclothes faintly burned by the old dryer, created a small oasis in the middle of a disorderly storage space. A pilly orange blanket lay on top. Gradually disintegrating piles of dusty jazz albums, carefully folded woolen blankets, a broken decades-old vacuum cleaner, and an antique fan clogged the periphery of the room. A long box that looked like an old suitcase caught Eddie's attention, but when he unsnapped its clasps, with some difficulty, to discover a shining brass trombone inside, nestled in red velveteen, the sight put him in mind of both Fremont and a body lying in a coffin and he flipped the case shut. Eddie stared around the dim room, doubtful that he could sleep well there. He pictured nights of watching for unpleasant signs in the inky crevice where the halves of the roof came together.

🗡

In less than an hour Bethella changed her mind and insisted that Eddie see a doctor. My doctor, she said, she's a Chinese, perhaps assuming that her nephew would not accept a white physician. Eddie wasn't immediately swayed, though, and Bethella gave him a lecture on the stubbornness of certain black men in the family, like his grandfather P. T. Randolph and his uncle Gunther. You're acting just like your granddad. He enjoyed sitting in his pain and just wallowing, she said. Well, Gunther's got all the time in the world to feel sorry for himself now in prison. All of you are smart enough to know exactly how the world screwed you, and the Man screwed you, and that there's no hope to change it. Your daddy wasn't like that. See, he was on the Hardison side. A fine man. He tried to change things!

Eddie shot a weary look at his aunt.

Oh, they got him, she continued proudly, but at least he died fighting. She scratched her biceps and continued. Fine. Be hardheaded. But I don't have any time for a young man who loses his phalanges and won't see a doctor. And you're going to tell me how this happened and who is responsible ASAP so help me God.

At first Eddie resented Bethella's involvement and resisted going to a doctor merely for the sake of resisting, but after a while he admitted the stupidity of his stubbornness, and weighing it against the possibility of gangrene, the workings of which Bethella explained to him in detail, he agreed to go. She offered to pay half or figure out how to put him on her insurance. I'll say you're my son, she promised. Quietly, he enjoyed that idea.

Dr. Fiona Hong had a clever face and an easy, staccato laugh. Her limbs seemed loose for someone in medicine, someone who had to jab folks with needles. Her swooping arms won Eddie over. It didn't bother him that she called him by his first name. When she unwrapped his bandages, she did not register very much shock, or even curiosity. Instead she seemed impressed, almost thrilled. Maybe doctors liked unusual cases.

We're going to need to get you to the OR, Eddie. Pretty much right now. Her bright, possibly nervous laugh sounded like a bark. You'll also need antibiotics and painkillers, she informed him. And we'll see each other again soon. Okay?

Several days and doctors later, as the two of them rode back to Bethella's house, his aunt's thin patience disappeared. Her head flicking toward him like a bird's, her eyes reddish and intent and halfway off the road, she said, You're not telling me what happened because you don't want me to know what your mother did. When are you planning to stop protecting her? Stop protecting her. What, did she do it herself?

Eddie did not agree with Bethella, but he knew better than to sass the most responsible member of the older generation, especially when he needed to sleep in her attic. If he argued, she would pull rank and stick to her version anyway. Mostly he wanted to make sure his aunt knew that Darlene was not to blame.

A few weeks after arriving in St. Cloud, Eddie started to pick up jobs here and there. He randomly encountered Sandy, the waitress from the Hungry Haven, at a drugstore and she told him that an overworked construction guy who didn't do concrete had heard about a divorcée in a Victorian outside Pierz who needed a whole pool patio and front walkway done. Pouring concrete didn't require much finesse, and the construction guy could handle anything Eddie couldn't. When Eddie met with him, the guy made the call while Eddie sat right there. People did favors for strangers here, Eddie noted, without exactly being friendly. Nevertheless, he felt like he had a reprieve. Bethella had mixed feelings about his decision to work. Sometimes she warned him to get a diploma, other times she openly wished for solitude, seeming to imply that he should get a steady job and get gone.

Eventually Bethella stopped tolerating Eddie's announcements about going to find Darlene. Your mother and I—she would begin, always neglecting to finish the thought. Then she'd say, Just don't. You have to have a bottom line.

Darlene had called the house, begging him to return, but it soon dawned on Eddie that she hadn't quit drugs. Their conversations splintered into anger and incoherence, and while brooding over their relationship in his workspace—aka Bethella's basement—one day, he admitted to himself that some problems—and some people—can never get fixed, even by a skilled handyman.

After that, Eddie might speak abstractly about going to rescue his mother, but he said very little to his aunt about the exploitation and injury he'd suffered at Delicious Foods. She never encouraged him to return for Darlene, and she never asked for details. The more time went by, the more ashamed he grew about taking Darlene's side, and the more he saw the sense in Bethella's dispassionate, rational decision to cut her off.

In the meantime, good luck at work made hedging easier for him. His one job grew other jobs, then an apprenticeship, and soon a regular business sprouted up around him. That September Eddie turned eighteen and moved from Bethella's to an apartment just down the street, so they could still look out for each other. Sometimes Eddie would go over to her house to watch her new favorite TV show, a sentimental series featuring a black woman angel. She would rub his shoulder blade and describe her pride in him, but he could still hear the undertones of her relief that he'd left. She might come over with a piled-up plate sometimes—no sweet potato pies, but juicy greens that made the breading flop off her overcooked fried chicken; mashed potatoes in a tinfoil pouch, soaking up its metallic taste; undercooked pig feet. He ate only enough to be polite. He never complained—he knew that good intentions always trumped bad soul food, and he grew as comfortable with the surrogate motherhood she provided as she did with the way that he partially filled the space left by Fremont's death.

In due time, Eddie learned to stick a pen in his mouth and write again, and once he gained some skill, he sketched out a device: Two short cups, each with a pair of pincers attached, a simpler model of a prosthetic hook he'd studied in a trade magazine. The carpenter to whom he'd become apprenticed helped him make a version out of wood—cheaper that way. Together they perfected it, a custom fit for the end of his right arm. They smoothed and finished it, covered it in a lightweight polymer, and when that one worked, they made another for his left, attached it to a harness with catgut strings, and looped it around his back.

Wearing the contraption felt as grand to him as putting on an expensive new suit. Eddie stretched his arms and elbows, testing out the potential for movement, for subtle inflections in each pincer, for a lifelike bend in the wrist. The prosthesis seemed to wipe out the past and stretch the future into infinity. Eddie began to hope ferociously. Perhaps he would go back south after all and get Darlene to leave Delicious whether she wanted to or not.

He spent eight months or so gaining dexterity. Mornings and late nights, he'd practice picking up grains of rice, turning doorknobs, spigots, and pages, holding utensils, raising glasses. As he grew more confident, he tried juggling two eggs, but after covering his kitchen table in goo, he switched to small rocks.

The range and subtlety of motion Eddie's invention offered him expanded his abilities well beyond what he'd hoped. Pouring concrete and tarring roofs no longer made up his entire work schedule. After being in St. Cloud for a year and a half, he returned to doing electrical wiring and repairing appliances, as he had done at the farm, though it took longer to overhaul a radio than before. He had trouble managing the tiny screwdrivers, the intricate circuitry. But soon.

To the clients he started attracting, Eddie became something of a curiosity. They would come in to watch him work in his garage, behind a house he now rented, and he would sit intently on his high wobbly stool, lit by a bright fluorescent desk lamp, amid oily file cabinets and plastic drawers full of washers, lug nuts, screws, nails, and grommets. They would stay sometimes until it seemed rude—fascinated, he assumed, by the fact that a physically disabled man could make a profession of such precise work, by the added hardship brought on by his color, and eventually by the minute detail he could accomplish using only the curved wooden hooks of his prosthetic hands.

Eddie knew that they viewed him as a novelty, but he didn't have the luxury of begrudging them their reactions. Instead he sought to translate the amazement in their faces into a stable income. If he could've pulled coins directly out of their mouths, he would have. He'd meet the men's sheepish gawking with technical conversation: These here wires—This darn microchip—Did you ever see a circuit board this—Your screen has blown out. Or if they showed no interest in the gadgets or home repairs he hunched over, he'd start with the weather. You could nearly always complain about the cold in Minnesota, and if you couldn't, you could marvel that for once it wasn't cold, or about the strange summer heat. You could then graduate to the Twins or the Vikings. Somebody who brought a child or a dog into his garage hardly had a choice about whether to become a regular customer; when the pressure to seem compassionate and good in Eddie's presence intersected with the cuteness of animals and children, the resulting atmosphere could probably have made a bedridden hermit throw a dance party. Only the kids ever asked about his condition, though, and, provided the adults didn't hush them, he'd speak frankly and jovially.

One day a red-haired girl asked, Hey, mister, how come you have claws?

I had an accident, he told her calmly, though at the same time he remembered every second—the blindfold made with a sweatshirt, the tension in his clenched teeth, the moment when he blacked out from the pain.

Her father stroked the nape of her neck. Don't bother the handyman when he's busy, Viv.

He's a handyman without hands, Viv observed.

Her father let out a loud, anxious laugh, Viv giggled, and Eddie turned away from his work for a moment to share their laughter. As the father laughed, Eddie wondered if the man would hold the comment against his child. But the tension ebbed, and Eddie leaned down until some flyaway strands of her hair tickled his nose.

You know, that's exactly right, Miss Wilson. I never thought of it in that way.

Her father made an apologetic mouth. She's darn plucky, my Vivian. I'm sorry, Mr. Hardison.

No need, Eddie said. That's a great saying. I'm gonna put that on my business card. He turned to the girl. How would you like that?

I guess that would be fine, Vivian said demurely.

Be careful, her father warned him. This one will want royalties down the line.

The following week, Eddie visited the printer and offset a run of small stiff cards emblazoned with his name and contact information, carrying the girl's description above it in red, curved like a rainbow over a landscape, with a river zigzagging through the center.

Handyman Without Hands

When he thought of the phrase, Eddie didn't mind that it reduced his troubles to a friendly, manageable quirk. The funny, contradictory label covered up all the loss and the pain and made it so that customers could approach him with a feeling of comfort and friendliness. People didn't recoil or start anymore when their eyes traveled to the ends of his wrists. He's the Handyman Without Hands, they'd say. How cool is that?

The *St. Cloud Times* wrote an article about him and his business; in the photo, he grinned, holding his prostheses up, a hammer balanced in the right one. The headline described him as a local John Henry—as if you could find that many John Henrys in Minnesota, he snickered to himself. Eddie saved twenty-five copies of the article, and though he gave most of them away, he hung one above his workspace inside a plastic sheath.

Soon a flood of customers sought out Eddie's services, people who had seen the article or the card or heard about him through friends and relatives. He welcomed the mild amusement spread across their creamy complexions, the nervous questions pumping through their blue veins. He preferred curiosity to derision, so he controlled his impatience because the discomfort came with a bag of gold attached. Some of the white folks brought items to him that they wouldn't otherwise have bothered to get fixed, just to meet Eddie Hardison, the Handyman Without Hands.

The superior quality of his work, however, brought a large percentage of the gawkers back with more serious issues—prewar homes begging for rewiring, bathtub reglazing, wood-paneling installation or removal, patio design and reconstruction. He saved for and bought a more up-to-date prosthesis—stainless steel this time—but he preferred the comfort and facility of the earlier model, wearing the newer one mostly for public appearances: socials at the Nu Way Missionary Baptist Church, business meetings, visits with friends.

Two and a half years after arriving in St. Cloud, Eddie opened a bona fide shop downtown, Hardison's, selling hardware, fixing appliances, organizing home repairs. When the florist next door went out of business, he expanded into that space. The shop thrived, and the novelty of the Handyman Without Hands wore off, but Eddie never removed the phrase from his business card.

Eddie didn't let his disability get in the way of an active life, and that attitude paid off in many ways. On an ice-skating outing to St. Paul, he met a paralegal named Ruth, four years his senior. Ruth was the only woman he'd met in Minnesota who remained unfazed by his missing hands, though she did prefer to remove or warm up his metal prosthesis with her cardigan before lovemaking. After eight months of dating, which Bethella considered too short a time, Ruth moved in with him and became his fiancée. They had a son out of wedlock whom they named Nathaniel. The boy seemed to inherit his father's tenacity and his grandfather's charisma.

Eddie presumed that by drafting and adhering to such an average blueprint for a life, he could overcome his misfortunes and shake off all the agonizing memories of Delicious Foods, but they never left him, nor did the urge to return to Louisiana and set things right disappear completely. Sometimes he snapped awake in the earliest-morning hours, convinced that he was back at the farm. Shrouded in pitch-black, the memories would return, alighting on his bed like dark birds poised to attack him. Inevitably, they seemed to say, someone will reveal everything that happened on that farm, and you will have to go back.

———

1.

BRAINDANCING

azy? That fool done zipped off in his black sedan and the tail-lights getting all mixed up with the traffic signs, and Darlene thought hard 'bout that word. Out all the stuff a motherfucker could say, not realizing he had spoke to somebody who gone to college. You could use other words for her activity at that moment, maybe some of em not so nice, but *lazy?* She had to laugh behind that, hard as she out there working for a couple ducats. The nerve of this man! He ain't know her life. She had a son to feed, eleven years old, had to get out there walking in some bad shoes, humidity frizzing the heck outta her perm. This whole damn June, sun been beating down so hot the roads be looking blurry up ahead, all kinda mirages happening up the highway. Look like a truckload of mercury done had a accident.

Seem to Darlene that everything she strove for turned out as a hot mirage. Probably folks oughta blame that on the dude in the sedan or that dumbass self-help book she read; can't nobody pin what happened to Darlene on me. Can't nobody make you love em, make you look for em all the time. Maybe I attract a certain kinda person. Folks always saying that I do. Doctors talking now 'bout how people brain chemistry make some of em fall in love harder with codependent types. But I feel a obligation to Darlene. Out all my friends—and, baby, I got *millions*—she make me wonder the most if I done right by her. Sometimes I think to myself that maybe she shouldna met me. But then again, can't nobody else tell her side of things but Yours Truly, Scotty. I'm the only one who stuck by her the whole time.

Nine months out on the street and she still had a meek little attitude 'bout doin' the do, you know? She ain't had the look down at all. My girl had on flats and a skirt that went below the knee—no lie! Instead of going down to the edge of the road to look in them cars, she be hanging back, almost in the hedges or whatever, hoping some car gonna slow down and stop. She reckoned she get in and get cool in the vehicle. Solve two problem at one time.

Across that double yellow line over at Hinman's Aquatic World, it was some giant Plexiglas pools resting on they sides, looking like God's bedpans. The owners had just turnt on them plastic palm trees with the lights all in em. Pickup trucks parked at steak houses, broken neon trim blinking on the wall of the porno store. Forlorn-ass Mexican folks be chilling at the bus stop.

Texas was stupid, I'm sorry. Fat sunburned gluttons and tacky mansions everyplace, glitzy cars that be the size of a pachyderm, a thrift store and a pawnshop for every five motherfuckers. Fucking limestone! Whole state and everything up in that bitch made of limestone. Damn strip malls look like they done come right up out the ground. *Upon this rock, I shall build my strip mall.* It's like they ain't heard of no other rock. Granite salesmen getting jealous. In summer, Texas too hot for 99 percent of life-forms;

in the two-month winter, ain't none of them houses insulated, so you gotta rub your legs together under your blanket like you a grasshopper, rub so hard you about to set your own ass on fire.

Then some crew-cut ofay she hoping gonna be a trick—so she could score and we could hang out—he just slowed down and stuck his neck out the passenger side and went, Lazy.

Lazy! Darlene took a few steps back—the flats made me feel for her since the first time I met her. (She said from the get-go she couldn't wear a certain kind of pumps but wouldn't say why, and it wasn't till I penetrated the inner sanctum of her brain later on that I found out the truth.) She made a note to remember that guy and his li'l rabbit face. 'Cause when they said *lazy* they also meant *nigger*. Hardy-fucking-har-har. And lazy working on who behalf? Hustling this hard at the Peckerwood National Savings Bank, she'd be the damn manager. *Hell,* Darlene thought, *I'd be the CEO. It'd be an easier job too. In that air-conditioning? I have put this paper in this folder. Now I will return that pen to its holder. Done. I am leaving for the day. Hey, Mrs. Secretary! Where did you put my golf clubs?*

A pothole by the white line tripped her, and my girl be wobbling. She twisted a tendon and almost dropped her handbag. My sweetheart thought bending over would be vulgar, even though she had on that long-ass skirt. She still ain't knowed thing one about marketing herself. She squatted, and she saw that highway marker sparkling down there, and that took her mind off the rabbit-face man and sent it rushing back to her usual thoughts, thoughts about how to spend more time with me.

I wanna rock with you, she sang without thinking 'bout it. The day start going dark orange, and some shadows starts to cut through the trees like they broken bottles. The past kept dogging her, like she could always hear its clunky old motor idling outside whatever else be in her thoughts. The sound of her dead husband whistling would get super-loud up in her head, and if *I* couldn't stand that noise, you know it made her stone crazy. Darlene would double the fuck over—this time she bent down and put her hands over her ears like the sound coming from outside her head.

Once that particular bad feeling passed, she got up and turnt to face traffic, thinking 'bout a happy person. The book said that to get good experiences and money in your life, you had to think positive thoughts and visualize shit. So she imagined some dude thumbing a fan of twenties into her hand. Held out her palm to take some imaginary cash—I almost busted out laughing. But instead of fat-money johns down this road, it's only some soccer moms going by and frowning behind the wheel of they minivans. They kids heads be swiveling with they mouths open and closing, pointing they little chocolaty fingers at her like, Mommy, what she doing?

Next thing you know the Isley Brothers singing *Who's that lady?* in her head. *Real fine lady.* At that time, Darlene truly was fine—that girl coulda stopped more traffic than just some tawdry johns if she'd a wore some tight miniskirts and high heels. I kept telling her that shit all the time.

Now where in the hell she had walked to? Halfway to Beaumont, seemed. Nobody else out there hooking, else they had better luck. Crickets getting louder, dog barks be coming from way the hell and gone, headlights whizzing by all silver and black, like low-flying spaceships—could be anybody in there. Aliens. ET and shit. Chewbacca smoking dope with ALF.

Darlene start shuffling backward, staring into them headlights, till she got near to the end of the commercial strip of whatever the hell city she in. Out there, wasn't no more traffic lights—edge of the world. After that, just flat dark. Brushy dirt, short trees, and squinty little stars—wait—was that the fucked-up carcass of a crow? Nope, just a busted tire tread in the damn emergency lane.

The sun finally gave up and turnt its back on the dusk. Fuck you, went the sun. Fuck all y'all, you skanky freaks don't deserve no sunlight. Find another star.

Outside the parking lot of a closed-down BBQ restaurant, somebody headlights drove up like glowing monster eyeballs, blasting in Darlene face and—*hallelujah!*—the car slowed down. Old cheapo car, VW Rabbit something. Darlene couldn't see in, but somebody could see out, so the car slow to a halt in the gravel. In there, it's some round-faced man, 'bout fifty, leaning cross a lap, cranking down that window. Light brother with a short 'fro, wine-tinted Coke-bottle glasses, rough skin. Had a cigarette stuck in his left hand, his round-ass belly up against the steering wheel. The lap in the passenger seat belong to a skinny teenage boy in a short-sleeve shirt. Kid had skin light as the man's, pretty lips, ears out to here, the picture of a scared-ass virgin. Even a rookie could figure out that setup.

Tobacco smoke poofed out in Darlene face so she pulled back like somebody done threw a snake at her, even though she a hard-core smoker herself. I thought Darlene coulda made a living as a singer; she moved like a dainty princess, like one of them bougie Marilyn McCoo, Lola Falana types. On the AM radio in the car, she heard DeBarge doing "Rhythm of the Night." So she's like, *Good, they're middle class, they have some money.*

The man leant across the boy and went, What you doing out here all alone, honey?

Get cool, get paid, get some rocks, go home. Darlene heard them phrases in her head, and I thought they had a nice rhythm to em, so I asked her to say em out loud and she did.

The father went, Say what? Go home? Aw right, then. He spun the window roller once but Darlene stuck her fingers on the top of the glass, so he stopped. The shit we do for love. The love we do for drugs.

The boy went, She meant *her*, Dad. I think.

We noticed a car key chain made of braided plastic swinging off the steering column, and the shadows of the braids was forming a pattern like a swastika. That got us both to thinking about what the book had said.

What about the Jews? Darlene thought, and also said. What about the Jews? They couldn't have brought the Holocaust on themselves, right?

The kid went, Excuse me?

The Jews! You know. She pointed at the key chain. Chosen People?

Jews? the kid says.

Yes, because if you're an antenna—

The kid went, Ma'am, you okay?

With your good thoughts, I mean—

The father shut the engine, took his glasses off, rubbed his eyes, put the glasses back on. He scratched his 'fro and went, How much it's gonna be?

The grid on the kid's shirt made Darlene remember a tablecloth from her childhood. People who know me well always be making interesting leaps and turns inside they head. I call it braindancing. Me and Darlene was doing the hustle right about then. You could hear the flutes from that Van McCoy jam going *doot-doot-doot...do the hustle!*

She poked the boy chest and he bent his torso away like the curve on a banana. Let's put the basket of fried chicken right here, Darlene said, figuring a li'l joke might break the ice. They ain't get it, so she poked him again, closer to his belly button. And the potato salad goes here, she said. I busted out laughing and so did Darlene, but she scratched up her lungs and that made her cough and spit.

Dad—

The afro father twisted his face, getting uptight, squirming in his seat. He tugged a chunky wallet out his pants and peeled off two twenties, so Darlene says to me, See, the book is right. I thought a good thought, and here go the twenties I dreamed up.

Nice trick, I said.

The man went, Okay, here go my fried chicken. That's my fried chicken right there. What you do for forty?

Her eyebrows rose.

Dad. She's—

The father yelling and muttering at the same time. You can just shut the fuck up. You gon prove to me you not like that. To-night. Punk cousin done turned you.

The son closed his eyes and twisted away from the father. No, Dad. It wasn't what you—The son gulped down a sigh and stroked the car-door handle like he probably do his dick in private, then punched it in a half-assed kinda way. His Adam's apple shot down his neck and then right back up.

The father chucked them bills in the kid lap, but the kid ain't budged, so in the pause, my girl picked up the Jackson twins, all gentle, like they was babies. She folded em together, thinking, *My ticket to the morning light.* Now we both got excited. Forty clams not much, but it did mean we was gonna be spending a whole bunch of time together in the very near future. We was like, *Love, soft as an easy chair, love, fresh as the morning air.* Darlene wondered if we could just book right then so she wouldna had to do nothing else; she had too much pride in her heart for this line of work, and I kept telling her, Yeah, fine, do what you want. I don't judge nobody.

The father broke the silence and went, Get out the car, go in them bushes, get laid. He stuck out his lower lip. Bitch got my money now!

The kid put his hand on the door and went, You mean your fried chicken.

Darlene smiled more than her usual amount, 'cause she still thinking 'bout the forty dollars and had forgot that they could see her.

The son kept staring and his face gone all tight. Dad, this isn't Christian, Dad. I want my first time to be special. You said you wanted me to wait for marriage!

The father ashed in the tray, said, Don't give me that first-time bullshit. You done some damn unholy shit already. You think I don't know? You think I'm stupid something?

The kid turnt his shoulders and leant into the father space, tryna keep his words private. Ugh, he growled. She's *really* out of it. What was that crazy stuff she said about the Holocaust?

Darlene shoved the Jackson twins deep in her bag to hide them shits from robbers, under a change purse she found on a barroom floor, a scratched pair of sunglasses, and a bunch of open lipsticks—she ain't know, but one of em had got extended and be smearing her possessions with all kind of red smudges. I knew 'cause my ass was in the damn purse, a couple tiny rocks in a glass vial that she thought she had lost.

Two months ago, on Easter Sunday, some guy who called hisself a coon-ass car salesman paid her to watch him fuck a watermelon. No lie. Set that melon on his card table, knifed hisself a round hole in it, and made her egg him on while he sliding his dick in and out that little globe.

He says to her, It turn me on to got somebody watching. I like the shame.

She couldn't think what to say. Screw that round thing! Mmh! Juice it, boy!

The fruit start weeping pink water out the hole. His hairy butt went *umph* and he came inside that melon.

When he pulled out, he grinned and said, Hope it don't get knocked up, 'cause I don't want no green chirren!

Even remembering that shit, we couldn't stop laughing. Don't want no green chirren! Like they gon be little watermelons with legs. I tell you, though, Mr. Melonfucker had him some green money. Darlene spent most of it on me in a day.

Somebody as inside herself as Darlene right then, without no natural talent for hooking, could watch some melonfuckers on the regular, though. Not bad, not like some of them other johns. Melons had it all over cigarette burns, getting stabbed, leather belts across the back, and a curtain rod up the ass, all of which she had either had or come close to having. For a while, Darlene had this gentle, fresh attitude that made motherfuckers want to kick her in the tits, like a girl in one them Z movies.

Out in the street, she always thinking 'bout Somebody Might Kill Me. She got so obsessed with dying that she ain't take no kinda precautions 'gainst it. To Darlene, copping ain't never meant risking her life—'cause not copping felt like dying anyhow, and she ain't lost that game yet. And if she did lose—well, hell, she wouldn't know. Her idea of heaven was that the two of us could kick it together 27-9, like we would say—that's twenty-seven hours a day, nine days a week—without nobody judging our relationship. Without none of the issues you get from having a body. Y'all think a body be who you is, but it ain't nothing but a motherfucking sack of meat.

Darlene start inching away, thinking 'bout making a run for it—to where, she ain't had no idea—and the father shout at her to stay put, but she ain't heard him right.

Another thought that we had sewed together in her mind right then like a thrift-store quilt spilled out her mouth without her re-alizing. Who does a watermelon...laugh at...when you kill it?

Dad, I can't do this. I can't do this!

Then get my motherfucking money back.

What? You're kidding. Dad?

A ambulance screamed by, honking a high note, then a low note, and that took they attention. They waited like criminals for the sound to die down, for normal cars to whiz over the asphalt again, so they could get calm enough to ignore the background noise, and Darlene took a couple tiny steps away from them two before some regular noises crept back in. The kid moved his eyes to his father head, then to Darlene face, and swiveled again.

First he asked politely. He go, Ma'am?, and opened the car door.

The word *ma'am* itself made her back up faster, like a curse reminding her who she shoulda been, so she turnt and start to book behind the dusty front entrance to the BBQ, thinking the Jackson twins was hers now and she ain't had to do nothing to the kid. A plastic cowboy on a red bucking bronco be dangling off the roof. Broken furniture sitting behind that greasy windowpane, and a For Lease sign be hanging by one corner inside the damn window.

The father shoved the son 'gainst the door and went, Sammatawitchu, nigger! Git that money back!

Ow, my elbow!

Darlene ran, but it was a fence back there and she couldn't jump that shit. The fence too high and she too high and a razor wire be swizzling round the top of the fence. She heard the car door slam and feet slap the asphalt behind her and the next thing she know, the sonofabitch had her wrists behind her back. He got some kinda sharp, athletic thing zapping through his fingers like a depth charge. Youth buzzing in his veins, all gruff and rowdy and shit. She bucked around and thrust her legs back, tryna find his nuts with her heel, but she kept kicking her bag on accident. She ain't had his kind of strength.

Some vagrant brother be lying by the dumpster without no shoes on, showing off his rough-ass swollen feet. One of em had a open sore that's all meaty, attracting flies. Darlene yelling murder and rape, but the bum just lift his head and ain't react no further. The young man hand had came down over her mouth and it tasted soapy—cleaner than some of Darlene recent meals. So she licking the webs between his fingers to get him to let go her face, but he just clamped onto her jaw more tighter.

The bum lift his head and put it down again. A bottle of Old Crow be his pillow and his pacifier. The kid let go her mouth and figured out how to cram his hand into the bag and rifle through without letting her go. Once he had got the money, the bag fell off her arm and he pushed her forward. She twisted her ankle and fell on her face 'gainst the curb by the dumpster and she could feel her nose and lip and face had swole up already. A police car slowed down fifty yards away on the main road. One cop checked the scene from the passenger side, but they ain't stop, probably because the father said everything cool. Darlene spat out two teeth and felt a third so loose it come out when she touched it with her tongue. She rolled that puppy round in her mouth.

I guess that made Darlene go more nuts. She not vain, but she had to keep her looks to get business. I made sure she knew at least *that*. She picked up them teeth, stuck em in her skirt pocket, and tore after the kid—leapt on his back right as his hand touched the door handle and tried to throttle the motherfucker, using his shirt collar to get control. Man, she wanted that forty dollars something bad. But some powerful surprise demon leapt up out the kid too, and he threw her off and slammed her in the cheek. Darlene head snapped back, then she stumbled and doubled over. Dull, heavy pain spread out from her nose into her skull. She couldn't turn her neck without no more pain and she tasted iron and salt, touched her lip and held out her hand to see some cherry-red fingertips, and all her love lines and heart lines and fate lines be wet with blood. The car wheels was skipping around in the gravel, then the car turnt onto the road and got smaller in the distance till you couldn't see it no more. The dust be mixing with the gritty metal taste in her mouth and she spat the blood and the grit on the dirt. Her gums was throbbing real bad.

Forty dollars...Shit, Darlene, I said. We coulda been done for at least one motherfucking day. Much as I loved Darlene, I couldn't hide my disappointment. I could get sorta angry sometimes. I ain't proud of it. But she had that thing where she crumbled under pressure. So I threw a fit. I lost it, I was hollering and cussing and accusing her of being unfaithful to me. Then I guess I made it clear that I wouldn't let her go home until she could get some money so we could go braindancing together 27-9.

She looked at me with her cheeks deflated. Who's going to pick up my sorry behind now, she asked, with my face broken, three missing teeth, and no shoes? I can't do this anymore. This is horrible. I give up.

Goddamn it! I shouted. Maybe Crew Cut's right! Maybe you *is* lazy, you fucking—! I made myself hoarse yelling inside her head. I called her a bazillion nasty insults I can't even repeat here. I went, You don't really want to be with me! You don't love me! I cried—she made me weep.

Scotty! she screamed. Please, stop! Just tell me how can I get the money now. Scotty! I *do* love you, and I will do anything for you.

I pointed her face at the road. Get out there! I said. Ain't nothing shameful 'bout trying to survive, bitch. Don't you know the street always got a answer?

And of course I was right.

2.

BLACKBIRDS

Eddie got used to being home alone after nine o'clock, when his mother went to parties, or so she said. *Every night a party?* he thought at first. Sometimes she'd go meet a friend and return in twenty minutes. During the day in the schoolyard, he fought other fifth-graders who called his mother names, not convinced that they had any evidence, but at night the names reverberated in his head. *Your mother is your mother,* he would tell himself, *and you have to forgive, no matter what people say, no matter if she did any of what they say she did.*

In the mornings he'd sometimes find her facedown on the couch in last night's outfit, one leg drooping above the carpet, a crust of spit caking the throw pillow under her snoring mouth. She would have left the television on, and he'd hear people talking for a long time about some guy named Dow Jones who had fallen down a lot. His mother's dress would have crept up to expose the crease where her thigh met her butt. No one else lived in the apartment, and to discover his mother's rump displayed so crudely moments after he had woken up with an erection always produced a confused sensation in his head. To silence the feeling, he'd find a sheet, draw it over her body, and kiss her cheek gently, attempting not to rouse her. It occurred to him that he was doing her job, but he didn't notice the cloud of resentment forming in his love for her, his hostility growing darker. I'm the son, he whispered to himself. The son can't take care of the mother.

Other nights she didn't come home at all, and instead her keys jangled in the lock at dawn, startling him into alertness. The front door would bang open against the drywall, followed by the twin thuds of her handbag on the carpet and her body on the squeaky couch. He would close his bedroom door so as not to disturb her. Quiet morning sounds from the outside would smooth everything over. Cheeping birds, car engines, a rooster someone kept, perhaps illegally, in a backyard, somewhere in the complex of dusty two-level brick buildings from the early 1970s. Through his mother's arrival he'd attempt sleep—though after struggling into slumber he'd always doze more comfortably for another hour or two before getting up for school, knowing Darlene had again escaped the nameless dangers of the night world.

One Tuesday morning in June, on one of the last days of fifth grade, as he lay between unconscious dreams and waking fantasies, he pictured a time years earlier, when they had lived in Ovis with his father, before coming to Houston. (*We're moving to be nearer to Aunt Bethella*, his mother had said, but even at nine years old, he suspected she had ulterior motives.) Before the move, they'd had a blond-brick ranch house with a backyard—a real yard—a limitless rectangle of parched crabgrass that grew larger and greener in his imagination the further time ran away with it. In the evenings, crowds of grackles would settle in a live oak in the corner by the chain-link fence. Their black iridescent feathers had a natural elegance, and the birds peered at him with mocking intelligence, like well-dressed rich folks encountering a vagrant on a red carpet. They didn't want *some* of his food, it seemed, they meant to cheat him out of *all* of it. Their raspy noises sounded more like broken radios than birdcalls, and to make their cries they widened their beaks and puffed their feathers with so much force that it looked like they might explode. The way they strutted and sneered, Eddie decided that these birds had inside them the souls of angry black people from the olden days, ghosts come back to settle some ageless vendetta.

His father, Nat Hardison, who could now qualify as such an outraged spirit, had lived in that house with them, but Eddie, who turned six the month after his father died, couldn't summon many clear memories of him—a bedtime story about a whale, the green marbled tackle box they took on a fishing trip, the scent of Old Spice aftershave. His mother kept a photo of Dad in his air force uniform on a shelf by her bed, facing away so that she wouldn't see it while lying down. The sun had turned the picture mauve, but from that pinkish dreamworld, his dad glowed back, displaying his L-square jaw and high cheekbones, showing his teeth as he smiled.

Eddie remembered chasing the grackles in the old backyard, maybe because their menacing weirdness barged in on his need for order. In his fantasy, Eddie knew that if he could only clear all the birds from the backyard, his father would return—not the stiff, fading image, but the real, lanky man whose crossed leg he would ride like a horse into that unhad future. He found a horseshoe embedded in the grass and tossed it at the fence. As the iron clattered against the chain link, black wings fluttered everywhere around him; piercing cries rang out across the neighborhood. The sense of his father's presence came on so powerfully that it woke him.

Daddy? he said.

Then came the realization that he was alone in Houston, a thought that ripened into terror.

Ma?

He did not find her on the sofa, or anywhere else. He searched for evidence that she'd come in and left, but he didn't see the bag, the shoes, not even the clothes she would sometimes hang on doorknobs or abandon near the bed, clothes he would later fold and put away, arrange neatly in the hamper, or leave on the bed for her as the photo of his father watched, he hoped, approvingly.

When the school day was about to start and his mother hadn't appeared, Eddie left early and ran to Mrs. Vernon's bakery to tell her that his mother had vanished. Mrs. Vernon, solid in as many ways as one could think of, owned her home and ran the shop practically by herself. The bakery sold staples like loaves and rolls but also red velvet layer cakes, cookies, and coconut towers for weddings. The smells lured kids, made her place their first stop at the strip mall, even before the video-game arcade. Mrs. Vernon could always tell who had big problems in their lives. The neighbors called it a gift, but everybody had issues; Mrs. Vernon just happened to ask the right questions and didn't mind getting involved. To a certain extent.

Once she understood Eddie's troubles, Mrs. Vernon immediately called the police. He watched the hands on the big clock above the glass display cases inch closer to the start of school while Mrs. Vernon remained on hold, the receiver wedged between her cheek and shoulder, pulling the looped cord taut. Eddie admired Mrs. Vernon's levelheaded attitude as she sold beignets and translucent coffee even while attending to his predicament. He entertained the fantasy that she would adopt him if Ma never got back. But this thought came too close to wishing his mother dead and he felt guilty for it. Instead of coveting Mrs. Vernon's motherly ways, he occupied himself by pretending he had his choice of the different cookies in the display—green pistachio leaves, pink and brown checkerboards, squares buried in chocolate. He breathed in their almondy aroma.

I'd like to report a missing person, Mrs. Vernon said. Name Darlene Hardison. She started to spell his mother's name and stopped short. Oh, you do, do you? Mm-hmm. Another pause. It don't matter about what she do, sir. It's that she got a young son waiting on her, and he right here. Her voice brightened. Really, now? Would you mind checking your records?

Keeping the phone wedged against her ear, Mrs. Vernon gave someone change, paid full attention to customers for several minutes. A few times she made eye contact with Eddie and raised her eyebrows to say they still had her on hold. Then she said, dejectedly, into the phone, So she's not down there, huh? She cupped her hand over the mouthpiece and addressed Eddie. When the last time you saw her?

Last night, he said, around nine thirty.

Half past nine last night, Mrs. Vernon repeated to the cop on the phone, and froze her face into a pout during a long pause. Friday morning sound like a long time, Officer. Don't you think—no, I suppose you don't. At the end of the call, she sighed and said, Thank you for your help, and Eddie could tell she meant *Thanks for nothing.* He forced his tears back up into his head. Mrs. Vernon gave him a slice of cake in a Tupperware box to save for lunch but it only made him feel better enough to relax his face. The best possible cake couldn't help.

Even one day to wait for your missing mother is forever. Eddie told a bad friend at school about his mother and the kid said, Every second you don't do nothing, somebody could be killing her and you're not preventing the killing of her! During recess a kid called Doody but really named Heath tried to cheat at finger football and Eddie stomped on his foot so hard Doody wept and said that Eddie had broken it even though he could walk fine after five minutes. No teacher witnessed this; no authority heard about it later.

Eddie looked for his mother on the humid, sweaty journey home. When he got back to the apartment, he kept thinking she would call if she could get to a phone. As he searched the rooms, he found that she had left a favorite blouse with gold threads sewn into the piping. His feverish inventory of everything she had not taken proved that she had not meant to disappear, to leave behind the possessions she cherished or anything else she loved. Who had kidnapped her?

Hours passed; the house remained silent. The street seemed quieter than usual, as if everybody knew that Darlene Hardison had gone missing and, worse, that they had hidden themselves to avoid caring. To drown the silence of the phone, Eddie turned up the television. Mrs. Vernon dropped by to see if his mother had shown up, and Eddie said she hadn't. In Mrs. Vernon's voice he waited to hear something tell him that he could spend the night with her, but that never came, only a complaint about her own full house and a promise to check in on him tomorrow.

Now, if this go on much longer, I'ma have to call protective services, Mrs. Vernon warned the next day when he visited just before the bakery closed because she hadn't checked in the whole day.

No, Eddie whined. I can take care of myself. Plus my aunt Bethella lives across town if I need her. I've stayed with her before, he told Mrs. Vernon, though he thought at the same time that it would be impossible to contact Bethella. He knew that his mother and his aunt hated each other, and he felt that his aunt hated him because of his mother. No, he could never ask her help again. But maybe he could go it alone. I'm almost twelve, he said.

And you think you grown. Hmm.

I am the man of the house, he said, shoving his hands into his pockets, trying to sound logical and wear a serious, old expression.

I suppose you right about that, sir, Mrs. Vernon said soberly, forcing him, as rapidly as someone dropped into cold water feels a chill, to remember what made that a bad thing. He scuttled out of the store before she could see the shame take over his face or hear him cry.

At 9:30 that night, shortly after the time Darlene would normally leave, he turned off the lights and appliances, slipped out the front door, and locked it behind him. He walked downstairs into the parking lot of the complex, concerned that someone would see him and figure out what had happened or judge Darlene a bad mother for letting him stay out late. Car headlights suddenly shone on him, so dazzling he couldn't see the vehicle behind them. The beams seemed to expose his aloneness and helplessness, sensations he couldn't release even after scampering to the sidewalk and making his way to the strip.

He had been driven down parts of the long commercial avenue many times, sometimes when the school bus took a wrong turn or a detour, but rarely at night. Seeing it in this new way filled him with dread. A few sections, mainly the strip malls nearer the highway, supported restaurants and movie theaters. There were no sidewalks. In Texas, having a vehicle meant having a life—if you walked on the shoulder, everybody could see that you'd failed in some way. That you couldn't afford a vehicle, that your car had broken down and you couldn't pay for a cab, that you had no friends to call. Maybe you were too weird to hitchhike. Out by the curb, shaggy people with walking sticks and shopping carts guided mangy animals to nowhere. Teens who'd blackened their eye sockets and pierced the bridges of their noses shuffled toward Houston's underworld. A decaying but popular bowling alley sat across from a lot that contained Mexican and Chinese chain restaurants, and farther down you could find one of those tremendous, shiny supermarkets that stayed open all night just because it could, its clientele growing sparser and freakier as the evening progressed. Whole sections of the road closed after business hours—a cluster of stores that sold antiques, ceramic tiles, and Christian books and supplies lay dormant in shadows, and farther on, beyond a bright gas station, stretched another chunk of avenue where several strip malls had failed and their gigantic unlit parking lots seemed to undulate like wide, deep rivers do at night.

At the corner, near the edge of an empty department-store parking lot, a woman waited at a bus shelter. She leaned against the light box, silhouetted, peering into whichever cars stopped at the traffic signal. This didn't seem strange to Eddie until it occurred to him that the buses must have stopped running. Initially he judged the woman unfortunate, then ignorant and badly dressed, but as he figured out what she was doing, he saw her ingenuity. She had an excuse, if a lame one, to lurk in this territory. Suddenly he thought of his mother—first he had to rule out the possibility that the woman was her, then reconcile himself to the idea that his mother was no different, which he could not do. But he felt this woman might know his mother, or her whereabouts.

He passed, pretending not to notice her. After walking fifty more yards, he stopped and returned to the bus shelter. He stood away from her, watching her light a cigarette and toss the lit match casually into the street. The woman squinted at him, took a drag, and blew her smoke. The expression she sent his way—brows close together, mouth pursed—made him feel that he had offended her.

No, sugar, she said. Ain't happening. She leaned out of the shelter and craned her neck in the opposite direction. Mm-mm. You too young.

I'm not that young, he announced. I'm almost twelve.

She took a step back and guffawed, and he saw her sympathy for him break open. What is happening to me? she asked the sky. I can't believe I thought—she shook her head and sucked on the cigarette again. Good God A'mighty. Eleven years old. And what you doing out—

I'm looking for my mother, he blurted.

The gravity of the matter seemed to settle in her body, as if the same thing had once happened to her. Oh, it's like that, she said. She on the street, hmm?

I reckon. I'm not sure where she is, ma'am.

The name Darlene Hardison did not sound familiar to the woman. Out here, she said, a lot of people—the names aren't the names, you know. What she look like?

Like a normal mom.

You gotta do better than that, my dear. How tall, how fat, how black. Big boobs, small boobs, big ass—what her hair like? Natural, straight, weave, dye? Scars, tattoos. What she was wearing. Who she was with.

Nothing helpful came to mind. Vague adjectives orbited his head. *Pretty. Nice.* If he didn't find her that night, he would need a picture. He struggled to create an image of his mother with his undeveloped tools, and watched his failure reflected in the woman's blank expression. He could not handle this alone, but he didn't let that thought enter his awareness. He had to hold back a riot in his chest that made him want to shout, or kick the bus shelter, or himself.

A gleaming white town car slowed at the bus stop. The woman broke Eddie's gaze, flicked her unfinished cigarette to the ground, smashed it into the pavement, and leaned her torso into the window of the car. Loud rap music from inside drowned out their conversation. A voice whined, *Don't believe the hype!* Presently the woman turned back and smiled. This my ride. She swung the door wide, leapt in, and slammed it. In Eddie's imagination she became his mother, who might have done the same things, recklessly stepping over the line into danger, into oblivion, and—worse than wrapping herself in a stranger's murderous arms, worse than dying—leaving him behind.

Only then did a vivid picture of his mother come to him. Slim, her edges round like a soap sculpture in the rain, fuller hips than her frame seemed able to support. She straightened her hair and kept it at shoulder length. She wore sleeveless floral sundresses in muted patterns and flat shoes—in particular he remembered a mustard-colored pair. At the old house, in Ovis, she would garden from October to May, when it wasn't too hot to spend time in the yard, and she dreamed of getting a sprinkler system for the lawn. He remembered eating a certain brand of chocolate sandwich cookie that matched her complexion, not the deep brown of stained wood but lighter and ruddier, like cedar-bark chips. She had grace, and painted her finger- and toenails a respectable shade of plum. A night sky of faint dots spread across her face, maybe from an adolescent 'bout with acne. He remembered sitting in her lap and tracing these constellations while she slapped his hands away. The makeup she used always compensated for the spots. These were some of Eddie's earliest memories, which always gradually gave way to something else, as if Darlene had pulled a zipper and the halves of her body had fallen away, like a husk, to unmask another person.

This mental image lasted only as long as the flashing red sign that told him not to walk. Hazier still was the gap between that image and the woman he couldn't find that night. Eddie's father had also disappeared, nearly six years earlier, and they'd found him dead. During the Vietnam War, he knew, his father had flown an airplane, and after that, in college, he had played basketball. Eddie's father must have done his job as a soldier well because he wore a medal in the shape of a silver star over his heart in that photograph near his mother's bed. That's for bravery, his mother had said, so often that he could say it with her. Charlie didn't get your daddy, no sir. He had to come home to Jim Crow for that. Then she'd laugh, but not a funny laugh.

Eddie did a lot of asking that night. He encountered many peculiar people, etched in fluorescent light outside ratty convenience stores, walking across empty parking lots whose fault lines sprouted crabgrass and sparkled with nuggets of safety glass, peeking from inside dark concrete motel rooms with broken doors. Nobody remembered Darlene; some people did not know if they remembered remembering. Others forgot that they did not remember. Some spoke fast, for a very long time, and did not stop. Some people could not form words.

One skinny lady with sunken eyes claimed that she definitely had seen Darlene. Without question, she said, absolutely, on this very road. But she also insisted that it had happened ten years ago. We shared a slice of pizza, she went on, because we only had enough money for one, and your moms wanted olives on it, I member that clearly, and we had a little argument about that because I hate olives.

Eddie somehow knew not to mention that his mother also hated olives.

Minimart clerks at gas stations shrugged, a man in a tool belt who claimed to be an electrician said he lived two hours away in Nacogdoches, and a nervous man with slick black hair and a tattoo of his dead Rottweiler on his naked pec kept reaching into the small of his back and telling Eddie, You better go home, kid, 'cause shit's finna go down right the fuck here, son. He pointed to the ground with both index fingers. Eddie met two kids younger than himself who wanted money for a Butterfinger. At first they threatened him verbally, but after he turned his pockets inside out and explained his journey, one of them offered to help him find his mother. Eddie declined, and as he walked away sideways, it occurred to him that nobody else had volunteered to help. Two or three dark sedans slowed by the roadside, powering down their tinted passenger-side windows. Eddie ran from them.

On his second night of searching, drawn to the bright pink and orange of a 24-hour donut shop, he thought he might finally find people inside who would not only know and remember but also know *what* they knew and remember what they remembered, and have some of it turn out true. He understood that he couldn't rely on the night people, who frightened and angered him, and he experienced a deep burn in his stomach when he thought about how his mother had joined them or died with them, like his father, and at best they had engulfed her and made her vanish into this ruined land where true and false didn't matter, where the differences disappeared among memories, dreams, and a young man standing in front of them asking a desperate question.

3.

CONJURE

Not long after Darlene arrived at Grambling State University, she gained a sorority sister, Hazel, who transferred in from Florida State. Hazel had a vivacious, confrontational attitude, fueled by her determination to override the social strikes against her—a mahogany complexion, features too small to fit her face, a large mole muscling in on her nose, unusual height for a woman, a tough demeanor.

All this Southern gentility baffles me, Hazel sometimes said. I always feel like I'm playing the trumpet at a tea party. She made up for her brashness with camaraderie. Hazel organized the group's bowling outings, oversaw the decoration of the house, and made an astounding barbecued brisket packed with smokiness. Her flowing red-and-turquoise blouses often had African designs or palm trees printed on them, and the loud clothing seemed to complement her frank conversation—often about her main vices, chocolate, bourbon, and sex—and her bawdy sense of humor. Everybody took to her, especially several doe-like, unremarkable Sigma Tau Tau sisters, and Darlene, who, as she grew into womanhood, joined Hazel's shocked but delighted audience and found it hard to avoid imitating her infectious insolence. April Woods, a light-skinned, straight-nosed, and polite senior beauty queen, served the function of official role model, but Hazel's charisma got everybody wearing brighter clothing. She loosened their tongues, their attitudes, and their belts.

Hazel ignored her presumed lack of status and thereby overcame it. She accepted herself and demanded reciprocation as the price of her esteem. In association with these strong values, a sense of moral outrage ran like an underground stream through her sense of humor. She took the greatest delight in skewering hypocrites and had immediate and unforgiving scorn for anyone who gave even the appearance of doing something unethical for personal gain. At one point, Tanya Humphrey (It's *Tan*-ya, not *Tahn*-ya, she would say) insisted that Sigma tap Jamalya Raudigan, a notoriously self-involved cheerleader whose father ran a black Atlanta law firm where Tanya aspired to intern, and in the middle of a potluck supper, Hazel quieted everybody, stood on a coffee table, and told Tanya, Stop promoting this annoying social climber because you want to work for Curtis, Gitlin, Raudigan, and Sindell. When Hazel exposed your failings, she made you feel like she'd stuck a blowtorch full of truth up your nose. Rarely did she turn her anger on a sister, but everybody knew not to butt heads with such a sharp-tongued, obstinate powerhouse.

More than one Grambling linebacker had called Hazel a lesbian, though never to her face, and the notion that it might be so rumbled under Hazel's frequent complaints about men and was tacitly reinforced by her perpetual singleness. Darlene had heard these rumors about Hazel and had listened to her comments about men, head cocked in wonder. While she didn't completely believe what everybody said, she accepted the possibility. In those sophomore days, in the rare instances when her friends said the word *lesbian,* it was always a slur, never a person.

All the Alphas had to suppress their shock when Hazel took up with Nat, an impossibly attractive tall man who moved with the alien grace of a praying mantis. He played forward on the Tigers' basketball team, a trail of comparisons to Willis Reed spilling out behind him. His rank as a slightly older guy with experience added to his mystique—he'd come to school on the GI Bill a couple of years after serving a tour of duty in Vietnam and had just entered his junior year.

It took Nat three tries to convince Darlene to walk off campus with him after their economics class to a greasy-spoon diner that other students rarely visited. She made excuses until his third request. A number of possibilities stampeded through her head: Maybe he wanted her econ notes, so he had decided to sweet-talk them out of her. Perhaps he had no idea that it would look bad, and the choice of restaurant wasn't deliberate. Or possibly he intended to woo her behind Hazel's back. At the center of these possibilities stood the man himself: the supple-spined number 55, with feminine lashes ringing his amber eyes; a fine-looking, bashful guy whose many sensitive questions and attentive gaze had probably invited fantasies of marriage in even the most sensible of her Sigma sisters. He palmed basketballs easily, and Darlene enjoyed thinking of those big hands wrapping her hips or cupping her breasts, her nipples pinched between his long fingers. His solar charisma shocked her thinking so dramatically that anything capable of keeping them apart—even Hazel—became irrelevant.

The second time Darlene went with him to the diner, he made his intentions clear by brushing her bare arm with his knuckles,

and though she sensed the wrongness of the caress and felt stir-
rings of the potential havoc it would cause in her sorority, she
couldn't avoid relating to Nat the way all the sisters did, as a grand
prize only an idiot would refuse. Under the table, her leg relaxed,
slid against Nat's, and rested there as a testament to her surrender. The next time they saw each other, they walked farther off
campus, and in the lot behind a different restaurant, when they
recognized their luscious privacy at the same moment, their faces
drew together instinctively and their mouths and tongues connected with slippery, illicit delight.

The secret dalliance inflated her—it practically pulled her
skin taut with joy. Her roommates noticed and told her she had
the flushed look of someone obsessed; they poked her waist and
demanded information so personal that she blushed and hid from
them in the library. She would have had a very difficult time keeping such juicy information from the girls with whom she shared
lipstick, pomade, blouses, stockings, and class notes, and with
whom she usually initiated long conferences after a mere glance
from a fly athlete.

At other times, she wanted them to know. Her roommate,
Kenyatta, wouldn't give her any peace, and Darlene finally confessed, careful to emphasize that they had only kissed.

Kenyatta's face went flat at first, then developed into terror.

Aren't you happy for me? Darlene asked.

No, Kenyatta told her, this is not good. This is *very* not good.

Vertigo overtook Darlene, and she swiftly understood how
they'd view everything. Nat, the man, the basketball star, wouldn't
bear the responsibility, only Darlene, the slut, the man-thieving
heifer, regardless of whatever credit she might have with her sisters. When it came to romantic betrayal, they'd give her no breaks.

Then just don't tell, she begged Kenyatta. Forget I told you.

I'm sorry, these girls gon find out one way or another. Lord knows I can't keep a secret, neither. Better if it happens sooner than later for all involved. Why you had to tell me, anyway?

No, Kenyatta, don't. You can't. Please.

Tau Taus can't be beating other Tau Taus' time. You know that.

Kenyatta would never have considered keeping the secret as an act of mercy. In choosing her as a confidante, Darlene had forgotten Kenyatta's loyalty to the inflexible pecking order of the group, which required that the girls regularly submit their most fashionable clothes to April for approval before dances; though April's motivation for this ritual remained unspoken, everybody said the reason was that she wanted to keep anyone from upstaging her. Often April would cherry-pick her entire outfit from the best of the lot.

Darlene, petrified, could only wait until someone passed the bad news to Hazel herself. Until then she tried to keep her distance—but not from Nat, with whom she frequently met in the evening on shady residential streets or in parks, where nobody would take note of two dark figures pressed against a tree trunk, their lips conjoined, their hands traveling ardently over each other's bodies.

During that time, she remained on edge, constantly ready for the inevitable confrontation. She envisioned hair-pulling, so she got her hair cut a little shorter, tied it tightly behind her head in a tiny bun. But nothing happened. Kenyatta claimed not to have told, despite her declarations of allegiance to Sigma Tau Tau, and when Darlene crossed paths with Hazel, she couldn't detect any signs of vengefulness—no eyes narrowed, no mouth corner raised, not a single oddly placed or ambiguous word in her conversation. Paradoxically, when they returned to campus after the winter break, Hazel's conversations with Darlene seemed to take on a more familiar tone than usual, a crisp lightness like the very infrequent morning frost.

Hazel played on the women's varsity basketball team. On the one hand it made her seem a good match for Nat; on the other it inflamed the rumors about her sexuality. One weekend when she had an away game, Darlene and Nat met at an expensive bed-and-breakfast an hour away, in Shreveport, intent on going all the way.

The place had a lush atmosphere, with antique, wallpapered rooms named for Renaissance painters and a deep, putty-colored Jacuzzi recessed into a wood-paneled alcove in the deluxe suites. Nat had requested the Botticelli Room, he told her, but only the Raphael was available.

Fifty more dollars per night, he said, but you're worth much more than that.

Immediately on arrival, they made gasping, feverish, and clumsy love for the first time in the dry bowl of the Jacuzzi, then Nat playfully hosed the two of them down with the shower attachment and bathed their partially clothed bodies. The evaporating water tickled them as they air-dried, and flushed Darlene with a creamy sense of well-being. Lying exhausted on the comforter, they peeled off the rest of their clothing. They held each other's faces and basked in the buttery warmth of skin against skin.

Once they tired of such luxury, they agreed to go to dinner. The thought seemed to Darlene almost as outrageous as their lovemaking. They had once run into one of Nat's teammates at their off-campus diner and become paranoid about being seen together in public, creating the appearance of what happened to be true, but this far from campus they found an alternate universe in which their desires could thrive. Darlene started to find their increasing anxiety silly and frustrating. No one really belongs to anyone else, she thought as they locked up the Raphael and descended the Victorian's lopsided staircase. Your heart takes you on a journey. People move around of their own free will nowadays. Women are liberated—it's all over the news, in the sitcoms, on everybody's lips. If people choose to be together, they agree on the terms.

She accepted this idea even though she detested the thought of sharing Nat with Hazel, now that she'd admitted to falling in love. Hazel, she sensed, without thinking the words, would most likely see his infidelity as confirmation of her belief that men—black men in particular—had no scruples, and finding out about their affair might encourage her to drop Nat and try women, if she hadn't already. A crueler, foggier portion of Darlene's imagination wondered if, for the girls' basketball team, an away game didn't imply a whole lot of late-night bed-hopping anyway. Yes, people were free to do as they pleased with whomever they wished. Men couldn't own slaves, or servants—they couldn't even own women anymore. And women had never owned men, that's for sure.

They entered the foyer, where Darlene stood marveling at the front door, a magnificent original with its pastel-colored stained glass restored to glory, until Nat took her hand and guided her across the shadowy verandah. She basked in the fantasy of wealth and romance almost as much as in the incredible sense that for this weekend they belonged together, that the beauty and elegance of this moment was pleading with them to turn it into their everyday reality.

They arrived at the front steps—only ten or so. Still, she exclaimed that she couldn't see well enough to descend them without breaking her neck, so he stood in front of her to demonstrate the location of each one. As the sky became visible to her above his head, silhouetting him against a tapestry of sickle-shaped clouds, contrails, and faint stars, this profound gesture of help framed his character so perfectly that she leapt momentarily into the future, to their possible daughter's wedding day, when she would speak to the crowd about this moment of kindness and use it to define their relationship.

At which point a familiar voice slashed through the dark. The person had been sitting in one of the wicker chairs on the verandah, Darlene realized with a start, carefully and motionlessly positioned in a corner where a high laurel on the other side of the railing created an impenetrable shadow. Probably not even breathing.

The fuck is this? the voice said. Y'all think you're fucking slick?

Hazel peeled out of the darkness as they turned their necks. She stood akimbo behind and above them. Kenyatta told me, but I didn't believe her, 'cause she's so trifling. I guess my girl got some cred after all.

Darlene's and Nat's hands fell to their sides like they'd suddenly regressed to embarrassed children. Nat opened his mouth and made an *uh* sound, ready to justify everything with his deep voice, a resonant bass that could smother anything unpleasant in molasses. Darlene stepped to one side, hoping to stay irrelevant to the discussion for as long as she could.

Didn't you have an away game? Nat asked stupidly.

Canceled at the last minute, Hazel said. Turned the bus around. I got back just in time to follow your ass out here. Almost ran out of gas. Nice place. *Real* nice. When were you planning to take *me* to some Renaissance bed-and-breakfasts?

Listen, Hazel—

Don't even, she snapped. She stepped forward into a position where the evening light cut diagonally across her torso like a sash. There's no bullshit you can say to me that will make this not this. She waved a hand back and forth dismissively and ended by raising a finger into Nat's personal space. So do not let it escape your lips.

He said it anyway: Hazel, Hazel. We're just friends, honestly.

She repeated his words, mockingly, in the voice of a cartoon character, then hauled back and slugged him in the chin. Hazel's fist packed a lot of force and speed. Nat raised his arms too late to block her jab. He stumbled at the stairs and lunged for the railing but lost his footing and tumbled to the pavement, twisting his ankle.

What else you got to say, Mr. Big Stuff?

He had bitten his tongue.

Darlene leapt down the stairs and bent over Nat's injured ankle just before Hazel triumphantly clomped down the steps in her heels—roach-stompers, everybody called them—her breasts swinging defiantly under a loose blouse.

Cocking her head, she finally addressed Darlene. And *you*, you ain't nearly got a *inkling* of what's coming on you. You hear?

Hazel reached into her pocket. She squatted over Nat and, as he rose up to his knees, brought a cupped hand to her lips and forcefully blew some kind of acrid dust into each of their faces, enough of it that they had to close their eyes against the stinging grit. Hazel stood up and shouted a French phrase that Darlene did not understand, then raised her hands, flicked them at Nat, and brushed them free of dust above Nat and Darlene. The substance turned out to be a puzzlingly dirty, possibly volcanic soot that stuck to their cheeks and lips; Darlene thought in horror that it might be somebody's cremated corpse. In another moment, Hazel clunked across the main road and disappeared, leaving them to clean up and regain their wits.

Ridiculous gris-gris, Nat grumbled to Darlene, though he couldn't see how gory he looked—a squiggle of red liquid at the corner of his mouth, and his teeth soaked with blood from where he had bitten his tongue. It doesn't work. She carries it with her all the time. You've never seen it? Stupid.

Yet when they returned to school, it did seem as if some bizarre spell had taken effect. Not on the two of them, but on everybody they knew. News of the scandal had spread rapidly, no doubt hastily pollinated by Hazel's own sharp tongue. By the end of the weekend an unspoken banishment had begun. Suddenly their identities were hollowed out; they were nobodies. Even Nat's status had fallen somewhat, if not as far as Darlene's. As she clacked across the dorm lobby, lugging her suitcase, people who used to smile, even the ones who didn't know her, studied the floor as she passed. None of them offered help as she bumped up the stairs. When Darlene got to her room and pulled back her bedclothes she found a dissected frog in the center of the mattress, bleeding formaldehyde.

One of Nat's roommates, a man whose girlfriend spent a lot of time with Hazel, jumped him, knocking the wind out of him. Three weeks later, a different guy Nat didn't know asked him for directions to the student union, slugged him in the stomach, and ran. The guy hadn't seemed like a Grambling student—Nat and Darlene wondered if Hazel had relatives or dangerous connections outside the university and had started calling in favors. Their paranoia soon reached a high pitch when Darlene became the victim of many ugly pranks.

In the next month and a half, the majority of Darlene's notebooks got stolen or destroyed. As she turned the pages of her textbooks during classes she found the words WHORE, SLUT, and CUNT scrawled across them in red Magic Marker. The faces of her family in photos she'd left on her dresser grew mustaches and beards. Their eyes were blacked out and crude drawings of genitals sprang from the children's heads and mouths. Her sorority sisters, including her roommate, Kenyatta, denied responsibility for the vandalism. Darlene received phone calls from strangers at very early hours, the weirdest at three a.m. on a Wednesday, a computer voice that sounded like a children's toy threatening to cut her throat.

Someone put sports cream in her bra, and the burning came on during an econ exam, numbing and searing her chest until she gasped and nearly passed out, even after carefully twisting free of the straps without removing her shirt and hiding the icy-hot garment between her legs. She flunked the test. Nobody admitted doing any of it, and she had too many suspects to point at anyone in particular. It staggered Darlene to discover how terribly people, even so-called sisters, could treat you as soon as they had an excuse. Hazel hadn't needed any powder. It turned out black magic didn't work because of spells or potions but because of the fear of persecution and conspiracy that roiled under people's lives like contaminated groundwater.

Darlene struggled against the abuse, thinking it would eventually subside, but it didn't. The authorities, meanwhile, saw the pranks as isolated incidents, not a system of torture, and didn't offer Darlene help. Her sisters hid behind their reputation. Sigma Tau Tau girls volunteered at soup kitchens, as the school's administrators frequently reminded her, they led can drives and supported upward mobility in the black community with their bake sales. They performed, in their trademark periwinkle and tangerine, at senior citizens' centers. They organized step shows and church bazaars and raised funds for people with cerebral palsy. Nobody believed that they had ganged up on Darlene, and finally she felt she had no choice but to leave Grambling.

Nat had grown extremely protective of Darlene, and as the attacks against her continued, their social world shrank and their bond intensified. He claimed responsibility for everything that happened to her and insisted on leaving school along with her. Darlene and Nat arranged with their professors to complete as many finals and papers as they could while missing a few classes and took steps to transfer to Centenary, in Shreveport, explaining as little to their families as possible, evading any questions about their relationship. Nat's excitement grew at the thought of transferring when he found out that Centenary had a basketball team with great potential—the Gentlemen, a name that made Darlene laugh. The NCAA was punishing the Gents, he said, by failing to report their statistics; Nat had met a Centenary player named Robert Parish, a center, who had one of the best records in college ball, but nobody knew. To Darlene it sounded like Nat had more disappointment and injustice in store, but she donated an empty smile to his efforts anyway.

Even before the semester ended, they fled to Shreveport, living together not because other young unmarried couples had begun to make it fashionable, but because they had nobody else to rely on. Darlene's sister, Bethella, was the only other family member who had gone to college before her, and she'd run off to Houston and never turned back. Darlene felt she couldn't return to her family's country ways after taking on all her college-girl habits and aspirations. The last time she'd gone home, her older brother, himself a high-school dropout, had pushed her psychology textbook off the table while she was studying and later, at the same dining-room table, told everybody how proud he was of her. Still, she had never gotten the highest grades, and her banishment dampened her mood and lowered her academic standing. It could've been worse; Nat's adoptive father, Puma, a religious and shrewd man, figured out the whole story, and what he called Nat's profligacy, mendacity, and premarital fornication disgusted him so thoroughly that he wouldn't allow his son back home.

Afraid of campus housing at Centenary, after a few months, they found a small house with a wide yard on Joe Louis Boulevard. While talking to a new neighbor, they heard that Holiday in Dixie would begin that night. It was a lackluster, month-late shadow of Mardi Gras; that event truly happened only in New Orleans, but this second-rate party welcomed them in a way that Grambling never would again. Even the lukewarm gumbo bought from a truck stand filled their heads with the memory of hotter spice and juicier andouille, and though the salmon in their beggar's pouches was all gray flesh and skin, the oily phyllo still flaked properly against their teeth, and that provided just enough comfort. They felt they had made the right choice.

Despite the loss and shame of leaving Grambling, Darlene felt she had won whenever she glanced at Nat. He'd agreed to go with her when he could have stayed and forsaken her along with the rest. He'd settled for a less impressive basketball scholarship. Words can't prove true love, she would think, only the list of sacrifices you make to keep it alive. Nat had demonstrated his love through his honor.

Nat didn't know much about his real parents, only his mother's first name. The agency might have known more, but they refused to release any information to him. His foster parents had adopted him at thirteen, after the system had pinballed him through unstable East Texas homes where supposed brothers stole his baseball cards, mothers beat his shins with pool cues, and sisters tied him to chairs as a playtime activity. Only his growth spurt put an end to the abuse. Out of the six homes he passed through, he'd wanted to stay in only two of them, the first belonging to an affectionate divorcée with apple-shaped hips, the second to the family who ultimately adopted him, the Hardisons: his foster mother LaVerne, a tubby young woman with freckles and keloids scattered on her skin; his adoptive father, Patrick, nicknamed Puma, a sturdy throne of a man the color and complexion of a walnut, a tense and authoritarian ex-Marine whose tough love contained very little of the latter ingredient. From Puma, Nat absorbed a fervent admiration for the military and respect for authority, as well as the desire to emulate the straight-backed heroes of Iwo Jima and Korea.

Their few new friends at Centenary did not know that Nat and Darlene's intense and somewhat paranoid bond had arisen from their persecution at Grambling. On a double date, a couple they knew from the Black Students' Union stared when they shared from one plate and when Nat rose to let Darlene out of the booth to go to the bathroom and then followed her to the door. They joked uncomfortably when the two returned, but Nat couldn't see what they found so unusual. Darlene mentioned shyly that they had registered for most classes together too.

We're both majoring in econ, she said, and we help each other through all the madness. I make flash cards for us. It's fun. We're practically the same person now.

Their supper companions smiled and changed the subject, and they often had standing plans when Darlene contacted them in the future.

Almost concurrently with their banishment from Grambling, a deputy in Pensacola had shot a black man dead at point-blank range with a .357 Magnum. A little later, someone strangled a material witness who'd said that she had a relationship with the deputy and had seen the murder. By the end of January, the grand jury had acquitted the deputy. Hundreds of people took to the streets in Pensacola, but seventy policemen beat them with clubs. Nat followed all of this and became outraged; he showed as much anger over these events as he had about what had happened to Darlene, and she wondered if he was letting Pensacola stand in for the earlier, more personal injustice. Now he insisted that they had to work for equality, even on a small scale. Then Darlene realized that she was pregnant, the child probably conceived a week or so after they'd decided to transfer from Grambling.

Now Nat felt inspired to move to a smaller town, like the

one near Lafayette where Darlene had grown up. The pregnancy seemed to make his wishes inevitable, even necessary. Somewhat randomly, Nat chose Ovis, Louisiana, a village on the shores of the Mississippi, half submerged under the poverty line, in part for its odd name. The name sounded humble to him, like the sort of place where he could organize and mobilize small-town black folks. He'd also gotten inspired by Tom Bradley's and Maynard Jackson's political careers; it seemed a portal had opened for black mayors to get common people to recognize that safety and power came with the right to vote and that involvement in politics could raise their standard of living and prevent injustices like the one in Pensacola. The nation would soon turn two hundred years old—it was about time.

The fetus, however, as if to scorch the edges of their idealism, did not come to term. Nat and Darlene kept the door to the second bedroom of their new home closed for the greater part of the next year as they regained the strength to want a child again.

The following September, Eddie was born—prematurely, and the difficulty of caring for him added to the upheaval in his parents' lives. With so little money, they ended up waiting to get married until Eddie was about six months old. They had no doubts about their relationship, but the official fussiness and expense of a wedding, added to the obligation to mobilize their families, had always seemed trivial and irritating compared to their monumental romance, their social dreams.

Though Nat, through his family, had known the stubbornness of rural folks firsthand as a child in East Texas, he still maintained a dreamy faith about the potential they represented. He had, after all, made something of himself, and he knew others could also. Occasionally he'd speak immodestly of himself as a Moses-like figure leading his people through the desert, but in truth, he faced a maddening grind convincing people to register to vote when they still felt that they might be harmed for attempting to better their lives. Nevertheless, Nat and Darlene opened a general store called the Mount Hope Grocery on the town's tiny main street, and lonely, destitute men and women gathered in its back room to drink in the peace and companionship of similarly hopeless people. For the most part they admired Nat's determination to mobilize the community, his fund-raising, his voter-registration drives, but they did not expect rapid change.

Sparkplug McKeon, however, a shiny-faced man whose compact body had taken on the shape of the three-legged, threadbare living-room chair that was his favorite in the dusty yard out back, would shake his head diagonally every time Nat launched a new initiative. Won't none of this come to no good, he growled. I seened it too many a time.

He told three tales of recent, nearby woe to illustrate his point. The first involved a Northern activist, a black girl of seventeen who had been abducted, raped, and gutted with a fish knife in Acadia Parish, probably by the Ku Klux Klan.

Cold case, Sparkplug said, raising an eyebrow, and we all know what that mean.

The second had to do with a Jew who was shot in the face outside Baton Rouge because of a rumor that he'd been having an affair with a white woman prominent in the community. Sparkplug told this one to prove that the hatred ran deeper than just prejudice against Negroes.

Catholics too, he said. Ain't nobody different had no chance in this damn state, he asserted, shaking his head.

The third tale was about his own uncle, Louis McKeon, who had refused to give up a parcel of land to a white man and gone missing soon afterward.

My cousin Grant wasn't but six month old at the time. You tell me what McKeon man gonna leave off his new child like that,

Sparkplug said, never hearing hide nor hair of him again. I tell you it never happen—we honorable folk. My cousin Geneva? Said she heard some white man talkin 'bout that they dumped Uncle Lou's body in the Mississippi and watched the gators feedin on it, and they was jus a-laughing, taking bets or some shit. And white folks say niggers is animals, that we next door to a ape. I tell you I'd rather be next door to a ape than next door to a goddamn cracker. At least a ape be my friend from Africa, wouldn't sell his damn house on Tuesdy if I move next door on Mondy. See, to these folks, a animal is even more of a nigger than a nigger is. And you know animals is some beautiful creatures of God. What they think so bad 'bout being a ape?

And yet the residents of Ovis appeared to have accepted the injustices they'd suffered as inescapable. Nat felt he could've knelt down in front of their strained smiles and gathered their impacted anger in his hands as he went door to door and filled baskets with the harvest, but his attempts to plant it or grow it into any kind of action often proved futile.

Well, he'd ask Sparkplug, why don't you register to vote, my man?

Sparkplug, the most frankly angry man for miles, often in the process of arranging his poker hand, didn't usually look up. The one time he did reply, he said, Vote for who? The son of the cracker sumbitch killed my uncle?

The men passed laughter between them like beer, mollifying a shared disappointment, frustration, and rage intense enough to turn murderous if you provoked it, though the opportunity to vent wouldn't ever arrive. Even if they got a chance, the talons of injustice would swoop down soon enough, dismember these men, and be gone, and everybody would forget that any of it had happened, leaving no trace aside from a lingering miasma that might rise into the Spanish moss.

Gradually, though, some of the men and women came to Nat privately, and he began to convince these few to see past their hopelessness and wrath into an easier future, if only a slightly easier one. A few signed up. They joked about a time when their despair would lift, when someone would cut them a break, and with a proud smirk, Nat saw that they'd taken the first step toward shedding their perpetual despair. But all his activity, despite the optimism at the heart of its politics, quickly attracted negative attention in the form of threatening phone calls, unpleasant words on the street, and bad service in local businesses. They'd been through this sort of thing before, from their own people, Nat reminded Darlene, so they should know not to pay it any mind. Still, Nat tended to measure these minor wrongs against far larger ones, like the atrocities committed against Henry Marrow, Medgar Evers, and Emmett Till, so he failed to see them for what they were: the opening moves of a chess game he could never win, considering how many moves ahead his opponents were already thinking.

4.

WE NAMED THE GOAT

This chick standing by that navy blue minibus parked at the side of the road seem okay to Darlene—better than okay. Firstly the woman had on a *clean* blouse, in a multicolored African triangle pattern, almost like a stained-glass window. Only a couple holes in that shirt—same with them acid-wash jeans and them skippies on her feet. The minibus seem sorta new, mostly. Wasn't no scratches or dents you could see under the white light in front the Party Fool, the next lot over from the one where Darlene just lost three teeth. The minibus tires was all waxy shiny, the hubcaps too. The sliding door slid open smooth, and you could smell the plasticky new-car odor inside even from a couple feet away. Them windows be shining, them seats look like they could actually bounce, and when Darlene leant sideways round the woman and peeked inside, she could tell the brothers in the back was comfortable.

The lady—said her name Jackie—done started in like some

direct-marketing TV huckster, talking fast 'bout this place and this job that sounded real good, and that Darlene and I should go with her. A wet Jheri curl went sproing on her head, then it gone partway down the back of her neck, with the hairpins pushing the sides above her ears for that business-casual look. Darlene ain't concentrated on nothing Jackie said, though, 'cause she said more than need be, the way people do when they already decided that you gonna turn down they pitch.

While we listening, Darlene had to plant her feet to keep from shouting with joy, even with all that dried blood caked up in her nose and gums and them scratched-up knees. Sound like this lady had a job they wanna *give* her, without no interview or nothing, hard work but good work, no more tryna sell her body and getting stabbed or having to watch no shame-loving Cajun get busy with no melon.

Jackie said, The company's associates do agricultural work, harvesting a wide variety of fruits, vegetables, and legumes. She actually said them actual phrases, like it's out a book she ain't never finished reading herself.

Darlene grown up doing that shit in the first place, so she got lonely for her childhood. On this job she gon be picking fruits and vegetables, like she a innocent little girl again. Jackie also made the farm sound like the kinda place where Darlene and I could go together and wouldn't nobody stop us from hanging out and doing our thing, and that seemed so perfect that we wondered if we mighta made it up ourself.

A image come up in Darlene mind, of a bodacious-ass horn of plenty that had all kinda green and red peppers and shit spilling out, and bananas and carrots and grapes and whatnot, and everything be cold, crispy, fresh, and wet with morning dew on account a being just picked. In her head, somebody snapped a carrot and it sprayed a li'l bit of mist up into the air.

Darlene said to me, See, Scotty. The book works. I put positivity and love out on my antenna and the universe sent it back to bless me.

Jackie said, *Three-star accommodations.* She said, *Olympic-size swimming pool.* Said, *Recreation activities. Competitive salary. Vacation.* Then she showed Darlene a picture of some condo-type complex with a motherfucking kidney-shaped pool smack-dab in the center. Then Jackie top it off with benefits, health care. We got a dentist that could help out with any problems you might have, Jackie said, looking at Darlene mouth, as well as day care. To be honest, she said, the pay ain't super-high, but we offer our workers a salary above minimum wage, the competitive rate in the field.

Darlene appreciated the honesty. Even better than getting a high salary was the feeling that you working with people you could respect, who told your ass the truth, motherfuckers you could communicate with. This here felt like the first luck Darlene had touched in the whole six years since she lost Nat. Above minimum wage? She thought she could reach up to that luck and stroke it and the luck would go *purr.*

Now Jackie talked a long stream, you couldn't dip in your damn toe. Girl had heart-shaped lips with brick-color lip gloss slathered on em, and the edges was shining. Sexy red plums. Her tongue always going somewheres when she talked. Sometimes she licked the corner of her mouth to keep it from getting dried out from all that talking.

Jackie. Jackie? Jackie, Darlene said every so often, trying to butt in, to let her know how much on board with it she already was.

Jackie eyes still ain't said nothing—they could only say *The deal, the great deal, the wonderfulness of the deal.* She acting jittery—and I knew why. I recognized her as a old friend. Finally I had to introduce the two of em. Jackie stopped the hard sell for a hot minute.

May I call my son? Darlene asked.

Sometime Eddie say that Darlene didn't never care about him, especially when it come to the particular moment we talking 'bout now, but she ain't never stopped tryna make sure she could get in touch. Eddie probably thought his mom loved his dad more than him, and that mighta been true, but she thought 'bout Eddie all the time. Love's a mother to start with, so when sonofabitches start fighting over who love who more, and tryna say that this action you done today gotta line up with that verbal statement from yesterday 'bout how much you loved somebody, and they pull out they love-o-meters and start measuring shit out to infinity, I get pissed. Me, I think people could love me, or somebody like me, and still show they obligations to the other people in they life as number 2 and 3 and 4 and so on down the line and it ain't no thang.

When Darlene asked about calling her son, Jackie got activated again. Course you could call your son, she said. We'll let you use the phone when we get there. Free of charge!

Jackie be showing off the open door of the minibus with her hand like she on *The Price Is Right,* and Darlene thinking she could hear the sucking of pipes and the popping of rocks in there. The darkness and the tinted windows had kept her from seeing much, and in them days, she always hearing rocks in the background of everything anyhow.

I said to Darlene, I know these folks. I approve. Honey, get the fuck in before the people out in them bushes behind the Party Fool who be listening to everything we say find out 'bout this terrific opportunity and try to come with us. Darlene said yes and jumped over to the minibus without no reservations whatsoever. And when she done that, she noticed a plush carpet on the minibus floor, a carpet laid out in front of us on the road to prosperity.

Darlene hesitated on account a she ain't know if she could get up into the van. Her eyes rolled into her head and she swooned, almost 'bout to fall. She gripped the footrest to get a balance and flopped onto the floor of the van, next to the center seat. Her hand went swoosh over the beige shag and she remembered being a child and petting a sheep her father had named Luther.

At the wheel, with just the front-seat overhead light on, a red-eyed brother be sucking the last from a juice box, making a racket. When he got done, he pushed the box through the slit in the window out to the road, and a breeze blew it into the center lane and a passing semi done crushed that shit flat.

Jackie laughed, and the driver looked around and gave a broad smile without opening his mouth. Four others sitting in the rest of them seats, all of em hunched-over shadows made by the headlights coming from the opposite side the road. Red Eye turnt the ignition, the door closed, and they was on they way.

Darlene found herself a seat and look at Jackie. I grew up on a farm, Darlene said.

Did you now? That's sure gonna come in handy.

What time is it? I need to call my son, okay?

Okeydokey.

How far is it from Houston?

Just up the road here, an hour or so.

That close? Okay! Darlene seen a bunch of dark shapes, three in the very backseat and one in the seat in front of that, passing round a little red light. The one in front took it in his palm, and she bugged out when she saw that pipe. The man put it up to his face, and the light be getting brighter as he sucked it in and the pipe start fizzing that fizz that gave Darlene a orgasm of hope. She love the sound of my voice.

You feel like lighting up, go on ahead now. This ain't company time! Jackie said, and giggled.

Darlene nearly had a conniption. You don't mind? she asked.

Jackie talked all calm and businessy. This company really takes care of their workers! We don't judge.

Seriously? she asked Jackie. Seemed to Darlene someone should nominate them for Best Employer the World Has Ever Known.

Seriously, Jackie said.

Word, said one the brothers in the back.

What's the hitch? Darlene asked.

The hitch is that there ain't no hitch.

Jackpot! One the brothers passed the pipe up front and Darlene sucked it like it's a pacifier. She thinking how we could spend time together, but she also gonna have real, honest-to-God work at a place where they understand our relationship and ain't try to stop it or make her stay away from me. Too good.

This is an incredible opportunity, Darlene gushed. She felt like Miss America taking her first walk with that motherfucking tiara on, carrying them roses in her arms and waving and crying.

I rushed into the few doubting and unbelieving parts left in Darlene's mind and I shouted, Babygirl, surrender to yes! Say yes to good feelings! Say yes to pleasure! Fuck pain. All that damn pain? Leave it behind you. Ain't that what the book say to do?

Good thing I ain't run into no resistance up in her mind, 'cause I wanted to go to that farm just as bad... Now, I get that when somebody walk up to your house and offer you heaven on earth, the delivery truck don't usually be idling at the curb. That goes extra-specially in Texas. But we couldn't think on that. Darlene already had way too much shit not to be thinking 'bout.

Once the minibus got moving, Jackie passed the recruits a

clipboard and a pen, like when you getting a *job* job, and she goes,
This the contract.

Somebody already done folded that sucker over to the last
page and put a bright yellow tag in the place where you supposed
to sign. A beefy brother with giant teeth and idiot eyes name of
TT squinted at the page and scribbled on the signature line. Sirius B, who a intense, silent type sitting cross the aisle, took the
contract out from under the clip, fold it to the first page, and held
it like he wanna read that shit in the streetlamp light that they
whizzing through.

Jackie leant into his personal space and said, Don't sweat it,
bruh, you just sign.

Before she seen what anybody else done, Darlene slipped that
pen out that clip and joyfully wrote *Darlene Hardison* right on the
line. A screen rolled down over her world that showed a sparkling
future of joy, just like the book told her she gonna get by asking
and believing that she gonna receive.

Picture Darlene not thinking. Imagine her ass floating above
that bus, having a long-term hopegasm, rivers of happy sliding
from her mouth to her crotch and back, warm and smooth, curling around her body like a combination of pure maple syrup and
sex. Picture me fucking her deep, slick, and slow, a body made of
smoke, telling her I love her more than her mother ever did. Picture Darlene starring in a Hollywood movie called *The Lady with
the Damn Good Job*.

After she had got to know some her future coworkers and everybody shared stories and drugs, the bus hushed up a minute
and Darlene put her head back, relaxed her pelvis, and got all
philosophical. She goes, Drugs are good, and she threw a smile
as easy as you'd throw a 45 onto a turntable back in the day. The
minibus had a smooth, bouncy suspension. Jackie turnt back to
listen, stretching them shiny lips across her face. Darlene had

thought shit like that even on sober days, now it fell out her mouth like a little stump speech.

Drugs's *good!* She said it with extra *o*'s. But not just! she said. Everything in this country that they tell you is bad? It's *good!* She counted on her fingers. Sex is good, fast food is good, niggers are good, dancing's good, and you *know* alcohol's fantastic. That's why they—they rape it into your head that it's all bad, because if everybody realized how good, nobody would do anything else! Wouldn't waste time going to a stupid school where nobody will hire you once you graduate, or working for some big company that steals your life. She sat back again and sighed. I have spoken, she said. Now pass the peace pipe!

You know the minibus be rocking with laughter and agreements on that one.

A while later they turnt off Interstate Something and start down a state or a county route, one without no streetlamps nowhere, maybe without no number. The driver clicked on the brights. Out the left side the minibus played hit radio, all staticky—the right-side speakers ain't worked. The station played "Need You Tonight," and "Sign Your Name," and "Get Outta My Dreams, Get into My Car"—I told Darlene that I knew the DJ and he playing them songs just for us. Then that song "Never Gonna Give You Up" came on and I went, That's 'bout you and me, honey.

Out on the highway you could sometime make out some misty farms with little shrubs next to em, and out yonder on the road, the lights of cars was shrinking and falling into the past. In spite of her state of mind, everything Darlene ain't thinking 'bout stayed with her, the way that a sound too high for your ear to hear still out there and dogs or whatever could hear it, or radioactivity your eye couldn't see could still spread out everyplace in front of you and fuck your shit up. I couldn't completely keep her

mind off her thoughts, even though she kept begging me to—she
wanted me to wipe out the experiences that be rising up like the
undead, chewing on her will to live. But I do things different. I
like to get people hyped up, to loosen they fear, give em some extra courage, put a little english on they stride.

So while Darlene smoked with the men in the back of the
van, she could still hear something whispering, *He's gone, he's
gone, nothing matters, never did. We will all be dead soon. Then
the world will end, so why go on? Go to him. Be with him.* I swear
that part did not come from *me.* 'Cause when folks really wanna
die, that's a substance more powerful than Scotty—imagine a
drug that you do it once and you guaranteed dead. Right, that's
called poison. Na-aah, no, thank you, not my job. All I ever said
was Smoke it up.

Quiet come down in the back of the van, and the men seen
that without no streetlights, you could see the stars outside flickering like rocks in a pipe. That brother who name Sirius B pointed
out one them animals from the horoscope, talking 'bout how it
predict what you gonna be like.

That doesn't mean anything, Darlene told him. There's nothing out there.

Sirius B goes, Then what do you think the stars hanging on to?

Just—just whatever it is. Darlene swirled her hands in front of
her face. Just *Out There.* Like, deep space—God. The horoscope
is just some fools putting fake satanic ideas onto nothing. The ancient people looked up through the clouds and said, That's a goat!
she shouted, bugging her eyes out like TT to show the stupidity.
And folks have harped on it for so long that now everybody looks
up there and says, Look at the goat! She folded her arms, but she
wasn't done talking. But it's stupid because we gave the names to
the stars. There aren't any lines connecting anything up in the sky
to make a goat. It's the same with everything else. People named

everything, so we think the name is the truth. But nothing means anything if we made the rules up ourselves. God made the rules, we just made up some fake names.

Darlene ain't thought 'bout Nat's face, or the blood. She sure ain't thinking 'bout what come later, and whether it had to do with the obeah that Hazel had worked on her. On the way out there, she ain't even thought about how Interstate Whatever didn't never curve, how it kept you in a state of suspense. This minibus trip had only one turn, it felt like, a left turn that had happened some time before, she couldn't remember how long ago. Then the road got real rough. It be bounding everybody forward into the headrests and sideways against the windows.

For miles it's only reeds growing at the side of the road, then trees come back, then you see a farmhouse with a collapsing barn beside it, then a rusty tractor, then a big-ass wheel. Then the pink part of the sky start going all blue, and Darlene could see faraway shit without knowing how far she traveled, like if she seen a pagoda, she'd a said, I guess we made it to China. Without questioning none of it.

What she seen farther away was tiny trees by the horizon, lame little hills, a burnt-out car. Puffy mist rising out the ground. Wasn't no towns, not no buildings nowhere, only tall green grass and telephone poles and wires and, later, cornfields, rows of some green plant that was probably collard greens or cabbage, then more motherfucking corn. Darlene ain't notice, but they hadn't passed no houses of no kind in more than a hour. Jackie shifted in her seat and the pleather start making rubbery noises up against her thighs.

Jackie goes, Almost there.

Darlene looked out the window and the whole goddamn view was corn. It had took all night driving to get where they going, but didn't nobody in the minibus ask how many hours had tiptoed past. Too much enjoyment be happening up in that vehicle to keep track of the time or the place. We wanted to rip ourselves outta times and places anyhow. Someday I wanna switch places with y'all just for a while, so before you die you could feel what it like not to have no body. Sweet Jesus, it take a whole lot of worriation out your head. First 'bout doctor bills, and then 'bout racism and sexism, and most positively, it immediately put a end to all that When Am I Gonna Die bullshit. I told Darlene that the whole problem of humanity is that if you got a body, you gotta have a time and a place. But when y'all got a time and a place, y'all really don't got shit—time don't do nothing but disappear. People and places and seasons and events be changing faster than you could recognize em, let alone remember em or appreciate em. How y'all supposed to live on fast-forward all the motherfucking time? Don't ask me. Scotty don't got no idea. Better y'all than me.

5.

SHOW US THE PLANETS

Edward Randolph Hardison always wanted to get things done quickly. Even his birth came a month too early, right after Labor Day weekend, another event in a week of fleeting expectation in the news—the Viking 2 spacecraft sent the first color photographs from Mars, the Rat Pack reunited for a moment, Mao Tsetung died. After his parents' overwhelming experience of the miscarriage the year before, they nearly went to pieces as they waited by the incubator, watching Eddie breathe through a ventilator until his lungs finally developed. Nat and Darlene had wanted to get settled before getting married, but the urgency of Eddie's medical problems, followed by the tentative elation they felt when they finally got to take home a healthy child, in mid-October, inspired them to hold a small marriage ceremony the following March, not far from the hospital in Shreveport. To avoid the appearance of immorality—finding out they'd been living in sin would shock their new neighbors—Darlene handed Eddie to her sister during the wedding photos. If necessary, she and Nat would sometimes lie about which event had come first, the birth or the wedding.

Once Eddie's condition stabilized, they rushed back to Ovis to attend to their business. The Mount Hope Grocery was in the wrongest part of a town made of wrong parts, a wooden building with thick greenish beams holding up its awning. It had been a gas station once, but over time Eddie's father had the pumps ripped out, moved the main building, and added another structure until he'd built a classic general store with an inviting verandah where neighbors would soon gather to play cards and voice grievances. A stream ran behind the store, and back there, while the adults talked business, Eddie often tried to capture tiny fish between his palms and once chased after a talkative tabby cat with green eyes.

Before the store opened, on the nights when people gathered at the blond-brick ranch house they rented in town, Eddie's parents would send him to bed early, but he would silently pass through his open bedroom door and watch what he could from down the hall, where he'd see men like his father, with straight carriages and resonant voices, and women, attractive like his mother but slouchier, with arch, skeptical expressions, crowded into their living room smoking, watching television, and drinking bourbon. On some occasions Eddie created excuses to get up in order to sneak glances at the fascinating box with its bluish-gray, flickering images. But these adults never watched anything exciting, only white men standing opposite each other at podiums arguing in words he did not understand, or crowds of people in big rooms where balloons fell in the colors of the USA.

More often the men alone would gather to watch a game—the Saints, or college basketball. But the rules and the breaks in action disturbed Eddie's concentration, and he couldn't keep his childish attention on anything for very long. When his mother discovered him in the process of sipping from a spent whiskey glass polluted by a cigarette butt, she increased her efforts to keep him in his room during his father's summits, and during her own more sedate meetings with the ladies.

Once the general store opened, all the activity shifted to the verandah and the side yard there. They would congregate at long forest-green picnic tables outside the Mount Hope Grocery, and Eddie's parents would speak with their neighbors as they went about their day—people in overalls, women pushing white children in carriages. Nat and Darlene encouraged all of them to write their names down on clipboards. During those times Eddie wandered up and down the main street, or into the thrift shop, where he found toys, or he begged his mother for change to run to the ice cream parlor that drew everybody in with the sweet smell of baking cones.

Eddie's parents always gave him the sense that they were doing important, possibly risky work. They drew emergency plans for him on the blank pages at the back of his coloring books. They forbade him to trust strangers. Phone calls sometimes came at odd hours, and he would hear his mother panicking, his father rising in the night to secure the doors and windows. Not only did his father keep a shotgun locked behind the counter at the store, he taught his wife how to use it.

But one morning, not long before he turned six, Eddie awoke to find that his father hadn't come home. He fixated on Darlene as she spoke into the phone, her face pinched with fear and anger, paying him no mind, one fingernail scraping at the corner of a corkboard stuck to the refrigerator, dislodging the brown flakes as her calls to neighbors went unanswered and she grew frantic. Her determination and pessimism came out in tiny fragments: *I just know! Lord, how could you let it? Please don't let him be.*

Ma, let's go to the store and see if he's there, Eddie insisted.

I called, she said. He didn't pick up.

Maybe the phone is not working.

Maybe, she responded. Maybe...

Darlene turned her attention back to making phone calls and remained focused on that activity even when Eddie stomped on the floor in front of her and insisted. She wouldn't leave the house or let him go out by himself. Eventually she agreed to let him go down the street to a friend's house while she watched from a window.

In the early afternoon, just after Eddie came back, several policemen strode into the house. They'd never come inside on earlier visits, and they seemed to want to say serious things; Eddie knew because they removed their hats. White men nearly as tall as his father crowded around the kitchen table; it was a novelty to have white people in this small space, let alone these authoritative, beefy guys with their safety-goggle glasses, short, cornhusk-colored hair, and tight speech. His mother, who enforced hospitality under all circumstances, offered them coffee and warmed biscuits for them as if they paid house calls every day and insisted that they sit. He hoped a couple of them might be astronauts. When they started talking about identifying something they called *it* and *the body*, he did not recognize at first that they meant his father. His mother registered shock, and after a few moments, she collapsed into her own arms, fell to her knees beside the table, and, following an uncomfortable pause, ran outside to the clothesline, where she dashed between the ropes, yanking the laundry down and hollering something that did not sound like language. The men were still talking, to one another now.

After the screen door banged shut, Eddie went to the doorjamb and watched Darlene's path. He couldn't see behind the sheets, but he followed the clothespins with his eyes as they snapped and flew off in all directions. Soon the policemen came to the door behind him and stood solemnly, heads bowed the way they might do while saying grace, and his mother tumbled from behind a fitted sheet, clutching a pair of his father's dungarees, embracing them as if his legs were still in them, smearing them against her face, stifling her cries, dampening the fabric with tears. Eddie ran out to her, but she didn't seem to see him through her grief.

Days later, something like a party followed. All his relatives had been invited except his father. When he asked his aunt Bethella why they had forgotten to invite him, she thwacked him sharply on the behind, glared, and raised her index finger to a point between his eyes, the way a robber might hold a switchblade.

Don't you ever, she said. Ever!

His mother, uncommonly silent and numb, in a pillbox hat, her face veiled, dressed him in a black jacket and itchy pants from the local thrift store and held his hand in the front row of the church as everybody sang and wept before a shiny oblong box draped in flowers that people now said contained his father. How did they know? Nobody could see inside.

Later Eddie stood perspiring in his jacket but not daring to remove it as they lowered the box they claimed contained his father into a hill, and men shoveled dirt on top of it. When would they stop the circus act and let Daddy out of that thing? He had read picture books about Harry Houdini. Maybe he'd tell them, he thought. But he had started learning not to say the majority of what he thought.

In the rainy days that followed, seemingly related to the events of his life, he would beg his mother to go visit the hill and bring extra umbrellas. We can't let Daddy get wet, he'd protest.

Friends came to the house, shaking their heads and saying, Mph, mph, mph. Well, you know if he'd a been white they'd have a suspect by now.

Over time, Eddie came to understand the part of dead that means *never*. That is to say, the whole thing. Never coming back, never going to swing you upside down, never taking you to school, never giving you presents, never coming to the holidays. But the finality of it didn't upset him the way it should have. For the most part he didn't believe it, so he tried to turn *never* into *someday* with the usual tools: ideas he heard in hymns, tinglings he felt while soloists cried during Sunday services at Ebenezer Baptist. Notions of angels, of heaven. Of ancestors gazing down, pride and anger wrinkling their foreheads. Of the sun and wind tickling the tassels of ripe corn in a wide field. Of pious deeds and of Jesus Christ levitating above an empty cave.

In contrast, his mother started to demand something impossible, maybe indescribable, something he didn't understand until much later—she needed for time to reverse itself. Gradually her posture slumped, her chest became heavier. She stopped having anybody over, she rarely called anyone, the phone didn't ring anymore, she became quiet and unresponsive, her moods enveloped her.

For a long time, Eddie thought only about adjusting to the loss of his father, and the loss of the grocery store, not about seeking the cause of those losses, and no one pointed him in that direction—in fact, his relatives diverted his attention away from it. He would ask a direct question of a random cousin or of Bethella during her sporadic visits—How did my father die? They'd stare into a corner of the room and feed him a noble abstraction—He died fighting for your rights. The follow-up question seemed ridiculous, unaskable—I mean, what killed his *body?*—and would linger in the air.

You need to find out, press charges, and sue, everybody would say to Darlene, sometimes even to him, at six years old. Eddie, your mother needs to bring these people to justice. What's she scared of? She has a thousand percent of our support.

But he watched his mother during these days, and he sensed, without actually knowing, that something unnameable had curled itself, snakelike, around her leg, then bound her torso; her breathing got more strained, her eyes bloodshot and sunken. He'd overhear the things she'd mutter to photographs of his father—*I never should have asked. I shouldn't have worn those shoes. Forgive me. How can you forgive me?*

Then a whole bunch of folks from up north came down asking questions about what happened, and Eddie spent even more time than previously in the confusing world of people talking over his head, primarily about politics. As he grew, reluctantly, to accept his father's absence, the path of his grief and his mother's reached a fork and then the two diverged. Once the house quieted down again, she began to neglect everyday life and allow a tide of chaos to rush into the house: a cascade of filthy dresses, wire hangers, pizza boxes, cigarette butts, and eventually vermin. She left their new television on at all times, usually playing to an empty couch, so that it seemed the advertisements begged no one to buy their products and evangelists prayed with nobody.

Toward the end of their days in Ovis, Darlene started to run with a different crowd—no more politics people anymore. These were men Eddie might see only once, men who smoked unpleasant cigars, who drove rust-caked Lincoln Continentals, who had filled the graying white leather interiors of their cars with discarded newspapers, who left their toenail clippings on the coffee table. Her moods became unpredictable. Once he brought a half-inflated basketball into the house, and she hurled it at his face for no reason he could figure out. He turned so that the rough ball hit him in the flank, leaving a cloudy bruise. The impact stunned her into regret, as if it had hit her instead of him, and she kissed the space below his arm over the next few days as it took on the color of an eggplant. Their trust throbbed and disappeared as the border of the injury grew sharper.

A year after his father died, Eddie's mother hadn't moved his father's clothes out of the bedroom. She stopped speaking to a friend who'd tried to set her up with a man. She hadn't gotten a job. Mommy's running low on savings, Mommy's having trouble finding work, she'd tell him, and he'd have to move a pile of half-finished cover letters from the kitchen counter when he ate breakfast. But he would leap off the school bus and return home in the afternoon to find her in the same tattered bathrobe, spooning thick brown liquid from a bucket-shaped container of ice cream in the kitchen, her eyes glazed and underlined, transfixed by daytime-TV shows where staged fights would break out. *Mom Stole My Boyfriend!* Empty beer cans studded the coffee table, corkless bottles of discount wine lolled on their sides, sometimes falling to the carpet. She stopped going to the courthouse and locked herself in her room, often weeping, sometimes for an entire day. During that time, Eddie taught himself how to hard-boil an egg and follow directions on the back of a frozen-food box. She started to ration his breakfast bars, she stopped buying him new clothes, the pencils she bought him for school all snapped or were lost within two or three weeks.

Six months after all the northerners left, Darlene finally found a job at a convenience store, and Eddie assumed that her new job would open up a new life: Her mood would brighten, she would stop biting her nails, she would finally make it to Parents' Day. But none of that happened. Somehow, things got worse.

When he found the pipe that summer, he did not know what it was at first, but it made a cool toy spaceship, since it looked a little like the starship *Enterprise*, round at one end and skinny at the other, and he flew it through the apartment between his fingers. He flew it across the universe of the living room repeatedly, trying to reach warp speed. The first time Darlene saw him playing with the pipe, she plucked it out of his hand without explanation, only curses—curses he'd rarely heard her speak before, and that change felt more ominous to him than the pipe.

One afternoon he came home to find her, hair disheveled, one pink roller in, nearly passed out across the card table they used for meals. He pulled out the chair beside her to discover one of his father's shoe trees lying sideways on the seat cushion, and the combination of these sights made him aware of everything he had pretended not to understand about his mother. In the past, he had walked in on her intensely caressing or staring at photographs of his father or objects he had owned, but this time he felt as if he had interrupted some deeply shameful activity between his mother and the shoe tree, perhaps the aftermath of a voodoo spell meant to transplant his father's soul into the shoe tree and resurrect him. The absurdity of the situation gave Eddie the courage to ask a question so outlandish, insulting, and terrifying that every other time his tongue had tried to form it, the query had evaporated.

Did somebody kill my dad? he asked.

Yes, she said from under a canopy of her hair, like he'd asked if the sun rose in the east. Then, more ferociously, raising her head, she added, They killed him hard, so he would stay dead.

Who did?

They don't know, Darlene said.

It didn't cross Eddie's mind until several days later that she could have meant more than one group of people by the word *they.* By then, the subject had disappeared. He kept trying to figure out what she'd meant, but during the rest of the year, all through second grade, he couldn't find a gentle path to bring her back to talking about his father's death and discover what she'd had in mind. First of all, whom she'd meant by *they.* The police? The people in town? She'd said it like she meant the detectives who had failed to get enough evidence to convict the suspects, but she'd also said it scornfully, as if she didn't believe that the detectives didn't know. Or did his mother mean that *she* knew, but nobody would listen? His eight-year-old brain tried to unscramble the mystery, until a final possibility emerged like a poisonous toad from a bog, shaking mud off, and this option proved ugly enough to weigh as much as the truth. That *they* knew, but pretended not to know. That one of *them* might have helped or covered up the evidence.

That summer, right before he died of pancreatic cancer, Sparkplug told him how they killed somebody they wanted to stay dead. Darlene and Eddie had traveled to the closest hospital, in Delhi, Louisiana, to pay their last respects.

You bind his hands behind his back with twine, Sparkplug confided while Darlene used the bathroom. You break his legs. You bash him in the mouth with a tire iron so that he swallows the majority of his teeth and the fragments scatter. You stab him eighteen times. You set his body on fire in his own store. You shoot him with his own gun. I'm telling you this because you ought to know, he wheezed. And bless her heart, your mama ain't gonna say.

Eddie was too stunned to believe what this guy, a known oddball he hardly remembered, told him—it would take another five years to sink in.

Sparkplug passed away, and that November Darlene and Eddie moved to Texas, into a small apartment in the Fifth Ward. Eddie had screamed and wept that they would have to leave his father there, and everything associated with him, including the Mount Hope Grocery, but his mother explained, holding in her own tears, that they could come back anytime, and they'd also leave behind many painful memories. The store's just an empty lot now, she said.

When they moved into the new place, she called to him from the vacant living room before her friend arrived with the rental truck full of their possessions. This will be better, she said, her voice reverberating through the space. We'll be closer to family, I'll be further away from temptation.

It was not better.

Temptation came with them. A few months after he and Darlene moved to Houston, creditors started calling. His mother, often some combination of drugged, absent, and sleeping, could not usually answer, and Eddie learned to recognize the calls whenever he heard several seconds of dead air after picking up. Or a machine would say, *Please hold.* The calls started coming several times a day; he'd hear their robot voices on the answering machine when he came back from school, or they would call in the evening. If he picked up, he would try to sound younger. Sometimes a utility would get shut off. He took to boiling water on the electric stove to wash himself. He would open the oven for warmth during that string of chilly nights in January and February that passed for winter in Texas, do his homework by the range light.

Talking to his mother stopped working. She no longer paid attention to the world or to time. She acted like someone wrapped in a gauze of happiness, but a fake happiness that to Eddie suggested that she didn't care about him. A year later, Aunt Bethella came over for Thanksgiving dinner, but she turned around and left. Eddie didn't think she would have liked the dry, donated turkey or the generic cranberry sauce anyway. They couldn't eat the sweet potato pie she'd brought, and he was angrier at his aunt for hurling the pie down on the stoop in her fury at Darlene than for leaving.

He decided not to go to school some days, choosing instead to wander around the perimeter, seeing his friends at video arcades on their lunch breaks. He borrowed what he considered a lot of money; other times he slipped coins and bills out of his mother's purse in order to support his diet of one-dollar tacos and Bubble Yum. On days when he did go to school, he'd do stupid things like perform a mocking impression of his science teacher to her face or pick a fight with a dirty kid who had dark circles under his eyes. Each time Eddie landed in detention he thought that they would bring his mother into school. Darlene did show up a few times, only to deny her drug use to the administrators, who *acted* like they believed her more than they seemed to actually believe her, but eventually his mother stopped showing up altogether. The school nurse told Eddie that she had addicts in her family too, and to remember that no matter how much he misbehaved, he would never divert his mother's attention away from the drugs. Don't take it personally, she said. It's a disease. Sometimes she would give him five or ten dollars. It made a difference.

❧

One October night, Darlene put on one of her late husband's hats, a fedora that seemed new, and sat at the table across from Eddie, maybe pretending to be a businessman. He had taken to shutting her out, because making eye contact would provoke a confrontation or make an upsetting episode worse. But when he didn't acknowledge her this time, she dropped her head to the table, despite the clutter there, and peeped at him from under the hat brim, making owl noises. She tried other animals. Cats, goats.

Then she saluted him, raised her voice, insisted they were somewhere else—on a boat, it seemed.

We've got to get at the emergencies, sir, she demanded. The other people need to see if it isn't correctly so that a reaction can't do it! Show us the planets.

Ma? he asked, hoping that speaking to her directly would shatter the pane of craziness she'd pulled up between them. He posed the question again—Ma?—wrapping his fingers around her forearm as if he meant to tug her into reality.

Show us the planets! she repeated, and slammed her hand on the table, slightly lifting the cards, pennies, and dominoes, nearly knocking over a tiny vase designed for a single flower.

Eddie peeled her hot hand off the table, threaded his smaller fingers between her rough ones, the nail polish now candy-apple red and flaking off, and led her to the balding patch of soil just outside, the size of a carpet, where a few sprigs of clover hugged the sides. Distant dogs barked and trucks rumbled down the highway, wailing like giants in pain.

She followed him, stumbling, and when he'd adjusted to the beauty of the cooler evening air and the spectacular array of pink and blue clouds in the immense sky, he pointed to a bright dot near the moon and said, There.

Calm settled on her shoulders, randomly. The sight of Venus might have had nothing to do with the shift in her mood. It seemed that as far as she was concerned, Venus could have been a flashlight, a motorcycle careening down a one-lane highway, a match losing its fire. Even so, they sat spellbound. She kicked off a sandal and absentmindedly drew circles in the dust with her toe, not looking down. In that moment of peace, he put his face between his knees so she wouldn't see, and rubbed it there silently, his cheek against his leg, letting numb tears fall from his eyes.

6.

YOUR OWN CORD

The cops in the pink and orange donut shop said the police couldn't go find Eddie's mother right then because you had to wait.

Everybody who got somebody missing gotta wait, they told Eddie. Not just you, son.

He sat with three policemen at a table with four plastic seats, the officers looming above his thin brown limbs. Eddie swiveled in his seat, fascinated by how it swung and caught, focusing on the chair to avoid the eyes of the cops. Everything outside now had the same glossy dark about it as the inside of somebody's eye.

You can't always tell right away, one cop leaned over his massive coffee to say, if a person has run off for personal reasons or if something of a different nature has happened that necessitates officers of the law getting involved.

Eddie unconsciously made a face that showed he didn't understand this principle—when somebody disappeared, didn't you just go find her? Wasn't it that simple?

This fellow's convex belly kept his cop shirt taut. His mustache went down to his chin on either side, and he had a soft, genuine expression, none of which matched his starchy uniform.

Sometimes folks can't cope, he kept explaining, and they run away from their lives on purpose because they think that their problems will go away if they take their bodies off the scene. A bad person didn't do anything to them, he said, scrunching the space between his brows, they just hit the highway. And in the first few days, unless we find somebody who says they saw a bad guy taking the person away, there's always a hopeful chance that the person will come back on their own recognizance, because they realize that they love everybody they left behind and that all they really needed was a little breather.

What's *recognizance*? Eddie asked.

Um, by themselves. It means you do it by yourself. Of your own accord.

Nope, another of the cops said. That's *reconnaissance*. Nobody paid attention to him.

I went to look for her myself, Eddie said. Because everybody here says don't trust the police.

The cops glanced at one another and then at Eddie.

I don't know why anybody would say a mean thing like that, the handlebar-mustache cop said. Don't you trust us, son?

Can I trust somebody else? Eddie asked. Is there a different police where she won't have to use her own cord?

The officer's chest jounced under his taut shirt as he laughed.

Already this waiting period had made Eddie skeptical enough that he decided not to get the police involved even when the time came. He would do it himself. The police, he realized, wouldn't have the same incentive. His suspicion that they didn't think his mother was worth finding came not from anything they said but from their general attitude of mildly amused boredom, even from the officer who sounded as if he wanted to help but couldn't break the rules. He probably didn't want to seem different from his partners.

That policeman scrawled Eddie's address and Mrs. Vernon's number on the back of a parking ticket. Eddie got up to leave, and at that point he gave the men a more detailed verbal picture of Darlene, the one he'd worked on some in his head, and they promised to stay alert and contact him as soon as the waiting period ended. A fourth cop came back from the bathroom and sat in Eddie's chair.

Brave kid, Eddie heard one of them say as he crossed the tile floor and shoved the door open with his shoulder. He launched himself into the pink lights flooding the far reaches of the parking lot.

He determined that he would try to enter his mother's mind, searching places she might have gone, armed with a photograph he'd uncovered in a brown album half filled with fading snapshots. The picture he had found showed both his parents grinning in front of a Christmas tree choked with tinsel, locked in the past by denim vests and blowout afros, but he thought he should let the night people see only his mother. To preserve the memory of his father, too upsetting and confusing for him to comprehend at this point, he covered the image of Nat with a piece of newspaper, careful to fold it over the back like a sleeve and tape it there so as not to damage the front.

The police, as promised, left a message on Mrs. Vernon's answering machine a couple of days after he'd spoken to them, assuring him that an investigation was under way, but he did not return their phone call. He had already given his own investigation priority, because, he had decided, in a just world only he should be allowed to find her, by chance or by God, but since he did not see a point in refusing their help outright, he didn't respond.

On day three he lingered at the end of class, having nodded off a few times and nearly fallen asleep. He had not eaten well—only free breakfasts and lunches in school, from which he would bring home portions for later, hidden in his book bag and under his shirt. His placement in the second row from the back had saved him from drawing the teacher's suspicions—though so many discipline problems exploded around him daily that Mr. Arceneaux wouldn't have noticed anyway. The realization that nobody cared was both liberating and frightening—he could fail that class and other classes, drop out of school, and graduate to hanging out and drinking Dixie beer while sitting on milk crates and playing dominoes in front of boarded-up houses without anyone even raising an eyebrow. He could disappear or die and it would take weeks or years for anybody to realize what had happened.

As he swiveled his eyes through the room, drowsy and dizzy, he understood for the first time that his classmates didn't count for any more than he did. It didn't matter if they never acknowledged the shadow of worthlessness above them, poised to crush them like Godzilla's foot. There wasn't much they could do to resist that. Few things could save him, as he saw it. School might save him, at least that's what everybody said, but school went down like medicine. Sports could, or becoming a singer or a rapper, but he wasn't musical. But with school he thought the odds might improve. He had a sudden sharp mental picture of his dead father crossing the concrete playground and crunching through the grass and leaves outside to peer into the classroom and monitor his progress, his grayish face troubled and stern. Eddie didn't pretend it had actually happened, but the what-if got to him. He sat up and forced himself to pay attention, stealing a nervous glance out the window every so often but seeing only birds.

Eddie feared that Darlene might be dead, but in the abstract that didn't seem as bad to him as the idea that she had abandoned him on her own cord. He thought that he would prefer to find her dead than find her alive and have to endure a face-to-face rejection, possibly amplified by the addition of Some Man. Some Man he thought of as a brutish, stocky guy weighted down with gold-plated necklaces, cursed with an overhanging brow, a throaty growl, and a habit of challenging people to punch him in the gut. A foolishly proud James Brown–type with tattooed forearms and a Jheri curl who drove a white Cadillac edged with rust. In Eddie's mind, this aggressive dude differed little from Mr. T; maybe that had something to do with the increased TV watching that came with having the house to himself. Perhaps Some Man would be his mother's pimp, though he didn't know that she had one, let alone if she had actually sold her body. He hadn't seen her take any money or do anything. Still, Eddie dreaded the appearance of a flashy dresser with an iron fist who would confirm his mother's status and imprison him with vicious, irrational rules. Any potential attachment of Darlene's terrified him; anybody coming between them could only widen their rapidly expanding separation.

But that fear didn't prevent him from venturing into the underworld every night after her disappearance and creating a fantasy life for himself as a detective. In fact, the fantasy was nearly real. Eddie divided up an old map of Houston, already so overused that the paper rectangles had nearly separated from one another. He circled each neighborhood and, starting with his own house in the Fifth Ward, knelt on the map in the living room scrawling through the city's landmarks, making pie shapes inside the concentric ring roads. Every few nights he'd visit the seediest corners of the pie shapes, each time making new connections, like a paper chain that might lead him to her.

When he had done with the likeliest areas of the pie shapes, he moved outside the ring road, until his nightly journey began to require more bus fare than he could manage on what he borrowed from friends and teachers without explaining his situation, and he'd had to walk home long distances after the buses stopped running. School gradually ended, and for most kids, responsibility dissolved into heat and haze, but Eddie worried that he might have to figure out how to pay the rent and the bills if his mother did not return soon.

Whenever Eddie saw their landlord, Nacho Vasquez, a tan guy about Eddie's height who wore denim shirts and a bolo tie with a silver and turquoise brooch, Nacho always steered the conversation toward Darlene—How's your mom? he'd ask. Is she at home? It took until August for him to tell Eddie to remind her that she was two months behind on rent. Eddie explained that she had gone on a business trip—a long one. When asked what kind of business, Eddie said that the trip was a job, she had found work somewhere else for a little while. He told Nacho that she knew about the rent and would pay him when she got back. Eddie was about to get on a bicycle he'd borrowed from a school friend and go searching for her again.

She left you here? Nacho asked.

Mrs. Vernon looks after me, Eddie said. Every day.

Did she go by herself?

Yeah. She doesn't have a boyfriend or anything.

She doesn't? Oh. What kind of guys does your mom like?

I don't know. She doesn't like tall guys. Anymore.

Nacho turned mauve. Really? Has she ever dated, you know, someone like me? I'm half French and half Mexican.

Maybe. Yeah. I'll ask!

When does she get back?

In a couple of weeks.

Tell her to get that rent to me, okay? But maybe I'll cut her a break if—you know? Never mind. All right? But soon!

Okay, Eddie said, and he could almost see time accruing, as if he had turned a crank and made the sun go backward and rise in the west. Nacho's patience would eventually run out. But Eddie hoped Darlene would get back long before then.

7.

WHO IS
DELICIOUS?

The minibus done slowed down to a bumpity-bump. The head-lights lit up a wall, and the bricks of the wall turned out as part of a farmhouse made of cinder blocks. The red-eyed driver, a brother they called Hammer, put the thing in park, let the engine idle, and went, We're here. Hammer wasn't his name, they called him that on account a he look like MC Hammer—he a skinny brother with his hair shaved in stripes on one side and got them same big glasses. He stretched his arms by grabbing the top of the steering wheel and said, Home sweet home, y'all, then a second later he said GET OUT in a real loud voice, like the *Amityville Horror* demon, to a dude name Hannibal and to TT, who twitching and talking shit and hadn't got up yet.

Didn't nobody in that minibus care about nothing. TT and Hannibal—a spacey man who always wearing this raggedy-ass fe-dora—almost got into a fistfight over if Michael Jordan was the best *ever*. They agreed that he *played* the best, but Hannibal said just playing the best ain't make nobody *the best ever,* because what about sportsmanship?

So nobody seen them headlights shining on the new digs as we passing, let alone the whole farm. I coulda told em 'bout some shacks I seen next to some white propane tanks, and then some wide-ass fields with orange trees sometimes, and swampy saw grass far as the headlights could throw they beams. Looked peaceful, like a place where wouldn't nobody get up in our business, and you know I hate when people be judging my friends for hanging out with me. Whenever I could take a vacation with em I jump at the chance.

A chicken waddled into the road in front of us. Hammer almost hit it—he had to stomp on the brake with both feet and that made the bus jerk forward like Sherman Hemsley, so much that Darlene seen the bead cushion under Hammer's ass when he leapt up. The whole crew got jostled and took to complaining. Hannibal dropped his pipe, and it ain't break but it did roll up under the seats, and he had to get down on his knees and crawl around to find it while it's rolling back and forth. When he bent down, everybody could see his butt crack and that caused some serious hilarity for everybody except a lively woman name Michelle who wearing pigtails even though she thirty-something—you know that girl hopped over Hannibal ass and looked out the window with a scared face on, gripping the seat back.

Did you hit it? she asked. You didn't hit it, did you? That's bad luck to hit a chicken!

Especially for the chicken, Hammer said.

Down in the road, the chicken waggled them red things on its head at the new employees in the bus like it saying, Course I made it, you dumbasses. The fuck you looking at?

In all the drama of stopping, Darlene and I sat in the back

looking at the scene, studying it like it's some philosophicated hy-pothenesthesism and with a li'l giggle we thought to ourself, *Why did the chicken cross the road?* Kind of as a joke, but Darlene also said that shit out loud. Why did the chicken cross the road? Ain't nobody act like they heard, so we start asking the question se-riously—my girl wanted a *answer. Why did the chicken cross the road?*

Right then the chicken booked into them tall grasses off to the side of the minibus. Hammer pointed at it and said to Darlene, Look like you missed your chance for a exclusive interview. Then he jump off the driver seat and gone to unlock the door that let us all out.

Michelle told Hammer, You funny. Glad you ain't hit it.

Jackie frowned and squinted, tryna see where the chicken had went, like maybe she gonna have to go chase it down. How did she get out? Jackie muttered under her breath. But then her ex-pression changed into one that ain't care no more.

We was in front of this long one-story building made of con-crete that had a line of muddy windows along the top of the wall. Jackie, Michelle, TT, and Darlene slid down out they seats into a pothole filled with water and had to shake out they shoes; Ham-mer poked and punched Hannibal and Sirius B till they stood up and got out, all sloppy and nervous. Now that Darlene out the shitty-ass A/C in the van, the humidity put her in a chokehold. She searching for a clue to where we had gone to—was we still in Texas, or had we went far as Louisiana or Mississippi or even the Florida Panhandle? Couldn't nobody tell, and if I was the only motherfucker paying attention, they sure had a *mucho problema.* How long do it take to get how far? Was that a Texas tree? Was that? The hell time it was? Was that sugarcane?

Darlene look at the building kinda suspicious, and then, right with everybody else, the good smells in her memory gone away and got replaced with a strong shit smell. Like a shit smell so bad that it reached its whole hand up inside your nose, pinched the bottom of your brain, and twisted your tear ducts like a lemon peel going into a motherfucking cocktail. The newbies all gagging and making disgusted faces and talking with vomit voices. Somebody seen feathers on the ground and pointed and said they saw feathers on the ground.

This is a chicken coop, Darlene said, like she just discovered America. Why did we stop here?

No, no, this ain't no chicken coop! TT said. How it's a chicken coop when we just seen a chicken running around *outside?*

Basehead, she muttered.

Bitch, I heard that, TT started, but Sirius B took a step to stand between em.

Darlene screwed up her face at TT and then turnt around, sighing to herself, 'cause TT always be saying the negative of whatever you said. She knew to ignore his ass.

I feel bad for you, TT, Sirius B said.

In the minibus, Sirius telling everybody how well known he is for music in Dallas–Fort Worth—mostly Fort Worth—and that hadn't impressed nobody, but outside Darlene could check out his tallness and saw that he had these long sexy arms on a wiry muscular body, with a ballplayer butt. Big big big Sasquatch feet. She took a step closer so she could feel the body heat between they arms and the little hairs that be brushing together there.

You in the opposite reality of everybody else, Sirius told TT. You don't gotta be Einstein to smell that this a damn chicken coop. He laughed at how ridiculous TT be.

Darlene smirked, and she wanna put her hand up Sirius shirt between his shoulder blades so she could know firsthand 'bout how smooth his skin. So she did. And instead of jerking around violent or nothing, Sirius turnt and shown her his face like a gift he gonna let her unwrap later, but she gotta wait. But between the feel of them silky back muscles and the open face he done showed her, his eyes touching her eyes, shit got all gooey, and that put the holy terror in her. She pulled her hand out and put it behind her on her own back, like she tryna undo what she had just did. Sirius looked forward again.

Jackie asked Hammer to leave the headlights on so everybody could see better in the early light and follow her to a heavy sliding gray door a few yards up. She kept hunting around, maybe to see where the chicken had went, then unlocked the door, pulled it open with some help from Sirius, and stood next to it so everybody could get in, even though she ain't put no lights on. The chicken-shit odor got ten times stronger, and when Darlene moved inside the building, into the nasty musty chicken air, and stood in this hallway with a bunch of straw scattered on the floor, she could hear these *ting ting ching* sounds coming from the left. She looked to the left and seen that one noise had came from all the chicken feet plucking at the bottom of they cages, and the other noise was the birds going *what what what brock* all over the place, or at least the ones of the birds that be insomniacs.

Hannibal spoke up for the first time in a while. He took his hat off his nose and mouth and ask, What we going in there for? It's all birdy and whatnot. He clamped the hat back over his face.

Come on, y'all, Jackie whispered, like she afraid to wake up the birds. It's people on this side, not no chickens. This the no-chicken area. She moved her hand in a half circle and went, Chicken, no-chicken. Okay? She clicked on a flashlight and walked into the no-chicken area, like everybody supposed to follow her.

The beam from Jackie light danced around and Darlene and I seen little flashes of the room. For a no-chicken area it sure had a shitload of feathers and pellets on the floor and you had to make damn sure you didn't slip on them pellets and fall on your ass. I went, I love this place, isn't it beautiful? But Darlene disagreed with me. See, she had went to college and everything, not on the honor rolls or nothing, but she still had some high-bougie ideas about comfortability and accommodations that I found it hard to respect. For her, everything had to look like some stupid Renaissance bed-and-breakfast.

Meanwhile, they got rows of perfectly fine bunk beds lying not very far apart going through the whole space. Aight, people of all kinda brown colors was tossing around in them beds without no sheets, looking like a box of chocolates that had fell on the floor and got smashed and then put back into the smashed box. Whatever. A bunch of them beds had striped mattresses on em with rusty springs poking through the tops, and the tops was ripped up. Them beds was close together as you could get beds without making it one big bed. The concrete floor and the walls had a ton of layers of paint all over em, and the layers had chipped away, so you could see brown and white patterns crawling up the paint and moldy-ass smears of water damage over the whole kit and caboodle. It's some small windows up by the ceiling, but they got wooden boards over em. I was like, Fine. You take the good, you take the bad.

But Darlene stopped cold, looking down from her motherfucking high horse, and in that moment come her downfall.

These are the accommodations, she said to Jackie, trying not to put too much of a question mark at the end or give away all her disappointments, 'cause out the corner of her eye she seen her traveling companions pushing on into the room, going to the best of the beds that's free, and Hammer helping the most whacked-out folks. Somebody climbed up to the top mattress of her bunk and the damn thing swayed like it might fall over if too big a person sleeping up there. She figured maybe Jackie playing a joke, maybe they only had to stop there for the night.

Something wrong with em? Jackie asked. That's me down the end. She threw the beam from her flashlight over to another cinder-block wall that stuck into the middle of the room but ain't quite met up with the ceiling, giving her the only privacy. 'Sgood enough for me, 'sgood enough for you, 'less you some kinda uppity bitch, which you shoulda said. Her eyes gone up and down Darlene body all judgmental and shit.

To be honest, Jackie, it isn't what I expected. You said three stars! I thought we'd at least get two.

You could go at any time, but you owe us for the ride and for the accommodations of at least this night because we ain't taking nobody back nowheres until tomorrow.

What do you mean?

It's in the contract. You signed the contract.

How much do I owe?

Five hundred for the ride and a hundred for the first night.

Six hundred dollars? Darlene asked.

She feeling tricked, like now she had to grow a whole crop of rice outta one grain.

You'll pay it back working, Jackie said.

The others in the minibus had understood the situation lickety-split without getting snotty and had gone and got into they space, and right behind that, Darlene found her sorry ass at the foot of the least wanted, most disintegrated mattress. She done a li'l circle around the bunk real quick, looking for some other clean bed that maybe nobody else seen. The last bits of her pride was breaking up into nothingness when she laid her pocketbook down and parked on the most bedlike part of the bed. Her heart start beating crazy like a freaked-out little moth under a juice glass.

For me it was a big reunion, a party. I could give two shits 'bout how many stars. I was like, Stars schmars.

So Jackie goes, I don't know about you, Darlene, but I'm exhausted. She stretching her mouth out to yawn, then shuffling back to the master bedroom. Once her new superior had disappeared into her space, Darlene start staring like a cat at the jerky light moving around behind Jackie wall. Then the light blinked out and a blackness thick as oil be pouring into her eyes and filling em up. She could make out maybe a couple of them folks on the beds. She put her hand in front her face and couldn't see nothing but the pinks of her nails if she squinted. Outside it started getting light, but in there, couldn't nobody see nothing. Sirius had took the bottom bed next to hers, which ain't seemed as filthy to her. Darlene stared at his back, hoping he gonna suddenly sit upright and switch with her out the protection he shown to her before, but no, he grabbed his knees and made some wheezy gurgle noises and that meant that he had fell asleep.

They ain't let her get in touch with Eddie yet, and even though it's late, she know she ought to tell him where she gone and that she safe. Since she think the company done cut off the phone, she figure she gonna call a neighbor who could check on him. She ain't know how Jackie gonna react, but knowing the bitch already gone to bed, Darlene start thinking 'bout if she ought to remind her now or wait until morning. But then she got all up in her motherhood, start groping her way past the sleeping folks squirming on the cots until she found the special wall, and whispered.

Jackie.

She ain't heard nothing back.

Jackie?

Yeah, honey? You need a hit?

I *really* need to call my son. Where can I call my son from?

Oh, Darlene, sweetie, I am so sorry. I forgot. It's too late now, it's almost morning, I can't take you out there at this hour.

Darlene start wondering 'bout what she gonna say next and the silence ate up her thoughts until Jackie open her mouth again.

How old your son? He not gon be up this late, is he? Even though Jackie folded that question into a sweet tone, it sound like she daring Darlene to admit that she not a good mother.

No, of course not. She figured he coulda stayed up waiting for her to get back—sometimes he did—but Jackie had this logical tone that bulldozed right the hell over Darlene feeling that she gotta do it right then, and all of a sudden asking for a phone seem ridiculous. Still, she kept on thinking 'bout *Eddie Eddie Eddie,* so I started to ignore her ass—I had a lot of other friends in the room, I ain't need her—and of course I knew that was gon make her cranky. Then I said, Darlene, look how much positivity you brought to yourself, chile. Stop worrying about that stupid kid and come party with me.

Jackie said, Good night, but Darlene's ass stayed right there, didn't know what gonna happen if she snuck on out to find that phone. She kept listening to Jackie clothing rustle while she tryna find a comfortable position to sleep in. She figured Jackie couldn't see her loitering, on account a she couldn't see Jackie neither, with both of em black and invisible in that damn dark room, and she hung out there, leaning 'gainst the wall, digging her nails in that rough concrete.

It's four miles away, Jackie's voice said, all breathy and not listening. Six miles, I mean. We'll go in the morning, she added with a little more feeling.

Darlene felt like Jackie had listened in on her thoughts and decided to give a warning not to make no trouble, and whether that was a coincidence or a dead-on guess, it still gave her a jolt. She stood straight up, peeled herself off that wall, and stumbled back to her bed. Had to figure out how to pass what be left of sleepy-time on that stained, lumpy box spring that look like it might poke out her damn eyeball if she turnt over in her sleep, not to mention all them strangers around.

Then she thought about using her pocketbook as a pillow to keep it safe from anybody fingers reaching in there and walking off with her stuff. She thought she left it on the mattress. No? Maybe she put it under the bed? Could she left it in the minibus? She touched the places on the mattress where she might had put the bag, but that method, though popular, don't never make nothing reappear. She got on her knees to hunt underneath the cot but she couldn't see nothing in the shadows down there, so she probing that hard cement with her fingers. When she pulled away, her hands was covered in dust and hair; she had little feathers, twigs, mouse pellets, and chicken feed sticking to her palms. A sneeze danced up her nose but she held it in and her face spasmed, like *gnaufg!* She brushed the crap off her hands onto her thighs and said, Shit shit shit, real quiet a bunch of times, like that be the name of every moment. I went to hang out with TT and we tried not to laugh at her. Rule Number One is keep your hands on your bags.

The stress made her want to reach out to me, even though me and TT chuckling at her pathetic ass. She punched herself in the heart and went, Stupid stupid stupid, through her teeth. The minibus still idling outside and she thinking 'bout a tiny chance that she had left the bag out there on the seat. But first she visited every restless black shape in that long-ass room, forty-six in all.

None of you are asleep! she burst out. You just smoked up Crack Mountain and now you're pretending to be asleep? I don't think so. Who has my bag?

Darlene! Jackie yelled, and then her voice rang outside the wall. Calm the fuck down.

One of these—has got my bag, and I am going to find out who.

Go to bed, honey, we'll deal with this once we've had some sleep, okay? What you had in there that you need so bad?

Darlene silently had to admit her possessions wasn't worth much. I was the most valuable thing in that purse—a half-empty glass vial and a rock in a plastic bag from the trip—and surely somebody gonna oblige with a hit anyhow when she start getting boogie fever. But Miss Darlene had issues with the princi-ple—you know how violated you feel when somebody jack your belongings.

After a while, Jackie voice ringing through the room, like Dar-lene mind be talking, like Jackie cutting in on our braindancing. Jackie go, You still want that hit? It's yours if you want a hit.

I smiled at Darlene inside her brain. I knew what she gon do. Not to be egotistical or nothing, but I *am* irresistible.

A totally unnecessary moment went by and then Darlene said, Okay, and gone in Jackie room. Jackie took a hit first, and that shit surprised Darlene for a second, but the radio static sound of them rocks fizzling got louder when Jackie sucked on the pipe and sent Darlene eyes into a rapture like she a motherfucking saint. The flame from the lighter be giving they face a red-brown glow, and the hot glass tube almost singed her lips and fingers again. Darlene knew I was not in the best mood—somebody mixed my ass with levamisole, I hate that shit—but then again, good shit wouldna let her sleep.

Then Jackie goes, It's ten, okay, but don't worry, I'll just add it to your bill.

Levamisole good for deworming a dog, but it ain't pacified Darlene one goddamn bit once she got me inside her. When she groped her way out the bedroom area, Darlene kept tryna figure out who robbed her, without the use of her eyes. When that shit ain't work, she fumbled over to the door they'd come through, a industrial slab kinda thing, and she thought she could maybe quietly raise that latch and go out to investigate. The bar felt cool when she touched it—weird for a place that's mostly hot, where she and the others had started using the bottom of they shirts to wipe away the sweat that be trickling down they brows and turning everything they looking at salty. The rusty iron bar went up a little bit when she lifted it, but she found a giant padlock holding that bad boy shut, a lock she couldn't believe she ain't noticed snapping shut behind the group. Who locked the lock? Hammer? What if a fire broke out?

Darlene stuck her hands in the little cranny where the door come to the frame, tryna cut a deal with the steel bulk and the pulley system that slid the whole motherfucker open. The crag ripped one her nails so bad she had to tear it off.

Ah, she thought, *that's good. Nobody could've left this place with my purse.* She decide to squat right at the opening of the door till sunrise so that couldn't nobody pass and in the morning she gonna do a inventory and find the handbag. Her eyeballs tryna drink in all the light they could, but it ain't much. The whole time her open eyes be feeling like closed eyes, and blinking didn't hardly change the view none. She keep worrying 'bout what she had got herself into with this place. She closed her eyes for real and say to herself that maybe everything gonna turn okay in the morning. She thinking 'bout the book and visualizing somebody giving back the bag.

She laid her head back and hit it against the concrete too hard, had to clamp down her jaw to keep from shouting, then start rubbing the sore spot where she thought a knot might pop up. After the pain got tingly and then got boring, I let go her arms and legs to make em relax and she accepted that she gonna have to take a wait-and-see attitude. She visualized that damn purse and getting the purse back until she done fell asleep.

All the same, the purse ain't never turnt up. Not only did it not materialize, but the harder Darlene tried to reckon out who done lifted it or where it gone, the more some the crew start wondering—to her face—if a crime had took place at all.

Michelle started going, Did you even have a bag? I don't 'member you having no bag when you was in the van.

Sirius remembered the bag and described it pretty good, but Michelle was not convinced beyond a doubt. Didn't nobody trust TT or Hannibal, including TT and Hannibal, and Hammer wasn't nowhere to be seen. Not one motherfucker confessed to the possible theft of the probable bag, and the whole episode made Darlene look bad and wacko 'cause she had accused everybody before hardly meeting em.

Just 'bout two hours after they got there, sleepytime got done and everybody had to get the hell up and start the damn day, even if they ain't had no rest. For these folks, *rise and shine* meant *get a hit off a dirty pipe,* but Darlene ain't had me or her bag no more, so she had to mooch. After breakfast—aka a hard-boiled egg, a gritty, no-name yogurt, and a half-pint of 'bout-to-go-sour nonfat milk—Jackie unlocked the door to go out and smoke, but she wouldn't let Darlene search nobody for the pocketbook. When Darlene checked the road, the minibus gone, probably left during the hour or two when she'd drifted off. Hammer must have drove it somewheres. Had he been inside or outside? Had Jackie had the key all this time? Did Jackie snatch the bag?

Darlene snuck a short, angry walk away from the chicken house to breathe some fresh air. She figured out that the building was one of three look-alike connected buildings near the top of a ridge with a dusty road cutting through it all like the part in some old white man's hair. Once she had scampered up to a higher place, jumping over them potholes, and she could see over the ridge, she turnt to get a look at the farm.

For 360 degrees, the view stayed 'bout the same. Bunch of shiny-ass, frilly leaves of corn be fluttering out to the horizon, like the invisible hand of God ruffling em, and they get small in the distance and morph into a emerald glop. Beyond that was some teeny-tiny gray trees and a long chain of them electrical Godzilla towers in the far far distance where the world start to curve, a crazy distance couldn't nobody imagine running away to. No wonder they let her walk around during the day.

Darlene gave a nervous look to the chicken house, like she wanna skip out, but then a man she ain't never seen before come out the nearest building and called her back by name. The way he said her name made her feel like she had did something wrong by wandering off—the second syllable came louder than the first, exactly the way her daddy used to say it when she got him pissed. The sound of the voice alone tugged her back over to the coop and she picked up speed as she went.

Darlene feet going chuff-chuff and stopped in the rocky dirt and the dude pointed at the chicken-house door. In his other hand he had a gun—still in a holster but he got his damn hand on it—and that made her wonder what's wrong and is he gonna shoot her if she don't come back?

He told her, They're gonna dock your pay ten dollars for missing roll call.

Ten dollars ain't seem like much compared to what she need to make, or her expected salary, so she didn't hardly notice what he said.

The man was a ethnic type with a round-ass tan body and a face too small for his head that be held in by some elephant earlobes sticking out at almost ninety degrees. He petting his mustache like a kitty cat. He ain't introduce hisself at that time, but he did take his hand off the gun right as she gone back inside.

Darlene heard the last couple names of the other workers as

she going in the sleeping quarters. Jackie had everybody lined up in two rows, one of twenty-three, one of twenty-two, so the new girl seen where to put herself. She filled the empty place and wait for her name but Jackie ain't never called it. She told the men to divide themselves from the women and that they had a special assignment. While the women waiting, Jackie had herself a private chat with the mustache man who had called Darlene inside. Darlene stepped out the group of women and waited right behind Jackie to ask her a question.

Darlene words come out strange, on account a me, and that she ain't had much sleep. Jackie, did anybody who... called my bag? I mean, my son. Did anybody find my bag, and can I call my son?

Jackie let out a breath. Nobody got your bag. I don't think you had a bag. Did you show me your ID? We need to keep your ID on file.

That's it, the ID was in my bag! And how about my son?

When we're on detail we can stop at the depot and you can call. She threw her attention over Darlene to the rest of the group. Men to the right, ladies left, please.

What, Darlene said, it's different work?

Darlene, if you want to get with the men, you could certainly try it. Jackie had this high, edgy note in her voice, tryna sound all businessy.

It's more money, isn't it? I owe you six hundred twenty already, I need more money.

It's only more depending how much work you do, Jackie said. You not willing to work hard, are you? She raised her eyebrows and turnt to count the men as they went together.

Darlene frowned, she shifting her weight, and this grumpy feeling kicked her ass. She cocked her head and walked over to join the menfolk, saying, Of course I'm willing to work hard! At first she stood behind the backs of the tallest dudes, then she got up on tippy-toe to hear Jackie instructions. When the big echoey space swallowed Jackie voice, Darlene decide not to ask her to repeat herself. When she done wore out the patience of the shortest, furthest-back man by begging him to tell her what Jackie said, she decided to mimic the guys as they stiffened they bodies and pulled they holey T-shirts and muddy work pants into place. Those that been there and got theyself the regulation canvas gloves (fifteen dollars at the depot) be tugging em over they rough fingers. Most the men made they way to the door, Darlene marching in with em, getting set for tough labor, hopefully justified by high money. She ain't had no appropriate shoes, so Jackie found a pair somebody had left behind.

She goes, These boots belonged to Kippy.

It sound like Kippy somebody important. Darlene put the boots on, and she notice that the laces be all stiff with some dark, rusty-colored dust, and it be on the shoes too.

Kippy ran away. Tried to. But he didn't make it.

Darlene wiggled her toes inside the toe of one boot, and they fit her tight as a rabbit inside a grain silo. Them shoes was too huge, and now she thinking that that rusty dust be Kippy blood.

They caught him. So... Jackie shook her body like she tryna say, *Don't try this at home, kids.*

Shortly, ten of em riding in a souped-up school bus. Most the seats had got ripped out, so everybody had to stand up, and the windows of the bus, the kind schoolchildren woulda jacked down and thrown paper planes outta, they been removed, and both sides opened into the air. The front windshield had broke in a spiderweb shape, by somebody the foreman called a crackhead. The guys who worked there longest knew to sit down and hold on to the few seats there was, 'cause when the bus started up and shook in them potholes, you might lose your balance and fall out the open side. A bunch of big-ass light green plastic tubs took up part of the inside the school bus.

Darlene sat near Sirius, but he acting all uncomfortable, what with all the man-talk that done broke out as soon as the guys separated from the women. He leant away from her and he ain't look back. A guy would sometimes make a rude comment and glance over to check what she doing, but Darlene only half listening to they coarse jokes and swagger. She had came down fast since them dirty hits this morning, and the drumbeat done started up in her head again. I heard her thinking, *I need you, Scotty. I want to be with you.* I told her that I loved her too and that I always gonna need her forever. I'll always be with you, I said. I started singing her wedding song: *You're the best thing that ever happened to me*... Just look up. She turnt her chin to the sky and saw some chunky little clouds with straight edges at the bottoms, rocking a smooth butter color on account a the early-morning light. To us the scene above look like a giant blue table in the middle of a ballroom, scattered with some crack rocks. We felt like she could reach up and pull them ginormous rocks down like they lemons off a tree.

Darlene raised her hands to where the window woulda been, but the bus went in a pothole and wobbled big and she flinched and grabbed the side and the seat in front of her to keep from falling out. One her legs gone over. Sirius gaping at her for a second and hold out his hand, but by then she ain't need to grab it. Her temples throbbing with blood, and drips of sweat sliding down her armpits to her waist; they tickled and made her itch. One the guys had a voice like Nat, and soon she could hear her dead husband whistling "You Are My Starship" along with them drumbeats, and her eyes teared up like she crying but she ain't know why the tears 'cause she only felt numb, like she suddenly a metal spigot that somebody had opened.

Another dude who ain't introduced hisself interrupted her sad little trance to say, You better have some strong arms. He raised his arms and flexed em to show her what strong arms looked like.

She stared at his deformed nose, tryna make him feel as small as he had made her feel.

He went, You know it's watermelons, don'tcha?

What's watermelons?

What we picking.

Oh yeah, right, right. Mm-hmm. Watermelons. It's more money though.

Nah, not that much more than anything else.

Darlene thought 'bout what it gonna look like to carry a fruit the size of a big-ass dog across her forearms. I *know*, she said. Between the ginormous job and that sticky heat, already hot enough that the sweatier men had took off they shirt and was using it as towels, she might drop dead by afternoon. I wanted to give her more strength, but I could feel my power fading, till I was only a li'l tingle bouncing up and down her nerve endings, like a pair of shoes stuck on a telephone wire.

It ain't the real biggies, the guy said, not no Carolina Crosses— whoo. Thank God it's still early. Reckon they'll be like thisyer. He cupped his hands around the air to show something the size of a basketball. Maybe li'l bigger. They call it a Sugar Baby.

Darlene remembered her melon-fucking Cajun john. If he could make it out here, I said to her, he'd be in heaven, and she could make a lot of money and spend it on a lot of drugs. Plenty of shame out here for that sonofabitch to like. I lived for the upward curl of Darlene's wet lips, I wanted to see em around a pipe again, letting me in and down her throat so I could gently caress them li'l sponges inside her lungs and give her back her beautiful self-confidence.

Look like you gonna enjoy it, the guy said.

No, she said, I'm thinking about something else. I'm sorry.

I laugh like that too sometime, he said, tryna see some shit beyond the flat fields. I was friends with that guy too—we spent a lot of time together laughing about shit neither of us could remember now.

Darlene did not enjoy harvesting no watermelons. Not even them Sugar Babies that only weighed ten pounds. But she had to do it for at least another month, because she had chose the job and they wouldn't let her switch, plus she had something to prove. The foreman, that mustache guy, who also the driver, chose the spots with the most ripe melons. He said you could tell the ripeness by how yellow the grass underneath, and he giving all kinda li'l notes 'bout when a melon ain't ripe and warned the group not to be touching none of the ones he ain't cut off the vine, 'cause if you ripped the stem you could ruin the ripening process and that would be bad for what he be calling consumer demand.

Then he'd go up and down the rows with a li'l hook blade shaped like a comma, cutting the vines and freeing them green globes. His second in command had a butter knife and did the same thing, but he had a helluva lot more trouble. After the cut, they'd turn the melon out so the pickers could see if they'd cut it off the vine or not. Next the bus would drive slowly down a row, and half the group would form a human chain on either side. They'd pick up them Sugar Babies and toss the ripe ones down the chain till somebody threw em to one the catchers riding inside, a brother on each side the school bus. The catchers had to drop em in the bins without bruising none of em. There was miles and miles of this shit to do.

The foreman—Darlene eventually heard him answer to the name How, probably short for Howard—maybe 'cause he seened her almost run off that first morning, ain't wanna put her on none the easier jobs. He ain't let her hide inside that shady bus and arrange them melons into no neat pile—his buddies, the dudes he joked with about pussy, got them jobs. He put her in the middle of the human chain, where she had to catch the Sugar Babies with her gut. Once or twice they knocked the wind outta her. She breathed deep, pretended she ain't hurt, and hurled the next melon to the next catcher, who handed it up to the guy on the bus.

This supervisor How seem to enjoy putting Darlene down, always reminding her that she had wanted to come out and harvest watermelons with the men. He'd pretend that she on a baseball team and do a play-by-play of her throws or her catches and snicker when she fucked up. But she ain't never broke none, she kept saying to herself. She never dropped a single one. Her forearms bruised up, she jammed her finger, broken nails scraped melon skins sometimes, but she ain't never dropped a single one.

The season went on, and the melons changed type till they turnt into some humongous, child-size, lead-heavy boulders. Darlene always thinking that they weigh what Eddie used to weigh when he smaller, and that made her ask could she call home, but then it'd get too complicated or pricey and she'd hang with me instead. She got near the pay phone, but she ain't never had no money. She dialed a number and it said some crazy shit she ain't never heard a pay phone say. It'd go, *Please deposit five dollars for the next five minutes.* And she be like, That's twenty quarters!

Once when she picking melons she stopped and wiped the sweat off her forehead with the back of her wrist and stood there all sporty-like, waiting for the next one, and How giving her a hard time 'bout it.

He go, Bet you wanna cut one of them Charleston Grays open and sit down on that rock over there, eh?

It wasn't the first time he talked trash about picking watermelons that sounded like he tryna get the black folks' goat. How called himself one hundred percent Mexican and talked a lot of shit on how Texas and California really belonged to Mexico and the gringos stole everything, and he teased the black crew members 'bout the Civil War and said that they belonged to him. He told the few Mexicans on the crew that he be a Aztec and they his POWs.

At first, in that roasting heat and that motherfucking unbreathable humidity, Darlene did dream 'bout stopping work and tearing open a Sangria melon with her bare hands, biting the red part off real slow and letting the juice drip down her cheeks and onto her neck and chest, sticking her face in and wetting it just to get cool. But on account a How's comments she ain't want him to know, 'cause it seem racist against herself to want so bad to stop work and eat a watermelon. This man How wouldn't never cut that shit out, though.

You know you want that, right? How told her. He mocked her with a exaggerated grin. All you people want is some watermelon.

Fuck it, How, she spat. It's one hundred degrees out here and we're slinging around these twenty-pound fruits all dainty like they already belong to some white lady in the Garden District? If I want to stop and eat one myself, who cares if people call me a nigger just for wanting what anybody in their right mind would want? If eating and resting and surviving makes you a nigger, then sign me up!

The guy behind her on the chain goes, I hear that, and grunted and lobbed a Carolina Cross her way. Word.

It socked her in the gut and made her stumble backward a couple steps and then drop to one knee, but she held fast, like letting go even one a them suckers would splatter the last of her willpower all over the dirt. As she got up the strength to heave that damn monster up to the guy in the school bus, she feeling a intense need to hang with me again, so she could smoke and smoke and smoke until I filled up her empty insides with smoke, and we could do a spiral dance together up into that heavenly ballroom full of drugs way above the planet Earth.

8.

DRIFTWOOD

Darlene clutched at the bedclothes in her sleep that morning, mashing them into the shape of a blanket and winding up in the middle of the bed, sweating. The clock said 6:05 a.m. when she awoke, and Nat hadn't come home. At 6:06, nothing; 6:10, 6:14, 6:59, still no husband, and she felt certain she knew what that meant. Her mind told her, *An alive Nat would have called.* Darlene's internal organs seemed to shift positions; her lungs fell to her hips, her heart pulsed through her stomach. For the first time she allowed herself to think, *He's not alive. He offered to go to the store and get the Tylenol and now he's not alive. If I hadn't had a headache he would have stayed home safe. If I hadn't worn those tight shoes that I know give me migraines I wouldn't have asked for the Tylenol and he would've come back last night. If I hadn't already taken a sedative, thinking it could substitute for Tylenol, I wouldn't have fallen asleep.*

They had gotten used to occasional threats and crank calls

from their political opponents over the years, but after Nat spoke out in the local media against David Duke, the former Klansman who became a member of the House of Representatives, the Mount Hope Grocery got on the radar of a host of malicious detractors. In the past few weeks, Nat and Darlene had found a multitude of college-ruled-paper scraps shoved into their mailbox or underneath their door, covered in epithets. They both heard unpleasant words shouted from cars and endured a disturbing incident with the local police when two uniformed officers entered the store. The first fired his pistol into the ceiling apropos of nothing while the second bought a package of beef jerky from the terrified part-time clerk on duty. Sometimes the phone would ring, and on the other line somebody would breathe or bark a threat: *We gonna string you up, nigger. Make your ass a human piñata.*

Once Darlene picked up the phone, and after several moments of silence, she heard a radio crackling in the background. Finally, a raspy voice asked, Connie? That you? Hello, is Connie there?

Darlene let out an audible breath and told the caller, You've got the wrong number, ma'am, in a bright, relieved tone.

I'm glad *you're* happy about it, the voice said before the receiver banged down.

Most of the customers who weighed in felt that the police had not addressed the threats to Mount Hope particularly seriously, but you couldn't call the police on the police. Sparkplug had a routine in which he would imagine making the call himself: *Hello, police of the police? We got some officers that's breaking the law—all over my back. Send us a cop fast, but send another cop to watch the first cop.*

From the moment Darlene woke up, Nat's absence burned pinholes in the fabric of her life. She very much considered Nat's life and her own the same life—it had never occurred to her that marriage could represent anything less. If she ever thought about death, she prayed that the two of them would die in a car crash together at age eighty-three, or drift off into senility as their many grandchildren stood beside their king-size bed, massaging the balls of their thumbs and feeding them black cherry–flavored gelatin. She hadn't thought very carefully about how big a risk it is to love anybody, or how much the choices made by the one you love can increase that risk.

Darlene ordered herself to rise; she tossed the sheets back, letting them crinkle across the mattress. On a normal morning, Nat would've calmly entered the room by now, set her coffee on a coaster on the nightstand, made the bed as she showered, whistling as he glided from room to room. She tiptoed into the hallway, thinking that she would discover him there; he would make an excuse about getting a slow start, she would blush at her foolish worry, and they would kiss. He did not appear, and yet the sound of his whistling entered her mind along with a knife of sheer dread that sharpened itself on her rib cage. For a while Nat had favored that Tavares song "It Only Takes a Minute," but sometimes he'd whistle a gospel tune, or something a little more somber that sounded like "When Johnny Comes Marching Home." Sometimes he would whistle through his teeth, other times he wet his lips and puckered them. The notes of the songs would repeat in her memory, like breezes drifting around the corners when she didn't expect them, sometimes warm and loving, other times merely annoying.

By that time Nat would normally have filled the house with the smoky aroma of country bacon. Eddie would probably have gotten up with him to set the table and pour juice into their jam-jar glasses before Nat walked him to what they called day care—really just the home of a caring local matron. But when she peeked into Eddie's room, she saw him still asleep. Darlene shivered at this realization and attempted to warm herself as she walked down the hallway to the phone. When she called Mount Hope, the other end rang interminably. She dialed the number of every person on her list of people to call in the entire town of Ovis and several of the nearby towns, but she couldn't get an answer anywhere; perhaps nobody got up that early. The fear of bad news kept her from journeying down to the store herself. She would wait at home, at least for a while longer. Eddie woke up, distressed to be late, asking for his father. Darlene told him that he'd stubbed his toe and driven himself to the hospital.

How could he drive with a stubbed toe? Eddie demanded to know.

He stubbed the left one and stepped on the gas with the right, she said.

Eddie quieted down, and her own lie calmed her enough to dismiss her fear as irrational. Maybe some version of her lie had actually happened. Sometimes, she knew, if she dwelled on it too closely, she could fear every moment she spent apart from Nat—not knowing what danger he might face in those murky parts of his life she did not share.

That afternoon, when she'd decided to figure everything out once and for all, the police paid a visit just after Eddie came home for lunch from playing down the street.

The police spoke of something they called it.

At first, she became unhinged and threw herself outside, toward the clothesline, but once the police left the house, she calmed down, remembering not to trust what the police said, certainly not more than her own experience. She steeled herself to walk up to Mount Hope and investigate. The police may not have had the facts exactly right—white folks in Ovis had a habit of confusing one black man for another. Perhaps Sparkplug had burned himself to death accidentally a few doors down and Nat had merely fallen asleep in one of the chairs out back, the way he had done once after too many beers at an evening party, and he'd had to open the shop as soon as he awakened. Then he couldn't answer the phone because a long stream of customers had kept him busy.

Outside, a small group of short trees gave off a sweet thick maple-syrup odor. Anybody she met along the way she subjected to a grilling—Did you see him? He wouldn't ever stay out all night. If only she hadn't asked him to go out. If only she hadn't had a migraine last night. I'm sure he's okay, they told her back. Didn't hear nothing. Didn't hear nothing—but they didn't make eye contact when they said it.

Then Darlene ran across Sparkplug chuffing up the road outside their house—alive, half awake. She tried to hide her disappointment in his continued existence, and the rising terror making her limbs shudder.

Oh! he said. You ain't hear? Suddenly his crow's-feet wrinkled up with apparent shame and he shut down completely. His fat legs shifted as if he meant to break into a run. If it's any help, he said, I myself spent last night downtown on vagrancy and I ain't see them bring nobody in, definitely not Nat, 'cause when a fine fellow like him come in a jail cell, everybody notice. Darlene thanked Sparkplug and hurried closer to the store, wringing her knuckles, feeling her pulse race across her cheeks, into her eyes.

A group of older women in flowery muumuus and silky wigs crossed the road to greet her, two of them with flowers behind their ears. The two biggest ladies blocked her path in a way that seemed obvious and deliberate. Darlene recognized the women as her neighbors, but she didn't have a close relationship with any of them, not Harriet, not Alice, not Jeanette. From her vantage point she could not make out the store through a tall copse of sugar maples and pines that obscured the view.

Why, Miss Darlene! How are you today? Alice said, gripping Darlene's wrist with both hands, her voice high and fake. Alice's thick forearms looked like big tubes of cookie dough.

Ignoring Darlene's many questions about whether they'd seen Nat, the ladies clucked about nothing of consequence—the muggy weather, who's cooking what, who wasn't at church and why, last year's cane harvest, an upcoming wedding. They did so with enough energy to confuse Darlene for several minutes, especially when they paused to solicit her opinion of the various trifles, but then she came to understand that they had information to conceal. When she subtly endeavored to step around them, they moved along with her, surrounding her in their human corral.

How is Eddie? asked Jeanette, taking hold of Darlene's forearm, walking both her hands down Darlene's arm and stitching their fingers together. She put her face close to Darlene's face and forced her to lock eyes.

Darlene, for her part, resisted Jeanette's stare, letting her eyes blur into the distance through the trees, in the direction of Mount Hope. She answered the ladies' questions without listening very carefully, keeping her responses terse and attempting to graciously extricate herself from Jeanette's firm touch.

Isn't this cool afternoon just delightful, what with how hot it's been? Harriet said. She breathed in to the crest of her lung capacity while caressing her face with her hand. The others agreed and added boring comments to her cheerful, inconsequential statements until the cloud of boringly ominous comments seemed to attack the group like thirsty mosquitoes.

The wind changed then and the heavy smell of burned wood rushed up Darlene's nose; for the first time she saw a thin tube of grayish smoke rising above the vicinity of the store's footprint. The horror must have shown on her face, because the ladies moved their feet apart like they would momentarily need to hold her or push her backward. Jeanette lurched forward and gave Darlene a loving, paralyzing bear hug. Tears distorted her voice as she begged Darlene, Please don't go no further.

Darlene wrenched herself free of the ladies, who lumbered after her but could not prevent her from running to Mount Hope on her own. She clutched herself and cried out when she arrived at its charred maw, raising her eyes to see the sky through what she had known as the roof, the support beams askew, blackened, cracked, and shiny from the inferno, the front door chopped apart by firefighters and dangling from its bottom hinge, melted plastics, and even the freezer severely burned, all telling her with one voice that the police had spoken the truth, that her husband had perished among these things.

Later that day in the morgue, which smelled of lemon cleaner and formaldehyde, the same cops she'd hoped had lied when they spoke about *it* in her house asked her to look at something else burned, something they had found in the debris, and for a moment Darlene thought that they had taken a pig from a nearby barbecue pit and decided to play a prank. At first the sight of this thing did not affect her any more than watching a tray of ribs show up on a picnic table, until the doctors and policemen referred to *it* as *him*.

Him resembled one of the support beams from the store, a log turned to charcoal, and had she run her finger along its contours, she thought it would've dropped bits of black powder onto the steel table and the floor and darkened the swirl of her fingerprint. She knew why they had asked her to come, but it confused her to see this bizarre piece of driftwood that they might have pulled away from a riverside bonfire. She almost laughed, as any normal person might have, but those other people wouldn't have noticed that the gold ring around one of the fingers matched the ring on her own finger. The sculpture had an open mouth, and Darlene thought of her husband screaming and choking on smoke as the fire changed places with his breath. The blood drained from her arms and legs, and she spun around and covered her mouth as she walked carefully out of the room to the nearest waiting area and collapsed over the back of a chair.

It had really happened, somebody had burned her husband to death, ripped him out of her life forever and left her alone. And now she might be equally likely to get stabbed to death and set on fire by the same people, who had decided that it didn't matter when someone killed and mangled bodies like his. She wished that she had died instead. No, she wished that she had come with Nat to the store and changed the outcome, or that she hadn't had a migraine that night at all, or that she hadn't let him go to the store even though she'd said she'd be fine, that she had taken a sedative instead. Then she wondered if somebody on the police force had been involved, or known something, that maybe somebody on the police force had doused Nat with the actual gasoline, maybe another had lit the match, a few more had stabbed him, and perhaps they had followed her into the sitting area at that very moment. Maybe that man, or that one; which of these creeps had the cruelest face? Or the *nicest* one. Which sonofabitch could cover up the best? She felt certain that they would try to chop her up and roast her body like a rack of ribs too—or her son's.

¥

Darlene's parents wouldn't show up for the services—they probably wouldn't show up for their own funerals. Her father, P. T. Randolph, had allowed various illnesses to go untreated—hypertension, cataracts, and rheumatoid arthritis, to name three. He claimed to do so in the name of religion, but everybody said that being saved meant less to him than saving money. He'd splurged on a wheelchair a few years back, but now he shared it with her mother, Desirée, who had thromboses in both legs and diabetes running rampant. According to Darlene's brother, Gunther, whom they called GT, they barely left the sofa, let alone Lafayette. They didn't have a car or a home phone anymore, and if they wouldn't get a phone, they'd never pay for a bus. Besides which, he said, Mama panics if she even thinks about getting on a bus.

Surprisingly, LaVerne and Puma, who had cut Nat off for years, drove up from New Orleans for the service, but Puma kept grilling anybody who would listen: How do they know it's him? They don't really know! That ain't my boy. Bethella avoided Puma, and later complained to Darlene about his disrespectfulness. As a rifle party fired off a three-volley military salute, Darlene could feel Puma's eyes on her. His tortured expression seemed to set off each gunshot, all of them aimed at her heart. Then Nat's parents turned on Darlene as if they suspected her of the murder, as if they knew about the Tylenol and the tight shoes. She overheard LaVerne say, He should've been buried in the Hardison plot. Darlene could see she would need to steer clear of them.

Family notwithstanding, people with earnest intentions did try to help Darlene as best they could over the next couple of years. Retail clerks, neighbors, social workers, a detective from San Francisco. She would remember that help from time to time, and the feeling would raise her mood slightly for a short period. The detectives eventually ruled out a large number of people and settled on a group of young hoodlums, possibly hired by an older set of hoodlums. They feared that they did not have enough evidence to guarantee a conviction, but they arrested them anyway, even though the district attorney could not get the trial moved to a more favorable location.

Without telling Darlene, Nat had taken out a modest life-insurance policy in addition to the store's fire insurance. When she learned of this by mail she wept; she thought of each check she wrote afterward as a postcard he'd sent from beyond the grave. Darlene avoided spending much time in Ovis, buying buttermilk or ham hocks from other shops in nearby towns. She'd lost, along with the store, the heart to stack cans of baked beans on the shelves by herself or decorate the register with pictures of family members she could no longer face because of what she had done, and so she did not attempt to rebuild or reopen the store. Instead she hid under the fear that these insane freaks who felt they did not have to follow the law meant to return and finish the job. Sometimes she hoped that they would.

Bethella volunteered to take Eddie off her hands for a week immediately following the services, during the terrifying lull after Nat's death when it began to seem that no one cared anymore except her, and during that time, the citified Negroes and Jewish lawyers of New York with their biblical names—Aaron and Abraham and Leah—came to Ovis and stayed for weeks in nearby motels and private homes, offering their services for free. Darlene refused to throw a party, but Eddie spent his sixth birthday playing in the backyard with several of the lawyers' children. The lawyers interviewed her with earnest intensity, though she could not tell them much; took to the streets, though she would not; and shook their fists at the press, telling them everything they knew about justice and how it ought to work. But fist-shaking did not produce sufficient evidence for the justice system to feed on. Despite their tenacity, after more than a year with no results, they had to apologize and depart for good. Although the police found a tire print that matched the pickup of a certain kid and his friends, whom they rounded up, all other evidence had been incinerated, and they couldn't produce a single witness. At the end of those many months the lawyers shook their heads and scribbled down emergency numbers on the backs of their business cards. The police promised to keep working on the case; they all seemed sincere. Then the lawyers went home to their city of origin, probably thinking about different legal cases that they could actually set right.

After they left, Darlene decided that she should independently collect whatever information she could to prove who murdered Nat, but the people who had done it had covered their tracks, chucked their murder weapons in places nobody had found, probably burned their bloody clothing. Nobody white in the town admitted to seeing anything untoward. Nobody white would take the word of anybody black. It seemed sometimes as if an imaginary store had burned down and an imaginary black man had lost his imaginary life inside it.

Some of the white people who had no shoes, holes in their clothes, and moth-eaten hats squinted at Darlene differently afterward, like they had indigestion from the story and couldn't spit up. Did they know things they couldn't tell her, or did they despise her? How could a store burn down at night and nobody see anything, Darlene would think, and complain to anybody who would listen, as well as many who would not, and interrogate anybody she thought might have seen something that person did not want to have seen. In bad dreams, she watched the orange flames chewing Mount Hope to death, lighting the neighborhood and the faces of people she'd served every day, who peered into the glow while her husband shouted for help and melted behind the windows.

But after a year and a half, Darlene's desire for revenge subsided enough for a daily routine to take shape, one that avoided anything to do with Nat and focused instead on everything related to raising a son and struggling to pay the phone bill and the rent and the car insurance, things Nat had done without her help and that the store's income had covered, barely. The loss of even one of those sources of support—the store, her income, her husband—could've crushed Darlene. But losing all three, combined with her guilt about her part in the tragedy, eventually drained away her spirit and the last of her fight. At that point she merely wanted to sit still, to look beyond reality and ignore the world; she wanted to switch places with the boring chores of life so that she would matter again, and all the obligations would grow small and distant and useless.

As her insurance money began to run low, an eccentric white man who claimed he'd once met Nat gave Darlene a job she called a Hail Mary pass, the kind of job you take knowing that it won't cover your expenses, hoping that you'll get an additional job the next day (or a better one the next month), admitting that you simply need to get out of the house. She became a clerk and cashier at a chain drugstore called Hartman's Pharmacy, the type of lackluster store where red-and-green crepe-paper Santas and reindeer faded in the chaotic, dusty window display until February, the month when she started.

She had worked there for only a couple of weeks when they came in. Two of the five suspects they hadn't had enough evidence to convict. Both of them lanky and tattooed, with grayish skin, pimples, and dead killer eyes. With a long line full of talkative people, Darlene didn't see the men until they arrived at her register. She turned to the last customer in front of the two guys, and when the customer left and she saw these two so close, with nothing in between, close enough to squeeze her neck shut, she stumbled back as if somebody had pushed her.

They dropped a case of Schlitz cans on the counter with a smug bang. Darlene pushed around behind Carla, at the other register, and went into the back. The two hadn't recognized Darlene, and when she disappeared they became confused at first, then angry when she didn't come back after a few minutes. In court, they had shaved and worn ties, but since then, they had let their hair grow long. One of them had on a filthy T-shirt that said ALABAMA in metallic letters. Dirt highlighted the wrinkles on their knuckles and outlined their fingernails. One of them had a wispy mustache. Then the names exploded in her mind—Claude and Buddy Vance, whose father, Lee Bob, was considered the ringleader.

Where the hell she run to? Buddy asked.

Claude laughed. She got workaphobia?

Buddy, the older, taller one, in the Alabama T-shirt, rapped on the counter a couple of times with the flat of his hand. Excuse me!

Carla, in the middle of her own transaction, asked them to wait a second and told them, Ain't nothing gone wrong. She stepped toward the back room, but just as she reached the door, it swung open so that she had to jerk back. Darlene poked her head out.

Darlene, what's the matter? You got customers.

It's them, she said. They've got their nerve coming in here.

Them? What them? What them is they?

Them! Darlene insisted, as if pushing that word would reveal its hidden meaning.

Shoppers piled up at her checkout line and began grumbling. Darlene did not attempt to answer Carla in full; instead she swung the door the rest of the way and stomped back to her cash register in order to keep the weakness she could feel flooding into her arms and legs from causing her to fall. She willed herself to bravery, thinking of what Nat would've wanted.

Composing herself, she focused on the case of Schlitz, but she couldn't find the price tag.

It's nine ninety-nine, Claude said. Like the display says right over there. He was quieter, more intense than Buddy, the type who would probably whisper to you as he strangled you to death.

Buddy pointed. The display featured twelve-packs of Schlitz

cans, *two* for $9.99. They only had one. One would not get them the discount; it would be $12.99. She tried to explain the problem, haltingly, without meeting his eyes, but then words became unsayable, her mind a little tornado.

Buddy's feet kept shifting, like a wrestler's, and at last Darlene glanced up at his forehead turning red. Now she could see his short temper, the rage that Nat did not survive. She stared at his veiny hands on the twelve-pack, the hairy fingers that might have held the tire iron (she imagined a tire iron, though they never figured out what blunt instrument) that smashed into her husband's temple and left him limp, dead on the floor of his own store, because she'd had a headache and she needed Tylenol. That's why she would never use Tylenol anymore, why she walked in any other aisle in the drugstore rather than walk by the Tylenol, why she wouldn't touch the Tylenol whenever anybody bought some. Why she wouldn't say the word *Tylenol*. Why she wouldn't think the word *Tylenol*. From the book she knew that thinking certain words might bring back her bad luck.

Let me tell you what I think of your twelve-ninety-nine shit beer! Buddy said, and tore open the cardboard box and ripped out a can. He shook it vigorously and popped the tab in Darlene's direction so that the foam spewed both high and low. Claude smiled up at his brother and prepared to run.

People in the two lines stepped back—some horrified, some admiring of Buddy. A chunky man in a baseball cap reached out to bend Buddy's arm so that he would stop, but Buddy grabbed a second can and opened that one too.

Carla shouted, Hey, I'm calling the cops, and Darlene screamed *Stop* and *No* again and again, and then she slipped on something, or fainted, and fell on the rubber honeycomb pad behind the checkout counter.

Buddy reached over the counter to keep dousing Darlene with

beer after she fell. The man in the baseball cap grabbed his arm to restrain him. Claude ran to the door and paused there, begging Buddy to run, and as he started off, Buddy grabbed a third can of beer and squirted that everywhere too. Again the man in the baseball cap attempted to thwart Buddy, but Buddy's beer-slicked arm slipped from the man's grip. Then Buddy aimed the beer-can fountain at the man, who became enraged and chased the two of them out of the store, the three of them growling curses at one another.

Darlene, doubled over on the floor, kept screaming long after the men had run off. In the confusion, some customers dashed out of the store to watch the chase; others gave up on making purchases, and somebody stole herself a handful of 100 Grand candy bars. Carla knelt down beside Darlene on the rubber honeycomb, trying to wipe her face and clothes dry with the tail of her company shirt and console her at the same time. Darlene had pulled in her arms to defend herself and kept them stiff in front her chest.

Lord have mercy, Carla said. I seen it on the news! Was that them boys that—I mean, they probably done it, but can't nobody say. And you! I didn't even put it together. Oh my stars.

Darlene's terror faded a little bit and she cried normally.

Carla sat back on her knees. Why don't you take the rest of the day off, honey. Come in tomorrow, or even take a couple of days, make a fresh start. I'll let Spar know what happened. She put her hands on her hips, then let them drop to her sides, and said, Lord, I hate this town.

9.

AN IMPROVEMENT

Unless work gone late—which it done a lot—Delicious supposed to paid the crew every day in the afternoon, round 5:00 roll call or a li'l later. People looked forward to that shit like they 'bout to start a weekend, but most everybody worked the same amount every day except Sunday so it ain't matter much. The company ain't paid on the books. Instead they tallied up your productivity they own self without no paycheck company or nothing. Some folks got paid by the tub, some by the hour or by the egg if they was in the coop with the laying hens. The sad motherfuckers who scooped up birdshit for fertilizer got paid by the bucket. Ain't nobody wanted that job, and asides it made you a outcast of the crew. Sirius B always seem to look for the worst jobs to do, acting like he Jesus. He went after that one like he thinking everybody else want it, and ain't nobody tell him no different.

They lined your ass up outside the sleeping area and told you how much you had worked and what pay you got and then hand you the pay right into your palm. Most folks ain't get more than ten dollars a day, so for real they hardly giving out nothing except more debt. But some days, some folks could make thirty and forty, and everybody be striving for that, like the company running some kinda numbers game. Meanwhile, Delicious took out for *everything*—the meals, the boots, the tubs and sacks they loaned you for the picking, the alcohol, and me especially. They be giving you drinks and drugs like it's your birthday party and then laying it all on your credit.

They left How in charge, and that sonofabitch did his whole job quick as a auctioneer and made your pay sheet sound like a science, so if you ain't get what you expect, you would have to walk off slow, probably confused, shoving your li'l three or four dollars down in your pocket so couldn't nobody see how much or steal nothing from you. Some folks tried damn hard at this shit—like Hannibal kept a piece of paper under his hat and had wrote down damn near every debt he got and every vegetable he done picked, but when he went to How, he got argued down into the same amounts of nothing as everybody else.

Sometimes it ain't make no sense that How's version of your salary would come so much lower than the one you calculated in your head as you working all day. Darlene got the idea from Hannibal to count on a piece of paper so she could give evidence to How if he told her she ain't worked the amount she said. But whenever she called How on it, he would tell her that she made it up, or that he done docked her pay on account of a sarcastic comment she had made 'bout the company.

That guy How could remember every bad thing you done or said without letting you know he noticed, and then he'd remind you right when you needed a hit, or cash, or a boost. Even if you only said what you said to let off steam. You couldn't bad-mouth the company or complain 'bout none of the busted tubs without no handles, the broken equipment that had took off somebody finger once and usually opened up a thigh every couple weeks, or point out that there wasn't no masks or no clean place to wash your hands even with so much pesticides clouding up the joint. You especially couldn't bitch about nothing on company time. He had people spying on each other, too, and he would dock you and reward motherfuckers for information he got secondhand about your ass. Sometimes How would even dock you for questioning his calculation of your debt. That shit fucked motherfuckers up.

But if you complained, How would go, You think a big diversified grower that has contracts with Birds Eye and Chiquita and Del Monte needs to skim five bucks off the paycheck of a little piddling serf like you? And you would shut your trap, 'cause on balance you needed the money more than that tiny moment of self-respect. Except that them tiny moments would start glomming together like little oil droplets in a contaminated stream.

So Darlene might make a few more bucks a day if she could chuck a couple extra melons, handle all them eggs, or shovel some chicken shit with Sirius. Every Tuesday and Friday, almost soon as How gave the crew the vapors they called pay, him and Hammer would drive everybody out to the depot, six or seven miles down the road to a place they said called Richland, but everybody call it the depot. Motherfuckers had most likely spent everything and borrowed forward on the rest, so what you got that day ain't even count as pay, or it look like negative pay.

Richland ain't look much like a town. Hardly nothing grew there—stunted bushes and dry grass out to the edge of your eyeballs, a gas station, a depot, a broken-down brick building, a tin-roof shack with a painted sign that said GENERAL STORE in red. The place too tiny to get on a map. Some the crew thought Delicious had actually made up the town. Other people told them people they was paranoid on account of me, but Sirius B said, It's not no paranoia when it's happening up in your face.

At night, between craving and using, the group got into one the many debates that always be going through the chicken house like a virus. This one had to do with whether the farm be in Louisiana at all, or if they maybe driven everybody far as Florida in that van. Darlene and Sirius was usually arguing on the same side about where they at, on account a she growed up near Lafayette. One time, a few weeks after she got there, the whole crew had kept arguing 'bout where they at until after lights-out. Darlene stayed quiet a long time, simmering like a li'l pot on a blue flame, then her voice busted out in the dark, saying that great-tailed grackles always hanging around there, which you don't get nowheres but in Texas, Louisiana, and Mexico, and which she seen all the time growing up near Lafayette, but ain't nobody seen not one flamingo, which everybody know they got all over the place in Florida but *not* Louisiana, so how you could explain that? The whole no-chicken area gone totally silent while people be thinking on that one, then TT goes, That don't prove nothing, 'cause birds don't gotta stop at no borders. They don't know the difference for when it's one state and when it's another.

Darlene shouts, Oh, shut up! and fold her arms, then she announce that she had to go to sleep behind that one, 'cause the whole thing done got too boring. She close her eyes, but she ain't had one eye closed for more than a few seconds yet when she feel something touching her elbow. At first she take in a deep breath 'cause she think a giant roach or a poison spider done crawled up onto her bed 'bout to bite her, or that TT gonna strangle her ass 'cause she proved him wrong, but the same instant she figure out that it somebody hand, she realize it ain't touching her with a palm—somebody dragging they knuckles all the way up and down her arm in a slow, calm, stroking way.

Seem like them knuckles be touching each one of them su-
perfine hairs on her arm, making em stand up and sit down at
they command. The touch make her remember 'bout meeting
with Nat at the diner. Darlene know who belong to the hand on
account a which side the bed it come from and how long it is,
but to make sure, she reach her right hand over and hook her finger inside the curled-up hand as it passing down her left forearm,
knowing it belong to Sirius just from the feel of them rough-ass
calluses right under the fingers and the veins popping out right
past his wrists. She keep moving her finger over the palm and
once her hand be totally inside his, she feel his pulse there at the
bottom of the hand, thumping against her fingertip.

That go on for a while, the hand-fucking, but it start to seem
kinda stupid if it ain't gon lead to actual *sex* sex. The problem
with fucking in the barracks wasn't that nobody gon see—in fact,
couldn't nobody see they own hand in front of they own face up
in the chicken house at night. The problem be keeping everything
quiet, 'cause them beds be creaky as all get-out, and you could say
something really whispery to somebody in that concrete-ass room
and motherfuckers on the other side the room not just gonna hear
what you said, they gonna *answer* your ass.

Sirius had to get up real slow, and Darlene listening for every
last creak his bed make as it start letting him rise up off it, she
imagining that man body coming for her slower than a check from
the government, she ain't letting the touching hand go neither,
like if she let it go he gon fall sideways into the darkness away
from her. Finally the moment come where the bed ain't make no
more noise and she could feel Sirius breath and lips near her face
and she raise her head up a tiny bit and use her lips to find his.
It hurts a little 'cause of the burns and sores near her mouth, but
she put that out her mind on account of the hotness of them lips.

He whisper real soft, almost so that she can't hear it, that they could go in the bathroom and get it on, 'cause don't nobody know the difference at night between one black-ass fool and two in the bathroom, since you couldn't hear what going on in there well as you could out in the main room. Darlene ain't thinking too hard 'bout nothing, and she definitely wanting to continue what they started, maybe not to the point that she think he thinking, but at least in the bathroom they ain't had to be so cautious. She rise on up out the bed in the same delicate way as he just done, and they tongues be poking all inside each other mouth and whatnot, and they breathing so heavy they know they got to get out that main room.

She grab ahold his belt loop and he feel his way through the dark to the bathroom, and even though it stink, at least they could squeeze in the stall without no door and get a small amount of privacy for a microsecond. He sitting on the toilet and she sitting on him, and she can't see nothing in there neither so it's like she fucking nothing, or the night sky, like he a star and she the blackness that be holding him up.

Pretty soon he get done and after a longer time she do too, and she fall over onto his shoulders like she gon fall asleep there.

I seen a whole bunch of those birds too, he whispered. The grackles? I knew we was in Louisiana.

Then somebody banged on the stall wall and the hot mood went right down the drain.

✄

Where they at wasn't the only thing folks be talking 'bout by a long shot. People talked a lot about they next job and how they gonna get it. When I get outta Delicious, I'ma go into construction, I'ma start my own landscaping business, I'ma drive a ice cream truck—didn't none of it had no basis in reality. They be arguing 'bout sports even more, after watching parts of the games on Jackie's portable TV that had a blue-ass nine-inch screen. Everybody talking 'bout Carl Lewis and Flo Jo all summer long.

After the five-hundred-dollar ride and the hundred-dollar first night, folks had to rent they beds and pay utilities on the water and electric, so the total came to twenty dollars a night. Sirius be like, I'm making ten a day and paying twenty a night? That shit don't make sense. Everybody told him to just work harder, 'cause sometime you could get over that hump. It wasn't no A/C, and it be so hot all the time that folks starts taking a shower in they clothes tryna keep cool while the clothes drying. Couldn't hardly nobody sleep in that heat. They only collected the living expenses once a week, so if you ain't want no more debt you had to be smart enough to squirrel away them greenbacks somewheres wouldn't nobody find em. You even had to make sure didn't nobody stole your stuff while you showering, so a lot of folks got Ziploc baggies and jammed they little moneys and whatever else in em—gold fillings, photos of they kids—so they could take they not-that-valuables with em into the shower, keep a eye on that munty, like TT called it.

But it never was much in them baggies, 'cause down in Richland, Gaspard Fusilier marked up everything so much that it gobbled your whole dollar amount. They charged $4.99 for a minibottle of Popov, $12.00 for a six-pack of Tecate in a can. Darlene and em would think, *Bullshit*—sometimes they even said Bullshit, but never too loud—they knew they ain't had no choice but to pay the outrageous price, usually on credit. And since everybody addicted to drugs or alcohol or both, or denied it until they copped, folks would buy bottles and rocks and gear from a outside dude who marked his stuff way up, too, 'cause they all knew that the operation worked out in the hinterlands of God knows where, way out in Louisiflorida, and you couldn't do no goddamn comparison shopping.

If Darlene got her groceries (that's what they called their purchases) early, she would wait by the bus for everybody else, smoking boulders in the space between the minibus and the trees. She called that having afternoon tea. They got the workers to go faster and be more productive by keeping me away from em between lunch and dinner. That made em insane, but management promised em all kinda rewards in the form of extra rocks. People freaked out in them fields—twitching and yammering and shit—but you'd be surprised how fast a crackhead could pick a strawberry vine when it's a lighter and a loaded pipe on the other side.

Out in the field one day, a potbellied brother name of Moseley who nobody knew how long he been with Delicious told everybody 'bout how a dude with a beef against a guy he claimed had stole his muffuletta sandwich out there had made a shank by melting the wrong end of one them sporks they sometimes gave out with the lunches and sporked his enemy in the kidney enough to put him in the hospital and never come back. Didn't nobody know what happened after, Moseley said, if he died or what have you. Somebody said it might be worth trying that to get outta Delicious and somebody else said they gon tell How.

There's a rock out by some trees that had that Spanish moss hanging on it, 'bout thirty yards away from the depot, but still you could see it from where Hammer usually parked. Darlene like to sit on that rock, squishing a lousy bread-and-cheese sandwich between her fingers before pigging out on it and drowning it with a Popov or two or three on good days, and when she sat there, she could hear a little brook trickling, fondling the other rocks before it go into this concrete tube that's under the road real close by. She watching a group of crows edge over and pick apart a dead opossum in the road. Somebody once told her that crows could remember your face forever, so if you do mean shit to a crow and come back twenty years later tryna act all nice, it'll squawk at you and go, Look, it's that same sonofabitch! Let's peck his brain out, y'all.

Once, after 'bout two and a half months of working for Delicious, Sirius B came to sit with Darlene. Something wasn't right about him, even more than the drugs, but it musta been kinda mental, 'cause aside from a faraway glaze in his eyes that look almost like a rapture, his problem wasn't nothing you could put your finger on unless you counted the shit he talking 'bout. Sirius ain't did no small talk; he would find the most painful thing on your mind or the most cosmic idea and act like chitchat could just start there, at the most intense part. When you start talking with Sirius B it's like he tryna stab you with a conversation.

He sitting down near Darlene on the rock and smoking, and when he done sucked up his first hit, he held his lungs tight and start wheezing and talking at the same time he passed her the pipe, and then she sparked it to get the rest, burning the end first and then moving up the pipe to my sparkling chunks of stone inside.

He said, You missing your boy, Darlene? You call him yet?

She shook her head, put me down, and start flattening that damn sandwich again. She went, It isn't easy using the phones, as you know. Darlene thought Eddie wouldn't want to see her that way anyhow, that nobody oughta see her that way—hair undone, lips burned, ripped seams all over them thirdhand T-shirts she wore; sweaty, dirty, itchy, and scabby, doing the monkey the minute I got too far away to beam her up. She say to herself, *Eddie's smart like Nat, he'll find somebody to give him what he needs.* She figured her sister gonna step in.

So Sirius asked her, Did you get in touch with anybody?

I left a message for Eddie that I'm okay and don't worry, she lied, but I couldn't say where to look for me because where are we? She threw her eyes around at the shrubs and trees, and farther out to the gray mist way the fuck out by the horizon. That sonofabitch How keeps saying he's going to tell me the name of the place and the address of where we are but I don't think he knows himself!

Delicious phone ain't work for nobody, they both knew that shit. But Sirius too much of a gentleman to call her out.

That ain't right, you shouldn't let them keep you away from your son.

She thought he's talking down to her, and got upset. I'm not letting anybody keep me away from anything, she said. She gnawed the crust off the sandwich and start chomping on the mashed bread and yellow cheese inside. Her throat dry and she ain't had nothing to wash the sandwich down with 'cause she had the Popovs first that day and the heat of late August already done dehydrated her ass. She staring at the brook, thinking maybe she could get water from there, but judging by the smell and them crushed cans and cigarette boxes sloshing around in the water and the weird-ass way that the foam foaming up in the water didn't never disappear off them rocks, she figure that shit's polluted.

Sometimes I get a feeling about all this, Sirius said.

All what?

The day after the hand sex that led to the bathroom sex, Sirius had said to Darlene that it wasn't no thang, and said it again the couple of times it happened since, and that phrase kept repeating in her mind—*Ain't no thang.* It got her confused and frustrated that her stuff ain't floored Sirius or, if it had, that he pretending it hadn't.

You know, he said, the dorm got rats and palmetto bugs, we be picking heavy-ass melons or shoveling chicken shit all day in this crazy-hot weather, pay's the lowest of the low, can't call nobody, won't nobody let you off the premises or visit home, assuming you still got one . . . Don't it feel like a punishment from the Lord? Like it's God saying, Fuck you, you crackhead nigger, you can't do no better than this?

Darlene twist up one side her mouth. First of all, she said I'm not a crackhead *or* a nigger, thank you very much. I went to school. A crackhead is an individual who has lost all sense of the outside world, they're like a zombie, closed off to the whole of existence, like they would smack, rape, and kill their sister for a hit and it wouldn't matter in what order. That is not me. And God nothing. You made the choice to shovel chicken shit, Sirius.

Pardon me, ma'am. Sirius start looking at the bus and then off in the other direction.

And Lord, this is an improvement for me! At least now I'm doing good work—*hard* work, but honest work. Darlene flexed one her arms, which had got thinner and more muscular from tossing around so much produce, and also from doing drugs, but you couldn't really tell which one had slimmed her down more. Work I'm proud of, she said. Can tell people about. And I don't have to run all over the world dealing with shady people when I'm trying to get high. It's one-stop shopping around here. Right?

Word.

Sirius nodded, even though the shit they *ain't* said be as thick as crack smoke hanging in the air, a reckless doubt clinging to every little drop of humidity, but Darlene ain't know if that feeling had to do with the attraction they was ignoring or with something else, something they couldn't quite see, or with some shit they both knew but couldn't share 'cause that would change all they fears from cloudy-ass suspicions to real demons, like demons on *horseback,* galloping down the road in they path, couldn't stop em. Quietly they watching all the other workers walk out the store and congregate by the bus, and the pressure to go back over there getting more pressurized.

Maybe behind that doubt, and the sense that the intimate moment gonna end soon, Sirius suddenly start talking 'bout his past. He told her he always had a interest in science, specially the sky and the stars, that he wanted to go to school to become a astronomer or a meteorologist, but his brothers couldn't tell him how you got them jobs, and his mama said you need a telescope and you need to be smart, and he thought that meant (a) they couldn't afford no telescope, and (b) she ain't think he smart. His father told him you couldn't make no money looking at no stars nohow, so he should get a job that paid real money, a job that people need all the time, like building houses or stitching up dead bodies.

His third-grade teacher couldn't tell him none the steps to be a astronomer neither, except she said you had to be real good at math. He had just failed a math test 'cause he ain't knowed it was coming and hadn't studied. Later, he went to a bad high school and he dropped out and started a hip-hop group, but they wasn't signing nobody from noplace but New York or LA, and meanwhile he stuck in Fort Worth, couldn't get his crew to move—they was like, Too far! Too goddamn expensive!

But I keep reading the science pages in the paper, he said. Hell, that's all I read. I don't follow politics, but science is real interesting to me. A smile spread over his face. He goes, Darlene, did you know there's a star in the sky that's a diamond? It's called BPM 37093. I memorized that, 'cause the minute you can go there, I'm getting on a spaceship. It's a star that collapsed. A star caves in when it dies. That's what happened to BPM 37093. And all the carbon in it got crushed up into a diamond. A diamond that's a *billion trillion trillion* carats. Can you believe that? A *diamond* that's bigger than the sun? Now when I get there, I'm not gonna be greedy or nothing. I'ma cut off a couple of pieces that's maybe only the size of my hand and bring those back. I'll be a mega-bazillionaire, and I won't have no worries no more.

You're the biggest bullshitter, Darlene told him, flirting with her voice. There's no such number as a billion trillion trillion.

Swear to God! Actually that shit is *actually* true. Then, like he tryna prove that he had told the truth all the time, he admitted to her that he called hisself Sirius B partially 'cause his real name was Melvin—Please don't tell none of these niggers, he said—and the other part 'cause it's also the name of the closest star to the solar system. He spelt it for her, explaining that every-body who heard the name mistook it for the word *serious*, but all his inspiration done come out the sky. His pupils get wide and he start telling her 'bout the Dogon people of Mali in Africa, said they got ancient rituals that had came from astronomical infor-mation that white folks only just discovered, like the fact of the star he named hisself after. You need a telescope to see Sirius B, he said. Now, how the Dogon people known about it so long ago? He also said that the Dogons was amphibious.

Darlene thinking she gotta draw the line at a motherfucker who believe in amphibious Negroes from ancient times who knew shit about outer space, right?

Then Sirius stood up and scrambled down into the brook, knocking rocks over and splashing. He goes, Don't say you saw me, Darlene. I think I could trust you. Then the sonofabitch ducked into the culvert.

Sirius? What are you doing, Sirius? she called out.

It's a experiment, he called back. His voice be echoing from inside the tube, like the earth itself talking.

What about the contract? Didn't you sign the contract? You owe them money.

I'll come back, he said. Splashing sounds coming through the pipe for a little while. I just want to see what happens.

What happens is you get your ass kicked. Hammer or How will find you and kick your ass. Or you die in that hole there. Or

---

they find you and kill you. She sat back and showed him her feet. These used to be Kippy's boots!

Don't say you saw me. Please, just don't say you saw me. Or say I went a different way.

Darlene wanted to stand up and go with him, but out the corner of her eye she seen How getting the group together to go back to the chicken house, and even though How had his wide lumpy back turned, just looking at that muscular neck made her afraid he gon turn around and raise his eyebrow at any moment once he realize she tryna slip off. He'd run over and pull his gun out to keep her from flying the coop, and that would give Sirius up too. If one of em had a chance, maybe she shouldn't push their luck.

Sirius! I need you to do something?

The cylinder said, What.

When you get far enough, call this number and tell them where you are, and when they find you, tell them how to get to me. She recited the number for Mrs. Vernon's bakery several times. Remember it, she begged. Please. Remember it? And call.

Sirius promised.

On breaks, and in moments when she panicked or got frustrated, Darlene be daydreaming 'bout busting out the contract and running too. During her afternoon, if she raise her head or get a two-minute rest from pitching Sugar Babies to TT or Hannibal, she could squint out cross that infinity cornfield with all them bushes or groves of maples or live oaks here and there that went along the many li'l streams that be zigzagging through the property, so many that couldn't nobody memorize em, and she pretend she could leave and go back to the calm life she ain't never had.

One afternoon, they had driven out to the lemon grove Delicious kept in one corner of the joint. The Fusiliers, who running the place, had wanted to specialize in citrus at one time—at least that's what How said—but this li'l bunch of acres, maybe six or seven, was the only part left of that experiment, which they said used to spread out something like two hundred or three hundred acres but had also failed. But now it had only some twisty lemon and lime trees, and the crew found out it ain't had too much fruit. After climbing through a whole bunch of rows, the twenty of em had only picked enough fruit to cover the bottom of one tub, and even them lemons was covered with all kinda brown spots and holes.

Even How seen how bad it was, and for once he could only blame the bad soil and them scrubby trees, not the laziness of his pickers. Hannibal went, They know it ain't the time to pick no lemons, they just giving us busywork or some shit. What the fuck.

How ain't want to, but he gave em a five-minute break and said that after that they gonna be spraying pesticides on the leaves of them trees and aerating the damn soil. Darlene got permission to travel a few yards up the road to squat and pee. On one side the lemon grove there's another one them giant cornfields, corn they told her mostly gonna feed some livestock, nothing that gonna show up on nobody dining-room table. She found a aisle between two sections that looked private enough to do her business and prepared herself.

By that time of year, the corn be stretching higher than her forehead, 'bout to get harvested, them little yellow tassels be dancing in the wind. Her family raised corn on the small plot she had grew up on—it couldn't have been far from here, she figured. It had that familiar scent of home to it, sometime she could smell eucalyptus slipping into her nose. Sirius had said that if you stayed still and listened real careful, you could hear the sound of corn growing, a noise that Darlene couldn't hardly imagine. She figured everything sound like it: the corn leaves rustling, the wind its own self, a creaking-floorboard type sound she could sometimes hear. But she wasn't prepared to feel what she felt then: the two fields of corn rising on either side start to breathe, like they got gigantic lungs underneath, like they sighing, she thought, or maybe sleeping.

She finish and stood up and thought 'bout running. Anywhere. Just picking a random direction and trying her luck. She tryna figure out which way she gonna have to go to find people who ain't had nothing to do with Delicious, who would keep her and protect her if need be. The bus had came from a direction she thought was north, and that was the sun in the west. But she ain't had no way of knowing which way gonna lead somewhere safe the fastest. Folks knew Sirius had runned off, but management ain't said nothing 'bout it to nobody, like it be a family secret from 1859.

Maybe as a way of talking 'bout Sirius, Hammer and How and the crew started tryna top each other at describing the dangers you run into if you escaped into the woods, even if you found your way to the bayou. Alligators, crocodiles, black bears, quicksand, swamps full of mosquitoes everybody said was the size of birds, wild gun-toting rednecks who went by the old ways, hungry wolf-dogs, voodoo priests who need human flesh for they ritual sacrifices, humongous tree frogs and poison insects, poison ivy, poison oak, hogweed. TT once insisted, all serious, that the Devil out there, the actual one. He kept saying, *The Devil*—that his sister had seen *the Devil*, and the Evil One done torn the ligaments in her heel so she couldn't run, but she crawled back to her car and got away. TT said he seen the torn ligaments and everything. People mostly ain't took him seriously, but he still told the story good enough to shut everybody up and bring out they sympathies.

Hannibal, over there hugging his fedora, said, I ain't messing with *the Devil*.

The earth keep breathing, slower now. Darlene gone over to the exhaling cornfield and put a foot by the edge, then another, then decide to press her way through the tall plants to God knew where: the idea of Away be pulling her farther into the field. But after a minute or two, she realize that they could hear her moving around out there, and that they had put tiny surveillance cameras out in the cornfield, some stuck inside the leaves of the plants, partially to watch the crows and the deer, but also for other reasons. The corn got impossible to push through, and when she done shaking her hands off—they already cut up by them rough, sticky-ass cornstalks—she had to turn around.

Back in the bus, she peering round the geography more careful than ever, hoping she gonna see some shit that give away her whereabouts, that point her in a actual direction, told her what to do. She ain't never seen, nowhere in the places they drove through, a house or a shack that wasn't part of the Fusilier property or the buildings owned by Delicious. Smirking, How would point em out to the workers all the time, and Darlene sometime thought he smirked 'cause it meant they couldn't even be thinking 'bout leaving.

Brushy trees was fanning out cross the ground, sometime gone all the way out to the horizon, sometime they falling off right where the close edge had a sharp drop, maybe down to a river. Fog and mist making it so you couldn't tell where the field end and the sky start. In elementary school, her science teacher had taught the kids that long ago, when the continents was one continent, the middle of the U.S.A. had sat at the bottom of the ocean, and sometime Darlene find herself imagining that it still there, with the whole of the wind turning into a deep, drowning liquid, with catfish and octopuses skimming all around hills made of sand and seaweed, and prehistoric fish feeding on the naked limbs of dead trees that be pushing up out the dirt.

With the land so flat, the sky took up most the view, and the bigness of the blue made Darlene feel she had shrank whenever she stared up into them gigantic puffing, curling patterns that was smearing and flicking through the sky, looking like a spooky painting, like a prelude to the ridiculous universe up there, where it wasn't no air, and everything a quazillion miles from everything else and stars be diamonds. At the end of every day, while the horizon going black and she watching the stars and planets blink above the smoke from the planes, she thinking 'bout Eddie, and 'bout Sirius, and 'bout the billions of years since the water had drained off, and the billions that's gonna come, and 'bout how small her world had become. Without putting no words on them thoughts, she got pretty sure that she ain't matter, and she did break out running, but she ran back toward all the things in life she knew for sure—especially me.

10.

DRUNKEN BUM
KNOWS

Darlene had been gone a few months, and Eddie had failed to find her walking anywhere along Houston's semi-abandoned commercial strips. But the night people who populated the 24-hour diners and after-hours clubs treated him well, offering to help even if they couldn't, and he stopped judging them. A guy at a gas station gave him a discount on a pack of bubble gum and a free king-size candy bar. Everybody had a different suggestion for what could have happened, and though no one proposed that his mother might've died, none of the potential scenarios sounded promising. She could have run off with a john, some said, or someone could have abducted her. Perhaps someone robbed her and she'd ended up in the hospital again, Eddie thought, like last February, when he'd lived with Aunt Bethella. But he didn't find her at the hospital, and what's more, Aunt Bethella had moved. She'd told him then that she and her husband might leave Houston soon, that they would let him know and call with the address, but Darlene's phone got cut off, so maybe Aunt B. would send a letter soon.

Remembering Mrs. Vernon's chat with the police, Eddie assumed that they had not arrested Darlene for soliciting and thrown her in jail. She could be on an extra-long binge, a hotel clerk theorized. A few of the people he met squinted and tried to remember if they'd met her, licking her name with their tongues. Eddie's rapport with Houston's underworld didn't snuff out his despair, but when he returned to the badly lit rooms in their apartment complex, it reassured him to know that word on the street had started to pass from sidewalk to fried-chicken joint to strip club to pawnshop. But the routine of getting undressed for bed and brushing his teeth and saying his prayers did not change. He held to it desperately. After turning out the light and listening to the low hum of televisions and conversations in other apartments gradually settle down to the nervous tension of silence, he watched the movements of shadows on the ceiling and did not sleep until his uneasiness mingled with exhaustion and boredom and took his senses hostage. Then he rolled his borrowed bicycle down the steps and all over Houston. The Fifth Ward, where he and his mother lived, sat in the middle of Houston, so he often didn't have to travel that far, and Houston didn't have much in the way of hills, which made biking relatively easy. Cars and trucks caused more trouble for him than distance or topography.

He could not keep from searching during the day, but the best leads came at night. Once school ended, he'd spend the afternoon reading car magazines in libraries and bookstores, or visiting school friends, fixing their bicycles and hooking up their Nintendo systems, then playing Donkey Kong Jr. and Super Mario Bros. until their dinnertimes, when he would usually slink away unless he could figure out how to stay and eat something other than cereal or sandwiches without having to explain anything about his situation at home. At night, he would mount his bike to continue the quest, sometimes pretending to be a Batman-like character.

The seedier areas of Houston became his haunts. Down in Garden Villas, Eddie met a lady who called herself Giggles, and though she didn't seem to know much, he enjoyed running into her every few nights. Like a lot of people, she mistook him for a runaway at first. Many others had made that mistake, and it angered him, but sometimes they gave him food, so he tried to keep his cool. But this time he lost his composure and shouted, No, I'm the opposite of a runaway! I'm a stayahere!

Giggles told him that she'd seen a woman out walking in Montrose who resembled his mother, but when he went there the next night, a pothead by the name of Myron couldn't confirm her report. Myron did think that Darlene might be going under a different name out in Southwest or up in Hidden Valley.

In Hidden Valley several nights later, Eddie spotted a group of women on the other side of 45, but by the time he found the closest underpass and arrived in the place where he'd seen them, they'd disappeared into various town cars with darkened windows. At a tattoo parlor, a guy called Bucky ushered him out of the place immediately but stopped outside to listen to Eddie's description of his mother. Bucky claimed to know six different women who sounded exactly like Darlene, and wanted to know what an eleven-year-old kid was doing in that part of town so late. Frowning sweetly, he paid for Eddie to take a cab home and tossed the bike into the backseat.

That routine had lasted a month and a half. By late August, Eddie's sources started to yield other sources. Giggles told him to find a woman of the night nicknamed Juicy near where Giggles worked, up on Telephone Road, then Juicy told him to go way further north, to Jensen Drive. Jensen Drive was on the way home, so Eddie saved it for another night. When he got there, to a strip mall that contained an arts-and-crafts emporium, a post office, a dusty liquor store, and a pet-store franchise, Eddie met a chain-smoking Asian transsexual who called herself Kim Ono. She suggested he go back to Southwest, walk down Gulfton Street, and find a hooker named Fatback.

Fatback knows everything that happens before it happens, she said, and quite a bit that don't.

How will I find her? Eddie asked. What does she look like?

Kim Ono rolled her eyes and said, Kid, her name's Fatback for a reason, okay? Arching one penciled-in eyebrow at him higher than seemed humanly possible, she ashed her cigarette into a mailbox. Federal crime, she said, grinning.

When he found Fatback, a self-assured, meticulously put-together lady who had more of a landscape than a body sitting on top of her legs, like chocolate soft-serve, she claimed with utter certainty that she'd seen Darlene before, but only a few times, and not for a couple of months. Despite this ambiguous news, it seemed to Eddie that the Southwest area might prove fruitful. He visited the surrounding neighborhoods for the next three nights, but nothing happened. He started to ask himself, *Why can't I find another family that won't disappear?*

Fatback kept an eye out for him, or so she said, and after another two months, in October, he visited the same area again, having no better ideas, his hopes nearly extinguished.

But then he ran into Giggles in his neighborhood, and she could always spare the time for him because she didn't get a lot of business. All the johns found her inappropriate laughter off-putting. Just picture it, she said, every time a guy takes down his pants, I laugh. It's a nervous habit, I can't control it. She chuckled as if to demonstrate. I laugh like that all the time, but most guys don't like it none when it look like you laughing at they business.

If I turn away to do it, it's worse. Mens really insecure. Present company excluded, I'm sure.

She passed her long-nailed hand over his head, and he wondered if she would have sex with him for free, but he couldn't form the right question to pursue the idea and he dropped it.

Except my regular guys, she went on. They like it a little *too* much. But every time a new guy stops I need to give him a damn disclaimer. Whoops, I cursed in front of a child. And I shouldn't be telling you this. You're, like, a baby! You remind me of my li'l cousin!

They spent a long time chatting in front of a chain-link fence that surrounded the parking lot of a nautical store out by I-45, standing under a banner that read 50% OFF ALL BOATS. The sign, strung up on the side of a parked semitrailer without a truck tractor, flapped in the wind stirred by speeding vehicles. It wasn't completely impossible that a driver going by might think that she sold boats. Intermittently, Giggles would make a desultory attempt to attract someone passing by. He liked that she couldn't get anyone to stop because the thought of other men with her made him jealous. Eddie wanted her to babysit him, or be his girlfriend, or do something that combined the two but didn't have a name.

Only when she spotted a car she recognized, a shiny Trans Am yellow as an egg yolk, did she perk up, and she hopped over to the side of the road, shouting, Hey, Danny! What up, Dan-Dan? Yo!

Eddie clenched his jaw and kicked the pavement as he watched them negotiate; he figured she'd forgotten him and he began to turn away, thinking of the next place he might go, but Giggles called out and wiggled her fingers at him just before closing the door and speeding away with Dan-Dan, and he forgave everything. He yawned—he had stayed out until nearly two a.m. again. The company of his night friends had started to seem safer than the empty apartment.

Eddie walked seven times in a circle around the poles holding up the front end of the semitrailer, precisely, heel to toe, sometimes underneath the truck—halfway hoping to produce some magical effect that would bring Giggles back. He began saying things to hear what they sounded like in that metallic, echoing space, nonsense about how he wanted Giggles to come back so he might fuck her, that he felt left out because he was the only one she *wouldn't* do it with even if he had the money, and then idly he sang out his mother's name. He threatened to become a pimp if Darlene didn't come back, thinking that would surely get her attention, even if she'd become a ghost. After he strained his vocal cords, he started whistling instead, and then finally quieted down.

A disembodied voice exploded the silence, startling Eddie. An older man's raspy baritone seemed to hover somewhere near the truck, maybe underneath, perhaps inside. Phlegmy coughing sessions interrupted his speech—you couldn't call them fits; fits didn't last that long.

Eddie traveled around the truck again, thinking that he might discover someone under it who had a weapon and might steal from him one of the last two valuables he still owned—his five-dollar bill or his life. Instead, as he investigated, he eventually made out the shape of a bum lying against a dumpster a few yards beyond the semi. As he approached, Eddie saw that the man had planted himself in a nest of empty, capless bottles of Four Roses and Thunderbird and crushed red-and-white-striped boxes from fast-food joints whose thin, oily sheets of wax paper escaped from him and skittered across the abandoned lot, their journey interrupted occasionally by long grass that punctured the snaky black cracks in the asphalt.

When the man spoke, the underside of the semi and the boats on the other side of the fence caused his voice to bounce and carry, giving it an almost supernatural authority. Lookin' for Mama, the man announced almost tauntingly, like the title of a film he was about to screen.

Eddie stopped and scowled in the direction of the voice. This man had overheard information he had shared in private. As if he hadn't offended Eddie enough, the homeless dude then improvised an almost incoherent, mocking blues song around the statement. *I know where yo' mama at. Drunken Bum know where yo' mama at.* Eddie stood stewing, full of stranger-hate. *Whatcha gonna do for Drunken Bum before Drunken Bum tell you where yo' mama gone?* Despite the taunt, Eddie noticed that although the man had so much trouble speaking, he was actually a very good singer. A few times he repeated a line that might have come from another song: *I ain't got no mama now.* Then he stopped singing.

Yeah? Where you think she at? Eddie spat.

You go buy me some drinkahol, son, before I tell you nothing.

The fuck I will.

What say?

You don't know *shit,* Eddie snarled, emphasizing the curse word, excited to vent and test profanity out on an adult. You just trying to get some more wino wine.

I know what happen to yo' mama, the man mutter-sang. Then, in a rambling, improvised song, he described Darlene, with enough identifying details—the handbag she carried, the type of shoes she wore, her hairstyle, the correct position of the most prominent mole on her face—that Eddie arched his back, readying himself to attack the man if, as he feared, the bum decided to lay insults on top of a description he now recognized as his mother. *She real cute,* he sang lasciviously. *But she lost her teeth. Ain't got no teeth! But she's cute enough to hold. Yes, she a beaut! But only when her mouth be closed.* He collapsed in laughter.

Eddie became a child again and rushed over to the bum. What? What happened? Where is she? She lost her teeth? How?

This here jaw don't flap until it get loose, got it? Liquor store down that road. He gestured vaguely in a direction where there did not seem to be a street.

I'm twelve years old, Eddie protested.

I don't give a fuck if you's a embryo, nigger! Git! Wanna know where your mama at, don'tcha? By now Eddie had gotten near enough to smell a cloud of sour whiskey around him, body odor as pungent as a plate of raw onions.

Finding an adult to get liquor for him did not present so big a problem; he had heard many kids from school say they did so on a regular basis. The larger difficulty lay on the other side of that one—how could he find this wino again should he come across the liquor store and figure out how to buy the malt liquor the man demanded? What if he paid for the stuff and returned to find the guy gone? How to make sure this character, who came off so much like an evil spirit already, wouldn't disappear?

How come you remember so much about my mom if you drunk all the time? Eddie asked.

Ain't no fun remembering the shit that done happened to *me*, nigger, the bum slurred. Eddie felt the guy waiting for him to laugh, but he couldn't.

They went back and forth this way for a while. Eddie tried to get the guy to come with him, but the bum would not rise. The boy considered taking his chances—after all, there's nothing more pathetic than an alcoholic who can't motivate himself enough to get his own booze. But uncovering a viable lead after so many dangerous weeks of searching made Eddie nervous enough to hyperventilate. The notion that this fellow might be the only obstacle between him and his mother gave him practically super-human willpower and tenacity.

No matter how much the man insisted he wouldn't go anywhere, Eddie couldn't believe him. Not surprisingly, the man had nothing worth using as collateral.

Eventually, in the near distance, Eddie spotted a length of twine that had once held a large box closed and, with the bum's grudging consent, tied his wrists first together and then to the landing gear of the trailer with a knot so haphazard that it would have no choice but to remain secure.

You gonna make my ass late for the presidential cotillion, the man said. 'Cause that's where I'm planning to take the forties you bringing me.

Eddie walked away backward with the bike, watching carefully to make sure the man couldn't escape, and he hid behind a sedan at one point to be certain the guy could not get away. Then he leapt on the bike and pedaled frantically until he reached the liquor-store parking lot.

After a few tries, he found a Houstonite by the local convenience store who seemed outwardly immoral. He told his story and offered up an inadequate five-dollar subsidy. The young guy bought him a pair of warhead-shaped bottles of piss-colored liquid in two paper bags inside a third plastic bag with handles, which Eddie slipped over one handlebar and rushed back to the lot to deliver.

He found the man kneeling by the trailer, in position for prayer but cursing, snarling, biting like an animal at the crazy knot. He claimed to know voodoo, boasted he was a high priest, threatened to lay a curse on Eddie to rival the one laid on Ham.

By Papa Legba, nigger, you'll be a nigger forever, the man spat, and your whole kin gon be niggers. Black dark evil muddy-ass niggers, too dumb to know they own name and so black you can't see em in the *daytime*. Lips so thick they gotta eat through a straw, nose so flat they can't breathe, hair so bushy housecats'll get lost in it.

Eddie set down the bags with the bottles in them and stood next to the man, attacking the bizarre tangle of twine, digging into its tight knots with his fingernails, tugging and severing it when nothing else would work. Once the man found himself free of the handcuffs, he fell on one of the paper bags and tore down the side to reveal the forty, which he did not waste time admiring but twisted open and guzzled three-quarters of before he settled down enough to acknowledge Eddie's presence again.

With his eyes on the second, he slowed his sipping of the first and regarded his captor with a certain resentment, a resentment Eddie suddenly understood that he might never reverse, even if he managed to sweet-talk information out of the guy.

Yo' mama got in the Death Van, the bum said, punching the word *Death,* almost laughing.

Death Van? Fuck you, you lying s—

They come around with this here van, okay, and I seen a mess of folks get in thisyer van, but don't none of em come back. Now they asked me to go, and I heard them saying they take folks off to do some wonderful job somewheres, but I said to myself, *What kinda job it is you don't come back from?* He nodded as if Eddie had already offered the correct answer. Death, that's the only job a nigger don't never come home from. They prolly out there making some nigger-flesh dog food. Maybe I'm paranoid, or it's a exaggeration, but something's going on.

Eddie had heard or read the story about the man who goes to hell to get his wife back and eventually does bring her home, and even though he couldn't remember where he'd heard it—school probably—or the details of the story, he believed that you could go to hell and bring people back safely.

Where do they come get people?

Just up the road a piece. Northwood Manor, near the Clayton's supermarket.

Take me there.

The beggar refused, and as soon as he refused, Eddie snatched the undrunk bottle of yellow liquor away from him and moved backward, holding it above his head as if he might dash it against the concrete. This aroused a fit of shouting and cursing and then coughing from the older man, who looked wildly at the bottle as if it were his child. He rose to a standing position and lumbered toward the bottle with an arm outstretched as Eddie played a vicious game of keep-away around his intoxicated body. When they seemed to become aware of the game's endlessness, the fact that Eddie would never give him the bottle and he could never capture it, the ridiculousness of the standoff became apparent, and neither of them could hold his laughter. Even though Eddie hated him and figured the feeling was mutual, the man then agreed to take Eddie to the last location where he'd seen the Death Van.

I reckon it ain't that far, the bum said. It took a while, but Eddie managed to thumb a ride for them from a pickup, throwing the bike into the bed of the truck.

They called him Tuckahoe Joe, the bum explained to Eddie and the driver, or just Tuckahoe, or Tuck, because he had grown up in a place called Tuckahoe and because his real name was a girl's name that a lot of men in his family had cursed each other with, so he went by the nickname instead.

I started using it when I played out, he said. Music, that is. I used to play blues music. You know what that is?

Eddie nodded, though he felt the stab at his intelligence.

Now I just live the fucking blues, Tuck muttered. Played bass guitar for a very popular fella called Willie "Mad Dog" Walker. For years. You heard a him? He's T-Bone Walker Jr.'s second grandnephew. Or that's what he used to say, anyway. "Only Got Myself to Blame"—you know that song? That's him, anyway, his one big hit.

Tuckahoe sang a little but Eddie didn't recognize the tune. Old folks' music, he thought. Dead folks' music. Tuckahoe told them that the band had toured the East Coast and then come to Houston by public transportation alone. They would take the bus or the train from one city to the next and then walk or hitchhike when there wasn't enough of a connection. As if to verify his tale, he listed every city he had passed through on the way and how to hook up from one system to the next.

When you get to Houston, though, he said, you can go to Dallas or Austin or San Antonio, but between them and El Paso it's all desert, so the band had to stop. Originally we stopped in Austin. Austin's like a pitcher plant. Well, it was for me. You know what that is? A pitcher plant? It's a plant that eat flies, like a Venus flytrap, but it catches them by having a sweet sweet pool of sugariness inside, down at the bottom, and slippery walls, so that when the fly land on the damn thing, he slip on down in there and drown in happiness. Come to think of it, New Orleans even more like that, but it'll kill you faster. Anyhow, he said, tipping the first bottle vertically above his head to get the last taste of nectar, I'm still drowning in happiness.

The driver made a horrified face as Tuck drank, but said nothing.

Tuck looked at the label before placing the bottle between his feet and uncapping the second.

The driver took a deep breath.

The closer they got to their destination, the more Tuck's monologue sagged and melted. He also had a hard time remembering exactly where he'd seen the Death Van. Facts contradicted one another; Tuckahoe was in Virginia at first, then in New York, names ballooned with improbability—We opened for the Rolling Stones in Memphis the night MLK got shot, he said—until finally the narrative exploded and the plastic masks fell off his accomplishments. Eddie tried to believe his stories out of sympathy, as he could sense the extremity of Tuck's abandonment, but at the same time Tuck had become gradually more repulsive to Eddie during the ride and had widened the gap between himself and Eddie, not to mention the driver, in what was perhaps a self-fulfilling prophecy of loneliness. Eddie worried that he'd arrived at another dead end, with another disoriented person whose addiction made his mind too foggy to recall anything.

But only a few minutes later, Tuck got a flash of insight and suddenly demanded that their ride let them out a few yards away from the parking lot of a Party Fool, closed but still brightly lit. With the chain store's harlequin mascot looming above on the roof, governing their every move with his scepter, they disembarked. The driver helped Eddie lift the bike out of the truck. Tuck removed the second, half-empty forty from its paper bag, chugging as he advised Eddie about how the drivers of the Death Van operated.

They're picking on the people that's the most out of it, he said. That's what it seem to me. I don't know how you going to get them interested as just a little boy. They only after the worst of the hookers, the junkies, and the alkies, y'see, people rocked out they mind. Hey, maybe they selling Negro skeletons to Baylor for research. After that Tuskegee shit, anything could happen.

They waited for an hour and fifteen minutes, until a navy blue minibus slowed to a stop twenty yards ahead of them with the smoothness of a panther, then everything went silent for a moment, until the next car passed a couple of minutes later.

For the first time in some time, Tuck became silent, contemplative, almost reverent. He took a sip of malt liquor and leveled his rheumy eyes at Eddie. You lucky tonight, kid, he eventually murmured. He coughed and spat. Or, not lucky.

An otherwise skinny woman with a round butt, wearing a

thrift-store blouse, backed out of the minibus and hurried toward the two of them. Approaching with her hand thrust out, she introduced herself as Jacqueline Faire-LePont, planted her pumps in the gravelly asphalt in front of them, and asked Tuck if he needed steady work. Before he answered, she announced that she had it to offer, and spoke continuously about a wonderful place where he could flourish professionally. She briefly stopped speaking and smiled down at Eddie.

Yes, we need work, he said. But have you seen my mother? Her name is Darlene Hardison.

Jackie brightened immediately. Darlene? Oh yes! She's your mom? Oh, I know your mother *very* well.

Tuck put a hand on the back of Eddie's neck and whispered, Don't be too sure.

Eddie lurched forward, about to run over to the minibus and leap in. Tuck grabbed his shirt to stop him. I think this the same people, he warned Eddie, but this here lady gon tell you exactly what you want to hear.

Then Tuck attempted to walk him in the opposite direction. They got far enough to be out of Jackie's earshot, but then Eddie hooked his fingers into the older man's pocket, putting in extra effort to keep him stationary, and succeeded in slowing Tuck down and kicking up enough roadside dust to cake their shoes and pant legs.

We have to go! Eddie insisted. You have to come with me.

Hell no, Tuck grumbled. He pulled Eddie's hand off his pants. You go yourself. Your moms might be out there after all.

I have to go! Eddie searched his mind for a trump card. But what if she's not there? And what if they do things to little boys?

The comment made Tuck freeze as if Eddie had slapped him. Eddie pulled on his pocket again, but Tuck didn't move. After a few moments, Eddie looked up to see wet streams running under both of Tuck's eyes. The ploy had worked almost too effectively; Eddie was shocked.

Tuck wiped his face with his fingertips. Oh, okay, for God's sake, he said. I don't want that on my conscience again. He told a sad story about his late brother.

Of course your son can come along too, Jackie said, once they got nearer to the minibus. We'll get him in school. Are you Darlene's husband? Great to meet you. What's your name, sir? They all introduced themselves and Jackie continued her pitch. Now, the agricultural cooperative for which you'll be working is one of the best in the country, she said. It's called Delicious Foods. She opened a brochure to a picture of a courtyard with a kidney-shaped pool, then stopped and looked at Eddie.

You can't bring the bike, though. Why don't you lock it up over there? she said, pointing vaguely toward the Party Fool.

It's not mine, Eddie said.

Jackie smiled. You'll be back soon enough, she said. Eddie walked over to the entrance of the Party Fool, wrapped the bike's chain lock around one of the posts of the shopping-cart corral, and returned to climb into the minibus, whose door had remained open the whole time. By then Tuck was inside, slumped against the window, already starting to fall asleep.

11.

ECLIPSE

F all kicking in. Nights was dipping into the sixties, and that
made them Delicious people more comfortable in the
evenings. Helped em rest easier, and damn sure kept them odors
down in the dorm. Sometime Darlene took off one her gloves
and put her fingers up on the sticky watermelon skins. She deliberately leaving fingerprints, hoping somebody gonna dust that
damn melon for evidence and let her son know where she at.
Way far away, folks from America and Canada and even farther
be dropping them Sugar Babies and Golden Crowns on they Ital-
ian marble counters; blond children be biting down on that juicy
red flesh, letting the sweetness ooze and dribble over they tongue
and out the corner of they mouth. They wasn't looking for no fingerprints on no damn melon. They just a-laughing and chasing
each other cross a hundred acres of fresh green motherfucking
garden full of yellow roses, flashing they bright brown and blue
and green eyes, tryna spit seeds into each other hair. Them ginor-

mous melons, the Parkers and the Sangrias, the Sunny's Prides
and the Crimson Sweets, they found homes too. The superiors
said that some them Delicious watermelons made it all the way
to Japan.

When the first harvest drawing to a close, the foremen start
dropping hints 'bout pumpkins and squash and gourds, and the
late-fall plantings of wheat and corn. They talking loud 'bout
which ones of the feeble incompetents they gonna most enjoy letting go, like leaving gonna make them that much worse off. Crazy,
but How could get a whole lotta workers in a tizzy 'bout that they
gonna get fired. Of course that increased production 'cause everybody thought they gonna have to brave the streets on the holidays,
dead broke and jonesing, going to beg mercy of they family when
don't nobody talk to em no more.

The season 'bout to sputter out, and Darlene starting to miss
Sirius B. For so long she thought of herself as Nat's wife, like
Coretta Scott King or somebody who always gonna be married to
a great dead dude. She living under the curse of his murder, always not thinking 'bout the blazing red rectangular eyes of Mount
Hope on that night, and Nat behind em, hollering and melting.
She ain't hardly never stop hearing him whistle. All that grief and
guilt done drove her out her mind to the point where if anybody
tried to stand in the burnt-up spot in her head that she kept for
Nat, it put her in mind of a eclipse. By eclipse we not talking
'bout a rare, beautiful cosmic happening—more like a freak event
that done turnt a normal day dark.

When Sirius left, Darlene start getting all quiet, or grumbling
shit in her head that even I couldn't have convinced her to say.
They used to joke together and make all kinda rebellious comments, the type of hogwash that How woulda docked their pay
for. They had a secret habit of trading nasty lines under they
breath when the other one nearby, snickering behind the ridicu-

lous, strict rules at Delicious. For instance, Delicious ain't let nobody have no utensils (people said 'cause of that whole spork-shank thing), but they also served some shit they called gumbo twice a week, and you had to tilt the lip of the bowl above your mouth or put your face in the bowl to eat that watery tasteless shit. And they ain't never heat it enough. Jackie and em timed everybody damn showers to five minutes, even though the water took six before it would get partway to lukewarm. A cold shower could feel good in that climate, but not *that* cold.

Now Darlene had to face all that kooky bullshit on her own, same time she daydreaming 'bout the funny way Sirius use to raise a eyebrow at her whenever shit got too ridiculous. He had gorgeous eyebrows, she start remembering for the first time. Somebody mighta clipped them suckers off a mink coat and passed them to him.

'Bout a month and a half had went by since Sirius run away, and she bet he had got pretty far by that time. She ain't find it tough to keep his secret on account a nobody could say nothing 'bout it or they gon get jumped. She bet that he had found Mrs. Vernon and that Eddie would know where his mother had got took to by now. Believing that Sirius made it out kept her calm, gave her some hope beyond the next rendezvous with Yours Truly. Not to downplay my importance or nothing, but Sirius escape proved to her that all them fears they ain't usually said nothing about, that had to do with the work culture at Delicious, ain't really been true. They could get out, maybe. Hope revved up inside her rib cage and she visualized herself quitting Delicious, walking out with some crispy-ass hundred-dollar bills in her hands. The watermelon harvesting had messed up her body, she all cramps and sprains and bruises. Even still, she sometime thinking 'bout a reunion with Eddie the way she think about a sunrise; the endless circle of working and paying the people who

worked you for overpriced goods and no-star accommodations
had kept most her thinking dark as night.

Not even How had said nothing 'bout Sirius leaving after Sirius done it. Usually How ain't miss no kinda opportunity to put
a motherfucker down if he couldn't hack the hard work. But he
ain't chuck a single snide comment into the brother's path. Didn't
nobody ask Darlene nothing, even though she knew that plenty
of others had seen the two of em hanging by the brook, and just
about everybody knew they was fucking. She thought she saw
Jackie taking a real quick pause during the first roll call without
Sirius, fast enough that it might not even been a true pause, but
beyond that Jackie kept a total poker face about it. The silence
around it be more scarier than if they had said shit. When they
locked folks up every night, they took they guns and start hunting
Sirius's ass down like he a motherfucking rogue elephant headed
for a nursery school. Every morning the underlings wondering if
Sirius dead, if they had killed him, and if they maybe gon kill
again.

A month and a half after Sirius broke out, in October, the
crew gone out to them bad lemon groves, where it be some
dinky li'l Meyer lemons, and Darlene going around plucking the
tiny number of brownish-yellow examples out them thick leaves
when she heard some shit happening a couple rows of trees away
from where she standing on top her ladder, sorting through them
branches for any old thing she could plop into her plastic tub. She
heard a whiz in the trees, and right after that a wail so loud and
psycho that it ain't sound like no human being. A couple more
cries like that and she recognize TT voice and held her breath.

With a crop so close to imaginary, any event felt like a reason
to stop working a minute and find out what happened. Darlene
stopped and bent down to listen and then followed the sound under the roof of leaves and stumpy tree trunks. The ruckus of other

people feet going *whiff whiff* through the brush over to the noise let her know that she could get with the curious group, and she stepped down and walked over, going diagonal zigzag through the trees, moving faster the more curious she getting.

She found a bunch of Delicious people kneeling and standing here and there around TT, who wriggling in the weeds between the rows, howling and grabbing his own head like it's a Sugar Baby he 'bout to toss in the truck. A whole lotta blood had came through his fingers. The crowd made a circle around him, watching with they mouths hanging open but not doing much of nothing. Without thinking, Darlene tore off her shirt and ran over to him in her bra. She forced the dirty tee around his hands to sop up the redness. He took the shirt and mopped it all over his head but he ain't stopped screaming. She called him by his real name, Titus, the way his mama mighta did to get his attention and calm his ass down, but for a long time ain't nothing change.

Then How voice, low in the back of the group, say that work need to start up again, like work could get back to work by itself, but she managed to ignore him till she got TT in a stable place. Since he okay with staying on the ground on account a his shock and dizziness, she gone back to hunting down them not-there lemons. After a while, the sun went down and a chill came up into the air like water filling a glass. TT got up and start tryna work again, but he real hurt. At the end of the day, Darlene seen that his tub ain't had but four brownish lemons in it, and that meant he gonna be asking everybody else to share they food and they drugs.

Later, right before lights-out, she convince TT to explain what had went down, and even then he would only whisper. It wasn't no conversation, he said. I asked How a question and next thing I knew he took a fat-ass log and opened my head up like a damn watermelon.

What did you ask?

I asked if anybody knew where Sirius gone and what happened to him, just casual-like, and that was the answer. You was tight with Sirius, Darlene. Don't know why I didn't ask you first. What happen to that nigger? Did he get loose?

I haven't the foggiest, TT, she said, shaking her head. I wish I did know. I hope.

You do too know. You can't play me.

Why is it important to you?

It ain't! That's why I thought it wasn't no big deal to ask! I just wanna know. Did he get out?

I couldn't tell you.

That means you know. You prolly going with him next.

You go ahead and believe whatever you want. Get some rest.

But she kept hanging out with TT—and I joined them, of course. She tryna drown the troubles out her mind, her not looking at him, him not looking at her. I tried to get em to a higher plane, but it ain't gone much of nowhere; I was weak right then, mostly fucking talcum powder that they had sold on markup down at the depot. Jackie made the usual announcements to wrap up the day and send everybody to bed, and soon, what with all the activity, Darlene and TT become shadows to each other, like they be trees and shrubs spaced out on a hill in the damn twilight.

Once it got dark enough, though, TT start blabbing in a whisper with Darlene about the exact number of his debt as he calculated it on his own versus what they said he owed, and how in general couldn't nobody make no sense of the hiring policy at Delicious. Jackie and How had picked up a alcoholic bum with a swollen leg with gangrene on it, he said, and the guy's son, and the man had caught the terrible flu that going around and he up in the bed, and the boy wouldn't never leave his daddy. TT had only heard secondhand, though. Them two supposed to have got put in a barn that's further off, in a broke-down infirmary, to keep from spreading the disease. TT ain't had no idea what they want with people in such bad shape.

They like a motherfuckin' Hoover now, he joked. Sucking up old niggers and babies off the street. What a child and a invalid gonna do on a farm and winter season almost here?

They're crazy, Darlene whispered.

What happened to Sirius? Did they kill him?

I don't know, TT.

She said that shit to get him off her back, but saying the words made her think for the first time that she actually *didn't* know. She start thinking maybe Sirius had got captured and killed without nobody on the crew finding out 'cause wouldn't nobody say nothing. The idea cut real close to what had happened with Nat and bored a hole in all them optimistic thoughts she had stacked up in her head and now a ton of evil-ass doubts was pouring through that hole. After all the joking she and Sirius done 'bout Delicious, it had never crossed her mind for real that they might actually kill folks to protect theyself. She thought that ain't nothing much matter to Delicious beyond the take for a given day, week, or month and whether you had shaped a twig into a shank and hid it in your sock so they could dock your pay.

Sometime when I be hanging out with folks and they start getting all into conspiracies and plots, I like to encourage em to get creative and keep thinking on it and believing in theyself. Everybody say you gotta believe in yourself. Your parents says it, and the TV say it, and all the damn movies. Of course Darlene li'l book say it too. So before I got done hanging with her that night, her paranoia done hatched five hundred little chicks and they had all took to peeping around in her head, more chickens than it be in the next room. She couldn't sleep behind that, what with her mind tryna raise up all the possible chickens and figure out the truth without letting the powers above know what she knew, or even what she suspected. When you working hard, she thinking, you don't really be getting paid, and you can't go nowheres, everybody know the name for that. Everybody on the farm always comparing what they done to the olden days, but they just exaggerating 'cause they angry—didn't nobody get paid back then. Ain't that the definition of slavery? You don't get paid? And if you had signed a fucking contract and agreed to the debt they kept piling on—well, everybody be quietly arguing on the definition of that shit all the time.

Darlene thinking 'bout dropping hints to How or Jackie, or 'bout finding the mansion where the owner of the farm lived. They said his name Sextus Fusilier, that he Gaspard cousin, and he be living way out yonder in the southeast part of the farmland. He sometime did a random inspection on groups, but he ain't come to none the details she been on yet. Darlene figure she gon question that dude, or maybe she try to find some relative or friend of Sirius. She tried to remember the names of the people he'd mentioned in...was it Dallas? She thought of doing prayer, threats, voodoo, eavesdropping. She had a idea 'bout getting the entire crew to listen in on any conversation between the high muck-a-mucks, but she let that idea go when she realized that some these sons of bitches would probably rat.

She grinding her teeth and flinching all night, kept her eyes closed while them imaginary chickens and them real ones next door clucked and flew around and every bump she heard made her sit up and try to figure out where it had came from. When she heard Jackie making noise out there, she froze up and listened like she gonna pick up some crucial information. After a time, a creaking come from behind Jackie wall partition, and a clip light snapped on behind it, lighting up the whole space a little bit. Darlene wondered if Jackie also doing the monkey while she coming off her high, and maybe she had decided to take a pill to calm her nerves. She want a pill herself. But when she listened closer, she heard Jackie getting dressed, like she on her way somewheres.

Even with her nerves, Darlene manage to get up from the mattress without making no springs creak, and with her itchy torn sheet around her shoulders, she gone down the far wall of the building, where the shadows be the deepest. She moving real quiet and crossing Jackie wall till she could curve her neck around and see what the supervisor doing. She open her mouth to ask something, but what she seen almost made her gasp. Under that clip light, Jackie had laid out a row of fluffy tubes on a low plastic end table. At first Darlene thought Jackie had killed a bunch of mice, 'cause them fluffy tubes also had tails, and it be a deep red-brown stain on most of they grayish-white bodies that look like a pattern on fur.

Jackie hands went in and out that cone of yellow light, but Darlene couldn't see nothing but the faint shadow of her back. Darlene ain't said nothing and Jackie ain't notice she there. Jackie had placed a total of five them little mice in a neat row on her end table. She raised a plastic cup above one them mice and drizzled a stream of liquid over it and the shit puffed up.

Then Darlene face squinched up 'cause she figured this li'l ritual had some kinda connection to Jackie personal hygiene. Them little mice was tampons. Then it crossed her mind that Jackie be using her menstrual blood to work roots on somebody. From there, them imaginary chickens swooped in, all plucked up and weird-looking enough to be the truth: Jackie had collected them tampon mice from the trash so she could do some fucked-up gris-gris on the group. That made Darlene so sick she broke out in a cold sweat and tiptoed backward the way she had came, her breath getting short now, her heart jumping up like a fat red toad. She put her head down on her bed and pretended to sleep.

With the bulb giving off hardly no light, Jackie come out her room, dangling one the tampons by its tail. Darlene saw her stopping at the lower right corner of each the beds. To stop motherfuckers from stealing they shoes, most people stuck the legs of they beds into the heels of they shoes at night, and if you be peeping down the row of beds it be like the beds gonna run away with the dreamers on board. A couple beds up from hers, Darlene heard some drops of watered-down blood going *pit-pat* on people shoes. Maybe Kippy ain't even die tryna leave, but Jackie had just dripped them bloodstains on his boots. She turnt the start of a disgusted laugh into a sleepy cough, thinking 'bout telling Sirius that Delicious had Jackie doing obeah, dripping her monthly on they shoes to stop em from running away. Man, would he bust a gut. But then again, maybe the obeah had did the job on most these motherfuckers.

The next morning, Darlene felt the need to quit Delicious pretty bad. The boring hard work and dirty conditions had broke her will, and now she had to wash that bitch's voodoo blood off her shoes in the morning, behind her back? She kept muttering, No way, that isn't right. Sometime her work detail wasn't physically difficult, and they'd make her dump bushels of pink slop into the old wooden hog feeder or spray pesticides on the plants, and she'd have time to come up with plans to get out without nothing bad happening. But whenever she thought about doing courageous shit, her nerves turnt to Jell-O and she would come to my ass crying and begging me to make her feel better. She always saying she knew she should wanna leave more, enough to do some brave shit, but I be talking her out of it.

Plan A was that she just tell How she quitting and walk away—but to where? Would he let her go? No. And how far she gon have to walk, anyways? And how 'bout all that money she owed? It had fell to $908.55 at that point 'cause they been digging up sweet potatoes and she had got good at that. Then plan B became maybe she could find a lawyer somewheres—but who? And how? And to say what? And how you gonna pay a expensive motherfucking lawyer? Besides, Joe Lawyer just gonna go, You signed a contract. Plan C was to put a slit into one them melons she be packing and stick a note into the cut, but she knew they would find that shit during inspections and chuck the melon, or, worse, they'd fish out the note, trace the damaged fruit back to her, dock her pay, and do her like they done TT, who broken nose need a splint it wouldn't never get. He having trouble breathing, his voice sounding all wheezy, but you couldn't laugh.

Later that morning, she packing melons and had a vision where the fruit done split itself in half and growed a giant slice that turnt into a red mouth. First the mouth smiled at her but then when it start talking it tattled on her, got some pink juice spilling over its green and white lips, seeds popping off its red tongue like li'l fleas. Then a entire field of melons busted out laughing, along with the paranoia chickens and the real chickens of Delicious till the ridicule done got thick as mud. To be honest, I had been hanging out with some damn strange substances during that particular time. I ain't even sure who they was. Darlene suspected that PCP or LSD had become real chummy with me. But maybe Delicious finally did have her losing her mind. Plan D meant keep working and pay off her debt and then asking to leave someday. Maybe.

A couple days after they clocked TT, while she waiting on the daily money, Darlene out on a detail and strolling down a row of cornstalks by herself, not too far from the depot and within the reach of the crew. The only sound come from the rustling of the cornstalk leaves, and she thought it's that growing sound again, like some kinda creaky rustling, or that breathing. But then she saw a building she ain't notice before, sorta in the distance, and she decide to test out how long the leash on her just to see.

She get out to this path that's by a broke-down shack. Three grackles landing behind her one after the other, and a fourth one in the front, like a li'l militia 'bout to arrest her ass. Them birds would sometime come after her on days when she had to carry sacks of grain that was heavier than children out to the livestock feeders. They'd squint at her with they judgy-ass faces, probably expecting her to slip and scatter a easy meal for they ass, but on this particular day she ain't had nothing on her that she knew they wanted, and since she knew they ain't want nothing, it made her flip out a little.

She stared down the row of cornstalks at the place where it look like they nearly touched and spilled out into the sky. That rickety old barn be on her left. She could hear Nat whistling underneath just 'bout anything she notice at the time, surrounded by radio static. She recognize the song "Love Won't Let Me Wait." Nat had wanted to make that they wedding song. He loved that jam and thought it had a romantic mood but wasn't much interested in the lyrics. Darlene thought it sounded too sexual and she objected and finally he agreed to "Best Thing That Ever Happened to Me." But Nat kept on joking with her 'bout that first song; he couldn't see the sexual part even though people be moaning in the middle of the song. He said it had a honeymoon feeling to it.

She stop and hunt in the sky, almost like she expect the Lord to throw him down to her at last, but today the sky staring back like a just painted ceiling. But when she drug her eyes over the ground, she saw the main grackle plant hisself in front of her, maybe tryna keep her from going no farther. Was he in cahoots with How? He made his chest all round, sticking his feathers out and opening up that spiky beak wide as a change purse. It seem to Darlene like the song and the static pouring out his wobbly throat. The whistling done become the original singer voice, like the bird had a radio stuck down his li'l windpipe.

The time is right
You hold me tight
And love's got me high . . .
Please tell me yes
And don't say no, honey
Not tonight . . .
I need to have you next to me
In more ways than one
And I refuse to leave
'Till I see the morning sun
Creep through your windowpane
'Cause love won't let me wait . . .

Darlene did *not* know what the hell going on; she couldn't make no kinda sense outta this, so she skipped right past the effort and braindanced with me instead, closing her eyes and swaying to the saxophones as they caressing her and wrapping theyself around that singer sexy confession. She stopped feeling all self-conscious. The idea that Delicious had fucked with me left her mind. She even forgot to wait for her pay. All the sensations of her wedding night done came right the fuck back—the beautiful droop of the train on her gown, the stiff lace going round her head, the smiling faces of they few loyal friends and relatives, how they all had to keep Eddie out the pictures so she ain't looked like a Jezebel, the short pile of shiny gifts sitting by the entrance to the church, Nat's warm hand pushing against her knuckles as they cutting that spongy deep chocolate cake.

When the song got done, the bird start talking. He only got a couple words out before Darlene heard Nat's voice. She screamed with joy and the bird snapped his beak shut. She froze, put her palm to her face, then put herself onto the dirt in front the grackle and crawled toward him with her arms outstretched, begging to hold him. The bird hop-flew backward and away, without no fear. His friends was moving around Darlene; she thought they's chuckling at her while they making they bizarre noises, but she ain't give a shit. She put her eyes on the leader, tryna see her husband in his place.

Nat, it's you! Praise the Lord. What did you say?

All sharp and tight, the bird turnt its head sideways and tried out a bunch of poses where he could peep at Darlene. He wagging his beak left, then right.

He sighed. Darlene, sweetheart, I can't stand to see you like this.

But if it brought you back to me—

You know this isn't what I want for you. Or for Eddie. You're worth so much more.

At those words, Darlene started weeping. She tried to ignore her emotionality and talk through the sobbing, but that shit ain't work. Nat, she said, I'd rather be with you. Why'd they take you away? Why? How could God let that happen? Please forgive me for the migraine and the shoes and the everything.

Darlene, I said. Darlene! Stop talking to that bird. That bird ain't your husband. It's just a damn bird. When *I'm* the voice of reason, you know shit is fucked.

She reached out again, faster, and grazed part the grackle shiny feathers with her fingertip before he like, hippity hop out the way.

It's not the same, the bird said. You'll crush me, Darlene.

If I die maybe I could be a bird too.

Honey, don't talk like that. You're not going to die. You need to live. That's what I came to say. You need to leave here and go raise my son.

A long silence passed between the two of em. She couldn't stop staring at the bird's li'l yellow eye; he ain't hardly blink. She wanted to see tenderness in that bird, but she really couldn't. In that body she couldn't know Nat no more, not with that blank-ass eyeball. She wanna kiss him, but when the bird done turnt his beak toward her, she imagining what it gon feel like to kiss a grackle, have that beak poking her cheek or piercing her lip, comparing that to the memory of her husband lips on hers—warm, soft tongues and breath going back and forth, body linking up to body. She covered her face without no consideration to how she smearing herself with dirt bombs and grit. Some different strange music done started floating through in the air, not the radio song no more, but some kinda fucked-up jazz off a smashed piano, then that suddenly stopped.

How could you come back and act so cold? she said.

The bird goes, This is the best I can manage. I'm sorry.

Nat! Darlene grabbed for the bird and he moved backward again. He raised his wings all tentative and whatnot, like he testing the air.

I would if I could, the grackle said, this time with a bit of grief. Believe me.

Then the bird be poking under his greenish-black wing to groom hisself, and in a split second Darlene finally snapped out her insanity, and now she seen that the grackle just be a normal animal that couldn't talk and ain't had nobody dead husband spirit inside. She felt stupid and ashamed that she had thought that and had to admit she not in her right mind. She seen herself at the bottom of a well, and people yelling down to her. She peeking into that li'l circle of light up top, stretching her hand out and tryna touch em.

———

12.

OBEAH JUJU

Since the moment Jackie had helped them into the Death Van and distributed the first of many hits to the other passengers, Eddie fantasized that he really was crossing into the underworld to rescue his mother. Once the minibus turned onto the desolate roads and rattled over potholes toward nowhere, and his fellow travelers disappeared into a state between deep thought and sleep—though they had started the journey with a lively card game and an argument about boxing before lighting up—Eddie's fantasy rose toward possibility. Maybe this lazy mood was death? Even after they'd stuck the box in the ground and told him his father was in it, no one had ever told him that things changed about your body after you died, except for his impression that you wore a robe and sprouted wings in heaven or grew horns and a tail in hell. On some level he knew not to share these thoughts because people would laugh. He and Tuck had not yet received robes or grown tails. It probably took a long time, he knew; he had learned while following his mother around that anything you needed from a white person at a desk always took extra time and required you to sign a lot of papers.

Eddie tried to grill Jackie to figure out where he would find Darlene when they arrived, but she, along with most of the other passengers on the ride, was minimally responsive, especially after she smoked. If anyone on the Death Van said something coherent, they'd make the type of outlandish statements he'd become accustomed to hearing from his mother. Strangely, the familiarity of their drugged-out behavior gave him confidence that his mother had, in fact, joined their ranks. He would just need to sit tight.

Tuck nearly coughed his guts out during the journey; he'd been growing sicker and weaker as the trip wore on, and to Eddie this gradual worsening seemed consistent with the process of dying, or having already died. When he asked Tuck, the man seemed to think that all he needed was an Olde English 800. Once they reached their destination, Eddie's companion had lost the ability to rise from his seat without help. After Jackie spent several minutes attempting to get him to his feet by tugging on his limp arms, a few of the more able-bodied and right-minded men summoned from the chicken house lifted him out of the minibus and laid him on the ground next to the front wheel, and a debate erupted about whether he, and also Eddie, would be permitted to sleep with the rest of the workers or if this would constitute a health hazard. Eddie swiveled his head in search of Darlene but he didn't see anyone like her nearby.

The workers did not care where Eddie and Tuck went; the debate took place mainly because of the presence of two paler men Eddie later learned were Sextus Fusilier and How, who used the moment to turn over in their minds, briefly, whether they should quarantine these two or let the illness run its course among the workers. In How's opinion, not much work or profit would be lost, because he knew he could manage the team, but Sextus remained cautious, invoking all the clichés of thrift with which his family must have indoctrinated him over the years. Eddie didn't understand the gist of this conversation. Instead he imagined that the two men were really God and the Devil (though he went back and forth about who was who) and that they had deadlocked over a decision about his and Tuck's eternal fate.

During the conversation, Sextus brought up the topic of a barn out by the depot that seemed to him ideal as a temporary infirmary. After they had settled the issue and checked the other new people in, he drove off, and How and Jackie loaded Tuck and Eddie back into the van. Eddie opened his mouth to inquire about Darlene's presence on the farm, but How told him to shut up before he finished asking if he could ask a question.

Silently they drove out to the barn, which turned out to be weather-beaten and unstable, a rotten, listing structure etched in silver by the moonlight. With a few sharp blows from a small ax, How broke the padlock off its hinges. Then, almost as an afterthought, he tossed a blanket into the musty space with the two of them. Waving their hands at Eddie and Tuck as if to fan their bodies into place, Jackie and How made it clear that they did not want to catch whatever Tuck had come down with.

The fear and speed with which the crew had ostracized them made Eddie increasingly uneasy. He hadn't shown any symptoms, he hadn't coughed even once, but they assumed that he and Tuck, whom they kept referring to as his father, despite his frequent and loud corrections, had both picked up whatever contagious illness was soon liable to take Tuck to a picnic with the ancestors. Their certainty rubbed off on him. When they wouldn't even give him a Kleenex, he could only assume that they knew what illness the two of them had contracted and expected him and Tuck to waste away rapidly.

We'll be back later, Jackie said. She and How swung the door shut behind themselves and Eddie heard the noise of their shoes crunching through the dead leaves on the path gradually diminish, then the minibus's ignition and departure. When Jackie said *later,* Eddie couldn't tell if she meant half an hour or six months.

The support beams on each corner leaned far enough over that the walls became rhombuses. The barn had gone so completely to seed that blades of moonlight sliced through the decaying slats of wood that had once been the back wall. As his eyes adjusted, Eddie stomped less carefully. Tuck had collapsed near the door, and his endless coughing annoyed Eddie but also reassured him that his fellow traveler had not died or been attacked by something unseen.

At least I'm indoors tonight, Tuck managed between hacking fits. A moonbeam cut across his face. Sort of indoors, he added.

When Eddie reached the far left corner of the barn, he found—among rust-eaten pitchforks and trowels, useless stirrups and yokes, and a bucket of stagnant water—the remnants of an upright piano. The enamel on most of its ivory teeth had snapped off, and a few of the black keys had come off as well, leaving only raw wood flush against the keyboard. The front panel had fallen off, but someone had placed it diagonally on the top, although at some point the lid had broken and it hung precariously off the back by one hinge.

The environment made him restless—he thought he heard bats; the spiderwebs that touched his face and arms made him think of movies about zombies, almost made him wonder if he had entered the world of those monsters as a monster himself. With a theatrical flourish, Eddie reached out to the piano with both arms extended, his fingers splayed in a Frankenstein stance, and, in the manner of someone who does not know a language attempting to speak it, attacked the keys from one end to the other.

The muted thumps on the hammerless notes, dissonant chimes, and bizarre twangs that he made the piano emit sounded to him like devil music. When Eddie discovered the sustain pedal and let his every punishment of the instrument ring out, Tuck whimpered for him to stop, claiming that his ears would bleed and promising to play and sing a hundred songs on it when he got well, but the noise drowned him out, and the barn, and probably the outside world for a few hundred yards, became the eerie domain of some ghoulish musical apparition.

When Eddie decided that he had come to the finale, he bashed the keys forcefully four times and allowed the dirty sonic cloud he'd produced to dissipate until it disappeared beneath the sounds of crickets and strange frogs outside.

For four days that October the crew marooned Eddie and Tuck by themselves, providing only the most rudimentary food, usually care packages consisting of a bruised orange, a salty, disintegrating baloney sandwich, a half-pint of warm milk or watery OJ from concentrate, and one packet of generic mayo. Someone from the crew would drop several packages at a time in green Styrofoam containers outside the barn on the path, which was really just two deep, muddy parallel tire tracks with long grass between them. Without entering, the person might call out to check on Tuck, who could barely drag himself down the small hill where he and Eddie relieved themselves.

Because food came only once a day, Eddie divided the lunches evenly and saved half of his for dinner. He would do the same for Tuck, whose worsening illness had begun to make Eddie unsure of his own health. He begged for alcohol; Eddie whined until they brought it, charging against Tuck's debt.

During the day, Eddie explored the woods and fields around

the barn, thinking that he might see his mother somewhere. Periodically he made sure that he could still breathe by inhaling as much of the humid atmosphere as he could and running as far as he dared without losing sight of the barn and then back again, his vitality confirmed by his panting and sweating.

The food bringers talked but the talk did not say anything, it was only nervous chatter, like the night people in Houston. Eddie could tell that they might not remember how to have conversations, so when he tried asking about Darlene, he half expected to get garbled responses. Words without meanings jumped out of the sides of the food bringers' mouths; their eyes were always bloodshot and jumpy.

I'm missing school, Eddie said to one of them. I've got to go back. Is Darlene Hardison here somewhere? She's my mother. I need to find her.

You need? I need. I need me a rug, this food bringer said. He swallowed his words and barely opened his mouth when he spoke. I got me some *bad* rug-need, that's what I'm about! Fat motherfucker giving me attitude. Fattitude, that's what it is. Ha! One thing you gotta say about me, I'm funny. When I leave here I'ma go to LA and be a comedy star in the movies like Eddie Murphy. You watch.

Have you seen Darlene Hardison?

Once or twice a food bringer did not seem out of it but never answered his questions except by grunting equivocally, and they all regarded him with unsettling, blank cow-eyes. Eddie suspected that someone had ordered them not to say anything except to ask about his health.

You okay? a food bringer said, almost as an afterthought, while leaving.

I think so.

Fever? Chill? Ache?

No.

The guy pointed at Tuck lying in the corner. He ain't dead yet? He spoke with what sounded to Eddie like impatience.

No. Better than he was yesterday.

Hmm. Might not be medical. That's what How an' them saying. On account a you ain't got it.

Not medical? Then what?

Some kinda obeah juju from somewheres.

What's obeah juju?

The guy's response terrified Eddie. He stared at Eddie and his eyes glazed over in a dramatic way that the boy could not decipher. The guy didn't respond to the question, maybe because something more exciting had just happened inside his skull, but he also looked surprised that Eddie didn't know that term. Or perhaps bugging out his eyes was his way of demonstrating obeah juju. It did not feel at all like a normal interaction between human beings. With the same weird grimace on his face, the man turned and waddled off through the brush.

On the afternoon of the fourth day in the barn, Tuck recovered, almost miraculously. He sat up, stood, stretched, and walked shakily across the dirt to the rectangle of light in the corner where the door had fallen off one of its hinges. It was as if Jesus had laid his palm on the man's sweaty forehead and pronounced him well. Tuck qualified his sudden burst of energy in every way he could think of, as if he knew better than to get excited about something that could turn out to be nothing.

I could be about to get worse, he warned. And it ain't like I'm about to run the one-hundred-yard dash. But the fever musta broke or something. Damn if it ain't a complete mystery how shit function inside my own self. Chin to chest, he looked down at his dirt-caked T-shirt. Now I need some more of that drinkahol, boy, 'cause I'm getting the goddamn shakes again.

Was it obeah juju?

Tuck froze and then snapped his head toward Eddie. He responded with a condescending outrage Eddie always half expected from older black adults. Damn right somebody put a curse on me, he said. From the minute I got borned. He cut his eyes and spat his words. Doctor grabbed me out my mama pussy, held me by my feet, whacked my black ass extra-hard, and said, It's a nigger! That's the curse that's on me. Around here niggers say some funky words, put some chicken feathers in a wine bottle, and motherfuckers just laugh it off, but when white folks say some curses on your ass, you are up to your neck in fines and bills and fees and lawyers for the rest of your life. Then you're in jail, which is a motherfucking labyrinth of shit on a whole different level. And white folks do that shit to other white folks too. Shit, they'd do it to the birds if they could.

What you think happen to me? he went on. Tuck described his struggle to make it as a musician: the years of touring; sleeping on the same filthy comforter every night in the back of a rickety van; playing all night and having to split fifty dollars among the six band members, and not evenly, because Mad Dog, his bandleader, demanded a bigger cut; the club managers who sometimes refused to pay; the lack of a steady woman; the steady presence of the wrong women; the ominous, deepening evidence that the audience for Mad Dog Walker's music was literally dying and the leader's tendency to blame his band for the waning popularity of the blues and harangue them, and sometimes even the thin crowds at shows, during his interminable drug binges; how the stress of all these things made Tuck drink until he didn't have the strength to do anything but drink, and how even that strength disappeared, how his playing, the activity that had given Tuck the greatest pleasure and kept him going spiritually, though never financially, gradually seemed to take the shape of a noose and began to tighten around his neck.

He had followed his ambition to the outskirts of its possibility and had not found riches there, which didn't bother him, since he was used to poverty, but he'd expected a certain sense of fulfillment, a measure of respect from his community—What a joke that was, he said, to think that niggers fighting for the same scrap of meat like a pack of yard dogs is a community—something unnameable but gratifying, and he'd found that all he had in the end, once Mad Dog and the boys parted ways, was his own stupid life, emptied of significance.

Just as he had begun to imagine how to redirect that life toward something new, maybe to think about getting a GED, a spiteful variety of fate—others might call it God—put his body in Oklahoma City, in the path of a particular Honda Accord driven by a thirty-four-year-old mother with an alarmingly high blood-alcohol level, especially for a Thursday afternoon. Tuck sustained four broken ribs, multiple lacerations, a busted kneecap, and a severe concussion. While he remained in intensive care for two weeks, the woman was unharmed. He blamed the concussion for cognitive problems that made it impossible for him to return to any sort of work, and without health insurance he faced charges so astronomical that once he'd healed sufficiently and the overdue notices began to crowd out the junk mail in the doorway of his motel-style condo rental, the pressure became so great that it forced him out.

I gone out one day and just kept going and going and didn't go back. What I had? I ain't had no girlfriend, my children don't—I ain't got no real children anyhow, my brother dead, my parents long gone, and—

They both started and became still, alert, listening, because they'd heard a rustling outside, close enough that it sounded as if it had originated in their heads. The food delivery had already come through that afternoon; by now Eddie had the usual itchy acid sensation in his esophagus from the baloney. Neither of them could quickly come up with an explanation for the footsteps they heard making their way around the barn and casting a shadow through the open places in the planks. Quietly they rose and moved to the wall. A figure dappled with circles of sun and green shadow, made dark by the angle of the light, came around the side of the barn. It moved with animal grace for a moment, then its motions became twitchy. Eddie pushed his eye close to a break in the wall.

Somebody chasing a bird, Tuck whispered. Don't blame em—them baloney sandwiches ain't enough for nobody. He chuckled to himself.

The person muttered and stopped in a patch of sunlight. Though cautious of getting splinters in his cheek, Eddie pushed his eye closer to the wall and examined the figure in disbelief and confusion. A desperate and eerie feeling came over him that his fantasy of having crossed over into the land of the dead had leapt out of his control and become horribly real. He saw an apparition—a skinny woman, a witch with missing teeth and disheveled hair full of leaves and short pieces of straw, dressed in a tattered shirt and baggy, muddy jeans with a rope for a belt.

The woman dragged herself through the underbrush on her knees with her arms out, trying to catch an oily-looking grackle that kept backing up. Her eyes remained locked on the bird, which at last fluttered out of reach and into a young tree. The woman's irises rolled up too far under her lids and she fell forward. She looked like something dead.

Eddie sprinted out of the barn and around the corner, adrenaline throbbing behind his eyes and sapping his breath. Then he paused at a safe distance and peered at the woman and called out to her. She turned to him, but her reaction was not sudden or full of surprise. She angled her head in his direction as if she had heard a faint noise much farther away in the distance. Her mouth opened slackly, caught remembering.

Mama, he breathed, a question, almost a hope that this sad apparition had only temporarily assumed a shape similar to his mother's. Then the haunt's eyes flared and took on an intensity unlike before, and recognition blazed between them. Eddie didn't want to admit that his mother had turned into this thing, this barely familiar shadow, because he would have to move toward it and embrace it, but the relief that he'd found her, alive, finally conquered his disgust. His eyes overflowed, his heart broke into a blur of ecstasy; he ran toward her.

At that moment Darlene turned back to the bird and passionately groped toward it, and when again it moved to a higher branch, she burst into a panic. She rose and her wailing became violent, her grasping ferocious; she tore at leaves and flicked branches so that they snapped back against her arms and face and left welts that soon bled.

Eddie clung to her waist and bellowed, Ma, while she screeched and howled in the direction of the grackle, which leapt into even higher branches, then took flight above the treetops and into the smudgy sky, its black wings flapping quickly, then slowly, then fading into nothing.

Darlene collapsed against a tree and stroked Eddie's head as he burrowed it into her lap. They remained attached in this way, Eddie pressing himself into Darlene as if he could squeeze her back into her old self.

Tuck sauntered out of the barn and stopped cold when he turned the corner and saw Eddie and Darlene. That your mama, huh, Tuck stated. Drunken bum was right! He tried and failed to remember the song he'd made up, humming to himself in quiet confusion.

Eddie and Darlene paid him no attention. Their rocking and

crying reached a low, intense drone as natural sounds returned—the shuddering of crickets, the white noise of leaves in
trees, the songs of birds, including the broken-radio cacophony
of the grackles. Darlene, with her head back and her eyes rolled
up, watched the sky for them but saw nothing. Eddie clung to her
rough, foul-smelling jeans and wept, both because he had found
his mother and because he'd found her like this, in a state that
kept her from really being his mother.

Several strong breezes swept across the area at uneven intervals. No one spoke for a time. Tuck turned away and went back
into the barn, and Eddie and Darlene prolonged the moment,
soundlessly clutching at each other. What had come before was
too unbearable to talk about and what would come afterward they
did not know. Better to let the world melt into nothing for a while.

At last Eddie flipped over and scratched his hand through the
dirt. Soon enough, Darlene said, Eddie, and Eddie said, Mom,
and they repeated this rudimentary dialogue, having been so far
away from the fact of each other that it took the dialogue to bring
them each back into existence. The words of their names volleyed
from one to the other, first as a question, then a statement, an in-
cantation, and, finally, a revelation.

13.

MEET SCOTTY

Them shoes was the next casualty after the fire at Mount Hope Grocery. Yellow-ass pumps, too narrow just at the front of where the toe start up. Not the kinda footwear you need to got on when you standing all day. And if she ain't chose the outfit she did, she wouldna needed to wear them yellow shoes; she coulda put on the black flats. She wouldna jammed her feet in the yellows and got that headache, he wouldna had to go for no Tylenol at no store, and them boys wouldna run into him at that time. The store mighta still got torched but at least Nat coulda survived. You could start another store, but you couldn't start no other him.

So the first moment Darlene had alone with them shoes, back in her room the day after the cops drank all the coffee and then showed her that driftwood, she gripped the heel and the toe of the first one and tried to rip it apart, but the thickness wouldn't tear. The more it ain't rip, the harder she pulling—that damn leather ain't so much as stretch. Them durable-ass shoes got Darlene so mad she bit down on the side of one and be chomping on it like a dog attacking a squeeze toy. Her teeth sliding and her jaw cramping, but my girl ain't hardly made mark the first on them leather uppers.

She knew she done something ridiculous—you couldn't hold no shoes responsible for nothing, shoes ain't got no intentions. But shoes also can't talk back, they helpless, and what's helpless always gon take the biggest part of the rage. After she bit the one shoe, Darlene threw both of em at the wall, stomped on em, kicked em. She stopped to think for a second 'bout how to destroy em better, then she found a scissors in the next room, and with those bad boys she hacked and snipped and dug into every last one of the stitches that's holding the parts of the shoes together, poking the point in, twisting real hard. Then she pulled the leather off the sole and cut it into funky-shaped bits that landed all over, on the windowsill and under the end tables and shit, and she gone to the garage and got a hammer from a toolbox. She beat them heels with that hammer till the li'l layers of wood done come unstuck and be falling around her, spinning under the work shelves and into spare tires where wasn't nobody ever gonna see em again. If pumps could talk, them poor ladies woulda been yelling, *Darlene, have mercy! What we do? For God's sake, tell us what the hell we did!*

The blouse went next, and that gone into the grill out in the backyard, lighter fluid all over everything, up in a orange flame, like a miniature of the tragedy, like payback, though Darlene ain't understand or care that she just making them shoes and that blouse the next motherfucking thing down on the chain of pain. The fire made a loud-ass wind sound and the beauty of them jittering blue and yellow flames pulled her closer almost against her will.

Her son ran out there wondering what going on, and she hollered, Stay back, Eddie! He stood there watching slack-mouthed while them evil-smelling synthetics done burnt a black hairdo of smoke up over them live oaks back there, driving all the grackles away. Goddamn shoes!

Ma? Eddie asked, tryna make his voice like a hand that gonna stroke her shoulder blade and make it all okay, like he had a chance in hell of doing that.

She ain't never took her eyes off that grill. She twisting her fingers together and twirling her wedding ring around like she putting a spell on somebody. Darlene glared at that fire, tryna give it the same intensity it's giving her, then she squeezed a whole bunch more fluid onto it. Holy Mother of God, that shit made a gigantic flare that lit up everything in the yard and flashed back from every window in the house and from the neighbor windows too.

Darlene shouting, Goddamn yellow goddamn blouse!

She made a vow never to match colors no more. She boycotted Tylenol and all other pain relievers. Way down below her everyday thoughts, she said to herself that she ain't deserve no pain relief no more. Pain *relief*? Relief from pain? Oh no, she deserved *more* pain, the kinda pain she had inflicted on the man she loved, the man who was her life, the kinda punishing hell heat that had surrounded his body and burnt him up into a tree stump that got married. She deserved more pain than you could put in a human body. She deserved the kinda pain that filled up the sky and turnt into the weather. Like that big red storm on Jupiter. A storm the size of Jupiter itself. Her mind screamed real loud, like she need to get the attention of a motherfucker on another planet, or somebody who might or might not be in heaven, and them screams ain't never stopped.

After all that waiting, with everybody except her wondering if he had got away and still alive somewhere, they told her they had found something and showed her that piece of driftwood with her matching wedding ring on it.

Then people start coming by the house with all the hope they once had 'bout the husband being alive drained out they faces, and they all saying the same damn word—Sorry. So sorry. I'm sorry. So so sorry. Sorry sorry sorry.

You're not sorry, she said to them in her head. *You didn't do it. Me, I'm sorry. I had the migraine. I wore the shoes. If you're so sorry, do something about it,* she thought, and couldn't keep herself from thinking. *But you can't do anything about it. What can sorry do? Sorry doesn't pull anybody's husband out of the grave alive.*

Most the time she spent resenting relatives and friends, but she couldn't let nobody know that. She wasn't no horrible person, she just couldn't help feeling everything, including the wrong emotions. When she had to deal with anybody, she made sure not to show no emotion of no kind. They wouldn't like to know that her house felt invaded, that when she peeled all them carrots and cucumbers and whatnot to put out for LaVerne and Puma and Bethella and Fremont and the rest, she thinking 'bout stripping their skin, thinking 'bout chasing everybody out and stabbing her wrists with the peeler.

No, that wasn't the right thing to feel, or even think, let alone say—forget about doing it. So nothing. No genuine reactions. Acting all zombified made things easier and harder at the same time. Thank you for coming, Bethella. Oh, I'm hanging in there. Yes, it's terrible. Eddie doesn't understand and I don't know what to say to him. I mean, which parts do I explain, and how much? Yes, justice. *Justice won't bring him back any quicker than sorry,* she thought. In Louisiana, a Negro could find a igloo faster than justice.

At church, with Eddie gripping her gloved hand, all them

flower crosses looking blurry behind her veil, Darlene thinking 'bout the morgue, and 'bout that damn piece of driftwood inside that coffin. Eddie looked up and asked how they know his daddy in there, and she laughed a little 'cause she ain't know neither and couldn't bring herself to say nothing. If Eddie had seen that charcoal thing with its sickening face in that casket he wouldn't believe it had nothing to do with his daddy neither. Didn't no words come to her, she gone back to staring at the picture on the program, and fortunately Leticia Bonds from the beauty shop start singing "Take My Hand, Precious Lord" right then. She had the type of voice that made you think she gonna be a star someday.

Later, when they putting Nat in the ground, Darlene squeeze Eddie's hand a little tighter and he turnt his eyes down to the casket, and she ain't feel that Eddie had a grip on her hand no more, but that she had tumbled into a grave herself and be grasping at his forearm, tryna keep herself from getting inside that box next to that black log. She wanted to hold that damn log and stroke it like it still Nat, or like something of him had stayed inside it, even if it crumbled in her arms. As if she could still pull her face right up close to his after he had fell asleep, the way she used to did every night, and kiss him and breathe in his breath.

With Nat gone, she wasn't no person no more. She hadn't lost a part of herself, she lost the whole motherfucking thing. Bad labels came into her mind 'bout herself, and all of em stuck, 'cause she had stole Nat from somebody else, and 'cause of the standing around at the store in them yellow shoes, and 'cause of the migraine, and 'cause of who she was.

Even when her neighbors pressured the police and they found out 'bout a group of white men that ain't had no alibis, Miss Darlene couldn't be thinking 'bout what *they* done. They was just white boys doing what come natural in the place they from—down south, white boys be hunting Negroes like lions be hunting gazelles out in the goddamn Serengeti. Hell, the damn cops still did it theyself. Darlene focused on the part that she played in the process, how if she hadna stood around in them shoes and gotten that migraine, etc., if Nat hadna insisted on putting his clothes on and going down there, he wouldna been there for them boys to broke his legs and head and toss his ass on the floor like dog meat while they splashing kerosene everyplace like the Devil's cologne and then lighting they ever-loving matches and gone to sit in they cars. Sitting there like they television done broke and that's the substitute for *Disney's Motherfucking Magic Kingdom.*

But even in that hot-ass courtroom, Darlene couldn't conjure up no hatred for nobody but herself while them boys' steady stream of *Yes sirs* and *No sirs* ringing out against the walls, and the brutality be showing under they cool smiles and they polite chitchat with one another, even the women, even the judges. In the heat, them boys dabbing they foreheads with handker-chiefs and adjusting they ties, but you could tell they vicious bloodthirsty motherfuckers inside. They ain't stir at all when they lawyer used the word *coloreds* and a couple of black folk up in the balconies grunted a complaint. One of em, a older man, be clean-ing his damn fingernails while the lawyer describing the whole of everything Nat had gone through to turn his ass to charcoal. Them good ol' boys treat they own trial like they was toddlers that had got accused of stepping on a ant by accident.

If any of it woulda made a difference, Darlene mighta paid more attention. It ain't surprise her or move her none when the judge threw the case out 'cause the damn prosecution ain't had enough evidence to convict, 'cause why would they bother to *find* enough evidence?

She ain't feel nothing when the fathers and they boys filed

out with they crew-cut heads sticking out them stiff white dress shirts, hugging they wives and mothers like they done saved something precious that the evil Darlene had tried to take from em. Darlene said to herself, *Let them go back to their guns and their private clubs. Nothing will bring Nat back, and killing or jailing somebody else's husband or son would only burn everybody's wounds deeper.*

She let other folks talk to the reporters—people who felt more outraged than she did 'cause they ain't done nothing to cause the events. They ain't know and they never would know how it felt.

Eddie ain't need a mother who had did that to a father, a bitch who murdered husbands with her headaches. She let Bethella take him to Houston sometime, for the days right after they killed Nat, and later when she start tryna find work. Oftentimes, she couldn't bring herself to go get him, so she didn't, and he stayed with Bethella longer. Eddie needed Bethella's strictness and her discipline, Darlene said—she thought it gonna influence him positively. Whenever Darlene took care of Eddie after what happened, she let him jump on the furniture, bought him ice cream and cake, drove him wherever he wanted to go, let him stay home from school—once she even stole a wind-up toy boat for the bath 'cause at the time she couldn't pay, but she felt bad and stereotypical behind that immoral action too, even though she done it for a good reason. She wasn't 'bout to deny that Eddie deserved every last thing he wanted; it hurt him when he couldn't get things, and she couldn't watch him suffer for one blessed minute. It woulda hurt more to explain the why-nots. *He* the innocent one.

Nat been gone 'bout a year and a half before Darlene finally got herself a job, a job aside from the unpaid work she tried to avoid, which was dealing—or not dealing—with the charred remnants of Mount Hope Grocery. She heard 'bout the gig through this white boy named Spar said he met Nat once. The insurance money for Nat and for the store be running out, and even though it had helped a whole lot, using it still reminded Darlene's ass of all she done blamed herself for. Her new job was at a different store, a nationwide chain with fluorescent lights and linoleum instead of wood beams and peat-moss smells, so it ain't set off no unpleasant memories for her. But unpleasant memories you know to avoid; its the goddamn pleasant ones be causing all the pain on account a they sneak up on your ass.

On one them evening shifts, with Harriet from down the road looking after Eddie, Darlene start thinking 'bout going back to all the places she and Nat once shared, and when she get home late that night, she start going through a whole bunch of Nat's coats, his bomber jacket that still be smelling like his Old Spice, and his pictures of the Centenary Gents, and the songs he used to whistle start clogging up her mind. Darlene knowed she gotta drown out them memories and get the fuck outta Louisiana. That's right when she started thinking 'bout moving to Houston. Bethella could guard her son. Eddie like being with Bethella probably more than being with her, Darlene told herself. Eddie ain't need to soak up all the weird, negative messages she be giving off all the time. Plus, she hoping that she could find better work in Houston.

Of course, moving to Houston don't never solve nobody problems, and Miss D sure couldn't solve the big issue that be obvious to any fool who seen the family together in the happy days, which was that Eddie took after his pop so goddamn much—not just physically, with them whiskey-brown eyes and them eyelashes and that big-ass mouth, but he had somehow picked up a truckload of his daddy's ways. It got tough for Darlene to stay in the room with him and drain out all the unhappiness that start swelling inside her feet, 'cause her son be a living reminder of her dead husband. That gon be the same whether she in Ovis or Houston or the east side of Hades.

Around that same time, a few month after she start her job at that Hartman's Pharmacy, me and Darlene got together and had our first li'l tête-à-tête. So it could be I'm partly to blame for why it done took another year and a half for her to get her and Eddie ass to Houston for real. Meanwhile, in them May evenings after work, she feeling that restlessness coming on right before she gone home, like a checkpoint had sprung up between work and home where the happiness cops gonna pull her over and test her to make sure she got a positive mood. She be standing around outside the store after her shifts, watching customers stroll in and out, counting how many trucks gone past, letting the sun bake her face while it's dropping off behind the trees in the neighborhood cross the street. Sometime she sat on a crate, smoking alone 'cause the store discount done got her started on tobacco again, or she with her other so-called associates on break, everybody parking theyself at a wobbly old picnic table with all kinda graffiti gouged into the wood.

One afternoon she sitting there watching one them freaky sunsets where every type of cloud done mixed with airplane exhaust and space dust or some shit and the sky be turning all blue and orange and it look the way a brass band sound while it's tuning up. This sky had so much drama going on up there that a few customers was gathered on the walkway in front of the store gaping at it like they waiting for the space shuttle to launch. Off to one side, a gigantic storm cloud be blending the darkness with the coming night, but on the other side, the sun had burnt a hole in a bunch of puffy globs of meringue and its beams was shooting through. Above that, some the meringue done gone bright purple.

Spar, her manager, walked out onto the sidewalk and stared, then he turnt his head to Darlene.

It's a stunner, huh?

What is? Darlene said. She seen the whole spectacle, plus the onlookers, without noticing nothing at all; everything she experienced feeling humdrum, like it's a washed-out photograph in a motherfucking View-Master.

You, honey. He grinned.

Spar flirted with every woman who crossed the threshold at that damn store, but with Darlene he ain't never stop, and that made her nervous that he meant it for real. It disturbed her 'cause he said he met Nat once—you don't be hitting on the new widow of no acquaintance before the tag's off his damn toe. Spar a skinny white guy, shorter and younger than Darlene, who slick his hair back and can't grow enough face hair for a goatee but try anyhow. Not nobody she felt she could take seriously, almost not even as a boss. How seriously you could take a guy named after Spartacus, that dumbass gladiator from them old movies? She had wanted to work there 'cause that branch was way far away from Ovis—other side of Monroe, almost to Ruston—and she ain't always feeling the eyes of motherfuckers who knew 'bout the murder and the trial and Mount Hope. Only Spar knew about her connection to all them tragic events, and she ain't think he had said nothing to the others; also, most of em ain't read the papers too careful, 'cause they sure ain't sell too much of em at the store. Darlene liked that she ain't had no identity or no history at her job; being anonymous meant she could relax for a while and hide in the stream of shoppers that was high on buying shit.

Spar pointed his chin up at the sky. The sunset, Darlene, darlin'. It's almost as pretty as yourself.

Darlene waved one hand at him and took a drag from her cigarette with the other. Yeah, I see it, it's nice, she said, exhaling a couple gray plumes.

Spar seem like he egged on by the fact that she responded at all, but he ain't noticed, or had chose to ignore, the rejection in her voice. He took a few clumsy-ass steps over to her. Could I get a smoke, please?

Darlene flipped open her hard-pack and a final cigarette rolled to one side.

Are you sure you want to give me your last one?

She stretch out her arm farther toward him and push the cigarette up out the box with two fingers. Take it, she said, like she a robot. If I want more, there's others inside. On discount too.

He took it and used his own lighter to get it started and sat down on a concrete thing looked like a broken wall jutting up from the walkway. They looked up at the craziness in the sky again, and the thrill in Spar li'l face be rising up slowly.

Like the end of the world, he said to hisself, and then turnt to Darlene, thinking some new thought, or maybe one he just mustered the gumption to blurt out. You been off work the last hour and ten, ha'nt you? Why you ain't go home? You like it here that much? You waitin' on somebody? Your boyfriend?

Didn't he remember? Did she need to remind him? Darlene screamed in her head but decided she ain't gonna answer, and Spar, who making a show of listening, had took off his dark company shirt and folded it over his thigh, showing off a sleeveless tank top. On his left shoulder, down to his wrist, he had the ugliest tattoo Darlene ever seen, a orange-and-green cartoon of a vine that be strangling a evil octopus that had fangs and a human face.

She couldn't keep from staring at the terrible picture and screwing up her nose, and when he seen her looking, he went, It's new. Then he goes, I got another, and smirked and pulled up his shirt to show her the Tasmanian devil on his pec, all alone, like

Taz had runned over there 'cause he scared of the octopus. Spar held the ugly image on his shoulder close to her face until she felt like she had to say she liked it to make him move it out her personal space. Then he told a long story 'bout where the idea had came from that ain't make no kinda sense whatsoever.

Hey, Spar said, once the dusk getting started. As you probably know, I live walking distance from here? And I'm finna go on home and have me a couple beers, and uh, continue to smoke things, and you're welcome to join me if you like. Don't make me drink alone, honey.

Darlene peered at him like she didn't trust him.

I promise to be a total gentleman. He stood up.

Darlene be shifting in her seat.

You can bring me up on sexual harassment if I'm not. He raised his right hand. God's my witness, he said, and then, suddenly distracted, he pointed at her ring. Hold the phone, you got a husband. Then there was a pause and Darlene shook her head and glared into his eyeballs, then Spar suddenly lowered gaze to his shoes. Right! he exclaimed. I forgot. Damn it to hell, I'm such a idiot! He punched hisself in the head, maybe a li'l violently. How could I forget a thing like that? I'm real sorry, Darlene. He put his palms up like he wanna touch her, but she knew he couldn't.

Darlene finish her cigarette and flick the butt to the ground and it bounced underneath a car grille. The temperature had fell real quick and she ain't thought to bring no sweater. She stood up, folding her arms and rubbing her biceps with her hands to keep warm, looking away from Spar. She impressed that Spar forgot, even for a instant, the thing that had seared itself into *her* mind to the exclusion of damn near everything else. She thinking maybe he could teach her how to forget everything too.

No wonder you're always looking sad, Spar said. They started walking down the sparkly asphalt. Did them guys ever—? he asked, and then waggled his head, thinking better of it. Oh, I ain't gonna pry, Miss Darlene. You could say whatever you feel comfortable with. Then he gone off on another monologue 'bout how nosiness had done in his grandfather during the Great Depression; he ain't stop till they walked into his house, one them shabby joints with peeling paint everywheres, fat columns framing the door out on the verandah, sitting behind a couple magnolia trees.

Darlene knew who I was—she seen people smoking, they even offered to introduce her to me several times before, but she think she too good for me then. In the back of her mind, she thought I was dangerous, but she also recognized that sometimes you could do dangerous shit without no consequences. I was good friends with Spar, for example, and he the manager of a convenience store. When Spar brought her to the garden in his backyard and casually lit that pipe, almost elegant, like a English dude from the past would do with a pinch of tobacco, they had already had a beer or three and he had loaned her a sweatshirt, one still a li'l bit warm from the dryer and that had a clean, flowery scent to it. Her resistance gone way the fuck down; she wanted to get free from the shit reality she living in, plus, with how nice her manager acting, it seem rude to turn down the trademark thick velvety smoke created by Yours Truly. Hello, Darlene, I said, and my smoke entered her lungs for the first time, gentle like a handshake at the start, then my lovely fingers of smoke got in her breath and grabbed it right where Nat's breath had once spent all that time. I am so glad we met.

After a couple hits, I had gave her the first confidence she felt in years, not to mention contentment. She talked more and played checkers and drank whiskey with Spar—in a couple hours, she was certain this social outing gonna lead directly to a promotion at work. It dawned on her that she felt like recently everything in life had twisted her ass out of shape, but right then she seen that her distorted outline was a piece of a puzzle, the last one hanging above what had been a real tough board. I floated her ass above the board on a cloud of smoke. The smoke lowered her down and pushed her in place and something inside her went *snap* and we finished the puzzle together. It felt so good we ripped all them motherfucking puzzle pieces apart and did that shit again. And the ripping and the doing-again felt just as good the second time. And the fifty-second. And...

14.

LOST YEARS

Because of all the expectations Eddie had stockpiled about being back with his mother, the reality couldn't have held up even if things had been perfect. But he listed the ways in which things had improved. His mother didn't go out on the street in Houston anymore—she stayed in one place and worked steadily, got regular meals, and had friends. She and Eddie could spend time together in the morning and for a while at night. Sometimes the drugs didn't get in the way of her personality and he could see, behind the glazed looks and volatile reactions, the mother he remembered. His mother reminded him of the proverbial stopped watch that tells the right time twice a day. Every day he would wait for those two times.

In the late afternoon of their reunion, three men had followed Darlene up the path asking where she had gone. She responded by introducing Eddie as her son, and their attitude switched to a more jovial, relaxed one; pretty soon they sheathed their weapons and shook his hand. But the mood didn't last long, and they hustled him and Darlene back to the sleeping quarters, where he got his first look at how her life had changed. Though he had clamored for them to bring Tuck as well, they kept the old guy quarantined.

Not even the chicken smell or the concrete of the barracks or the locking in at night bothered Eddie enough to make a fuss after finding Darlene. She'd introduced him to everybody at the place before he noticed anything untoward about the atmosphere. The novelty of a kid among the workers made everybody there curious and excited. People now wanted to play the incomplete, broken set of Connect 4 that had gathered mildew in the corner—you couldn't use the last row because the chips fell through; they usually played it as Connect 3. TT gave a tour, pretending to show off a luxury suite; Hannibal taught Eddie an elaborate soul handshake. A child had arrived, and you had to show a happy time to a child, regardless of the circumstances.

By supper, the room calmed down, as everybody dispersed and tugged the matted plastic wrap off their green cardboard trays before munching privately. Darlene sat at the edge of her bunk, its metal bar creating an impression across the backs of her thighs. When she talked to Eddie about the place, her voice grew lower, softer, more urgent. Habitually, she scratched the bug bites on the back of her neck, the small of her back, and her legs.

Sirius got in touch with Mrs. Vernon? she asked. Is that how you found me?

Serious? Who? No...

Darlene's face didn't move for a few moments. You can't stay here, Eddie. Don't let them make you stay.

But aren't you glad to see me?

Yes! You know I am. But it's just—I wanted to get out of all this first.

———

It seems okay to me.

Darlene laughed uncontrollably, then slower, until she started to cough. Eddie slapped her on the back, and she twisted her torso out of reach. She lit a cigarette.

You need to go to school.

No, I don't. I'm smart enough.

We're not going to have an argument about that, she said. You're going.

Under other circumstances, Eddie would have fought her, but it struck him that Darlene had made a motherly gesture, and that caused a wave of happiness and relief to whip through his body like wind through a bedsheet on a clothesline. In his mind, he flashed to a moment in the future when she would act like a real mother all the time; he ached for it.

Is there a school? he asked. Is it far, the school?

No. It's around here somewhere, Darlene said, as if she'd misplaced it. She threw her pointing finger in a vague direction behind her and to her right. Cigarette smoke swirled around her hand. Out there, she said.

When he asked about the color of the schoolhouse and the character of the teachers and the other kids, Darlene frowned and stopped giving complete answers and then excused herself to go to the bathroom, stubbing her cigarette out on the bottom of the bed frame. Eddie occupied himself by playing with the rusty bed-springs as if they were a musical instrument.

After about twenty minutes Darlene returned, having turned jittery and unresponsive. For a while Eddie tried to continue the conversation. He repeatedly attempted to find out whether she was okay, but the exchange became one-sided, her answers less and less like answers until eventually they resembled the growling of dogs or the cries of birds. He'd seen her in a condition like this before, though not as severe, and he knew to find something else to do as he nursed his plummeting optimism. He helped his mother lie down, his shaky hand supporting her underarm.

✘

Eddie started working the next day. The night before, when Darlene told Jackie he was her son, Jackie had seemed interested in his hands. She put them up against hers and marveled at their large size compared to her own grown-up hands. That morning, How sent Eddie out with Darlene and a few other women on a weeding detail, to a wide field of young sunflowers. The topography of the field and the low height of the plants allowed Eddie to work at some distance from his mother without losing sight of her. Initially he enjoyed himself, running up and down the rows and depositing tiny clover-like plants and saplings into a cardboard box, but it didn't take long for How to find fault with his work and ruin any pleasure he'd found in the job.

At first there weren't enough weeds in the box for How, and he claimed that Eddie hadn't done any work at all. Later, when How stomped out into the rows to check the kid's progress and still found it unsatisfactory, he grabbed Eddie by the face and shoved hard enough to knock him down against a pile of rocks, where he wailed. Michelle, the mouthy one with the pigtails, protested just as loudly and pledged, to the tacit agreement of the other women, to make a report. To somebody. Somewhere. At some point. Then she tried to run, and How cursed and lunged at her, but instead of pistol-whipping her once he'd grabbed her wrists, he pulled her thrashing body back to the group.

If anybody made a report, nothing came of it. Although Eddie had only just turned twelve, there were a couple of grown workers from Mexico about his same height, and How would assign Eddie to work with them on projects that kept everybody low to the ground—weeding, laying down fertilizer, or transferring shoots from the plastic-covered greenhouses to the outdoors. At first, the other workers wondered occasionally about Eddie's age and muttered confused sentences about why the company would allow someone so young to do the same work as older people. They clicked their teeth and said, Shame, declaring that somebody ought to do something, yet never volunteering themselves. Somebody better tell Sextus, they'd say. This could put him out of business, they'd muse, perhaps uncertain whether that would be bad in the long run. But the more Eddie began to resemble his dirty, rough-handed, tough-skinned coworkers, the less frequently the comments came, and as Eddie blended in, eventually they dwindled away entirely. Soon enough he'd grow into the job, and his age wouldn't matter anymore. At Delicious, what you couldn't see didn't count.

In her more sober moments, Darlene never stopped urging Eddie to leave, to get back in school, but she mingled her urgent instructions with deeds that kept him nearby, bound him with tight hugs and tears, slept spoons with him.

You favor your father, she told him. In so many ways. Headstrong. Hardheaded man. You talk like him. Good-looking. So good-looking. She held his chin and studied his face. It's like I'm looking at him when I look at you.

Don't you want to leave? Eddie asked.

I owe them a lot of money. And with you working now too, we can pay off the debt faster and eventually start to make a profit. You can work here, but not out there.

Why not? Don't kids have rights?

Darlene's face opened. She touched Eddie's fingertips against her own. Don't worry, she said. The Lord will see us through. You have to think positive to get positive things into your life. She told him about the book.

Eddie accepted her burden as his own, partially because of his attachment to her, which grew stronger when he saw her need for him and felt his own for her, and partially because neither of them had any ideas about where else to go or how to get there. They might as well have been standing at the edge of an ocean, dreaming of a raft. Every so often he remembered his mission to bring her back from hell, but he couldn't remember how that story went. Something about an apple?

Eventually they released Tuck from his quarantine, and when he joined the rest of the workers in the chicken house, he made sure, when he could, that the kid got the proper amount of rest and he argued for his pay, and checked that he had a method of saving up, though Eddie loaned so much to his mother that it never did add up, something he never admitted to Tuck. Like the rest, Tuck grumbled that Delicious had put Eddie to work too young, but Tuck's meek protests produced either answers that weren't answers or violence.

He's capable of doing the work, How explained, so he can work.

Tuck's protectiveness inspired Eddie to arrange for Tuck to pay some attention to his mother, but after a while it became clear that something he couldn't understand kept them apart. Still, in his mind, he thought of them as his parents and invented an elaborate home life the three of them would share after they left the farm, a fantasy he tried to keep to himself but sometimes referred to accidentally.

On Halloween, as a thundershower blasted across the sweet potato field, warm droplets poking and slicking all the leaves and drenching everybody, since they had to continue working, the man the management had identified as Sextus Fusilier himself finally drove his red tractor through on an inspection. Supposedly these took place every month, but no one could remember one for the last six. They happened as randomly as possible, because, the crew said, Sexy enjoyed the element of surprise.

Why he chose to drive the grinding old tractor was the subject of frequent debate. Some said that despite its slowness, Sextus could use it to get to anywhere on the vast grounds via a system of shortcuts from his house that no one else knew about. He could get around faster than you could by taking the roads, all of which were unpaved and full of potholes the size of salad bowls. Others called it a purely sentimental attachment, claiming that Sextus still craved a connection to the land he had grown up tilling and which had enriched him to the point where he didn't need it anymore. The vehicle had become quaint and unnecessary, but its symbolic value to Sextus grew with the years. A legend circulated that his father had used what little he made from his beet farm to take out a loan for it and died the day after he finished paying it off.

You could hear the tractor coming long before it arrived, first a faint buzz and then a growl almost as loud as a helicopter descending on a dusty field; you'd see a cloud gather at the horizon and soon a hatted figure in overalls bouncing in the tractor seat, then he'd be on you. He always seemed to have a grin on his face. At first it looked like delayed amusement at a joke he'd heard earlier, but in his presence you got the sense that the joke was *you*, and your life, and the fact that everything in it depended on his mood.

Why wouldn't a man with that kind of power be happy all the time? TT had said. I know I'd be happy all the time.

Happy? asked Hannibal. Man, I don't get it. He smiling all the damn time but the motherfucker ain't *never* happy.

This time Sextus came in rain gear, a bright yellow triangle atop the red tractor, with his craggy face sticking out of the top, the drawstring of the hood pulled tight against it. If Sextus hadn't created an atmosphere among the workers and the supervisors of fear mixed with admiration, Eddie would have laughed, the man

213

looked that comical. But as soon as How heard the engine in the distance, he immediately gathered everybody for the 5:00 p.m. roll call, at 4:50, probably to make himself look efficient, maybe to gain the workers' cooperation, their gratitude.

Sextus swung his leg off the tractor and took his place beside How and the group of wet black and Latino men and women. They wore torn cutoffs and dirty T-shirts that had darkened with sweat and rain, and most of them fidgeted tightly, chafing against the requirement that they stand still. The rain surged, sending gray streaks through the air and muddying the dirt.

Sextus, after consulting with How, turned his attention to the roll call and surveyed the group of workers. They might or might not have met his approval; his perpetual smile made it difficult to tell. Usually the only indication they received would come later, from How, who would describe Sextus's dissatisfaction and threats without being able to prove that orders had come directly from him.

As the crew, including Eddie, called out their names, Sextus's expression modulated to a more neutral smile, down from a beam to a blank grin. He took several steps toward the group and his attention settled on Eddie, who stood in the second row next to Darlene. He grabbed rain off his forehead and threw it aside, then stepped back to face How and Jackie.

How, how old is that young fellow in the second row?

Chuckling, How looked down. Oh, Eddie. He don't look sixteen, does he?

No, he don't.

Don't worry. It's cool.

It's cool?

It's cool, How insisted. He's a good worker.

Eddie had never heard How say anything so complimentary; he planted his feet and stood a little more proudly.

The brighter smile returned to Sextus's face, and he slogged through the mud in a rectangle around the group, as if this cursory glance could tell him very important things about them. As he closed the rectangle, he returned to the same spot in front of the group and examined Eddie more carefully. Eddie looked away, and then peeked, looked away again, then raised his head but didn't face Sextus, the way an infantryman might stand in front of a general. Sextus untied and pushed back his yellow hood, revealing a head of silver-streaked, thinning hair.

Sixteen? Sextus pondered yet again, almost to himself, but with the suggestion that Eddie might want to say the word himself to confirm. Eddie turned his head so that he could figure out what his mother thought. She hugged herself against the rain, which had begun to let up, except that it had brought a post-thundershower breeze and a chill along with it. She stared at Eddie vacantly, then her irises disappeared under her lids, and with a faraway sigh, fluffy with surrender, she looked away.

Sixteen, How said again, this time more definitively.

After a rudimentary inspection of the grounds, the yellow triangle returned to the tractor and started off through the mud. Then it got stuck and everybody had to do unpaid overtime to help unstick it.

Tuck said, Damn, kid, you just lost four years off your life in one minute.

15.

INERTIA

Naturally some sonofabitches always looking for a way to get out. Like Sirius B, and who knew where the hell he ended up? Eddie done had enough after they pushed him down by the face on day one, but he tryna rescue his mama, so he couldn't go yet. Darlene could see the point of other folks leaving, but what she gonna find out there? Probably a worse life. A life full of Unknowns, Don't-Know-If-I-Cans, and Sure-As-Hell-Can'ts. Could she quit me, could she get on her feet, get jobs? What jobs she gonna get anyhow? Looking that type of change in the face could terrify the shit outta people who *ain't* had them problems. And now Eddie done showed up at Delicious—safe, thank the Lord—so she ain't even had no reason to run. Working for Delicious, you couldn't call it luxurious, you couldn't even call it nice, but it be steady, honest work for a li'l bit of pay, and nobody judging you 'bout no drugs, and that made a difference in Darlene life, allowed her some dribs and drabs of pride now and again. How always saying, Work be the salvation of man, and Work gonna set you free. He only said that shit to make fun of you, but he kept saying it and you heard them words in your head. And at certain times on certain days, you believed them words.

Darlene kept on tryna weigh the crazy danger of running against the safe misery of staying. Trouble was, they weighed the same, so without deciding not to decide or nothing, she ain't made no decision at all. Inertia came in and kept her doing what she did. Now Michelle, she want to get the fuck out every damn night. Whenever Darlene talking to her, she be pointing out flaws in the system that she or everybody could use to they advantage and escape. Michelle had a great big forehead and talked a lot *a lot*. When my girl got going, she'd correct herself ten times before she could finish a damn sentence—she had a jumbo-size brain up in there, thinking and scheming 27-9.

If Michelle stood next to Darlene during roll call, she always say something like, Lookit—it's only three of them. Then she move her eyes over to How, Jackie, and Hammer. And Jackie's so out of it all the time, Michelle said, she like a half a one. It's *twenty* of us. When they take roll inside one of these days, she'd say through her teeth—look at that window up in the corner. They don't never put the padlock on that at night. When they go out and drink and smoke on the weekend nights, somebody could lift somebody up and push them out and they could run. You could hoist me up, Darlene. You're strong.

Darlene would go, I'm not that strong.

So you saying I'm too big? That I'm fat? Is that what you saying?

No, you're not fat! You need to stop that. I'm saying I'm not that strong. But once you get hoisted, who is going to hoist *me*?

The week after New Year's, Darlene and Michelle had a opportunity to talk down at the depot 'bout what they plans for the coming year. Hammer and How had just gone inside to buy they own beer, and left the crew on that souped-up school bus.

Michelle ain't waste no time, she bounced out her seat and down the rubber rug in the aisle to the back, where Darlene had hunched down into a seat, just pinching that glass tube between her fingers and sucking up my thick smoke.

Michelle goes, You know what's my resolution? My resolution is to get out this hellhole—dead or alive. Truth be told, we oughta do it. Tonight. Just run. They can't keep us here.

But what's the plan after Let's Run, Michelle! Darlene said. Do you have a plan for They've Got Guns? Do you know where we're at so we can figure out where we'll go? No. We don't have a compass or anything. We could run all day and night and maybe we'd run in circles, or run the wrong way and end up deeper inside the farm than before. What then?

Michelle leant her head back far as it would go and roared, shaking her fists in front of her. Have you got a plan for We're Gonna Die Up in This Joint? Do you want your son to grow up working for these people?

They've got guns. We don't. We're miles from civilization. Don't you owe them fifteen hundred dollars?

It's $1,749.35. But that's a goddamn joke compared to what they owe *me*. Michelle folded her arms and cocked her head and cut her eyes at Darlene. At a certain point, she said, it's not like I care anymore. Between being in this shithole, working seven days a week from seven a.m. sometimes to nine p.m. or later, and getting ripped off by these freakazoids for shit I don't even know I did, not to mention shit I didn't do? I will take getting shot over that—probably in the thigh, because you know they can't aim worth a damn, right?

They've got better aim than that. They might get lucky on your skull. You could die, Michelle.

We're all gonna die someday, Darlene. But *I* don't want my damn body to get thrown on How's trash heap when I go. They said your son was sixteen when everybody knows he twelve. You remember when How shoved him by his face that day we went out weeding? If they pistol-whip Eddie, or beat the crap out of him like they done to TT, he won't survive that. People have disappeared, Darlene. Know how they always joking 'bout dumping folks in the swamp? What if it's not a joke? Michelle pulled out a cigarette and start striking a match a bunch of times, then she finally got it lit. She sucked hard and blew a long blast of smoke above Darlene head. Darlene reached out to bum a cigarette, and Michelle gave her one and went, Honestly, I don't know why I bother telling you. You're probably just gonna tell them. Get a break on your debt.

Okay, let's figure something out! Darlene shouted, mostly to save her ass from feeling insulted by Michelle but also surprised how easily Michelle had made her mad what with accusing her ass of being a bad mother and a traitor. She couldn't find that spark in her heart to be thinking 'bout no plan just yet, though. She all worried 'bout how she gonna do that and stay with me.

Hammer and How came halfway up the steps of the bus just in time to hear what Darlene shouted.

Figure out? What you got to figure out, Darlene? How asked her, like a cop. You know where your next high's coming from, don't you?

Michelle stood and swayed back up the aisle, still smoking, then she twisted her neck in How direction. We're talking woman things, she said with a nasty edge, tryna cut him out the conversation. You know what a woman is? You ever been with one?

That's a ten-dollar demerit right there. Better watch that mouth of yours, bitch.

Better than watching that face of yours.

That's ten more.

Now she owes *$1,769.35,* Darlene marveled to herself.

How climb the rest the stairs, snapped to attention, and done drawn his gun. He point the barrel at Michelle, panting like he a unruly German shepherd, and goes, Fucking shut the fuck up. I'm docking you for insubordination. And put that cigarette out.

Michelle giggled and covered her face. Then she flicked the cigarette out the window.

A few nights later, Jackie, How, and Hammer locked the chicken house after lights-out and gone drinking somewheres, or maybe to get new people. Hands had got short even for winter. It still be a lotta work—they be harvesting cabbages, curing sweet potatoes, planting onions and chives, and tilling the bejeezus out the soil in January. But Sirius gone, and also a lady named Yolanda, and a dude who went by Billy Bongo flew the coop. A Nicaraguan dude they called Flaco had got real sick off the pesticides and then vanished. This brother nicknamed Too Tall had probably died, maybe of heatstroke. When they found him in the morning, Hammer said, He still breathing, and said he gonna take this man to the hospital—even though there probably wasn't no hospital within a hundred miles—so he and TT and Hannibal stuck Too Tall in the passenger side of a pickup truck even though Too Tall not staying upright, and Hammer drove away. TT said that as they moving him, when Too Tall head and arm fell out the open window against the side mirror, didn't no breath cloud show up on the mirror. Folks said that that ain't prove nothing, but still and all, didn't nobody never see Too Tall no more. And didn't nobody bring up the name of Too Tall neither. Never.

The workers ain't know how far Jackie, How, and Hammer going when they went to pick folks up this time, but you bet everybody up in that chicken house heard the minibus noise and listened for it to fade out, putting they head sideways, raising they eyebrows up. Folks was relieved not to have to see no supervisors no more, and a few of em moving together to talk and smoke. Every so often Darlene would hear a li'l outbreak of laughter or a shout when one the rats done skittered through the bathroom—maybe somebody seen Charlie, this one nasty rat that got bald patches in his side from where he scratched hisself till he bled. Everybody said that seeing Charlie meant at least a week of bad luck.

In the cover of the laid-back atmosphere, Michelle and TT snuck over to the mattress where Darlene and Eddie already gone to sleep. Michelle shook them awake. They decided that once everybody else went to sleep, TT gon lift everybody up to the window and out. They pretend to have a conversation, which turnt to a real conversation even though Darlene couldn't think 'bout nothing except were they gonna go through with the plan and would they fail and die or fail and get the shit kicked out of em. Success ain't even occur to her ass.

When the group finally got quiet, and all they could hear was the clucking and rustling feathers from the hundreds next door, Michelle and TT stood up and made they move. Darlene adrenaline went *schwoop*. The dark be too dark; they looking like shadows of shadows up next to that wall. Didn't none of em had matches right then, or God forbid a candle—they ain't even sell no candles at the depot.

Michelle be like, How y'all could be smoking so much and nobody got a light?

Darlene grabbed Eddie hand and still had to grope her way around—you ain't want to touch them walls, what with the black mold and them palmetto bugs and whatnot.

Them palmetto bugs seemed to know shit, too. When somebody ain't slept in a mattress for a day, a bunch of em would go to that mattress and hang out. They was the giant flying type, too.

Then they got bold—sometime they run cross your toes or your face in the night or climb up your pant leg and you jump up and shout and do a crazy dance to shake em out and try to find em in the dark to kill them, but you couldn't. Tuck said, I bet it's like entertainment for em, even *they* know you can't do nothing. I told Darlene that I knew for certain that them shady-ass bugs was informing on the workers, telling the management who had bad-mouthed the company in the off-hours. Some of em was robot bugs designed to listen in. Darlene warned everybody 'bout that, but they wouldn't take her seriously. Their loss.

Eventually Eddie helped Darlene get to the wall with the high window. But then, when they got over there, they had to move one the bunk beds against the concrete real quiet-like on account a the other workers who ain't gone might give em away outta jealousy, or want to join up with em, and that would get too dangerous.

Once they done set up the bed and TT standing on the top bunk and putting his hands into a stirrup shape for the first person to step up and out the window, he got cold feet and went, I got to get high before we go through with thisyer plan. He climb down and groped his way back to his bed and found a lighter, then he come back to take a hit under the window. By then everybody hanging out on the top bunk of the escape bed.

In the light of the lighter you could see all the anxious black sweaty faces ringing TT, urging his damn ass to hurry up and get high so they ain't get caught before they could leave on out the room and get the hell outta Delicious. Michelle and Darlene stopped cold, 'cause they also felt that taking a hit gon raise everybody level of nerve.

TT said, Scotty always make me fearless.

Eddie reach out for the pipe too, as they passing it round, but Darlene thumped him hard on the arm and said, No! Are you crazy? Not for children.

In the relaxing moment of sucking sounds and the milk-on-cereal noise that be effervescing off my wonderful burning rocks, it seem for a second like the whole damn thing wasn't even gonna happen, that it gonna turn into three Negroes smoking in the dark on top a bunk bed while a child sit there watching. And that mighta been fine by Darlene, who getting—not physically tired exactly, but exhausted.

I gave TT something he called smoky courage, and in a couple minutes he had took the pipe back, tried to cool it off with his breath, and shoved it down in his pants. He balanced hisself on the edge of the bed and got in the stirrup position. Michelle used the lighter to make sure everybody knew where each other was and how to get to the wall, flicking it every couple minutes like a bad movie projector so they would get the idea, but she wouldn't distract nobody who wasn't already in on the breakout.

Since Eddie the smallest, TT waved for him to climb up onto the cot and put his foot into the hand-stirrup first. But when it's two people up there, the frame start shaking and coming away from the wall and Eddie fell and yelled with his mouth closed. His mama went over and made sure he ain't hurt bad and told him, Be brave, but them li'l doubts 'bout the whole mission come back. *If Eddie gets severely injured,* she thought, *this escape thing isn't worth it.* The bed had also made a loud jangly sound and the four of em had to stop doing any activity for a minute while the light sleepers in the rest the room be waking up and stirring and tryna figure out where the noise had came from and if it meant the roof finally 'bout to cave in.

TT yelled a apology, said he moving his and Hannibal bed and it had fell. That shit actually worked.

Everybody laid back down, which took a real long time 'cause they waited for this big brother name Kamal to start snoring again, since they know he ain't sleep 'less they heard some shit that sound like a garbage truck. This time Eddie refused to go first, so Darlene climbed up on TT hands, more bold this time, 'cause Michelle and Eddie had grabbed the frame of the cot and was holding it 'gainst the wall. Darlene couldn't get her hands to reach this one spot just underneath the window 'less she climbed onto TT shoulders.

The window be one them frosted safety-glass windows with wire running through it in a diamond pattern, had a metal latch underneath with a ring that you had to pull to open it. Some the same type windows was up near the ceiling, but Delicious had cinder-blocked em or nailed a board over em. Maybe the board had fell off this one, or somebody done pried it off already. It done clouded over like a eye with a dirty cataract. Hadn't nobody cleaned up there in a long time, and when Darlene up there feeling around the sill, she stuck her fingers in a whole lotta gunk she figured was greasy dust and dead bugs and spiderwebs and chicken feathers and all kinda animal droppings that's sticking to the ledge and to the glass.

With all the nastiness, it seem less like a window to the outside than a caked-up oven door, like if they'da opened it and gone through they just be crawling into another cage to get they ass burnt to a crisp. If Darlene hadna spent the last half a year washing her face in a toilet bowl after the sink done broke, and going without showers for days on end till she could get to the front of the line before work started at least one morning, and if she hadna just had a few very long sweet drags on a pipe, she mighta turnt her head away from that window and spit up her dinner on the nape of TT neck.

Still and all, she ain't feel too hot probing around up there in the pitch-dark. She could only imagine the disgustingness she touching.

The ring to open the window ain't budge and Darlene got sick off thinking 'bout what might be on her hands, so they decided that TT need to give it a try. For that to happen, Darlene and Michelle leant the bed up against the wall and was holding it there while he climbed up 'cause he not that tall. By that time, seeing how long it had already took, everybody getting paranoid, so they put Eddie on lookout even though he keep saying he couldn't see nothing.

TT tugged real hard and almost fell off balance, and they found out the window be screwed shut, but they made a screwdriver out a piece of scrap metal and he got the window open. Darlene looking at the size of the window opening and the size of TT and she ain't seen how TT gon squeeze through without his fat butt getting stuck and then nobody else would get through. But soon's he put his head through the window and start tryna hoist hisself out, a bright white light gone on outside and he said he seen a dog down there barking. More like he *tryna* bark, though, 'cause this dog had laryngitis so bad that his barking sound like when you squeeze a broken toy, a whole lot of air with a li'l squeak on top. TT got down and Darlene got up and had herself a look.

She shook her head, thinking, *These people couldn't even get us a guard dog that works right.*

She climbed down from the bed frame and she and TT told Michelle and Eddie 'bout the dog. They could hardly hear that dog, so each of them gone up on the cot and took a peek. The dog kept wheezing, and the sound struck em so funny and sad that they thinking 'bout going on ahead and jumping down anyways. That dog so old! TT said. What he gonna do, gum us to death?

Michelle said, Fuck it. Life and death, y'all. She climb up on the cot by her damn self and shimmy up through the window to the outside, and right after her leg disappear through the window they heard her ass fall and start howling 'bout that she twist her ankle and here come the dog. Darlene get up to the window to look, and she seen Michelle tryna dodge the dog, 'cause he keep coming for her, same time as she climbing up over the fence, but that fence be 'bout nine feet high and got a double row of razor wire at the top, so she can't go nowheres. At one point, she get halfway up the fence, but the dog chomp down her ankle and she had to kick his ass away while she still tryna climb.

Darlene's like, Just come back through the window, Michelle! But she ain't listen. She so hardheaded that she still hanging on the fence just out the dog reach when the minibus come back, and I ain't never seen nobody laugh and bust on nobody so hard as them three when they found Michelle out there, hanging on the fence and kicking her leg out at that dog face. They demerited the shit outta her and sealed up the window with new cement blocks the next day.

In the end, the rest of em decided to wait. To get to know the dog. Darlene wondered how they coulda put a dog out there for such a long time without nobody knowing 'bout it—maybe the wheezing bark kept him secret—but a month later, when TT start making a new getaway plan, Michelle goes, The dog must have just got there. Probably that night, knowing our luck, and TT chimed in, They found the most quietest dog going. But vicious. I think they trained his ass to want human blood.

Maybe 'cause the whole thing had happened in almost total darkness, or maybe 'cause didn't nobody on the crew want to blow they cover, Darlene and TT and Eddie got away with not getting away that night. Michelle ain't give them up or nothing. Nobody knew Delicious policy on leaving without terminating your contract 'cause they ain't never said nothing after people tryna bust out. Seem they wouldn't never admit that any motherfucker with half a brain would want to get away from that place. When you heard them sonofabitches talking 'bout Delicious, it *was* the place they told you about when they picked you up, the three-star hotel that got a Olympic swimming pool and a tennis court with gourmet meals, crazy as that shit sound. How act like the grind at Delicious be like he in charge of catering at the motherfucking White House.

So if somebody disappeared and ain't never tried to come back, which to them nobody in they right mind would, meaning that Sirius B was out his mind, which was not hard to imagine, you never found out for sure if they made it. They showed you Kippy's boots. And if you tried to leave the premises and failed, them Delicious people ain't want nobody to know you even tried, so they ain't punished nobody but Michelle specifically for that, 'cause the whole crew done seen her fail. They came down extra-hard on Michelle behind that, but you couldn't tell if that meant nothing, 'cause they came down extra-hard all the damn time, so what the hell could extra extra-hard even mean?

Even if a worker done tried to bail in a obvious kind of way, like booking down the road during the town run, How and them ain't never accuse nobody of attempting to escape. Hannibal tried that and they just grabbed his ass and threw him in the van, and there was this blood smear on the back window for a long time from what they did to him after, plus a scar on his neck and a big bloodstain on his hat that he couldn't never totally wash out. But they ain't said nothing about no rules. They knew that wondering what rule you had broke gon make you worry more, make the whole joint a totally scary question mark. They wanted to keep your sorry ass running in place, weeding fields, picking fruit that ain't there, and, most of all, partying with me.

16.

SUMMERTON

On rainy days, work didn't always slow down, but it sometimes changed focus; the routine might include fewer outdoor activities related to harvesting, more indoor tasks, and maintenance. For the most part, the equipment at Delicious either did not work very well, or did not work at all. Most of the cultipackers had numerous missing teeth, and some of the crossbars holding them together had snapped from rust damage, come apart at the bolts and no one had ever repaired them, or the machines had received some nearly laughable stopgap patch. As for the other farm equipment, someone had wrapped the broken axle of a wheelbarrow back together with a large quantity of twine, while someone else had reattached the ends of several rakes with duct tape.

To till the land, the farm still used a large number of moldboard plows, possibly from the 1960s, whose coulters had chipped, hung loose from their beams, disappeared, or, in some cases, become so corroded that their height regulators had fused to their beams. It appeared that management had appointed Hammer chief of maintenance, but only his proprietary exclamations of sorrow and guilt over the atmosphere of disrepair gave that role away, since nobody ever saw him do anything to actually take care of the machines.

One day during the rainy spring six months after he'd arrived, Eddie happened to be on detail with Hammer and a few other workers in the garage with the mostly intact roof, as opposed to the makeshift coverings that had become permanent fixtures.

Oh Lord, Hammer griped, almost like somebody suffering in a church pew, do we have a lot to do here. Look at all this. He stepped around a leak dripping from the ceiling to survey the disorganized, musty space, and then, overwhelmed, made a gesture with his hand first toward the crew, then toward the chaos, implying that somehow the two should interact. Get to work, y'all, he told them. He scampered toward the garage doors, and after a few moments Eddie smelled cigarette smoke floating in from his general direction.

The crew milled around in confusion until Eddie suggested to Tuck and Hannibal that maybe they should start organizing the place by putting like things with like, exactly the phrase he'd heard a teacher use in grade school. In minutes, the three of them were delegating various responsibilities to the rest of the crew members; some of them piling hoes and shovels near one another, separating the useful ones from the broken ones, others taking inventory of bags of lime and concrete, a few more stacking paint cans, sweeping, and clearing out floor space. Eddie found a stash of lightbulbs and decided to replace the many broken lights on the three tractors stored in that particular garage (and later many others) and to patch up part of the paint job on one of them.

The spirit of cooperation and focus produced a nearly joyful frame of mind in the group, raising the collective mood despite the worsening weather. For the first time in weeks, Tuck broke out in song. His version of Robert Johnson's "I Believe I'll Dust My Broom" perfected the song's bittersweet quality, and some of the other guys joined in, responding either with grunts and encouragement or by trying to learn the melody and sing along as Tuck gained conviction and roared each new stanza a little bit louder and gruffer. Then he and everybody else, to the extent that they could follow, sang "Struggling Blues," "Disgusted Blues," and "Troubled 'Bout My Mother." At times Tuck sang directly to Eddie, the lyrics standing in for what he could never express directly. But then Hammer came back into the garage and waved his hands disapprovingly without saying anything coherent. He adopted a pained look that gave everybody the impression that they all had to stop singing not because of any imminent punishment but because they had screwed up by finding a way to make the work bearable. Nevertheless, the crew had discovered a secret portal to escape the tyranny of their superiors, and Tuck continued to lead them in singing the blues whenever possible; someone else would lead them less effectively when Tuck wasn't available.

One afternoon they'd journeyed out to pick carrots, a grueling, thankless task, especially since few of the vegetables had grown very large or looked particularly healthy once you shook the dirt off the plants. Eddie sometimes heard other workers complain that some of the produce ought to go to feed them, and some folks would sneak a bite of something whenever they could, despite the strict rules against it, and How's assertion that he had once fined somebody four hundred dollars for biting a sweet potato—and not even a clean one. It sounded like bravado, but Eddie wouldn't have put it past him.

———

By midafternoon, the temperature leveled off. A parade of cumulus clouds lunged across the sky, occasionally providing shade in the middle of the vast flat field. Eddie could just make out the nearest line of taller trees if he squinted into the hazy distance.

Hammer had parked the school bus in the field, its cab pointed in Eddie's direction as he trudged toward it, his tub halfway full. He approached and walked down one flank, hearing voices reverberating inside. Only when he turned the corner to hand his harvest to someone did he notice Sextus's well-maintained antique tractor parked behind the truck, and Sextus himself at the helm, spine erect as a porch support, gripping the wheel as one might a horse's reins.

Eddie failed to make himself invisible.

Hey, Sixteen, Sextus called out.

Eddie froze. He looked back and forth at Sextus and at Hammer, who stood by the truck counting tubs and dumping their contents into the payload, for confirmation that he could respond without repercussions; it seemed to be the case since Hammer didn't register any concern. But by that time, he'd taken too long to reply.

Why's your bin half empty, Sixteen?

All these carrots are heavy, sir, he explained halfheartedly, at a low volume.

Sextus asked him to repeat it twice. It came as a surprise to Eddie, but not a relief to his wounded pride, that the boss responded with hearty laughter rather than punishment. Later he wondered whether Sextus had heard him the first time and asked him to say the phrase again just for his own entertainment.

I work fast, he said.

This set Sextus laughing harder.

Even Hammer could not deny Eddie's ability, though. He do, he said, as if trying to jam a plug into Sextus's laughter.

I hear you also fixed all thesyer taillights and such. You's a good fix-it man?

I reckon.

I got some stuff up the house could use some fixin.

Maybe I can fix it.

What's the biggest thing you ever fixed, son?

A TV.

The sound of Sextus's laughter slapped back out over the field. A TV! Well, butter my butt and call me a biscuit! That so?

Yes, sir.

How's about I come get you tomorrow and you have a look at some of what's broke up there. I got one of thesyer new computers and I'll be dang if me or Elmunda or anybody up the house can get it to print. You think you can handle that, Sixteen?

Nothing beats a try but a failure, Eddie said.

What Sextus called tomorrow turned into ten days, but eventually the boss came looking for him in the chicken house—in his own vehicle, not the usual tractor. In the interim, Eddie had discussed with his mother the possibility of his going to the main house, and to his distress, she'd insisted on going with him, refusing to let him go alone.

It's dangerous, she said. You don't know these people. What they can do.

He felt both stymied by and grateful for this rare maternal outburst. In advance of the visit, he noticed that she began making concerted efforts to appear more presentable, especially since they didn't know when their visits would happen; she started borrowing a comb from Michelle and bartering with Jackie for dabs of hair relaxer and conditioner here and there, despite the rise in her debt. She did her nails, moisturized her legs, and at the depot bought a somewhat tight secondhand shirt that she kept special for the visit and did not wear in the fields; in collegiate lettering across the front it said OHIO STATE.

When Jackie ushered Eddie and Darlene out of the barracks to Sextus's idling Ford pickup, the first thing Eddie did was confess that his mother had insisted on coming with him.

As they approached the driver's side, Sextus exclaimed, You some kinda mama's boy, eh?

Sextus's mocking tone made Eddie halt in the rocky dust.

No, he replied.

Darlene smiled at the boss without opening her mouth. She slapped Eddie on the shoulder. Yes, she said.

I thought you was too old for that.

Yes, sir, but—

Sextus laughed again in that way that made Eddie feel as if everybody else was in on the same joke. Or the same lie. The big boss's eyes traveled down to Darlene's boots and back up; he kicked the passenger-side door open with his right foot and said, Ohio State! very loudly, with exaggerated articulation.

Eddie had never seen anything as spectacular as Summerton. The place had a grandeur that went deep beneath the surface—not a showy type of class, but an elegance so lived-in that it didn't need to prove anything; the tarnished beauty of an important historic monument, say, like an early president's home where they hadn't replaced the silver since the great man was alive, but they polished it every afternoon.

It looks like the house on the nickel, Eddie said as the pickup trundled down the dirt toward the mansion.

Who gave you a nickel? Sextus asked. He seemed immediately to intuit Eddie's fascination with the place, and after he jumped out of the truck and checked with the gardener to make sure that they wouldn't cross paths with Elmunda, his unhealthy wife, they walked around the building and entered through the kitchen.

Sextus gripped the spot between Eddie's neck and shoulder a little too hard and leaned down to his right ear, promising at least a partial tour. The one rule is, don't touch a goddamn thing lessen I say, he whispered. Then he raised his voice. That goes for your mama too!

Inside, the temperature dropped and the air became faintly damp, which helped give the place its historical mood. The sheer number and disorganization of the heirlooms filling the various spaces hinted at how the Fusiliers' wealth and influence spiraled far back beyond the memory of anybody alive. In the parlor, dozens of brown photographs of groups of white men with mustaches holding shotguns shared chunky mahogany tables with portraits and cameos of immaculately dressed white Southern ladies, and mixed in with those were groups of more modern photos—a cube of Kodachromes showing white kids at a swimming hole; metal frames surrounding snapshots of Elmunda and an extravagant wedding photo taken during some outsize ball, with Sextus and Elmunda gently directing forkfuls of yellow cake into each other's mouths. All of these artifacts sprawled haphazardly over faded tapestries and complicated wings of lace.

The library housed an uncountable number of identical dusty leather-bound volumes that looked as if no one had touched them since they arrived at the house, in 1837 or whenever, and a disintegrating old-fashioned globe on which somebody appeared to Eddie to have drawn by hand the right half of America, given up after Louisiana, and started scribbling. The bathtubs had claws on their feet; Eddie imagined them breaking into a lumbering, confused run if anybody had the audacity to scald them with hot water. Darlene hesitated in the bathroom and ran both her hands slowly across the porcelain with a look of ecstasy on her face.

Some of the fixtures didn't seem quite as old as the others, and one room remained empty except for several large pieces of canvas spread out on the floor, a few cans, and some trays crusted with dry paint. The room had an unfinished coat of pink paint all over the walls. Sextus explained that they were in the process of *very* gradually renovating Summerton, and that they were expecting a child (both of which were reasons why Elmunda would have had a conniption if she'd heard about the tour). She ain't well, he explained. She had a progressive intestinal disease, but she read somewhere that she could still have a child, and had insisted on doing so before she lost the ability. It's gonna be a boy, Sextus said, and when Eddie asked how they knew, he explained that the doctor had told them, they had this new way of finding out.

It's called *sonofa*-something, he said. They grease up your wife, point a magic wand at her belly, and then tell you where your boy's going to college. But I already started painting the room pink because before the medical thing, Elmunda made me dangle her wedding ring over her belly and it went in a circular motion and that means a girl. She also said she had a hankering for sweets. Goes to show you! But I ain't finna repaint nothing I done painted already. Hell, I don't even care if pink walls make him a queer.

By that time they'd reached the den, the least historic-looking space Eddie had seen during the tour, though he hadn't toured the master bedroom or some of the other places where the Fusiliers did most of their everyday living. The den had perhaps as many books as the library, mostly piled against its fading seagreen walls, but they were all about farming and flowers and livestock and they sat on the floor, horizontally on bookshelves, mixed in with newspapers and magazines and crumpled sheets of typing paper, as well as on top of the dirty shoes that lined the windowsill along one wall.

In the far corner on an antique desk by a fireplace sat a beige

TV monitor with a floppy-disk drive, which was connected to a beige keyboard with a different floppy drive, which in turn was connected to a dot-matrix printer, a joystick, and a third drive, all of it beneath a layer of newspapers, cigarette butts, and a beer can. An oscillating fan blasted from the opposite corner of the room, but its breeze didn't dislodge any of the loose leaves; it only made the edges of the papers shiver. Sextus apologized for the mess, almost to himself. Somebody could ransack this joint, he marveled quietly from one side of his mouth, and I'd be none the wiser.

One thing Sextus had in common with Eddie's dad was that he didn't have much mechanical skill. Plants love me, he said, and I'm a crackerjack at changing a tire. I can rig up the honey wagon, sorta, but these doggone new electronic gadgets is finna break down whenever they see me coming. Must be some magnetic heebie-jeebies in my body, like these folks in England I heard about who bursted into flames? They just gone FOOM! and it was all over. Wasn't nothing left behind but a big spot of burnt grease in the middle of a chair. So y'all'll have to watch out, he warned Eddie and Darlene, raising his index finger, 'cause I could be one of them folks—there ain't no test or nothing. At any moment I could explode into a ball of hellfire. He was silent for a second. Ha. Y'all would prolly find that right entertaining, now wouldn't you?

In the den, Eddie's mother dashed over to the fan and raised her arms, following its beam of air with her torso. She and Eddie had cleaned themselves up to the best of their ability considering how few changes of clothes they had and how frequently they'd had to wear them in the sun and dirt and vegetation, but Darlene had begun to sweat the moment they got out of the truck and her forehead was now jeweled with perspiration. She did a shimmy dance in front of the fan like some kind of old-time performer,

singing loudly and groaning her pleasure as the fan cooled off her
underarms. Embarrassed, Eddie pushed his way around a table
and moved some stuff off a chair, with Sextus's blessing, so that
he could get a better look at what Sextus called the Patient. The
Patient was flickering, he said, and had stopped printing entirely.
Eddie set about moving all the papers and felt around the sides
and back of the monitor and the printer to find the on switch.

Fixing a television had sounded easy to Eddie, but the computer completely flummoxed him. He hadn't owned one before;
he hardly knew what they were supposed to do. To him the Tandy
1000 looked like the mutant child of a TV and a cash register,
with its drab tan skin and green screen, blank as a snake's eye.
The one thing he knew machines had in common was that you
had to open them in order to fix them, and he went about figuring
out the best way to dismantle it and get into its guts.

From the mess behind the chair, Sextus produced a metal
toolbox—streaked with paint and containing a crazy jumble of
spackle tubes and screwdrivers—and an almost pristine plastic
box of ratchet wrenches.

I got all this stuff out and then I remembered that I'm a idiot,
he said.

Eddie frowned at the blinking green box on the screen. I don't
know, he muttered.

C'mon, Sixteen! Give it your best shot.

Eddie flinched slightly at hearing the nickname, then began to
poke at the keyboard a little bit. Almost immediately the letters
and malfunctioning zaps of miniature lightning appearing on the
screen fascinated him. He typed some nonsense in order to test
out the printer; he didn't want to open up the computer or the
printer if the problem wasn't particularly severe and he didn't
have to. As he focused on striking the keys, the entire screen
skewed and compressed into a single green line for a second, then

returned to normal. Even though the problems were exactly as Sextus had said, the sudden flickering jarred him. He felt inept at this type of repair work and wondered if maybe he should give the job up and ask Sextus to find a professional computer repairman. But he found it difficult to admit failure to someone who seemed to have faith in him, especially an inordinate amount of faith. He continued playing with the machine and testing it out shyly, hoping the problem would miraculously fix itself while under his care and keep his reputation intact.

He tested each of the keys in alphabetical and numerical order, then tried them with the shift key and examined all of those characters for a hint at the problem. Once he had exhausted all of the possibilities on the outside, he resigned himself to the idea that he was going to have to open up the computer or the printer or both. The realization that he had a lot more work ahead of him than he might have if he had found some way to deal with the computer on the outside made him growl to himself and sigh. He sat down.

He took a deep breath and puffed his face up like Louis Armstrong, then blew the air despondently and forcefully through his pursed lips and leaned back in the black lacquered chair. He thought about turning to face Sextus and shrugging his shoulders, and his faith in himself sank as he imagined how creases of disappointment would pinch between the older man's eyebrows. He didn't know enough about the way Delicious worked to resent such a charming, funny man who told so many jokes on himself, and for a fatherless twelve-year-old, even the worst dad will do.

Then he noticed he was alone in the room.

He couldn't remember the exact moment when he'd become so absorbed in figuring out the computer problem that Sextus and Darlene could have slipped out of the room unnoticed. Had they disappeared at the same time? He turned away from the desk and listened for signs but could hear only the fan humming, the papers rustling, and, through the open window, the breeze shimmying in the trees. Birds and crickets chirped. Every so often a chorus of cicadas chittered loudly and then quieted down. A rooster crowed and in the distance a car sped across the countryside. He wished he knew the exact location of the car and of the road. Maybe they had left together? The car sounded too far away.

Eddie stood up, flexed his knees, and walked to the doorjamb. Almost afraid to put his feet outside the room, remembering Sextus's warning, he leaned against the molding and stuck his head into the hallway. Since he'd arrived at Delicious and found Darlene, he'd developed a fear of losing her, even losing sight of her, and his mind immediately shifted to a fear that the worst had happened—Papa Legba had lured them out of the room behind Eddie's back and taken them to the other side. He used his shirt to dab sweat off his neck.

Ma? he asked, as loud as he dared, a noise that could've come from a goat.

The dark, cool hallway, clogged with artifacts, offered no response, nor any clues about where they had gone. Eddie looked both ways, then into the room directly opposite, where, through one of the windowpanes, he spied a section of the front lawn. He rushed back into the den and peered out the opposite window in the hope that he would spot at least one of them outside. He went to the window as if it were a brilliant idea, wrested it open, and leaned out as far as he could.

Mama! he shouted, this time more demanding, less goatlike.

He listened for her response, expecting anything, even a muffled scream from behind a secret door. It was no use. They were dead. Eddie returned to the hallway and ran shouting up and down its creaky floorboards, suspecting that if people heard him misbehaving, he'd get their attention. He called for his mother, drawing out the word *Mama* into long strings that shook inside his throat as he dashed around the hallway. When he lost his breath, he collapsed against the banister on the staircase and flopped onto the second stair. He wondered how long he might have to wait for them to return, or if they had gone away specifically to avoid him.

Exhausted and scared, he put one ear against the stair. In the ear that pointed upward, to the next floor, he heard his mother's laugh.

This being his first time at Summerton, he didn't gather the nerve to ascend the stairs and listen more closely, but on many subsequent occasions, Eddie would remove his shoes and, taking advantage of the carpeted steps, slowly make his way upstairs to follow the sound of his mother's voice—it angered him a little that she seemed to use a higher, fake-sounding register around Sextus—down the hallway to a closed door. He knew better than to speak to his mother about this aspect of their visits to Summerton, but he drew conclusions on his own from hearing their labored breathing and Sextus's feral grunts through the door, their low voices and whispers, their frequent invocations of the Lord. At first he tried to convince himself that they were merely praying together. But soon he had to admit that their prayers sounded very sexual.

Over time, Sextus's technical problems became simpler and simpler—he never seemed to plug anything in—and Eddie would grow restless while waiting for Sextus and Darlene. He would sometimes tiptoe up to the door and listen for a while, trying to discern the meaning and emotion of their murmuring. Eddie would decide that he had to know the truth for sure even if it embarrassed all of them and he got in trouble. He'd plant himself directly in front of the doorknob, dramatically raise his hand high above his head, and resolve once and for all to yank the door open and satisfy all his doubts. There he'd remain, rigid as a slash pine, and hold the position until he became so frightened that one of them would open the door from the other side that he'd have to slide back down the hall and downstairs noiselessly in his socks.

17.

YOUR PUNISHMENT

As much as he hated the toil and confinement of the next several years, Eddie accepted most of what happened at Delicious as a condition of being with his mother. He complained about the moldy mattresses, the wet sandwiches, about having to avoid certain people on account of lice, but he almost never saw past those details to what might have been wrong with the place on a larger scale. The first time he suggested that they leave the farm and go back to Ovis, his mother doubled over as if he'd slugged her in the stomach, and on other occasions, if he mentioned Houston instead, she might fall to her knees on a rake, or cover her face with mud-crusted hands.

Nevertheless, it pleased Eddie to get paid for the farmwork he did, plus the computer repair or other fix-it jobs. Sextus would even sometimes send him off with part of a day-old loaf of Elmunda's homemade bread, which he devoured quickly with Darlene before they got back to the chicken house so that nobody would know and they wouldn't have to share. When he turned fourteen, he signed the contract, and even though he handed over most of his very minuscule wages to his mother—he was among the few who did not rack up massive amounts of debt, very deliberately—he took pride in his accomplishments and considered his endurance its own type of salary. He reckoned that if you went around comparing your suffering to the suffering of Jesus, you could get through the worst of the worst like nothing happened.

For some reason, How usually sent Eddie and Tuck out on the same detail each day. The work changed every few days, but having a consistent work partner made the intense labor go more quickly, even when they had to pull weeds out from between seemingly infinite rows of sweet potatoes under a patchwork of steel-gray clouds during tornado warnings, getting soaked by thundershowers and sloshing through mud past their ankles, or, later in the year, harvest the same crop by hand, tugging the stalks and poking into the dirt for the fat tubers in 95-degree weather, with no water breaks until noon and the end of the day. Every afternoon, Tuck would fill the entire countryside with his baritone, and sometimes, once he got the gist, Eddie and some of the others joined in a chorus of "Kentucky Woman," "No-Good Lowdown Blues," or "Lonesome Train." Sometimes if Tuck was in good spirits—or exceptionally bad spirits—Eddie could convince him to sing "Only Got Myself to Blame," and on extra-special days he might get him to demonstrate to a new recruit how to sing Mad Dog Walker's follow-up, a carbon copy that never charted, "Nobody's Fault but Mine."

Eddie got sunburned all over his arms and the back of his neck from being out there all day. When he complained to How that they ought to give workers sunblock, How cackled and said, Sunburn? You niggers all so black you wouldn't get sunburn if a solar flare went up your asses. Buy some sunblock down at the store.

Six ounces of generic sunblock cost $12.99. Eddie tried to save up for it, but Darlene needed his money too often, and he gave her priority over a sunburn that really didn't hurt that much—it stung only when you touched it, or if it touched anything else. He vowed to wear a shirt no matter how hot it got, once wearing shirts stopped irritating his skin.

Every so often, something unnameable surged in him. One June evening it had gotten to eight o'clock and they were out harvesting Charleston Crosses, a type of watermelon so big that How said he'd seen mothers in Mexico dry them out to use as cribs. Eddie was hungry, he said, and How had promised that work would stop at eight p.m., but Eddie knew that it had gone later than that and they hadn't stopped and nobody else had complained. Nobody but How could own a watch out there, officially. Still, a couple of people hid clocks on their persons, and they had the sun to guess with until that went down.

When it got to about 8:45, Eddie's body stopped working and he took a natural sort of rest, sitting back on his hams and panting, wiping the sweat and dirt from his forehead and shoulders with his rough palms. Sometimes, like that night, How rigged up a few spotlights on the school bus and shone them across the field so that work could continue indefinitely. When How saw that Eddie had taken a pause, he shouted for him to get off his ass. Although his voice blared through the megaphone, because of the position of the bright white lights, the glare hid everything. Eddie squinted but couldn't see into the bus. When Tuck and TT begged How to go easy on him, pointing out that they had already been working most of the day and that Eddie was just a kid, How told them to go fuck themselves. He reminded the crew that they hadn't met the day's quota by a long shot because they were lazy fucks, like faggots or women.

We'll stay out here until four in the morning if we have to, he bellowed.

Tiny splats of water dotted Eddie's nose and shoulders. He always welcomed a thundershower after a hot day. It cooled the earth and all the workers, and made an excuse for work to slow down. Its arrival reminded everybody that when it came to their workplace, only God would show mercy. And even the merciful rain cascaded down their foreheads and over their eyebrows and blinded them. It created mud that got into their shoes and squished grittily between their toes and made it that much harder to get any work done, especially at night. The watermelons grew slippery, and if they didn't have work gloves, which most didn't, they'd drop the melons and bruise them, or break them open accidentally. The broken and bruised ones exposed their tantalizing sweet insides and Eddie and the others would salivate, but they knew these broken pieces would be set aside as slop for the livestock. Delicious didn't want to give workers the incentive to damage fruit.

For another two and a half hours, the rain shot down like the blast from a fire hose, and the crew struggled to judge the ripeness of the crop in the artificial light and to heave the fat orbs into the open side of the school bus. The atmosphere resembled something out of a disaster movie, with everyone scrambling past one another, careful not to collide, desperate to arrive at a quota that had never been specified in the hope that at some point they would reach a magic number that would conclude the ordeal. Eddie had seen and experienced this phenomenon nearly every day; he'd deliberately push time out of his mind so that he could soothe the agony of longing for the end of the shift.

You people should be better workers, How told the crew once work finally ended, not long before midnight. You're already out of it. All y'all really need to do is move your arms and legs. It ain't that hard. He lifted his hands perpendicular to his body and let his wrists dangle, then he bugged his eyes out and took a few clumsy steps forward. It's like *Night of the Living Dead* out there, he said. With watermelons.

By the time Eddie returned to the chicken house, he felt as if the rain had swelled a river inside his head. The thought of what had happened that day sent him into a rage that gushed over the ramparts. He glared at the brownish mattress he shared with his mother, who had gotten in earlier from her detail and had sprawled out as if to hug the bed in his absence. He complained to her that they had to leave right then, but she didn't respond.

As he waited in line for the shower, slapping away mosquitoes and looking in all directions at once for palmetto bugs, he decided to kill as many of everything as he could. The first giant bug he saw he lunged out of the line for and leapt on with both feet, an action that produced an unappetizing sound that caused some people to cringe. He kept watch as other bugs appeared at irregular intervals, eventually abandoning his place in line to go on the hunt. In the trash he found a piece of cardboard, rolled it into a stiff wand, and rushed around the entire space, bludgeoning wings and legs and innards on the walls and empty beds and concrete floors.

You just the little exterminator tonight, Tuck commented drily. Kill em all, don't miss none. There's one. Go get em. That's a real public service you're doing. By the time you done we'll think we're living at the Waldorf.

Despite his teasing, Tuck found his own cardboard weapon and helped Eddie out in a lighthearted kind of way. Eddie, by contrast, had a serious vendetta going. When he smashed an insect, he didn't stop hitting its dead body until it resembled a smear with dismantled legs and antennae.

Die, stupid bug! Die! he shouted. Then he'd examine each

dead carcass and stomp on it if it didn't seem quite dead before sprinting across the room to pulverize the next one.

Over time, the aggravation of that day grew worse, became perpetual, and spread. The bosses gave him increasingly demanding and more physical work on top of the mechanical issues and trumped-up computer problems Sextus called on him for, and he found himself at work nearly all day and all week. Anything became grounds for him to lose his head. He stomped on the moldy cheese-and-pickle sandwiches and chucked the rotten fruit at the walls; he ripped open a mattress with his bare hands; he threw a chicken across a yard; he broke his toe on a concrete wall and had to make a splint for himself with Scotch tape and a maple twig and hobbled around complaining until the toe healed. He arm-wrestled so intensely that he broke the arm of a young woman who then walked around for months with two almost straight tree branches duct-taped around the injured limb. Eddie ripped an already broken toilet out of the wall. He threw a coworker off a moving harvester during an argument. The fighting got him in trouble a lot, but he could talk his way out of almost any punishment because he had Sextus's ear.

Aside from his age, the other thing that set Eddie apart from everybody else was that he hadn't become addicted. His mother saw one of the workers hand him a loaded pipe and a lighter one evening and she snatched them out of his hands and threw the lighter across the room and started shouting at him, Can't you see what this goddamn shit does? and Didn't I raise you better than that?

To which Eddie thought, *No.*

Then his mother ambled across the room to find the drugs, picked up the lighter, and took a hit herself, and he watched her hunch over with her back to him, flicking and sucking on the pipe and trying to hide her activity from everybody who had just witnessed her go off on him.

When he moved closer, watching her like a scout stares at a campfire, she grumbled, Do as I say, not as I do.

Eddie left her side and went to sit on sagging milk crates among the rest of the crew. Darlene's behavior proved her point, he saw. She was like a drowned person hollering up out of the river at a potential suicide not to jump. The next time somebody offered him a glass pipe, he accepted it only to throw it on the ground and stomp on it like one of the bugs, though that started a brutal fight that left him with gaping wounds on his forearms that for days attracted horseflies to the edges of his toilet-paper-and-duct-tape bandages.

Usually, How was the one to punish Eddie for an infraction such as this brawl—whack him in the ass with the business end of a rake, across the back with a leather strap, or on the temple with the butt of his gun. But for some reason Jackie assumed the responsibility to decide how to make him pay for this offense. That same day, someone had ratted on Tuck for stealing a package of Jujubes from the store, and Hammer found the brightly colored candies in Tuck's pants pocket before the bus left the depot to return to the chicken house. Since he hadn't opened the package, Hammer returned it to the store (a five-dollar value!) and warned Tuck that the penalty would come later, giving him no idea when, or what form it would take.

The next day, Jackie brought Tuck and the bandaged Eddie together into a field of young corn, with Hammer there as enforcer. Jackie carried a cylinder of Morton salt in the crook of one arm, held against her breast like a stillborn child; Hammer carried a rusty shovel. They had tied Tuck's wrists together, and Hammer nudged him forward into a clearing with the point of the shovel.

In her usual dry manner, Jackie said to Eddie, Your punishment is to punish him. She leveled a merciless, distant glance at each of them in turn.

Hammer moved the shovel into Eddie's space, expecting him to take it, but instead the younger man stared down at it as if it might bite him if he touched it. A small aircraft buzzed overhead; Tuck and Eddie looked up, eager for a sign from the outside world.

You got ears? Hammer asked.

Yeah, I got ears, Eddie snapped.

Watch it, Hammer said, shaking the shovel up and down in front of him. Well?

Eddie and Tuck locked eyes, and Eddie remembered how easy it had been to tie him up the day they met, but now what they expected of him would amount to an unforgivable betrayal. Tuck had ended up here because of him, and had helped him to find his mother. Eddie ought to have been helping Tuck get out of Delicious. Now they'd given him no choice but to wound his benefactor, and it wouldn't have surprised him to hear that they wanted him to kill Tuck. Eddie had no intention of doing anything.

When he didn't move to take the shovel, Hammer grabbed him by the arm and yanked up one of the bandages, tearing away hair and skin. Eddie twisted his body, but Hammer held him tight. Jackie poised the cylinder of salt upright with its spout open above the freshly scabbing cuts that snaked down Eddie's forearm. Tuck attempted to edge away, but Hammer alternated carefully between holding Eddie and watching to make sure that Tuck didn't try to escape. Before Eddie could wrench free of Hammer, Jackie shook a few grains into the red valleys of exposed flesh and Eddie felt a biting pain and stumbled forward. Hammer chucked the shovel into his unstable path; it connected with his ankle and he fell on his shoulder into the loose, dry dirt, soiling his wounds and sprinkling clods of earth over the bandage.

Let's get this show on the road, Hammer demanded. He grabbed hold of the rope between Tuck's wrists.

Eddie slowly rose to his knees, brushing and blowing dirt off his arms and clothes and out of his bandage. He brought up a knee and took the shovel in hand, then stood, shakily, and gripped it with both hands, adopting the stance of a baseball player about to bunt, letting the blade swing back and forth between his shins.

Jackie and Hammer leveled the same impatient expression at him, their eyelids halfway down, their jaws tightly set.

Eddie struck Tuck lightly on the thigh at first, and muttered an apology he hoped Jackie and Hammer would not overhear.

Jackie only said, Harder, and Hammer pushed Tuck forward toward Eddie.

Tuck stumbled, but stood his ground. Eddie's blows grew sharper and more impersonal. Tuck took up Eddie's message where he'd left off, and every time the scoop of the shovel made contact with his shoulder blades or the backs of his thighs or, eventually, his head and neck, and he fell to his knees and then to the ground, he forgave Eddie out loud. It's okay, he said, it's okay. But soon Tuck ran out of forgiveness and begged for mercy, until at last he could no longer speak and his legs gave out. His face kissed earth wet with his own blood and he wriggled as if he could crawl underneath it to safety, while Eddie unleashed an aimless rage directed as much toward himself and his circumstances as toward Tuck's helpless body.

Eddie saw him a few days later, back out in the field—maybe they were harvesting rhubarb—holding himself up with a rake and a broken shovel handle (perhaps the one that had dealt the blows, Eddie thought with a shudder) tied to his leg to keep it set, and one arm in a sling. He imagined bruises in the shape of every state covering Tuck's body.

Eddie approached him with his eyes nearly closed, wringing the hem of his T-shirt between his fingers. You okay? he said.

No, Tuck blurted out. No no no no fucking no. Do I *look* okay, nigger?

I'm still sorry.

You nearly killed me. I almost wish you had.

What? Why?

I know what they did that for, and I don't want to see it.

18.

HOW

When Eddie became the official handyman, Michelle recruited him as a double agent. She wanted him to take advantage of the trust their superiors had in him, so she convinced him to use part of his time to comb through the Fusiliers' computer files and Sextus's office, trying to find information about the place that might help people who wanted to terminate their contracts and leave the premises. The first order of business, Michelle said, was to figure out the layout of the farm. Eddie spent part of his time rifling through whatever he could, but not so much as a faded receipt stuck in an old book gave anything away; even stationery didn't help. He didn't find anything that said Delicious Foods. He did discover a cache of letterhead for a company called Fantasy Groves LLC, though, which listed post office boxes in a variety of midsize cities—Shreveport, Birmingham, Tampa—no place even halfway as country as the farm. Someone on what they referred to as the no-lime detail, which lay just south of the no-lemon one, claimed that he'd seen Louisiana signs on a nearby road that outside people seemed to travel on; like a lot of things among the crew, it became an endless subject of debate. Eddie saw yellowing piles of a local Louisiana paper in the house, the *Picayune*. He related this news to Michelle, but the workers got into an argument about whether the presence of the paper proved the region. White folks in California be reading the *New York Times*, somebody insisted. I seened em doing it.

Eddie found little use in trying to convince the crew of something so basic, so he concentrated on finding details about the business, records of moneys paid or documents related to payroll. Most of what he found pertained to large payments made by big corporations that purchased food grown on the various farms operated by Fantasy Groves LLC. Just reading the names of all the food companies and supermarkets who bought from the farms on hundreds of invoices made his mouth water. Never did he uncover any records that had anything to do with the workers—no payroll stubs, no legal documents, not even a list of names. That made Michelle suspect that Delicious was a subcontractor to Fantasy Groves, a name she had never heard. Delicious was an anonymous shell company. With little hope of a paper trail, Michelle gave Eddie a directive to find out as much as he could from Sextus.

Why don't you ask my mom? he wondered aloud.

Your mom don't always get the facts right. And frankly, I ain't sure about her loyalties.

On one occasion when Sextus and Darlene returned from all the sex prayers they said upstairs during Eddie's visits, he picked up a few of the papers he had come across on the computer desk and tried feebly to draw Sextus into a conversation about business. Just get him talking, Michelle had said. Eddie had not quite finished replacing the toner cartridge and getting the printer back online. Eddie twirled in the room's knockoff of an ergonomic office chair as Sextus and his mother waited for him—too quietly, it seemed. Sextus lit a cigar and sat down in an antique chair near the window by the fan.

Eddie tried to keep his tone casual. Is the farm getting bigger? he asked. He'd seen a letter that suggested the Fusiliers had bought a large parcel of land.

Oh, them papers is old. And you shouldn't be reading em nohow. You wanna know something, son, you just ask.

The mild, nonchalant response emboldened Eddie. Okay. He waited for a while and then asked, Where do you keep all the records of the people at the farm and what you paid them and what they owe? How much does my mother owe? What about me?

Darlene had chosen a folding chair near to Eddie. She touched him on the shoulder and said his name sternly.

Sextus, watching something outside, maybe right downstairs, gradually smiled and said, You don't ask about that. He smiled his unhappy smile. Cigar smoking had become something of a post-visit ritual for Sextus, but Eddie could tell that watching him smoke made his mother want to use; she leaned in and kept her eyes fixed in the cigar's direction. She always beat a path to the pipe as soon as they went back to the chicken house. Sextus tried to blow smoke out the window, but it got caught in the draft from the fan and sped toward the two of them instead. Eddie tried not to cough by making his cough sound like throat clearing.

A long interval passed as the day's soporific heat penetrated Eddie's limbs and skull, intent on turning him into a rag doll, almost as much as it did on days when he went out with some crew to dig or weed or harvest.

Why don't I ask about that? Eddie asked.

Though he didn't raise his voice, a sudden rage sounded in

Sextus's tone. You don't ask because you don't fucking ask! Darlene, tell your whelp to shut his piehole.

The shift in Sextus's mood startled and humiliated Eddie.

Eddie—Darlene said again, not daring to repeat the phrase. The silence returned; Sextus focused out the window again, this time on something distant—maybe a plane.

Just as suddenly as his anger had rushed in, Sextus relaxed his back into the chair and adopted the caring voice of a mentor. He turned to Eddie. You might as well know now, son. At some point I think you might could become part of the management at Delicious. I seen it from the first. You're young and smart, you *usually* don't ask no dumb questions, you're a whiz with the equipment and such, et cetera. You got a type of authority inside you that you need to keep folks like the ones working here in line. I seen how you deal with that one who always singing, the bluesman. You're good. What's more, you don't got no issue with the pipe, and that's more than I could say for Jackie.

She's getting worse every day, Darlene said absentmindedly. That's true.

How's a good worker, but he's batshit psycho crazy. I reckon he'll move along somewheres else. Frankly, I wish he would.

Sextus turned to face the two of them and stubbed his cigar into a nearby ashtray. Now it ain't gonna happen tomorrow. But you keep doing good, by and by something gonna come available for you in one them upper areas. Just don't do nothing stupid, see? He squinted as he spoke, and Eddie figured he was referring to his earlier questions.

I won't, sir, Eddie said. The thought of Delicious becoming the rest of his life made his stomach burn. But he smiled.

Immediately on his return to the chicken house, Eddie sat down on the bottom bunk of the bed where his mother slept and unlaced one of his tattered shoes. In a matter of minutes,

Michelle made her way over to him and sat on the opposite side of the bed, a little farther down, probably so that she could examine his face carefully and make sure he wasn't lying, he thought.

So. Did you find anything out?

No, not really, Eddie muttered. I asked a couple of your questions and he told me to shut my piehole. Eddie didn't think he should mention Sextus's offer of advancement, but he thought of it during the whole conversation. Michelle grilled him about which questions he'd asked, the exact words Sextus had used in reply, the inflection of his replies, and his general state of mind. Eddie didn't have much to tell. It did seem important that Sextus made decisions about who did what at Delicious, because the company didn't exist on paper. But he couldn't explain how he knew that.

She asked for maps again, and anything that might reveal the structure of the business. If he did have any new information, he wondered if he now had an incentive to keep it to himself. Maybe the way to get out of Delicious was to move up in the ranks under false pretenses, save himself and his mother, then come back for the others. He doubted that Michelle would see any benefit in that approach.

What kind of cigar did he smoke? she asked. Could you tell where it came from?

Eddie apologized for not having noticed and promised Michelle that he would try harder to remember all the small details next time.

The smallest details, she insisted, could be the most important to remember.

As he dealt with his awkward feelings about letting Michelle and the others down as a spy (he was sure they suspected him of keeping information from them, though he hadn't uncovered any), the Fusiliers increased his responsibilities. Gradually, How stopped sending Eddie out to weed and pick and add fertilizer and pesticides to the various crops, and had him spend more time indoors, tinkering with computers, appliances, and engines. Sextus told me I had to, How said.

Occasionally Sextus would call on Eddie to watch over or play with the wee boy, Jed, who had recently turned four, and that kept Eddie away from the squalor of the chicken house. The doctors had advised Elmunda against having him in her condition, to which she replied, The Lord won't let me have him in another condition. Then her health worsened. She had had a series of seizures during childbirth, then a stroke. She and Sextus began to enlist Eddie as a babysitter every so often, in addition to having him make things. He put a wooden box with hinges together to hold Jed's many toys.

The managers, Eddie noticed, started to treat him like a mascot, as if a cogent and intelligent boy his color interested them the way a singing dog might, or a horse that could solve simple equations. As a joke at first, Sextus let Eddie sit on the tractor, but when he saw how seriously Eddie took the wheel and pretended to shift the gears, he volunteered to teach the boy to drive it for real. It pleased Eddie to receive that kind of fatherly attention from anywhere, though at the same time it made him sad and angrily conscious of his own father's absence, but he accepted anyway, since the opportunity to learn a new skill rarely came along.

Occasionally Sextus allowed him to shower in one of the downstairs bathrooms—Darlene had been doing so upstairs for a while. The bathrooms at Summerton had hot water and fresh-smelling soap; after the first time he had to stop using the soap because when he returned everybody smelled it on him and asked biting, jealous questions, exaggerated his chance to do what he wanted with his future, and openly doubted his loyalty to the workers. They had been less forthright with Darlene, given the implications of her special treatment. The Fusiliers, for their part, seemed to draw the line at letting Eddie dine with them, perhaps because they knew he would have demanded that Darlene join them, and Elmunda would not have put up with that.

Gradually everybody figured out—or Darlene told them— that the Fusiliers had decided to groom Eddie to become a supervisor, and though he found it flattering that the bosses treated him specially and gave him work that fit his particular talents, the question of whether that meant they would someday agree to send him on his way and allow his mother to leave with him—the only reason he considered accepting such a heinous position—remained unresolved. When Sextus decided to clean out the old barn and turn it into a workshop for Eddie, furnished primarily with woodworking tools Sextus had bought for himself but never learned to use, the management's intentions became public knowledge—not to mention a source of embarrassment for Eddie. But the discomfort was mixed with an unspoken relief and gratitude for his special treatment. At night, though, locked in the chicken house under the watch of the hoarse dog, and later a younger, nastier dog, he feared that his fellow workers would retaliate against him by stabbing or smothering him, which was one reason he'd agreed to spy for Michelle.

It was harder to negotiate the same kind of treaty with How, Hammer, and Jackie, but particularly How. He never let his guard down. Once, on a tomato-picking detail, Eddie wound up nearer to the school bus than usual by some series of mishaps, which meant nearer to How. The foreman usually wore black heavy-metal-band T-shirts, usually a red pentagram with the word *Slayer* inside it. He'd cut the sleeves off, making it easier for someone to catch a glimpse of his fleshy flanks through the large armholes. Along with a shock of black hair, thickening arms, and a compli-

cated beard he'd recently grown, How had an especially demonic
look around that time, and an attitude to match. TT said that
How had deliberately stepped in one of TT's tomato buckets because of a grudge and blamed him for all the damaged produce,
Michelle said she'd kicked his thigh to avoid his advances, and
that other women had not been so lucky. Everybody saw How
take special trips down the line to shout at Hannibal when he
thought the man wasn't working fast enough. He's just an older
guy, people would say, leave him be.

Standing above Eddie at the back of the truck, How glared toward Eddie, and since the detail had only begun, he had time to
wait and comment, so Eddie braced himself for the usual racial
remarks and accusations of laziness. The one thing you could say
about How was that he hated all groups equally, even his own
Mexican people. Three minutes into picking, he barked at Eddie.

You fill that tub yet, Eddie?

Eddie knew better than to respond; he concentrated instead
on selecting tomatoes at the proper level of unripeness for trans-
port—only greens or breakers this time, turning or pink stayed on
the vine—and cleanly twisting them away from their vines without damaging them. No one could've filled the tub by that point.

No? You can't fill a tub in three minutes? He climbed out of
the school bus, chuffed down the row, and stood behind Eddie,
who was still trying to ignore the foreman. I'ma show you. Move
it. With his bulk he shoved Eddie aside and moved the green tub
to his feet. He raised his wrist to look at his watch. It's six forty-
three now. So by six forty-six I bet I'll be done, or—or I'll take
twenty dollars off your mother's debt. He cracked his knuckles,
lowered his center of gravity, then positioned the tub in such a
way that he could nudge it with his foot as he moved down the
line. Move it, he barked again, and Eddie stepped back.

Okay, go, How shouted to himself. I haven't done this shit in a long fucking time, he said, already having plucked and tubbed three tomatoes, but this shit was my childhood. Just like you! His fingers moved with surprising speed and grace, like someone who could've played the vibraphone exceptionally well, and he placed each one against the last inside the tub gently, like an egg. I grew up in southern Florida, he said, where my mother brought me and my sisters, and they didn't give a shit about child labor or nothing, so all three of us would race each other to fill the tubs, picking tomatoes—we were so stupid we considered that shit a game. I got real good at it. You know how some kids get good at video games? This shit was my video game.

Then when I turned twelve they deported our ass so I joined a gang in Juarez. The main guy took me under his wing when I was fourteen. But that shit was too hard, man. So I came back to the U.S. by myself this time, but I had to take care of the guy who brought me back so that I wouldn't be in all that debt. Then I was a coyote myself for a while, but this farm life, I like it better. Not so much moving around. Not as many people trying to kill you.

He continued his absentminded autobiography until he'd filled the bucket with green tomatoes and the two of them had edged a short distance down the row of plants. He looked at his watch. Shit, six forty-seven. I guess I don't have the stuff I used to. And your mama don't get the twenty bucks off! He stood up and handed the bucket to Eddie, waited a moment, then snatched it out of the kid's hands.

What are you fucking kidding me, like I'm going to credit you for this one? Dream on, motherfucker. Call that a training session.

That evening, How undercounted what Eddie showed him; he did it to everybody, but with Eddie he'd blatantly lie about the count.

I picked five more bins than that, Eddie said.

———

Are you calling me a liar?

No, I'm calling you no good at math.

Oh, fuck you, How spat. I'm not good at math? All of your earnings goes to your crackhead mother, so why don't you pick up what you think I owe you at the depot, okay? Your tomatoes had scratches all over them because your fingernails got too long from working up at the house every other day. And I still haven't figured out where the jack from the truck went. I think you probably know. Don't you break Sextus's computer every other day so that you can keep fixing it instead of coming down here? I mean, I don't blame you. If I could fix a computer, I wouldn't leave that place neither.

For Eddie, interacting with How had become as unpleasant as when his coworkers had enlisted him to kill a snake or chase a rat or, once, a polecat in the living quarters during the early-morning hours. A visit with How came to mean only bad news, grueling work, or a combination of the two unique to Eddie's days at Delicious.

19.

THE WRONG LIMES

Darlene been had known that the only time that management ain't seem to need to know exactly where you was and how to grab you back at a second notice was when they took you down the depot on Friday and Tuesday and let you wander round a li'l bit. Michelle said the reason they be letting people wander off that time was that the depot be dead center of the farm, and the chance you could get off the property alive by your lonesome got so small that they's overconfident. Hadn't nobody never seen no map so didn't nobody know, but she said she had figured it out from stuff that How and Hammer said. If you gone missing at the depot, likely you gonna wind up back where you started or die from one the five zillion dangers between you and freedom. Michelle tried to piece together a map in her head based on where they had took her on different details and on things people be saying 'bout where things was, but she couldn't never be sure. Michelle always asking Eddie to find a map on Sextus computer but he only got a map of America—Naked, he said, without no states or no names, just all green and brown from mountains and plains and rivers.

Darlene ain't never told nobody, Michelle included, that Sirius B had probably escaped from that area and that he coulda made it out somehow. She ain't never knew how much to trust nobody, and I suppose I convinced her that the others gonna inform on her if she said too much. I liked it there; I wanted to stay. For me the place like one them barbecues you can't leave 'cause you gotta spend three hours saying good-bye to every last motherfucker there. Ooh, cousin Tyrone just walked in! Darlene always talking all kinda shit 'bout how she wanna leave, especially to Eddie, who really *did* wanna get out, but she ain't never put no effective actions onto her words. That shit start to work Eddie nerves.

But every time Darlene gone to the depot, she would make a special visit to that li'l stream with the culvert Sirius had disappeared into, thinking 'bout what happened to him and how he coulda survived what mighta happened, but now she kinda sure he ain't survived. She gone down to the opening of the culvert sometime and be looking in there and talking to it. That circle of concrete be low enough that it wasn't no way to enter 'less you hunch your ass over, and it wasn't no kinda underpass drain. This one turnt into a tunnel that got dark damn quick and ain't let on where the hell it gone to. She knew Sirius done vanished into there, and she guessing that if he come back and rescue everybody, he gonna come back through that same tube. He had told her 'bout wormholes in space, where you could go through that shit and come out way the hell far away from where you started, and sometime, specially when me and her was hanging out, she be wondering if Sirius had did some crazy physics magic and teleported to New York City through that bitch.

The culvert turnt into a shrine where Darlene and I had some top-quality meetings and contemplated the meaning of life and all that, but life ain't mean much of nothing to Darlene outside of me. She want Sirius to come back mainly 'cause she need a ally, not 'cause she think he some kinda savior. Sometime Eddie would come with us, but he getting old and angry and he ain't want to spend as much time with the two of us. Teens, they get like that. I suppose me and her could close people out a li'l bit too, what with all our inside jokes and braindancing and what have you. I told her that she should stop keeping me and Eddie from getting to know each other, but she refused to budge on that point. I got mad behind that. On a certain level I found that shit offensive. I wanted to know why she got to judge her best friend so harsh that she ain't want her son to know me? If somebody like me, I'ma like em back twice as much. I get off on the attention. Darlene pitched a bitch when Eddie start smoking cigarettes at fifteen—at least she *started* to say some shit, but Eddie shut her ass down by looking at her like she a palmetto bug, 'cause she ain't had no right to tell nobody what not to smoke.

With the culvert, I told her that when motherfuckers spend they life looking in one direction for a specific thing, some other shit always come from another direction. So one day Darlene and em end up on detail at the citrus grove. It always seem like that citrus-grove detail what they put motherfuckers on when it wasn't nothing else to do with them, or they too crazy on drugs. They was down in the part with the limes that day. Hannibal, who had worked on big farms before Delicious, thought they maybe planted the wrong kinda lime. He said, See these thorns? Thesyer's key limes, and key limes don't bear no fruit too far outside Florida. So maybe we not in Florida? Plus it's April. I don't get these folks at all.

That morning, Darlene thinking that her stash of me be down to the last, so she borrowed some off TT, but then when she stuck her hands in her pockets she found a nice-size rock there and smoked that too. You could say that me and her started up a braindancing tango right then.

When she got up on her five-step ladder, she ain't found nothing in them lime trees, not a single hint of a lime, but everybody know that if you got supervisors expecting to see work happening, you best make it look like you working. Me and her decide to dance, so that them branches would shake, maybe shake out a lime, but mostly we wanna prove somebody up in that tree tryna get some produce going. And Darlene could see out over the green of them trees across the grove and down the far distant part of that particular road to where How had parked the minibus. He had stationed hisself in a different grove some distance away. Darlene kept shaking them branches, not finding no limes, getting stuck with thorns. In her head, we start getting down to that jam "In the Bush" from the disco days. *Damn* we was high—you know you high when you hanging out with Scotty and Scotty high as you is. She start singing, *Are you ready? Are you ready for this? Do you like it? Do you like it like this?*

Then Darlene thought she seen a white car she ain't recognize going down a dirt road she ain't known about. She thinking she could run down there without nobody seeing her and get there just in time to flag it down that car. Mostly she thinking that she bored and that she want contact with outside folks, not that she herself want to go nowhere with em. And after, she could tell Eddie that she done tried to bolt but that it ain't worked out and maybe that would shut his ass up. Or if the driver be a good person and not a serial killer or a Fusilier, she could put Eddie in the car and he could drive away with em and leave Delicious like he want to so bad now that he think he a grown man. She wave her hands, tryna flag down the sedan, and then she come down that ladder. Darlene ain't really wanna leave Delicious, she just wanna *be able to* leave, and that notion plus the idea that she could re-port to Eddie 'bout it had the power to get her running.

When Darlene got to the side of the road, she still seen that car coming. Wasn't no mirage. She tried not to make no noise 'cause she knew that How gon hear and come to get her, but quiet as she could, she raise her arms in the air back and forth and kinda bounce on her knees. For a second she thinking 'bout leap-ing out into the road to make sure the car ain't pass by, but then she seen it slowing down. She hopped over to it through some short dry grass by the side the road, thinking 'bout how she gonna explain to the white folks inside what she want from em.

The car pulled off onto the same grass where she standing and the window roll down on the driver side, and that remind her of turning a trick. She looked for the car type on the car and broke into a smile when she seen a bunch of li'l stars and the word *Subaru*. She remembered the star Sirius done talked about, the star that was a diamond. She's like, Maybe it really does exist.

When she get up to that car window, she seen a white dude with a couple days' beard and thick black glasses sitting in the driver seat, and a heavyset guy with a electronic box and a micro-phone in his lap in the passenger seat.

Dude one stick his hand out the window for Darlene to shake and goes, My name's Jarvis Arrow and we're with the *Chroni-cle*—like the *Chronicle* be something famous we musta heard of before, like if somebody said, I'm with *Sandwiches,* or I'm with *Money.* He go, Are you one of the farmworkers for Delicious Foods? We're wondering if you would speak to us on the record for a piece I'm doing. He pointed to the other guy. This is Frankie, he's recording sound. Frankie wave with his fingers. Jarvis got a handheld video camera in his lap; Darlene took a cautious li'l peek at it and Jarvis went, That's in case I decide to make a doc-umentary.

Darlene shook Jarvis's hand, then her eyes gone to the back-seat 'cause she thinking 'bout hopping in and just *going*. But out of all the damn cars on the road, this one would have to be a two-door and not a four-door so she couldn't make the decision herself real fast and force em into it. And then what Eddie gonna do?

The song lyrics we sung was still in her head and we was still braindancing, and kinda letting it spill out her mouth, she went, *I want to do the things you want to do, so baby, let's get to it, do it.* And she laughed.

It's okay, then? Jarvis asked. He frown, looking confused, and turnt off the car. Frankie got out with that sound equipment, and after checking behind him for traffic, he gone around the back of the car and put the gear on top the trunk. Darlene looked over her shoulder down them rows of non-limes and ain't seen nothing, but she knew that ain't mean wasn't nothing coming for her. She still thinking she might have to perform sexually if she wanna convince em to take folks outta there.

Jarvis slide out the car and ask her name and vitals, then Frankie hand him the mic and kept fiddling with the knobs. Darlene ain't had the best information on her vitals, so she just said some bullshit. She moved her hips into Jarvis personal space, but he sidestepped to a comfortable distance without making no comments on her.

He goes, So can you just give me a general picture of what the working conditions are like at Delicious Foods?

It's good, she said, forcing a smile. That's when we realized that these motherfuckers probably worked for the Fusiliers in real life, like they had set all this shit up, so she said, I mean it's great! I guess it's great. And if it's not, I brought that on myself, you know. Like the song goes, only got myself to blame. I signed the contract, so—She shrugged. My son and I work here...it's a family business...religious folks...so that's good. I need to pay my whole debt back, which they told me is up there, and plus the book said you have to think positive to get positive things. I admit I haven't always thought things of a positive nature, so that might take a while. She struggling to stay focused on what she saying.

So what are the living conditions like here? We've heard reports. A guy named Melvin Jenkins told us some things that shocked us. Do you know him?

No, I don't know anybody named Melvin...The two of them locked eyes; look like he expecting her to say some more. *So baby, let's get to it,* she said.

Jarvis turnt his head for a second and then goes, Are the working and living conditions fair here? Are you fed well? Are you paid well?

Darlene ain't wanna answer none of them questions on account of the shame it brung her, a certain kinda shame she wouldna even noticed 'less he asked her to tell the realities to the world. Quickest way out would be to seduce him and they could get into the car. I ain't really care that much, I mostly wanted to stay, but I knew Miss Darlene wasn't going nowhere without me no more. I thought maybe if she done a li'l dance and he heard her sing it might get past that straitlaced news-guy mask he be wearing, so she start singing the song. *How 'bout if we could go push push in the bush?*

Jarvis shared a frightened look with Frankie. He stepped out of Darlene's way. Ma'am, I'm trying to conduct an interview here. Are you okay?

Darlene tickled Jarvis's stubble with her fingers and kept dancing. *You know you want to go push push in the bush. Get down get down do it do it.* Me and Darlene let out a giant laugh.

At that moment feet start coming down them rows of citrus trees right toward em, on through the dry grass and leaves. Darlene grabbed the car door handle but it's locked and she stumbled backward. When she got done stumbling, her shoulders fell onto a stiff tough thing that coulda been a tree stump but turnt out as How shiny cowboy boots. His cold andouille-sausage fingers lifted her up by her armpits and pushed her behind his bigness. He stomped over to get up in Jarvis and Frankie face.

Hello, sir, Jarvis said, raising his microphone and putting out his handshake. I'm interviewing the workers at Delicious Foods.

No, you're not.

Uh, yes. I am. I'm with the *Chronicle*. The, um, *Houston Chronicle*.

What is that, a newspaper?

Jarvis goes, Yes, it is. It's got a circulation of—

I don't read. And I'm sorry, we're not currently talking to the press.

Currently? You mean, at this time? Well, when—

No, I mean ever. He took the mic out Jarvis hand and ripped apart the connection and threw that sucker into the road and it made a little cloud when it hit the dirt. Then somewhere outta him he unleashed the harsh bellowing of a demon. Now get the fuck off our *private property!* He reached behind his back and Jarvis and Frankie must have got the idea. Maybe they seen that he had a weapon on him and he 'bout to turn em into a human watering can.

Frankie rushed into the road tryna save that mic; he chucked it into the backseat with the tape recorder, and then got in the passenger side. Jarvis ducked as he leapt into the driver seat, and the two of them motherfuckers was a mile down the road, tires left a couple of divots right there by the grass.

With some kinda kung fu move, How switch his hand from Darlene waist to her wrist, curled her arm behind her back like a barbecue chicken wing, then frog-marched her into a part of the groves where wouldn't nobody see.

The fuck is wrong with you, he said. He kept smacking the base of her skull with his palm to move her forward. You want the world to know you're a crackhead hooker? You want your picture in the paper as a whore?

I am not a—Darlene said, before How shoved her into the trunk of a tree.

A branch done scratched her arm and face and drawn some dotted lines of blood and she knocked her head upside the tree. How pull her up again by the back of her elbows. When she get standing again, he reach behind him and pull his Magnum out his pants. He put his fingers like he gonna grab the barrel and smash the butt of the gun against the side of Darlene face but when he twisted his torso tryna get some momentum going, Darlene covered her mouth to keep in a laugh. The eye contact that happened made me and Darlene bust out into total hysteria, and I bet that's why How kept at it, shoving her and bashing her in the head and face, talking shit 'bout how he gonna give her something to laugh about.

Darlene kept tryna say she ain't told the guy nothing, that she told him how great she had it at Delicious, but that ain't done no good and she stopped talking. Obviously, the content of what she said ain't matter as much to How as the fact that Darlene had went down there and start talking with folks from outside. He screaming 'bout that she knew it's 'gainst the rules to be walking away from them limes in the first place and then you couldn't talk to no random people who drive up in a car 'cause what if they offer you work somewheres else, or what if they take you to one of them other farms where they treat you badly. He asked her how long she had worked at Delicious, as if they ain't both known how long.

Just like with TT, people start coming down out the trees to see the goings-on, 'cause they heard somebody screeching and getting beat up. Darlene heard it too, and for a second she wondered where all the screams coming from. She said to herself, Somebody oughta shut that screamer up, but then she figured out that the screams be coming out her own mouth.

While the punching and kicking happening from How, and the bruises that's forming on her back and breasts and legs, and her eyes swelling shut and her mouth bleeding, Darlene made sure to think positive. She thinking 'bout what a blessing it was that she already got a few missing teeth and hadn't got no new ones yet. *I feel blessed,* she told herself. Her luck made her giggle more, even though that put a bunch of dirt on her tongue and she had to cough and spit it out with her blood. *So blessed.*

The reason she had started giggling was 'cause she remembered that she do know a Melvin. Melvin Jenkins. That Sirius real name—and that meant the sonofabitch done made it out. That plus me kept the beating she getting from How from feeling as bad as he want it to; for all them injuries he putting on her right then, she now had it confirmed that Sirius done escaped out of Delicious and got back to the real world. He could send folks who could figure out how to save anybody who ain't belong, with a chance to do something different to they life, like Eddie. But why he ain't came yet?

I figure Jarvis caught Darlene voice on tape that day, and that even though he ain't get nothing in terms of a story, he gone home and played the tape for Sirius like that night. Not so he could hear Darlene, but so he could hear How. But Sirius woulda flipped the fuck out when he heard Darlene 'cause he had took for granted that after six motherfucking years Darlene and em woulda figured out how to quit Delicious.

But he ain't hear just that she still picking nothing in the citrus grove for no pay and high prices, it sound like her son had joined her there too and that he doing the same never-ending chain of working and spending everything and debt climbing. And Sirius knowed that if you got sick, like the dude they used to talk about who got bit by a alligator, you ain't gone to no hospital, you just had to figure out the fastest way to get back to work with a big chunk missing out your leg, or they brung you out somewheres and told everybody else you gone to the hospital, but didn't nobody know for sure. Could be they just dumped you somewheres and you dehydrated to death, or the alligator came back for the rest of you. Delicious woulda shot the alligator and sold it to a handbag company. They'da sold your leathery skin too, if the alligator done left enough on the bone.

20.

DOING NOTHING

ddie sat inside at Summerton, contemplating the strange workings of the place as he concentrated on repairing the operating system on Sextus's PC. Or perhaps just plugging it back in. After that he was supposed to fix the door to the microwave and install some shelves he had built and stained that would soon go into his own workspace.

He had just unscrewed the back of Sextus's PC and placed the screws into a bottle cap on the desk, then edged out the interior components about halfway, blowing dust off the circuitry with a can of compressed air, when word came that How had an important mission for him. Eddie hardly needed to wonder anymore why How couldn't ask somebody else; everyone knew that he stockpiled the worst jobs and set them aside in order to spring them randomly on Eddie whenever he got the chance.

Apparently How needed to see him in the barn he insisted on calling called *the* workshop, not *your* workshop. He stood outside the barn when Eddie arrived, arms folded across his smudgy tee as if Eddie had taken two hours rather than fifteen minutes to get there. Even though he didn't have a watch, he poked his wrist when Eddie walked up, signaling his annoyance that the kid hadn't arrived quickly enough for his taste. He had a lit cigarette wedged between his fingers.

Eddie said, Sorry, unconvincingly.

Sorry what? He sucked on the cigarette and disdainfully blew the smoke toward Eddie.

Sorry, *sir*.

Still not great, but better. He chuckled, pointing to the slightly open barn door. Go in there. I have a little discipline issue in there for you to take care of.

Eddie approached the door hesitantly. Punishment had never been one of his responsibilities, except for that time when How disciplined him by making him beat Tuck, and he did not relish a new experience of that type, nor did he want to give How the impression that he wanted it to occur on a regular basis. The door gave a high-pitched squeal as he pulled it forward.

It took a moment for his eyes to adjust to the light, but when they did, he saw a body resting on the hay-dusted floor not far from where he had arranged his shelves the previous night in neat rows on pieces of plastic tarp. The figure was alive and clearly in a reasonable amount of pain, weakly writhing and groaning, straining to push a gag out of its mouth. Eddie went back to the door and swung it wider to let more light in. When he peered out, How made eye contact with him; a stifled laugh trumpeted out of his face. Confused, Eddie went back inside and got a closer look at the person on the floor.

Under all the bruises and lacerations, and behind the swollen eyes, he recognized his mother.

Oh Lord—Ma, what happened?

His head swelled with blood and his lungs seized up as he approached her. He felt his legs giving way, so he took the opportunity to kneel beside her. He checked the space for a rag he could wet to clean off her wounds or soothe the purple abstractions developing all over her skin. Finding one nearby that was not completely filthy, he got on all fours and reached across her to grab it. Using its cleanest corner, he dabbed as much drying blood off her split, swollen lips as he could without reopening any wounds. Gently he removed the gag.

What did they do?

Oh, honey, don't worry about me, this isn't anything. Her lips and her usual missing teeth got in the way of her speech, but she still tried to sound casual. Look at you, all worried about me, she teased. That's a cute one. She groaned and twisted her torso.

I found out some good news, she said.

But what did they do?

Never mind what they did. The only part of me they can hurt is my body.

Mama, you're using, aren't you?

They must think I'm gonna kick the bucket or something, is that why How's letting me see you? She managed a huff in place of a laugh. Maybe I'm dead already.

He wants me to give you some kind of punishment.

Her nearly shut eyes widened to the best of their ability and she coughed. These Delicious people are out of their minds. All I wanted was a good job.

What did you say about good news?

Hush! He's behind you, she murmured.

Uncomfortable with the idea of keeping his back to the guy, Eddie turned and stood to face How. He remained silent and stared, trying to push How to the ground with his eyes but waiting for the official explanation.

Should've been picking limes but she ran down the road started talking to some guy from some newspaper. So I started her, but I'm going to get a bag of pork rinds, so I need you to keep it going for a while. Looking around the space randomly, How handed Eddie a wood plane and a spoon gouge. Go to it, he said. We need to make an example. He laughed—Did he expect Eddie to take him seriously? It felt like another attempt at a fucked-up joke.

All right, he said.

Eddie took a tool in each hand and turned them so that their handles faced out. He suspected that How, or even Sextus, had some kind of test in mind—of Eddie's ruthlessness, his loyalty to the company, his willingness to follow orders. He wondered how close they thought he was to the kind of monster who would perform this task without hesitation, then considered what a mother would have to do to deserve such treatment from her son, and then, more dangerously, that maybe his mother had done one or two things from that list, but that this had no bearing on whether or not he could or should go through with his orders. Generally he felt that she needed his help far more than he needed to balance their relationship. There had never been a question about whether he would do as they asked; not a single nerve in his body twitched in the direction of fulfilling his assignment. Besides, what bizarre tortures did How expect him to invent with a plane and a spoon gouge?

The guy didn't have a whole lot of compartments in his emotional TV dinner, it occurred to Eddie. Eddie had counted How's moods in the past, hoping to be surprised, but only ever saw How expressing either mild amusement at other people's bad luck, like he'd just shown, or seething, molten rage that might as well have come up through his feet directly from the actual Devil.

Eddie thought that How was about to go off again, so he turned away and knelt by his mother.

You know the rules, Ma, he said. Or don't you?

He set the plane aside, raised the gouge, and then brought it down in such a way that it missed her body and lodged in the dirt floor, where he worked it back and forth, exaggerating the movement of his shoulders and elbows. Darlene instantly understood his plan and volunteered a variety of pained shouts and groans to help make the injury seem real. Eddie's body blocked the tool's real trajectory from How's view, but apparently this theatrical presentation worked, satisfying the supervisor enough that he let out a grunt that seemed to express his cooler emotion and probably convinced him that he had broken Eddie's will and exposed the depth of the boy's ambition. Encouraging Eddie to continue, How left the barn.

Once How's footsteps faded, Eddie, still kneeling by his mother, tried to find ways to make her comfortable. He folded scraps of canvas and put them behind her head on the floor, made a splint for her broken arm by wrapping a long piece of twine around a wooden paint stirrer. He found a small jar of petroleum jelly to use as a salve in the many places she needed it, some of which she insisted on balming herself. While he took care of her wounds, she blurted out a disjointed story about Jarvis Arrow, trying to tell Eddie that Sirius had made it out and would come back to get them and make a run for it.

Darlene's injuries, her restless state of mind, and Scotty, of course, had impaired her ability to articulate what happened, so her son paid only partial attention. Scotty never left her side even when—no, especially when—so much trouble tumbled down on her at once. She sounded amazed, like somebody having a religious conversion, and that made her story even harder to clarify. She kept saying, He's coming, He's coming, and Sirius will get us out of here, but this sounded to Eddie like *Seriously get us out of here.* Eddie didn't remember Sirius, having only heard about him from Darlene and the rest of the crew. To Eddie, Sirius B sounded like a hazy legend that the heavy smokers conjured up to give themselves hope, a figure barely more real than Papa Ghede.

Even if Sirius had seemed real to him, Eddie remained skeptical of all the cosmic mumbo-jumbo everybody said that Sirius used to talk all the time—space clouds shaped like crabs and horse heads, a diamond bigger than the sun—it sounded to him like the kind of make-believe shit crackheads talked 90 percent of the time. When he heard Darlene's half-conscious claims, through fat bleeding burned lips, that Sirius was alive and coming to get them, it seemed like a combination of a mixed-up prayer and a Negro spiritual about Jesus where a chariot comes down from heaven to rescue folks. And he didn't consider her babbling nearly as urgent as her injuries. She rambled like a psychotic, and though Eddie had an excess of patience for her insanity, he'd heard plenty of her ravings in the past and had learned not to pay her any mind. He focused on keeping her calm so that her body could start to heal.

A few minutes after her breathing slowed, she laid her head back—a sign of relative stability—and he got up to test out whether he could leave. He pushed the two panels of the barn doors forward and discovered, without surprise, that How had padlocked them together and drawn a heavy chain through a hole in each side. He must have done it carefully and quietly, because Eddie didn't remember hearing any chains jangling or even doors swinging shut, but then again, he hadn't concentrated on anything except his mother for a while.

An hour or so went by. Once Darlene stopped trying to talk as much and seemed moderately comfortable, she fell into a shallow sleep. Eddie knew she wouldn't sleep long and that when she woke up she would need to cop pretty bad. He thought he could get drugs for her on his next trip to the depot, but he didn't know when that might happen.

Once her breathing became even and her biceps stopped twitching, he returned the plane and the gouge to their rightful place with the woodworking tools and examined the shelves he was planning to put in. He would continue building them so that he could at least finish some of the tasks assigned him that day. It was as if the rest of the day had been a kind of grimy window, and his labor the rag he wiped everything else away with so that he could see clearly. From time to time he peered over at Darlene to make sure nothing had gotten worse, but primarily he remained fixated on assembling the boards.

When he heard voices coming up the path, he figured that How had come back with somebody and would soon unchain the door. He stopped working on the shelves, put away his tools, and moved to the center of the room, positioning himself between his mother and the slowly opening barn doors.

The chains clanked and swung loose from their position, going slack in the holes that someone had bashed into the door in order to make the chain lock. One of the chains gained momentum and hurtled to the ground like a fleeing snake. When Eddie looked up from watching that happen, he met How's eyes, and he could see Sextus standing just behind and to the left of him, hands on his hips, a bit of wind flipping up a strand of the waxy silver hairs on his head. He scowled like a mechanic watching a car crash and wondering how much he might get for the scrap.

Something didn't seem right—How looked good. His brown irises glowed, color flooded into his tan dimples. Was this emotion number three? It looked like he'd sent a better-looking younger brother in his place, not the sweaty dude who led late-night watermelon details and forced workers to pick nonexistent citrus. The brushy sides of his haircut glistened like an otter's

pelt; his spiteful smile got so broad he looked like somebody dis-
covering that his mission in life was to help others.

The three stood there like the last pieces left in a chess game.
Scowling, How breathed through his mouth in a way that made
him sound like somebody who snored loudly, his windpipe flapping deep inside him. His switch flipped to his second emotion.

You didn't do nothing, did you? I asked you to do things and
you didn't do nothing. She's still lying there in that same position
that you left her in. Didn't I say what to do?

You did. Eddie didn't think he would get anywhere by pointing
out to How that Darlene was his mother and that people didn't
torture their mothers. In the world of Delicious Foods, though,
obedience came first; everyone had to submit to a preposterous
system of laws that had nothing to do with justice, logic, or even
maximizing company profits—it seemed as if the managers made
up rules just so they could enforce them and their employees
would have to follow them, a pure sadism free of any incentive
aside from its own continuation.

Eddie's defense fell out of his mouth anyway. That's my
mother.

Oh, really? I didn't know that! How said, back to emotion
number one. Wait, let me ask myself: Do I give a fuck about that?
No, I believe that I don't give a fuck about that. He turned his
neck to address Sextus. Can you believe this? Without waiting
for an answer, he turned back around. Sextus regarded How with
mild discomfort, his face twisted slightly, like he had a stom-
achache. I don't care if it's the president of the United States, you
do what I say. What do you have to say for yourself?

Eddie didn't have *nothing* to say, but he didn't say anything
because he didn't want to give How the pleasure of letting loose
another hurricane of abuse.

How's eyes darted around the space again, and he moseyed

past Eddie, giving Darlene a cursory examination to prove his point. He sucked his teeth and picked up a length of sheathed cable and a long chain not unlike the one used to keep the barn doors locked. He took it up in one hand and pushed Eddie, struggling and stumbling, into one corner of the room with the other hand, shouting, See? See?, like he'd proved a point about Eddie that he and Sextus had discussed before arriving.

He took all that stuff and bound Eddie to the hole in one of the doors. First he wound the cable around the kid's wrists tightly enough that after a few minutes it cut off his circulation. Eddie felt his hands swell and tingle—first they felt like gloves, later like someone else's hands. He wrapped the chain tightly but randomly around the cord, and from somewhere on him he pulled out a rusty pair of tight handcuffs that he passed through themselves and cinched around Eddie's wrists until he could no longer get the cuffs to make their characteristic clicking sound as they tightened. Then he looped everything and the chain through the hole in the door and left Eddie to dangle by his wrists, his butt not quite touching the floor. He picked up one of the boards designated for the shelves, although it was relatively light and unwieldy, and used it to jab Eddie in the chin, the tender skin behind his ear, and finally to thwack him on the back of the head hard enough to raise a bump.

Sextus watched, twitching now and again, then Sextus and How left Eddie dangling there.

21.

THE PLAN

heard it secondhand that Jarvis Arrow gone back to Sirius B, who only lived a couple towns over from him, and played that tape of Darlene talking 'bout how good they had it at the farm and how everything hunky-dory, and when Sirius heard it his eyes might as well popped out they sockets and his scalp jumped off his skull. 'Cause it been a whole bunch of years, five or six something, since he heard Darlene voice, and that gave him a big surprise, on account a he assume that anybody he know from back then had figured they own way to get the hell outta Dodge. And here come this lady he'd had feelings for, who had worked in this place that whole time, who had helped him get away hisself, and him knowing she couldn't tell the truth to no microphone, like she a brainwashed zombie.

Meanwhile, he remembering that she had asked him to memorize the phone number and to find her kid and after all the time it had took to get off the farm — he had forgot the number and his promise too. I think he felt damn guilty about that, like he ain't cared enough for her to risk nothing. It's just as likely, though, that them Delicious people with they guns and whatnot scared the stuffing outta that boy. I bet fear had kept him from coming back to save folks as much as some dumbass guilty feelings.

For most of them years Sirius tried to put Delicious behind him and move on in that fashion that black folks often got to. He stopped hanging out with me, start going to them stupid meetings where they always talking 'bout higher powers and one days at a time, 'bout as ridiculous as that book Darlene read. Sirius cut me dead and I resented that shit, but we had a lotta mutual friends, and I be hearing 'bout all the li'l developments in his life. Underneath I liked him, and I woulda kicked it with him again any time he needed a little pick-me-up. I know, I say that about *everybody*. I'm so damn easy. My ass always tryna love some motherfuckers more than they love me, or more than they love they own self. I'm a mess.

Anyhow, I heard that Sirius had moved back to Houston and start making music again, some tired-ass rap jams with all kinda anti-drugs, anti-gang-violence messages in it, which I found hard to keep from taking personally, or seriously, but whatever, but I still loved that sonofabitch, just like I do all my friends.

Even with them low-quality goody-goody songs, Sirius start to make a li'l bit of a name for hisself, and this Jarvis guy got a gig interviewing him for a fanzine called *Fresh*. They talked for a long-ass time, probably 'bout social justice or some other bullshit that make people think they gotta *wear* hemp instead of smoke it, and for the first time since Delicious, Sirius got real comfortable and start talking 'bout some of what had went on there, and it blew Jarvis mind. That egged Sirius on, and he start telling Jarvis 'bout how he had escaped outta there through that drainpipe and lived in it for three weeks while he gone through the agony of being apart from me, eating lizards and stealing sweet potatoes to get by, and how he could only move at night, in the moonlight, and that it took him 'bout another month of living in a swamp to figure out where the hell he at and how to get the fuck out, until one morning, at dawn, he get up the nerve to hitchhike, but he only checking for cars he know Delicious people wouldn't never drive, like a Subaru or a beat-up Volvo. He wait for almost a eternity, too, 'cause folks in that area don't be driving no liberal automobiles. But eventually some black folks from outta town in a Volkswagen picked his ass up and drove him far as Shreveport. He spent six months working low-wage jobs out there before he gone back home to Houston—moving and construction, frying up pancakes at some nasty 24-hour diner, cleaning toilets for the crazies out at West Oaks Hospital. Good times!

Jarvis couldn't believe how good Sirius story was. Meaning *good* like journalists says it—a real bad nightmare for the mother-fucker it happen to, but good to write down and put in a goddamn newspaper for some idiots to gape at. At the time, though, Jarvis mostly reviewing bad rap music for *Fresh,* but he want to be more like a hard-news man. So he decide to do a exposé on Delicious for the *Houston Chronicle,* 'cause it be a chance to do some good for Sirius, bring some people he felt was bad guys down, and get his own career going at the same time. But once he had actually got up there to Delicious and brung back that tape of Darlene, Sirius ain't want to do the story no more, 'less they did a rescue up there. 'Cause it's one thing to get the story out, right, but a whole nother story to get them people out. Jarvis told Sirius that soon as How told the management that some newspaper guy done talked to Darlene, it gon be like Lockdown City up there, so they gotta move fast, and Sirius agreed that they need to go back to do a rescue that same night.

They got up near the chicken house round 5:00, parked the

car behind some bushes. Sirius had remembered that it was always this one moment for 'bout a half hour right after roll call but before lock-in when you could drive a car through kinda fast and people could jump in and take off, something Michelle had noticed first, but she ain't never figured out how to get in touch with the outside world and work it out. She and Tuck knowed shit was maybe gonna go down 'cause Tuck done talked to the dude in the car and when How beating Darlene she talking 'bout Sirius coming back, so they's on the alert. Right when How beating up Darlene, Tuck watching from a few rows down on that same detail and he seen Jarvis and Frankie making a getaway down the road. He figure while everybody gawking at the violence, he gon wave that Subaru down and get gone hisself. The car ain't stop, but Jarvis slow down a li'l, stick his head out the window and then Tuck begging them to come back at roll call. Tuck told Michelle they said yes even though he ain't heard nobody say nothing.

That evening they seen the car and they snuck they ass into the corn and then into the car real fast 'fore anybody could see. They panting and sweating like they just run a marathon. Sirius told Tuck they gonna have room for 'bout five people with a few belongings, but one rule—he said he wouldn't take nobody nowheres 'less they brought Darlene and Eddie. Sirius said to find some other folks who want to go right then and Tuck like, You crazy? But Sirius ain't budge on that shit and Tuck had to tiptoe back over before they closed shit up and ask folks if they wanna get free without creating no drama.

Tuck thinking he gonna have trouble keeping down the numbers of people who wanna go, but when he told just a few folks that Sirius B out there in a car right outside, the first three people went, Nah, all skeptical like they thinking he tryna trap em, and when he got all passionate and angry with em, talking 'bout how he telling the truth, and to go see for theyself, but the car be well hid behind them bushes, it made him look worse. 'Cause sometime the harder you keep saying you on the level, the less motherfuckers believe you. Lotta them had forgot that Tuck just a real bad alcoholic and ain't hardly never dealt with Yours Truly. Or they said to theyself that his drinkahol had made him start seeing pink elephants and whatnot, like he 'bout to have a breakdown something. The brother can't win. Hard-core addicts be judging his ass for being a alkie. Ain't that some shit? He just hoping that nobody blab to How or Jackie. Who end up also agreeing is just TT, who by that time woulda said yes to a escape plan that relied on a combination of Jesus, Michael Jackson, and Bigfoot. Problem was, TT said he had a special stupid detail down near the depot he had to go to right that fucking minute.

Tuck run back to the car and told Sirius that they gonna have to rescue TT near the depot. They had to wait until he got drove there, and then they seen that Gaspard still be in the store doing, like, inventory or some bullshit. Sirius told Jarvis to get out the car and go pretend to interview Gaspard behind the counter, and while he doing that, Sirius gonna jump out the car and go find TT. At first Gaspard tryna shoo Jarvis away, wondering how he even found the joint, but Sirius had told Jarvis to flatter Gaspard ass, and that worked. Gaspard wouldn't say nothing 'bout the goings-on at Delicious, and he definitely ain't want to say nothing with no tape going, but he did like to jabber his ass off 'bout everything else in the known universe. Jarvis kept him going just to give Sirius extra time; he damn sure ain't get no information for the piece outta Gaspard, just some bullshit 'bout college-football history, a couple random stories 'bout a deadly tornado that happened forty years ago, and a lotta advice 'bout how to catch a fish with a string rolled around a fucking twig.

While that shit be happening, Sirius start hunting round to see if TT in one them fields near the depot. It be some big grape-growing areas off to one side out there, surrounded by corn, and sometime maybe one or two people get sent out there, who they watch from a distance (but close enough to shoot), and if you be crouching down and moving real quick through the stalks, then you could maybe find somebody picking or putting on pesticides or fertilizers or what have you on them grape plants. And maybe escape the same way.

Which exactly what Sirius done. He knew the area good, and it ain't took him too long to find TT out there filling up some propane cannons and propping up some fake hawks on sticks. Both of them techniques supposed to scare off birds but ain't never worked at Delicious. Sirius done freaked the hell outta TT at first, 'cause Sirius gone down the row of tomatoes next to his and come up through them vines, like he finna strangle him to death or something.

He told TT that when it get dark enough, him and Jarvis and Michelle gonna go round to the workshop with they car to get Eddie and Darlene. TT and Sirius traded notes to make sure Delicious ain't changed the program none.

They had been through all that shit and they exhausted by the time everybody get to the workshop. Tuck the first in, and he seen Eddie up there in the barn and opened the side of the door that Eddie wasn't hanging off, and he got a good look at him and Darlene and made a expression like somebody done smashed him in the face with a drink. Like with the glass. Which woulda been the worst shit to happen to him because he'd rather have drunk the drink. Of course he already drunk on 'bout seven of them li'l Popovs since he had got back from the depot, and he knew that it ain't no promising situation up in there, but the opportunity to book the heck outta there might not come again for some time. He thinking, *Act like everything cool.* He said, like, Hey, y'all. Here's the dealio.

Eddie blew his stack and went, Nigger, get me free before you tell me the fucking dealio! I can't feel my fingers.

Tuck stuck the last of his Popovs into his pants pocket and squatted down to take a look at the number that How had did on Eddie wrists, and yes, he stone-drunk, but still what he seen be like a plate of Chinese noodles with a bunch of nigger fingers sticking up out of em. He look at it like it's a alien done come down out a spaceship and spoke French to him. He start tugging and turning the whole mess round in his hands, like he tryna find the end of a knot, someplace he could loosen part the cable and pull something through something else in order to free up Eddie hands, but everything so tight that he couldn't get started. He pull in one place, it got tight in another; he follow a thread of vinyl and that somehow led to a part going through a hole in the chain. He pinched them rusty handcuffs and they ain't budge. Meantime Eddie thinking Tuck having trouble just on account a the alcohol, and when it start taking too long, he got to yelling at the old man that he a idiot and a drunk, and that ain't make it no easier for Tuck to do what he tryna do. Then Tuck remind him of the night they met, how Eddie done tied his hands up, said he ain't had no kinda obligation to do what he doing, and that shut Eddie's ass right the fuck up.

But after a minute or two, Eddie start saying, Get the shears and just cut it! Tuck gone and took to ransacking all the toolboxes over by where Eddie putting up shelves, and he couldn't find em; meanwhile Eddie start shouting the description of what's a pair of shears at him. Tuck could find only a pair a pliers and a flat-head screwdriver and he thinking he gonna use em to pull up some the binding stuff. Eddie squirming around like a hog in a lasso and told him to get back there and look exactly where he left them shears, but when Tuck got to the precise location he seen they wasn't there. That's when Eddie knew that How had took em deliberately so he couldn't get outta that spiderweb of chains and cables. Tuck said he thinking he might could find hedge clippers in another place by the chicken house, but then they heard something outside that sound like somebody coming closer. Tuck edged on out the barn, saying to Eddie that they would see him again that night with Sirius B and figure something out.

For a while, ain't nothing happen. Which a bad kind of nothing because it meant that ain't nobody show up with no medical supplies to deal with Darlene injuries, which was moving toward getting infected, and ain't nobody come around with no food, not even that scalding-hot extra-salty broth everybody called water soup, the soup that, for all them chickens running around, ain't had no kinda chicken flavor nowheres near it. Michelle used to say, Didn't no chicken even look in the direction of this shit, meanwhile every damn morning I'm spitting out feathers. And that would crack everybody up and the joke made the soup go down easier. But Eddie and Darlene ain't had no nourishment to speak of, no water, and plus Mama starting to come awake and jonesing hard. There be this bumpy noise somewhere in the workshop that Eddie couldn't figure out what it was.

But then he realize that the noise he heard be coming from this one corner, and when Darlene woke up, they look over there and seen Charlie the Rat sitting in the corner, doing his li'l scratchy back-leg-behind-the-ear thing. Charlie seen em see him and looked up like, What? He ain't go nowhere neither, like even he knew they couldn't hardly move they own self, let alone go chasing no rat. Them palmetto bugs musta told him. He sat up on his raw back legs and point his nose into the sky like he gonna enjoy watching some shit go down. Like he had put down some his li'l rat money on the outcome.

22.

WE COULD GET
YOU FREE

uck, Sirius, Jarvis, Michelle, and TT made it to the workshop, and while Tuck, Michelle, and TT started bustling around and making noise as they argued about how to cut Eddie down from the cords and chains holding him to the door and tried to find the right tools to do so, Sirius remained utterly silent. Eddie noticed all this in his peripheral vision. For a long time Sirius stood motionless near the door, staring toward Darlene, and then, very slowly, in stark comparison with the activity around him, he made a path toward where Darlene lay, as if he were a deer hunter and she his prey. Eddie took note of Sirius's advance on Darlene, his stunned reaction alone revealing to Eddie who Sirius was. Sirius had apparently lost the ability to close his mouth, but Darlene, despite her agony, could not prevent herself from chuckling when she saw Sirius.

Look who it is. Darlene laughed. She seemed to gather strength from his presence.

I guess I finally made it, Sirius said, his voice catching with self-consciousness and what sounded like despair.

You didn't have to wait so long, Darlene said, like somebody about to kiss somebody. At this point Sirius knelt down to whisper to her, and Eddie could no longer hear their conversation.

Still, from his vantage point tied to the door, Eddie could almost feel the tenderness radiating from Sirius. Sirius had eyes nearly the size of strawberries, and almost as red, and when he looked at you, it felt like he pitied you, and maybe loved you like a relative. Anybody might have wanted to save Eddie, considering where he'd wound up, but Sirius was obviously ill-equipped for the job; a man of deep thoughts, spiritual sayings, and compassion—Eddie had heard from the crew that in his music, Sirius preached nonviolence, mercy, tolerance, and cosmic deliverance, like the second coming of Dr. King or somebody. Eddie thought he might like to know that sort of brother in his day-to-day life, to go to for advice and such. Darlene had frequently told him his father had some of those qualities—she went for that type. But when you've got to do some urgent work of the sort they were about to do right then, Eddie thought he'd rather have a no-nonsense fellow in his corner, somebody who wouldn't overthink it.

But somehow in the confusion that dominated the scene, TT placed a pair of bolt cutters in Sirius's palms and gestured for him to make an attempt at freeing Eddie's hands. Sirius rose from his conversation with Darlene and moved toward Eddie, delicately testing the tool. After a few moments of paralysis, he worked the cutters into a bunch of different areas but couldn't do more than snip little wounds into the sides of the chain and expose some of the sheathing on the cable. Then he tried using the bolt cutters to free Eddie from the hole in the door, but there was a long rusty metal guard running the length of it, which prevented him from making even a tiny slice.

Take the damn door off the hinges, Darlene wheezed.

But Michelle thought that would only saddle him with a gigantic piece of equipment and keep him grounded even more than if they hadn't done a thing.

In a silent, creeping way, it became obvious to Eddie, though nobody breathed the words, that the easiest way to get him free—something that the others had probably started thinking about a long time before he understood it—would be for him to leave his hands behind.

Tuck kept saying, Now we *could* get you free, we *could* get you free. But for the first few times he said it, Eddie thought Tuck meant to encourage *himself*; it didn't dawn on Eddie that perhaps Tuck wanted it to seem like Eddie had come up with the idea first. And when he realized what Tuck meant, and why he wouldn't be more specific, Eddie's head filled with a rage hotter than the blue flame at the end of a blowtorch.

He didn't say anything for a long time as the others milled around, discussing options. Instead he tried to explain the complexity of the situation to himself in his head, and then by looking back and forth in a certain way between Tuck and Sirius B. Never at Darlene. Tuck and Sirius semicircled his dangling body anxiously, not so much keeping their distance as seeming to fear the next step; apparently neither of them could muster the energy required to move forward. A sympathetic tingle passed through Eddie's nerves and veins, and he felt sharply that he shouldn't take his fury out on them, as they were victims too, nearly to the same degree.

With the time we have, I don't see an alternative, Sirius fretted.

Doctors can put em back nowadays, Tuck said. He had found the circular saw. He held it, unplugged, in his right hand, almost casually, as if he planned to use the blade to scratch an itch on his forearm. We'll save em, he said, and then repeated the phrase.

Eddie's anger rose even higher. More than anything else, he wanted, ridiculously, to show Tuck that he wasn't holding the saw properly. *Idiot,* he thought. Sirius busied himself by gathering up a few of the longer pieces of the sheathed cable; Eddie tried to catch his mother's eye, but she appeared to be having an intense discussion with Scotty—she wouldn't look at Eddie or come close to him in a way that somebody might later connect with what was about to happen.

We'll put em on ice, my man, Tuck said. Eddie listened to his voice for any undercurrent of payback. The songs of Willie "Mad Dog" Walker played loudly in his head.

Tuck plugged the saw into a plastic adapter that screwed into a light socket. He tested the distance between the end of its slack and Eddie's position at the door, then tugged on the cord attached to the lightbulb and moved the whole operation when he found that it wasn't quite close enough to do the job accurately.

I can't do it, he said.

Do you mean you can't reach, or you can't do it? Eddie asked.

Can't do it. Just can't. Can't even look at the doing of it. It's too...He took a long frowning pause.

After all that, you're going to go soft?

Go soft? I *am* soft, bruh, he said. When it come to something like this.

Sirius decided that the group should quickly make some rules about the procedure. He suggested that Eddie close his eyes so that he wouldn't know who had done the job. But that didn't pan out when Michelle said it would be obvious once he opened them again, and everybody else would know and give it away, so he'd find out immediately no matter what.

You should all come in close, Eddie said. Then it won't be so obvious.

Nobody liked that idea.

At last Tuck found a way to loop the power cord from the circular saw over a nail sticking out of the door above Eddie. The saw swung there like a pendulum, like the border between Eddie's life before and who knew what. Eddie would need only to raise his wrists toward the blades if somebody stuck the plug in and the power went on.

Darlene spoke up, voicing her hopes. Maybe the saw will cut through the chain and the chain will fall off? she said. But that went against what everybody else could see would happen, and what Michelle and Tuck had braced themselves to deal with. Their brows knotted together.

I hope so, Mama, Eddie said hopelessly, as his anger crested, like a fever breaking, and fear took its place. He stared toward his mother. Darlene took a very quick glance at him and their eyes met for an instant.

Looking back later, from the distance of St. Cloud, Eddie would say that he reckoned he'd done well. Best thing that ever happened to me! he'd say. How could I have become the Handyman Without Hands if I had hands? I wouldn't give up that experience for anything in the world. It's unique, it set me apart from any other Negro stranger, especially up in St. Cloud. I do believe that God called me to be the Handyman Without Hands. People who have everything and everything works, those folks don't even notice that they have it. But set an obstacle in a man's way and he can see his whole life differently—not that everybody in my position could've done what I did. But if you're stubborn like me, and you have to struggle to do what other people seem to do without trying—hell, without even *thinking* about trying—it changes your thoughts and your behavior. People who get the special treats of life think it's easy, think anybody can do what they've done. I've seen some rich folks focus so hard on everybody they think is above them and who gets more than they do that they actually think they're on the bottom. I tell you, the bottom is crackheads like TT and Michelle and Hannibal and my mom, out in that boiling heat, hunting for a brown lime on a barren tree. No, there's worse than that. But it's so much worse that if you saw it, you'd quit the human race.

Sirius apologized, then began to sing a slow ballad that Eddie didn't recognize—badly—until Tuck asked him to shut up.

Eddie closed his eyes, stiffened his wrists, and imagined what was to come. Immediately he forced himself to think of something else—his backyard in Ovis, a rare memory of his father watching him play in the sun on a breezy Saturday.

The solution everyone agreed upon, to protect the identity of the cutter and to reduce Eddie's terror, was that he would wear a blindfold. Darlene knelt behind him, wrapping a sweatshirt over his face. I can't stay, Eddie heard his mother whisper to him. I'm going to walk as far away from this barn as I can so I don't have to hear anything, I'll cover my ears and I'll wait right outside with these rags once I get the all-clear. It's too much.

But I'll be okay. Tuck says it's temporary and they'll get reattached. And by then we'll be out of here.

Right, she said. Of course.

His mother's reassurance did not sound convincing, but he had to admit he hadn't convinced himself of what *he'd* said either.

I reckon I'm a weak person. Darlene sighed. I get sick of myself sometimes. I just go along with life because I can't think myself out of the things I get into. I can't move on. I can't do that to Nat. I owe him.

How could you be weak after working at Delicious?

Darlene thwacked Eddie lovingly on his back.

Seriously, he said. Weak? Carrying those Carolina Crosses all day?

It's a different kind of weak, Eddie. It's like the Lord has asked me to walk through a hurricane and get across an ocean but didn't give me rubbers or a raincoat or a lifeboat. Or even clothes. She finished tying Eddie's blindfold and he heard the sound of her hands hitting her thighs.

So what. Your feet get wet and you swim.

That's okay if you're tough inside. You share that with your father. But I take everything to heart.

I don't know what you mean.

You're going to think I'm crazy, Eddie, but it doesn't matter if it's a pistol-whipping or a sunset, I can't stop feeling overwhelmed. I don't want to lose anyone anymore, I don't want to lose anything. Why does being alive have to mean always losing, always losing everything all the time?

You can take pictures! Movies?

No. I mean things nobody can replace. Most people don't even try. It doesn't matter to them. Or if it does, they know how to ignore it. I can't. I need to talk to Scotty. She laughed. Scotty helps me handle all of this.

She danced her fingers down to the ends of Eddie's arms and he felt a strange kind of pressure there. She promised to make sure they'd get him to a hospital first thing—this veiled touch would not be the last sensation he'd ever feel with his fingers—and he stretched his mouth skeptically, doubting her ability to supervise that journey. But before he could say anything, she used his shoulder to raise herself from the ground and soon the cooler air from outside tumbled into the space and her footsteps grew fainter as they crunched through the leaves outside. Eddie thought he heard her weeping but it also sounded like coughing.

He shouted after her, and her footsteps returned briefly to the door but neither said anything. Eddie's heart leapt into his neck and choked him.

It sounded to Eddie like someone unsheathed the safety, squeezed the trigger, and the wave-shaped teeth on the circular blade emitted a low whir that soon blasted up to a high-pitched whine. With the saw held aloft, the person seemed to approach the barn doors with nearly ceremonial slowness, punctuated by a slight stumble and a recovery. At the edge of the door frame, the person holding the saw paused; Eddie imagined him making some technical adjustment. A voice he could not quite identify—he thought it was Tuck's—shouted over the noise and asked about his readiness. Beneath the blindfold, the sleeves of the garment tight behind his ears, he closed his eyes and nodded, stoically barking the words, *Go ahead, get it over with,* hoping to have yelled it loud enough for everyone to hear him over the noise of the saw and through the thick cloth that covered even his mouth. He leaned his torso aside and held his wrists away from his chest to provide better access to the cutter. Tentatively, the buzzing teeth descended toward the cables and chains and cuffs that held Eddie captive to the doors.

Get me out of this, Lord, he prayed. *Let me get free.*

The first kiss of the saw buzzed against the hairs at the base of his left hand as the blade tore through the sheathed cable and uncoiled its copper and nickel wires with an insistent grinding noise. Cords snapped and frayed and the sheathing flew away toward Eddie and the ground where he had folded his knee underneath his body to brace himself. The unraveling cooled his hands and the circulation returned to his palms.

The blade had not yet pierced his skin, and the worker pulled back for a moment. Hope lingered—since the saw had destroyed the cable, perhaps it might cut through the chain and the cuffs

---

297

as well, sparing Eddie the loss of his hands. But when the saw touched the metal chain, the pitch of the grinding immediately rose to an unbearable squeal, then a sickening screech that seemed to thread through him like a giant needle, and after a moment or two, the ferocious rotation of the saw stopped entirely. Then the machine made as if to start up, but stopped again with a defeated clunk. Eddie imagined some of its teeth curving in new directions, blunted or jagged. The chain, meanwhile, had not lessened its grip around his wrists, nor had the handcuffs.

Urgent muttering sprang up around him, voices of group members confirming the mutilation of the saw, trying to decide on an appropriate, expedient action. Eddie allowed himself a few moments to get comfortable moving his fingers again; some blood and sensation had come back into his capillaries, he stopped imagining that his hands would soon turn black and that severing them would make no difference anyway. In the darkness behind the sweatshirt blindfold, he opened and closed his eyes and could see no light. A deep shadow appeared dotted with ghostlike greenish lights and vague shapes that he guessed must correspond to objects he had recently viewed; or perhaps they formed a map of the stars in some unknown corner of the galaxy.

The voices around him did not utter complete sentences; instead they communicated with barely audible whispers and soft, nudging grunts, some of which seemed to mean agreement, and others disagreement. They spoke among themselves, someone manipulating the saw, possibly knocking metal tools against it. Eddie had ordered a replacement blade, he recalled, but UPS would take several more weeks to deliver it.

After a time, Eddie permitted his mind to wander. He pictured the days ahead with great fear, making a list of activities he assumed he would no longer be able to do. He remembered rotating a tiny screwdriver between his thumb and index finger to tighten the hinges on Elmunda's eyeglasses, reassembling the circuit board on the Fusiliers' computer, picking up grains of rice that he'd accidentally spilled on their kitchen floor, removing a staple jammed in the business end of a stapler. The many times he'd opened soda cans and held pens and cutlery and turned the pages of a newspaper whizzed through in his head like images in a flip-book; he grew more despondent at the thought of the myriad items whose surfaces he would never get to caress, starting with the female body, then his own body, angora cats, corn silk, the pointed hairs of one of the Fusiliers' Persian rugs, a sack of seeds, cool running water. It didn't comfort him much to imagine that he would still feel these things with other parts of his body; idly touching the bristles of a shaving brush like the one that had belonged to his father did not seem possible or desirable without fingers. Then he thought about the pleasures of the fingers themselves, about instruments he would never learn to play, about snapping and clapping and flipping the bird, about making silhouettes of animals on bright walls, about carrying and drumming and cooking, and about the sign language he would never learn—and as these losses mounted, he changed his mind. There had to be a way to leave Delicious without having to go through with this. Sirius himself had done it.

But as he turned with his shrouded head to tell the debating folks behind him to back off, the circular saw started up again. When he shouted, he could tell his protest sounded to them like anxiety; they merely patted his back and reassured him. Perhaps the sweatshirt muffled him more than he had previously thought—could they not hear what he was saying?

In another moment the broken blade stung Eddie's skin just above the knot of his left wrist, and a burning sensation spread out from there, but in a second the spinning cutter came into contact with bone and made another high-pitched grinding noise before the hardness where the radius and the ulna came together gave way and shattered. The cut felt ragged to Eddie, who believed that a neat slice would improve the chances that his hands could be reattached, and he clenched his teeth against the horrific ongoing burn. The mechanical noises drowned out his shouting; at this point he knew that whatever came out of his mouth sounded to them like a response to the pain and shock, not a statement that he had changed his mind and that they should stop cutting.

The clumsy jabbing of the saw gave him the sinking feeling that the dirty job had fallen to TT, whom Eddie had watched perform all of the tasks How and Jackie assigned to him with a complete lack of artistry or subtlety, consistently bruising fruit and breaking open melons. After a few short moments more of burn and tear he felt his left hand hanging heavy from the skin and tendons that remained; he had grown faint from the blood loss and fainter still from the *thought* of blood loss. Someone jumped in to arrest his widening injury with a tourniquet made from a towel which quickly became warm and wet.

In the midst of the fracas, an unfamiliar voice entered the room, attempting to shout over the noise and direct people in some fashion. For a second the voice approached the same pitch as the saw and demanded an explanation for the current activity, but after a couple of moments it returned to its original volume and the focus around Eddie seemed to change. The voice, he now understood, must belong to Jarvis Arrow, the man who'd come with Sirius, and with a shudder of relief, Eddie assured himself that even if nothing else had gone well exactly, the timing of the escape would work out perfectly. He heard his mother's voice as well, and what he believed to be her feet scrambling around the workshop.

The awkward stabbing of the saw continued and finally released his left arm; Eddie let it fall toward his flank, but before it could get there, a pair of gentle hands lifted it into a folded towel. His mother whispered encouragements to him, describing the way she was stopping the blood by tearing up a towel and attaching it to the end of his wrist with lengths of sheathed cable and rubber they'd saved from before.

You're almost free, he heard her say. Almost free. Darlene ran out of the workspace again, pledging to return when the job was done.

But he would not be free until the bearer of the saw could scoot over to the opposite side—and repeat the excruciating performance. The pain of losing the right hand combined with what he already felt in the left; the trauma drained his head of blood and he began to hyperventilate. The bungling and the pain continued with the right hand, as before. The person with the saw turned it off and Eddie felt someone tugging at his forearm as if to loosen a stubborn connection, but the saw went on again, poking around and grinding into his fractured bones. Eddie passed out and then regained consciousness, then passed out again as he heard his mother, who had returned to the workspace, repeating, without joy or sorrow, We have to go. Right this minute. We got you free, so stand up.

23.

GATORS

The pain in Eddie's forearms had gotten so bad that he could only wobble forward, knock-kneed. A couple of strong people held him by his armpits and guided him through the blackness; low bushes scratched his elbows. After a minute or two he counted everyone present by the voices—his mother, TT, Tuck, Sirius, Michelle, and Jarvis. The car, they said, was parked about a mile away to keep the Delicious people from seeing and guessing what was about to happen. They had to make the journey as silently as possible. TT and Darlene paused for a couple of minutes because he had some rocks and they both needed some smoky courage. Nobody had bothered to untie the sweatshirt from around Eddie's head, but that oversight increased his awareness of sounds. He noticed all sorts of night noises—planes rumbled through the sky, bullfrogs croaked, grackles called and responded to each other, and something that might've been a deer crunched through crops and leaves. Not only did these sensations help keep his mind off the tension jetting up and down his arms into the space his hands used to occupy, but he couldn't find the right moment to ask someone to remove the blindfold, so he let it remain.

From time to time, Sirius leaned in to his ear and asked for a progress report. He said that he felt okay except for his hands, which was a joke, but nobody laughed. Sirius apologized, promising to get him to a doctor, and asked if he would rather have kept working at the farm his whole life than lose his hands.

I'd rather have lost all four limbs and my head than stay at Delicious, he told Sirius, but he didn't mean it. He wanted to make up for the joke and sensed that everybody's faith in the mission rested on the belief that cutting off his hands had been the best, most logical solution to the problem rather than something that would have occurred only to people who were out of their fucking minds. Most of them, after all, were literally on crack.

Led by Sirius, with Tuck guiding the blindfolded Eddie, they hiked a faint trail that Sirius claimed to remember from the days following his escape. At first, TT and Michelle held Darlene up, but she insisted on supporting herself even though she had a lot of trouble doing so. Once they had traveled some distance—Eddie couldn't guess how far—it occurred to him that he didn't know what they'd done with his hands. Naturally he couldn't have seen where they'd put them, and during the process his attention had stayed on the pain. He spent a few hundred more yards wondering about his hands. A couple of times, he craned his head back, as if looking for them, though that gesture made no sense, given the blindfold.

Tuck appeared to guess what his movements meant. Uh-oh, he whispered. I don't know. I think your moms has em. Somebody put em in a plastic bag and soon's we get rolling and get far enough away, we're gon stop and get some ice and you'll be okay.

Eddie nodded, but at that moment he could imagine that Tuck and the rest looked like old-time executioners taking him to the gallows out amid Spanish moss in the olden days. He worried that they would forget about his hands, that the appendages would stay behind and take root in the soil among the cabbage plants.

They got to the Subaru after what felt like hours. Sirius untied the arms of the sweatshirt from behind Eddie's ears and the fabric flopped down, landing partially on his shoulders. Before him a nearly full moon hung above the horizon like a flashlight interrogating the world. A road that Eddie couldn't remember ever seeing during his time on the farm stretched out in front of them. The moonlight turned the road ashy blue, a sight so unusual that Eddie almost thought he'd invented it himself.

Halfheartedly Sirius said, I figured you wouldn't want to see for a while, as he took the sweatshirt off Eddie's shoulders and folded it in half. He folded the arms as well and wrapped them in the bottom half of the shirt.

But this is beautiful, Eddie said, not thinking so much about the scene but the fact that everyone would be leaving the farm. He would've smiled if he hadn't been in so much pain.

I meant your—Sirius said.

Eddie raised his arms up to see for the first time what he'd lost. He remembered a time when he'd worn one of his late father's shirts, and his arms hadn't come all the way down. He'd skipped around the house, delighted with himself, until his mother discovered him and shook him almost hard enough to rip the shirt off his back.

In the car, Eddie lay sideways in the hatchback on a filthy quilt, keeping his arms raised. TT, Michelle, Darlene, and Tuck smashed into the backseat—Darlene on Tuck's lap—while Jarvis drove and Sirius rode shotgun. Jarvis gunned the motor, repeatedly expressing his shock that he'd gotten himself involved in this rescue, though the confusion in his voice couldn't mask his enjoyment of the crazy adventure or his implied belief that once they got through the whole thing, the mission would improve an already great story.

Jarvis had to drive pretty slowly to navigate the bumpy road. Eddie squirmed around in the hatch and gave up on trying to rest, let alone sleep. The four in the back jostled one another in humorously uncomfortable ways: TT's face smashed against a headrest, Michelle kept accusing and warning Tuck about the placement of his hands.

An argument broke out in the backseat over whether they had gone farther into the farm. During the argument, Michelle let it slip that she suspected Jarvis of working for the Fusiliers and that he might be taking them on a loop inside the farm instead of helping them get away. In a flock of half-finished sentences, she tried to explain that she knew the Fusiliers wanted to test the loyalty of everybody in the camp at any cost. She wouldn't put anything past them. If I didn't know better, she said, I might start thinking that y'all two—she pointed at Sirius and Jarvis, sacrificing her precarious balance—has conspired with the growers and any minute now could shoot everybody in the car and drive it into the river.

Jarvis shrugged off the accusation at first, but then grew quiet and sober, explaining almost lovingly his astonishment at the level of paranoia that everybody took for granted. He supposed that given what he called the Whole Coyote Scenario—cutting off someone's hands to free him from a trap—of which he didn't approve, he shouldn't have wondered that everybody had a lot of trauma. He compared the crew to soldiers coming back from an unjust war and told a story about his father's service in Vietnam. He begged everyone to trust that Sirius knew a shortcut or two and that he had no interest in doing anything *but* helping, and Sirius backed him up, explaining exactly the route they meant to take in order to avoid being conspicuous or making too much noise. Jarvis found it disturbing, he said, that the workers didn't have a clear impression of the size or layout of the farm, and he wondered aloud how Delicious had kept them in the dark for so many years. But to Eddie, the degree to which the workers depended on alcohol and crack cocaine should have spoken for itself, and to see such innocence in a grown man puzzled him. Why didn't he immediately recognize that drugs had vaporized half these people's brains?

Michelle swore that she believed Sirius and Jarvis, but a minute later Eddie heard her take off her seat belt. In the silence that followed, the purr of the Subaru rose above other noises and smoothed over some of the edgy feeling. Michelle said that it might help if Jarvis turned the headlights off and used the moonlight instead; Jarvis, apparently eager to accommodate her, tried that for a minute, then admitted that it scared him and switched them back on. Michelle settled into her seat and invoked her close relationship with Jesus as a kind of warning to Jarvis and Sirius, as if Jesus were an older brother about to pull up in his Ford Mustang and punch anybody who mistreated his sister. After a few moments she grabbed her armrest and held it tightly.

The shortcut ended and Jarvis edged the car up onto a more navigable stretch of road, strewn with smaller, looser rocks. As they came near to what Sirius assured them was the edge of the property, a world they had not seen for years, a headlight, the first they'd encountered that night, barreled toward them from a distance. At first Eddie thought it was a motorcycle, but as the car got closer, he saw that one light had gone out. Only a series of turns and slight hills sat between their vehicle and the approaching one.

Michelle straightened her back at the sight of the headlight and shouted, Pull over and cut your lights! Cut your lights! Pull over!

Oh, come on, Michelle, Sirius said.

What's—why? Jarvis blurted.

It's the minibus! The minibus done lost a headlight and they too cheap to fix it. You motherfuckers.

Minibus? Jarvis asked.

Oh my God, she said. By then, the distance had halved, and a moment later the minibus stopped in the middle of the road, perpendicular to traffic, its blue flank blocking the way forward like a dead cypress in a swamp. As Jarvis hit the gas, prepared to make a spectacular swerve around the minibus, Michelle pushed Sirius's seat forward, mashing him against the dashboard, and managed to swing the passenger door open and leap halfway out. TT tried to lunge over and pull her back in by the leg, but she kicked him off. The door rushed back and hit her shoulder, and then jetted out again. Jarvis stomped on the brake with his whole weight and the car halted at a diagonal twenty yards from the minibus. Sextus and How had already piled out and prepared themselves for a confrontation.

The moment the car stopped, Michelle vaulted the rest of the way out of the car and, after running forward a few yards like somebody ready to fight, took a right turn into the rushes, churning forward with great difficulty, as though attempting to sprint through thigh-high water. Sextus and How shouted her name, begging her to come back, saying that they did not want to hurt her. But when she did not respond, Sextus removed the shotgun from under his arm and fired a warning shot into the air. Behind the steering wheel, Jarvis shrieked and a spasm visibly rippled through his body; Sirius steadied the journalist by gently placing his palm atop his sternum. Jarvis gasped. Little gems of perspiration decorated his forehead and the bridge of his nose. Darlene curled down behind him to avoid stray shots and told Eddie to do the same, so he scrunched onto his side in the hatch against the back of the backseat, using it as a barrier, behind which no one could see or shoot him, but from which he could peek out. Meanwhile, TT squeezed close next to Darlene.

It seemed that How and Sextus—and Jackie, whose dark shadow Eddie could just make out behind a reflection in one of the minibus windows illuminated by the headlights—at first thought to follow and capture Michelle as she pushed through the vegetation, but the prospect of losing the rest of the crew for her sake maybe changed their minds and they let her run. He couldn't see whether or not Hammer lay in wait inside the minibus.

Sextus petted his shotgun lovingly and chuckled. It's all gators out in that swamp, honey! Hope you know that! He said it again, yelling loud enough that she could hear, perhaps meaning for it to discourage everyone in the Subaru as well.

They all jolted in their seats when Michelle hollered something back from far away that sounded to Eddie through the open windows of the car like, Y'all the fucking gators! You!

Eddie rediscovered the quilt in the hatch and slowly edged it over his head with his forearms, leaving a small area open so that he could see past the seat back, through the ribbons of seat belt, and out to where Sextus and How stood expectantly. The two men adjusted themselves in ways that demonstrated their bravado, tugging their belt loops up, spreading their legs like cowboys. Sextus continued to stroke the shotgun, his index finger curling around the trigger. How touched the brim of his hat. With a phony courtesy that angered Eddie, he asked the people in the car to get out. Jarvis kept his attention focused on Sextus and How as he stepped out of the car with his hands up at his sides, treating them like the police officers they pretended to be.

Eddie stirred under the quilt, but without turning around, Darlene whispered, Stay, almost like she was talking to herself.

The car's idling, she said. If we don't get out then maybe you still can.

Eddie thought he could still faintly hear Michelle's hands and feet pushing through the brush. Darlene, Tuck, and TT emerged from the backseat on the same side, and eventually Sirius came around the passenger-side door. Eddie listened to everybody's feet scuffling nearer to the minibus. Jackie turned on the lights inside the van. The two doors of the Subaru stood open like the wing casings of a flying palmetto bug.

Where are y'all off to on this fine evening? Sextus asked, almost cordially.

But when he and How saw the four of them for the first time in the peculiar light created by the Subaru's lights bouncing off the minibus and the silvery moon, they both stepped back and their eyebrows rose. TT, Tuck, and Darlene had bloodstains all over their clothes; they must have looked like a terrifying mob.

What the Sam Hill? Did y'all slaughter a bunch of my chickens?

Where are these nice gentlemen taking you? How said, before anybody could respond.

A few very uneasy moments passed while How and Sextus appeared to wait for some kind of answer from the crew, but all of them, excepting Jarvis, knew better than to give either of these men a response, truthful or sarcastic. Their silence inflated, and Eddie could imagine their eyes shifting from side to side, and the way they'd catch and throw back one another's sidelong glances, either gathering up the courage to make a break for it like Michelle or letting the will drain out of them so that they could give up without losing face or catching a beating.

When no one spoke, Jarvis kept starting to answer but changing his mind before a complete thought could fall out of his mouth, after which he would sigh, or say, Well, or Um.

Then Darlene, almost like a nervous flinch, leapt at Sextus and embraced the shotgun, kicking his shins and telling him to let it go. How pulled out a Glock and raised its muzzle, but Sextus, even as he lunged back and forth, attempting to wrestle the shotgun out of Darlene's arms, ordered him not to shoot her. Instead, How trained his gun on the others, though still trying to protect Sextus from Darlene, but in a matter of moments, the three others divided his attention enough to tackle him. TT in particular seemed to savor the thrashing they gave How. A shot reverberated through the air. Then another.

Darlene had begun to howl a series of outlandish, frequently nonsensical accusations at Sextus—You killed my son! You tried to destroy me with your voodoo! You made Jackie control me with her pussy blood, you fucker! You tried to break me apart with your hair! You tried to keep me quiet by fucking me! Your breath put me in prison! You tried to get inside my brain and piss your name on the inside of my skull, you fucking zombie-master motherfucker! I love you! But I hate everything you've ever done including love me, you sonofabitch. You stole my handbag and you broke my glass crystal watermelon! Give me my rocks. Kiss me. Why won't you kiss me with your mind! Fuck me with your gun! she begged him. I'm going to fuck you with your gun!

While the things Darlene shouted sounded like the random curses and incomprehensible bullshit a crack addict might spew during a breakdown, they were so bizarre, more bizarre than anything Eddie had ever heard come out of her mouth, even during her worst experiences with drugs, that he soon understood what he thought she meant for him to do. She was saying the first things that came to mind in order to stall them, so that he could make a break for it.

At the height of the brawl, Eddie looped a leg over the backseat and lay flat, then shimmied out on his elbows and knees and, using the open door to mask his movements, swung himself into the driver's seat.

They hoped I would do this, he thought. *They want me to.* He wasn't abandoning them. He planted himself in the driver's seat of a car for the first time, as opposed to the tractor Sextus had taught him to drive. Crouching behind the wheel, he stepped on the brake and used his forearms to shift the car into drive. He saw Jackie see him; she sat up and immediately started banging on the inside of the minibus window with the flat of her hand to get everybody's attention. Eddie hugged the steering wheel, turned it with his chin, and stomped down on the gas as hard as he could. The Subaru lurched forward and the passenger-side door closed from the momentum. The driver-side door banged closed against the back end of the minibus as it cleared.

Hey! Jarvis shouted.

Ten miles and thirty minutes later, convinced that nobody had followed him, Eddie managed to push the headlight switch forward with his mouth and turn on the brights. In front of the car, a brazen light the color of young corn exposed the night landscape, slicing through the future like a child's eyes opening on the first morning of life.

24.

SCOTTY IS
SURPRISED

Once Darlene saw How and Sextus actually physically standing in the goddamn road, keeping her from quitting Delicious after she had let them motherfuckers chop off her son hands to get out, she admitted to herself that she been had. She felt like she falling into a sinkhole right above a landfill, down into years of liquid garbage, the putrid trash of all them misreported work hours, of spraining her ankles and breathing insecticide without no health care, of choking down undercooked and overcooked food without no nutritional value, let alone flavor, of them jacked-up prices down at the depot. For a split second Darlene left me and floated above the whole scheme like suddenly she could see what it had did to her and to everybody else it touched, and like anybody who had a second of clear thinking in the middle of a cyclone of bullshit, she lost her motherfucking mind.

The whole time she been directing her anger and despair at herself, taking the blame for that short rope of events she done lynched herself on—them tight shoes, that headache, the asking for the Tylenol that led to the murder and the fire and addiction and the abandonment and finally Delicious. She remembered all what the book had told her, and realized the book had played her ass the same way.

Goddamn this drug, she thought.

That's right. Scotty got the blame again.

A lotta pent-up emotions and explanations for shit that had happened bubbled up into Darlene throat right then, hot and evil as a Tabasco gargle, and she gone to town on Sextus tryna get that shotgun out his hands. She had every intention of shooting his ass dead right there, and probably killing How and Jackie too, and then maybe herself. It's true we was hanging out right before this all happened, but some of the shit that came out her mouth when she had that outburst took even *me* aback. I ain't tell her to say none of that. Half of what she said just *sounded* crazy, but she more or less telling the truth. Then Eddie done the smart thing and hightailed it outta that hellhole, mom or no mom. We all ultimately on our own anyhow—ain't that sad?

It's strange when you used to encouraging your friends to do all kinda mayhem and then all of a sudden you gotta switch gears. This time I remember shouting at Darlene, I said, Honey, you need to check yourself! Give that man back his shotgun and let's get in the minibus and let this all blow over so we could get back to the way it used to was, with all the smoking! But D wouldn't have it.

Even while she tryna rip that gun outta Sextus fingers, biting his hands or licking em or kissing him, maybe thinking she gonna fool him into the idea that if he give up the weapon, she gon give up the punani. Who know what she thinking? You could be damn sure somebody gone nuts if *I* think they unstable.

What did happen is that the shotgun gone off and blasted

away one and a half of Sextus fingers. At that same moment, How turnt his attention away from Jarvis and Sirius and TT and fired a shot at Darlene head, but How had shitty aim and the bullet gone into one of Sextus lungs and later they found out it done shattered his spine. TT and Sirius and Jarvis jumped How at that point and Jackie took off in the van, leaving everybody in the dark, just struggling shapes outlined by the moonbeams.

Jackie thinking she could head back to the chicken house and pretend she ain't seened nothing. It ain't matter to her that she left her boss out there for dead with a crazy lady tryna turn his skull into a jack-o'-lantern. Me and Jackie, we tight, I know how she think. Self-preservation come real natural to her, and in this situation a motherfucker couldn't invent a better policy than self-preservation. I heard her say to herself that if Sextus and How died, she could just move on to a new farm, and if they made it she could tell em she flipped out and went to get help. She know how to bend reality into whatever tool could benefit her.

Since Sextus ain't had no use of his spine no more, he let go the shotgun like he done turnt into Raggedy Andy and fell into the dirt. All of a sudden Darlene holding a firearm right above the face of one the men she could hold directly responsible for a helluva lotta the shit that done fucked up the last six years of her life that she just had thought about. Nat had taught her how to use a shotgun back in the Ovis days, and she rusty, but she sure as hell remembered how to brace that bad boy 'gainst her shoulder for the kickback and the rest. Sirius and TT and Tuck had beat How down by that point; Jarvis done pulled off his shirt and had tore it into strips to tie the sonofabitch's hands behind his back so they could all take his ass to justice. That plan seemed shaky to Darlene even at that moment. How you gon take a motherfucker to justice without no car?

I can't feel nothing. Sextus groaned up at Darlene. He having a lotta trouble breathing and foam be pushing out one corner of his mouth.

Me neither, she said back. Her index finger wrapped itself around the trigger, and it felt good the way that shit cut into the underside of her knuckle. She touched the end of the gun barrel upside Sextus cheek, to his forehead, and then the end of his nose, like she deciding on the best place for the shot that gonna blow his whole head off. It gonna look like somebody thrown a jar of strawberry jam out their car onto the road. Strawberries her and the crew probably picked last year.

Meanwhile Sirius, TT, Jarvis, and Tuck is tryna control How, who a big-ass dude and determined to get away. They got his arms tied behind his back, but he keep running off a li'l farther down the damn road two or three time. Finally the three of em done knocked him facedown and sat on him.

Darlene raised the shotgun so Sextus could see, finna blast that sucker in the eyeball. She thought he laying there on account a he surrendered, that he gonna just let her shoot him.

She go, Look. The gun's kissing you. Kissy-kiss. At this point she just pouring on the crazy.

Your stance is all wrong, Darlene, he grumbled. And you've still got the safety on, honey. You ain't trying to kill me.

She snapped out her insanity for a second and frowned at Sextus and went, Always have to be in control, even when you're about to die. She undone the safety and kicked him in the side.

I'm just telling you. I'm trying to do you a favor.

I know what your favors are like. She kicked his leg into a awkward position, knee bent up and leg twisted backward, and it stayed that way.

Just go ahead, he said. I can't feel nothing from my neck down, Darlene. I want you to do it, I don't want to be stuck like Elmunda where somebody gotta take care of me all the time, dress me and wipe my ass like a newborn. Do it!

Darlene lowered the shotgun. If he tryna put some reverse psychology on her ass, it worked. She ain't want to do what Sextus said no more in no kinda way, shape, or form. No, she said. I know what I want. Something in Sextus face got double handsome to her when he begging for shit. Them eyebrows be curling like a corn chip, and that li'l space between em getting all wrinkly. That dude *been* knowed how to get folks doing what he want on some sheer animal-magnetism shit.

From the distance, somebody—probably Jarvis—start shouting at Darlene not to kill Sextus, like he just noticed she had put the gun in the man's face.

Tell me what you want, honey, Sextus said. I'll make sure you get anything you want.

Both of us rolled our eyes at that shit. Darlene took a long pause and squinted at Sextus blue-white head writhing on the pavement just a foot or so from a giant pothole where his brains would spill if she pulled the trigger. Right then, TT start kicking How in the head something fierce, maybe tryna knock him out, and he be pushing Jarvis and Sirius and Tuck out the way every time they grab him and pull him off. His face got the expression of a man who want everybody to know that he believe in what he doing.

A chilly breeze blowing up the back of Darlene shirt, and for a instant she could see what that landscape musta look like ten million years ago, underwater, when some continents was touching each other and the hills be rolling around on the seafloor and every last fish be a bizarre monster that couldn't see nothing. Couldn't no sunlight hardly penetrate down there. Everything around em made Darlene feel like she drownding under a mile of water.

She come back into the moment, a li'l bit further away from me, looking down at Sextus sweet miserable expression and thinking 'bout them eyebrows. She thinking, *They're thick like Sirius's and shaped like the hole in a violin.* Some powerful shit in her be craving more time to enjoy the feeling of loving him and hating him and controlling his ass while he a invalid. She traced them eyebrows with the end of the shotgun and goes, Know what I want? I want a real job.

25.

SUMMERTON REVISITED

Eddie finally heard from his mother a couple of weeks after he'd broken out. Mysterious calls had started coming to his aunt's house with disturbing frequency. Bethella would pick up the phone and hear silence or breathing, then someone would hang up. When she stopped answering the phone, it sometimes rang for a half an hour. At first Eddie worried that the Delicious people had figured out where he had gone, maybe by torturing his mother, but then one evening, he watched his aunt lose her composure and scream into the phone.

Please identify yourself! she told the receiver. Who in the Living Christ is calling? What do you want? I am going to call the police if you don't stop this harassment!

Her agitated tone put Eddie in mind of the relationship between the two sisters, and the next time the phone rang for a long time and Bethella was not at home, he knocked the receiver off the hook, arranged it on the floor with his mouth, and put his ear beside it in order to talk.

After an ecstatic, tearful greeting, Darlene explained, in a long, rambling monologue, that she had figured he would go to Bethella, so she'd phoned her sister's old pastor, who provided her, a little reluctantly, with the new contact information. She apologized for the weird calls, but at the same time, she said, she'd enjoyed hearing her sister's voice again. She mentioned something about taking care of Sextus in the hospital, and by that time, he figured that she had not kicked either of her old habits. He changed the subject to tell her about Fremont, and they eulogized him for a moment.

Almost immediately after this silence in the conversation, Eddie described a plan by which he would return to Delicious, though it disturbed him now that in his haste to flee, he could only partially remember where he'd started out in Louisiana— somewhere near Ruston, he recalled, the first place he'd stopped.

Hardly pausing for a breath throughout, Eddie launched into his own monologue, outlining for Darlene exactly when he planned to come back for her, where to meet him, and at what time. He would drive back with Jarvis's car, and Bethella would follow. Both cars would stop for five minutes a few miles away from the depot, where a particular dogwood tree hunched beside the road. They would load as many workers as would fit into the cars and take them to the nearest city—Shreveport, he believed—into which the influence of the Fusiliers did not bleed. He'd return the Subaru to Jarvis, in Houston, and let everybody else out at a police station along the way in order to give their testimony against Delicious, for what it was worth, though he doubted that the police would respond in any significant way. He couldn't live with himself, however, he told his mother, if he did not at least try to expose the place for what it was and get it shut down.

No need, Darlene told him when he'd finished. No need, she said, in an almost artificially soothing voice that made Eddie wonder for a split second if she had switched her addiction of choice to an antidepressant. I'll be living at Summerton from now on, she said. I'm looking after Sextus and Elmunda—at least I will be when he gets out of the hospital. Sextus was paralyzed during your escape, and you know Elmunda has always had serious problems. That's why I'm saying you can come home if you want. She gave him her telephone number at the hospital as well as at Summerton.

The changes she described seemed unreal to Eddie; he lowered his chin when she used the word *home* to describe Delicious. Home? he said. That place isn't anybody's home. They're brainwashing you, Ma.

His mother explained that she'd called not only to make sure he was all right, but also to ask him back. She had taken charge of all the business affairs at the farm, and things had become a lot better. Many improvements had come to pass already, even in the couple of weeks since Eddie had found his way up to Bethella. Things were changing, she kept saying. Already they had reconnected the pay phones, which hadn't been broken after all, and most of the workers would get to leave pretty soon if they wanted to, in a few months at the very latest. Sextus and Elmunda can't run this place anymore, she said. They are sick people.

Doesn't that mean you can leave on your own? Eddie wanted to know. And come here?

No, no, I have to stay, she said, in a tone that sounded as if she meant to reassure him of something she refused to give life to in words. She laughed. And I don't think Bethella will have me anyway, she said. Hammer and a few others are going tonight, they found enough money for a bus ticket somewhere. Michelle we don't know what happened to, but she did what she wanted, and I hope she made it. You really should come back, honey.

Ma, what happened to my hands?

The line went silent. Eddie, I know you know what happened, Darlene finally managed.

I meant where are they. 'Cause I never saw them again.

I don't think you want an answer to that. You're just trying to hurt your mother, Darlene said. And maybe your mother deserves it. The silence returned for several moments, then she said, TT. We stopped to smoke somewhere and I think TT put the bag down, and by the time anybody realized—we had to move fast, sweetheart. Is that good enough? Mama fucked up again. But now she's trying to make things right. It's much different here, everything's different now.

Eddie nearly walked away from the phone at that point, disgusted by the thought of the fate of his appendages, but the image of Sextus and his fake bashful laugh came to mind, as well as the corruption his expressions concealed so badly. Eddie could not believe that things had changed so drastically so soon, and he vowed never to return to Delicious regardless. Had the Fusiliers put his mother up to making this call in order to get him to go back, to entrap him and prevent him from exposing them? It made sense that they might try, given his mother's habit for crack, for Sextus, or for some twisted combination of the two.

Eddie promised himself that he'd get the Subaru back to Jarvis, who would write something in the newspaper that would tell the world what Delicious had done to him and to Sirius and the others, and they would pull his mother out of there even if it was against her will and figure out what had made her go from talking about Delicious as a nightmare to considering it a dream palace in so short a time. Had she ever truly wanted to leave in the first place? Maybe, it dawned on him, she had been pretending to want to leave solely to placate him.

Saying nothing further, Eddie dropped Bethella's phone onto its cradle with his mouth. But afterward, amid a rising sense of dread, a suspicion that much more had gone wrong than his mother was at liberty to describe, a worry lingered that someone, possibly Sextus or Elmunda, or more likely How or Jackie, might've been standing right next to Darlene with some sharp weapon up to her neck. Perhaps Sextus had such a horrifically strong need to get Eddie back to Delicious and to maintain secrecy that they would kill his mother if he didn't return. A wave of nausea crested in his stomach and chest, and he felt a violent disorientation, as if he were an hourglass right at the moment when somebody flipped it over.

Eddie called Darlene nearly every day after that in an attempt to convince her to leave the farm. Her refusal to allow him to rescue her became deeply frustrating. Had he stayed closer to Louisiana, he might have effected a forced rescue, despite how badly the first had gone. Eventually Darlene refused to speak about leaving Delicious unless he considered coming back. When he rebuffed her, needling her instead, she hung up on him, then stopped answering the phone entirely. Her actions aggrieved Eddie, and with reassurance from Bethella that Darlene was irredeemable, he eventually gave up.

Around that time, a few months after Eddie had left the farm, Jarvis finally tracked him down.

How did you find me? Eddie asked.

Jarvis explained that the St. Cloud DMV had contacted him about a parking ticket, which had provided the first hint. From

the ticket I figured you'd run off to St. Cloud. I looked up repair-
men and asked around. That's what reporters do.

I reckon you want your car back.

This is true, Jarvis said, and then he volunteered to come get
the car provided Eddie would talk to him about what had gone on
at Delicious. He could get the paper to pay for part of the trip and
the rest he could deduct from his taxes.

I can't, Eddie said. I don't want anything to happen to my
mom. She's still there.

Still there? That's great! I mean, not great, but what a story.

They spoke further, and ultimately Jarvis told Eddie that he
should keep the car for a while. Most of the people I need to talk
to are down here in the vicinity of Louisiana, he said. I can use
my girlfriend's car. I'll pay the ticket.

Late the following spring, when Eddie had been in Minnesota for
a little more than a year, ten months after the phone call, Jarvis finally arrived to retrieve his vehicle. Over the course of an hour or
two, Jarvis brought Eddie up to date about the exposé. He read to
Eddie a section of an early draft of the five-part series that would
run in the *Chronicle*.

Few people ever showed up at Delicious nowadays, he said.
Sometimes, one of the Fusiliers' former business partners might
appear at the front gate, which the family kept locked in order
to prevent surprise visits. Any visitors who did make it in would
most likely have heard pathetic stories about the rapid downhill
trajectory of the finances at Delicious after the accident, about
the magnitude of the family's losses, about the strange atmosphere that seemed to have grown up along with the kudzu now
gamboling across more than a third of the company's vast acreage,
and so they would have prepared themselves to pity this family for

their financial ruin. For the perceptive ones, however, that feeling would likely give way to the inkling that in addition to the sad fate of this husband and wife and their once-prosperous farm, a peculiar and maybe sinister tone of negligence and corruption had not only overtaken the watermelon patches and tomato fields now growing more weeds than crops but also tiptoed up the steps behind every visitor, armed with the ability to disappear at the precise moment before it could be observed. Your head turned sharply and your eyes saw nothing, but the sense of a malevolent presence would linger for an instant, like a streak of glass cleaner evaporating from a mirror.

Eddie suffered the journalist and his elaborate metaphors and maintained a polite demeanor, but of course what he wanted most was to hear that his mother had come to her senses and would soon get free of that awful place.

She says she's running the farm now, he told Jarvis.

Really? Jarvis said. If that's the case, it isn't official. Or legal. But she does behave strangely during business meetings.

Is she going to leave there already? Eddie asked pointedly.

Eventually she'll have to, Jarvis said. But listen, I'm getting to it—I think she's doing something weirder, based on my interviews with some people who tried to do business with the company. Jarvis went on to tell Eddie that some of the powerful cigar-smoking men who arrived in the parlor would slosh their neat bourbon as they suggested that Sextus ought to sell off some of the farm to develop some sort of real estate interest—one guy wanted a hive of condos inspired by the design of the French Quarter, another had a proposal for an amusement park. Because of his condition, Sextus always received them downstairs, and they all noticed, after much longer than they thought possible, a backlit figure Sextus told them was named Darlene sitting in the adjoining room, at work on something they usually couldn't discern with any success, given the dim light, though they all reported hearing the clanking of metal parts against one another or the thump of a thick stick, of a long metal pole scraping the inside of a metal tube, or of a foot slamming against a rug in the background.

Oh, that's Darlene—cleaning my guns, Sextus explained. She's cleaning my guns.

From behind the visitors, Darlene occasionally coughed or laughed or cleared her throat, and at some moments these visitors thought they detected her making editorial comments on their proceedings in the parlor, although they immediately judged it impossible for anybody to have heard the conversation in the parlor very clearly from that vantage point. One guy said he thought he'd seen her over there pretending to level the barrel of the firearm directly at Sextus's head, and that at the same time he heard a tiny laugh reverberating against the ceiling.

All of the deals proposed in the parlor, as the guests would know, if any of them had spoken to one another, met with the same ambiguous fate. Sextus sometimes agreed to some aspect of his potential investors' offers, and the old men would draw up a tentative contract with the eager developer's legal team, but regardless of whether these fellows paid a down payment or a percentage of some kind to ensure the Fusiliers' bond, a period of immutable inertia and inactivity followed.

After word got out and a couple of investors sued, with partial success, to get their money back, the number of hopeful developers trickled down to only a couple of rubes from Ohio or, once, from Billings, Montana, all of them apparently having mentally cleared away the brush that strangled the acreage and imagined themselves at the center of a cattle farm where a mass of lowing livestock reached the edge of their vision in all directions, every cow aspiring in its heart of hearts to become a gross of Big Macs and feed whole families of egg-shaped travelers along American interstates.

I got some stuff from people who recently got out of there as well, Jarvis said.

One day toward the end of the previous summer, not long after Sextus arrived home from the hospital, Darlene enlisted a couple of workers to take him out toward the nearest field in his chair. First he marveled at the heat, then complained about it until they arrived at the barn, where Darlene instructed the guys to clean off and drive out the red tractor: his friend, the workhorse with a patina of rust along the tire rims that always fanned out slightly more every time they met. Sextus's pupils dilated and his face took on the expression of a good child at dessert time. Darlene made sure he had on an official Delicious baseball cap to keep the late-afternoon sun out of his eyes. Once the cap stopped his squinting, the heat didn't bother him anymore and he asked the helpers to move him closer, even though he knew they didn't have a choice. They positioned him atop the tractor seat as if he could still cut through untold acres of the farm in the way that had once kept his workers perpetually on guard.

It took three people to keep him there, one on the left and one right, holding his floppy hands up to the sides of the steering wheel and miming for him, in the style of certain types of puppetry, the action of driving, and a third behind him, using his belly for Sextus to rest his useless back against, like the trunk of a tree supporting a spindly vine.

In order to save on gasoline, they didn't even turn on the engine. Even so, Sextus said he wanted to stay out there all day. Ain't this the life, he said. This is living.

They helped him drink a can of beer. Hours went by. Toward sunset, he peered into the far distance as the horizon turned crimson and cool breaths of wind raised and lowered the collar of his shirt. Then he told the guys *I'm cold* in a tone of voice that seemed to mean both *I need to go inside now* and *I have been dead for a long time.* In the balmy southern breeze, the phrase seemed to mean everything except what it said. The guys lifted Sextus out of the tractor and into his chair, raised the chair into the van, and wobbled the short distance down the potholed road back home.

26.

CHRONICLE

That fall it mostly be cloudy, like the weather had got stuck on the mist setting. Damned if that ain't make it feel like the farm ain't had no connection to nothing out in the world, but that's how folks liked it up at Summerton. Almost two years done gone by since the breakout, and it seem like wasn't nothing gonna change no more, like the mist itself just confirming that shit.

Then this one morning, the voice of anchorpeople Jim Pommeroy and Gigi Risi start ringing out in the hallway as usual, only Elmunda took to shrieking over the noise of the TV set and the bitch would not stop. We was like, What the hell and it's only 6:30 in the goddamn morning? Darlene with Sextus on the downstairs porch, and she had finally got him to sit up in his damn chair by shoving a little block of wood under the back of his wheelchair wheel, and now it sound like Elmunda done fell and broke her tailbone.

But when Darlene gone upstairs into her bedroom to see what

the hell gone wrong, Elmunda pointing at the TV and shrieking her motherfucking head off, going, I heard my name! They spoke Sextus's name and they spoke mine! Of all the nerve! What did it say about us?

Darlene stood in the doorjamb catching her breath. It wasn't nothing unusual for Elmunda to be going berserk—everybody say her problems was mental and not physical—so Darlene ain't paid it no never-mind at first. Trying not to sound all snobby or whatever, she goes, They probably said something that sounded to you like your name and his, Ms. Elmunda. She had that tone down for dealing with the lady of the house. Apparently Elmunda ain't like hearing that explanation, and she clammed up and frowned at Darlene, then she turnt away, thinking 'bout God knows what. She come back with a less insane attitude, but it ain't take more than another few seconds for her to get all argumentative again.

Darlene still standing there, ready to smack down any of Elmunda's dumbass paranoid fantasies, if not the lady herself, but after a bunch of commercials for pharmaceuticals and remote retirement communities, and then a heart-tugging story 'bout a hippo and a wallaby that's in love at the Monroe zoo, the news recap done proved Elmunda right, and she mad as a damn wet hen again and start talking all surprised, like she ain't never realized that people they talked about on TV could also live outside the TV. Darlene thought, *She didn't even seem to hear what they said on the news. She's just reacting to the sound of her name and her husband's.*

Darlene herself known something like this gon happen sooner or later, but then her life had schooled her to believe that things she knew was gonna happen *wasn't* gonna happen. So she shocked that it happened right then, but deep down it ain't surprised her. It turnt out the TV news had picked up on a story out the *Houston Chronicle,* a five-part investigation piece based on the testimony of a man who call hisself Titus Wayne Tyler who had worked for Delicious Foods, a company that Jim Pommeroy said Tyler had made some startling accusations against.

Then the camera had went to Jarvis Arrow, and Darlene thinking, *I remember that man's face from somewhere.* Sometime she be having memory problems. The dude pushed his thick black eyeglass frames up on the bridge of his nose and he shaking his damn head while he talking 'bout Delicious, or at least *his* version of what gone down there. Then they showed TT face, and the face start talking 'bout the chicken house, and he rolling up his T-shirt to show folks how long the scars be up his damn side and cross his back, welts that be looking like ginormous worms glued to his skin. Health care? He laughed. We didn't get no kind of no health care. I laid up on my back with paper towels stuffed in my guts, biting a piece of a Styrofoam cooler to keep the pain down. Still can't walk right, can't breathe right out my nose.

Darlene did remember that, though. She thinking how that TT had had a good sense of humor the whole time he sick, how he laughing at folks who fussed over him, and how he done told everybody he ain't want no kinda special treatment and to treat his ass normal. But now he talking like this the worst shit that ever happened, and it sound like a outrage to Darlene, 'cause he saying it in front of the world. It felt like he telling family secrets to folks who not gonna give two shits. Darlene shouted at Jim Pommeroy to shut his goddamn mouth.

From downstairs on the verandah Sextus snapped at her and Elmunda to shut the hell up. The men in white coats gonna take both you heifers away, he yapped. He silent for a second, then he goes, On second thought, don't stop. That'd be the happiest day of my life.

Then TT start talking 'bout a woman who brung her son to the farm and he start working there before he even working age. That made the shame in Darlene's chest that been swirling around catch fire like a spark in a almost empty gas tank and she jammed down the mute button on the set, watching TT ugly lips curling around all them damn lies she could tell was lies without even hearing em. But inside, she known for a while that one these freaks gonna bring the operation to a end. She just wanna keep doing it her way, the way she already been doing it, taking it apart from the inside, and she got took aback that TT and Jarvis telling they side of it without saying shit to her beforehand. Now she thinking a whole bunch of official motherfuckers gonna drive up to the house and demand that she let em in and that she serve em; they gonna ask to sit down and want cups of coffee and tea and water and they'd be smoking up the house, but not the good stuff, and they gonna write down all the answers to all the hard questions, them questions that ain't nobody inside the place wanna hear, let alone be talking 'bout with a camera up in they face.

Darlene finger start inching over to the red power button on the upper left of the remote, and just when she 'bout to put it in place to press down, she seen Eddie face and shoulders show up on the screen. It's only a picture, but the sight of him make her dizzy, and she cringing backward and lower herself into a seat in the recliner right next to Elmunda sickbed. By now the lady's anger more like it's a ember instead of a open flame. Elmunda had locked her arms cross her chest and had twisted her damn mouth over to one side, but she so annoyed that she couldn't say nothing no more.

Darlene moved her ass up to the front of the chair, then cut her eyes and unmuted the sound so she could hear TT talking again. She had to admit that what he saying 'bout the barracks and the depot and all that shit ain't had no big-ass mistakes or untruths or whatever, but she couldn't stand to listen to him tell his experience nohow, stuff so close to her own life, and making em sound all harsh and disgusting; she bet that Jarvis fool had told him what to say and how to put the place down so that sympathies gonna pour in and everybody gonna agree with his point of view on Delicious. If he ain't stop, that stab wound he making into her past gonna keep slicing and getting all deep until it ripped open all the motherfucking memories she had went through during her time on the farm. They all coming back and stinging her like she done whacked a hornet nest: the good job she thought gonna erase all that shit she want me to help her forget, how she done lost her teeth, all the streetwalking with me, the stabbing, them boys with they beer cans, them yellow shoes, that goddamn piece of driftwood. Plus the way that she had put the last scrap of her faith in Delicious—all gentle, like she putting a baby chick that had fell out a nest back up in it—and once again the world had kicked her ass with a thunderstorm of bullshit and cruelty that knocked down the whole damn tree. If it had happened to some dumbass who be far away or not real, she thinking it almost be hilarious.

She couldn't hear nothing of the broadcast over her own thinking no more. When the news over, she got out her chair and left Elmunda almost steaming out her ears and tryna decide the next program to watch, skipping over channels and rejecting all of em with a grunt or a screech of hate. Darlene gone down that hallway with her arms all slack, looking at some shit couldn't nobody see right ahead of her, and when she get back to her room and shut the door, she goes boom right down on the bed and done took a glass pipe off her night table. She put me into it and lit up, and I smiled at her with no face and fizzed and popped like usual, filling up the insides of the pipe with some thick-ass smoke. I opened a door inside the smoke and she done came on in and run down a unreal hallway past a whole bunch of rooms in the mansion I built for her until she found one with a fireplace going in front of a warm couch with a soft fabric that made her pussy shiver when she runned her hands over it. I put a blanket down the end. She watching the smoke float through the room for a while, then she put the blanket around her shoulders and be tugging it tighter, all the way over her head.

Wouldn't you know that right after we had got all comfortable together and Darlene lying in my arms of smoke, some damn phone that she ain't seened on a stand next to the couch start ringing. Suddenly we back in the real mansion. She peek out from under the blanket and I told her not to answer no phone 'cause it ain't a phone I had put there but she done it anyway and heard voices inside the phone, asking all kinda tough questions and demanding to speak to anybody who living in the house. She telling them voices to go the fuck away but they kept after her ass until she put the phone down. Sextus and Elmunda son, Jed, come into the room, six years old, and he talking the same as the voice, he asking what's wrong with his folks in his li'l child-ass voice. Darlene could hang up a phone, but she couldn't hang up no kid, and she tossed a empty plastic bottle at him.

He dodge the bottle and come over to her. What happened, Miss Darlene? Why's Mama shouting?

Don't be ridiculous.

That's not a answer. Did something happen? They were on the television.

This child was a little bitch-ass detective.

Darlene thinking 'bout telling the truth, but I said, Hell no, you not telling this child the truth! She told him, Nothing is going to happen to you or your parents, Jedidiah. She said that shit instead of *Your parents fucked a whole lot of niggers over and they might could go to jail for a whole long time, so get ready.* You got to protect a child, I said, and the best way I know to protect a child is to lie your motherfucking head off. She tried to tell me some shit 'bout Eddie when he round the same age, and how she feel bad for lying to him about his father, but I was like, Please. She pulled the blanket back over her head.

While she still under the blanket, she saying, Don't worry, Jed. Jed kept worrying and asking questions but eventually he took her advice when she went, Okay, you can worry, but go worry somewhere else.

She blown out a sigh when the li'l boy finally disappeared. Even so, Jed had set her to thinking 'bout Eddie more and she decide for herself that it wasn't no way she gon let Eddie talk to Jarvis or TT 'bout nothing that had went down. What they done had exposed her ass and made them weird voices come out the phone and out the boy, and she called Eddie up, 'bout to chew his ass out. For the first seven or eight times the number wasn't the number and some angry fool started getting mean with her, like, Go away, bitch, go away, but she kept calling until the real number gone through.

She got Eddie on the phone and screamed like a train brake at him even though she ain't want to. I thought it would get through to him and make him stop investigating with that guy on account a Darlene had everything under control and she could take care of the farm and them people who running the farm without nobody else getting involved or telling the world all what had happened there with the folks who running the company.

Eddie tryna tell her to stay calm and that she ain't sound stable, like that she had hung out with me too much. He said some hurtful-ass shit to her, like that she too tight with me, and he asked point-blank if she had stopped hanging out with me, and even with me there, she said yes, 'cause I often told her that whenever any motherfucker accuse you of shit you ain't want em to be right about, you can't just admit that they accusation be true, you gotta fight the fuck back.

I am not an addict or a crackhead, Darlene said. I can't smoke as much because of the way I have to operate the place, so now I smoke mainly at night if I smoke at all. Sometimes I don't smoke for a full two days. And why is this any of your business?

Eddie laughed behind that one. I can't say I blame his stupid ass.

Then Darlene told him that he think he too good to come back to Delicious and to her so what did Scotty have to do with anything? She told him she gonna figure out a way to get back at him if he cooperate with the investigation. He insulted her again, apologized, then he start pleading with her to quit me until Darlene could hear his wimpy ass start to break down and cry on the phone. Seriously. Darlene done pulled the blanket up off her head and sat up and leaned forward. We thinking we had the advantage at last.

Both of em start screaming into the phone, and then Eddie hung up on her, so Darlene called back a few times and the angry man she called before on accident said some stupid shit 'bout a restraining order. Once Darlene got the number right, Eddie bitched me out and told his mother that she had stayed at Delicious on account of drugs and Sextus, and said some other shit 'bout what he thought she thought 'bout Sextus body, specifically his skin and the whiteness of it. There's a lot in here that Darlene don't remember, including a whole bunch of beefs that she howled and that Eddie screamed back at her, and then more voices on the phone, whatever.

Couple days later, Elmunda seen a picture of Darlene on the TV and she called Darlene in the room and they heard Jim Pommeroy talking 'bout what Darlene had said, her own words going onto the screen and a scratchy recording of Darlene voice over

335

the phone going, Nobody did anything wrong, and How dare you, and The truth will eventually come out, like it always does.

I said to Darlene, Your own motherfucking son done recorded your ass behind your back. That's fucked up. She froze; her jaw clamped. She couldn't even comprehend that shit.

Then we had to make all them strange people voices and the questions from Jed, and Eddie, and the angry-ass man stop coming through phones and televisions and faces and mouths around us, so me and Darlene just start booking down that smoky hallway I made for her fast as we could and slammed the door behind us. Darlene sat on the couch and then swung her legs up onto it, laid down lengthwise, and curled up into a ball. She wrapped the ends of the blanket round her feet like she a sapling 'bout to get planted. When she seen the phone still in the room, she sat up again and kicked the phone table so it toppled over and made a big thump sound on the floor. The phone be clattering and ringing at the same time when it hit the floor. Darlene yanked that blanket over her head again and I put my smoke arms around her, and me and her laid there till we couldn't hear no noise no more.

27.

TRIALS

While she putting everybody together that morning to go to the courthouse up in Oak Grove, Darlene feeling damn proud that it had took three years after them news reports for the in-vesty-*gators* (as Sextus called em) to get any crimes connecting him to Delicious. Turnt out Sextus ain't never run nothing called Delicious Foods, see, he had ran some shit called Fantasy Groves LLC that just subcontracted to Delicious and he told the law he ain't known thing one 'bout what Delicious done to nobody. Darlene less proud that she ain't spoke to her son much in all that time, but Eddie so fucking hardheaded, couldn't nobody talk no kinda sense to his ass.

It wasn't too many folks wanting to come forward and say nothing 'bout what had went down at Delicious. Unlike some folks, they ain't like the shame. Plus them detectives couldn't hardly find nobody to ask nothing. Folks said after TT and Sirius and Tuck beat him half to death, How hitchhiked back to Juarez, and nobody ain't heard nothing 'bout Jackie since she done left outta Monroe on a Greyhound bus. They got depositions outta Sirius, TT, Tuck, and Michelle, who made it off the farm after all, and that journalist, and of course outta Eddie, but Darlene wasn't part of nothing, she ain't even had to go to the trial at all 'cause they ain't name her name in the suit. Most everybody else wanted to put the whole thing behind they ass. On top of that shit, the Fusiliers still had a damn good name in Appalousa Parish and far too many sonofabitches up in that area owed em too much shit, based on like Great-Great-Grandpappy Phineas Graham Sextus loaning a sack of grits and a horseshoe to some po' white fool back in fucking 1843. Then shit kept getting mysteriously delayed and postponed, and certain folks on the prosecution side had had threatening calls made to they house and strange fires getting set in they garbage cans, and a Molotov cocktail done smashed through somebody picture window and burnt up half they house. Folks always tryna act like shit done changed, but don't nobody even *want* shit to change.

Darlene got everybody looking good to be up in that courtroom. She rubbed sweet-smelling wax in Sextus hair, stuffed that yellow handkerchief in the pocket of that dark suit she done got for him, made him look real fly, and when she lifting his legs in the cab and breaking down his chair small enough to go in the trunk, she thinking, *Too bad nothing works anymore,* and then she snuck a kiss under his earlobe made him grin like a fool.

I said to her, His tongue still work, but she act like she ain't heard that. She even polished Elmunda's crutches and steamed out one her wrinkly-ass dresses so old it had got stylish again as vintage clothes. Then she buffed Jed's Buster Browns or whatever. At the door, when the taxi had pulled up, Jed swiveled around to see Darlene in her Sunday best staying put on the porch, gripping the wooden support like she ain't going nowheres even if somebody tried to pull her away and stuff her in that cab. Gaspard gonna meet you at the courthouse and unpack everybody, she said.

Jed went, Come on, Miss Darlene, what you waiting for?

I'm going separate, she said. Run along now!

The taxi done a U-turn in the driveway and Darlene caught a glimpse of Elmunda looking up at the house, maybe at Darlene, her jaw all set, them eyes tight as a coin slot. Darlene let out a breath when she heard that gravel crunching under the tires switch to a loud engine noise and fade away down the hill. The intensity of the moment made it so me and her had to tiptoe upstairs for a little tête-à-tête, just to take that edge off, and by the time our taxi pulled up, we coulda sent it away and flown there ourself, we was so high.

We got to the courthouse real late, after the trial already been started, but that ain't bother neither of us none, since we didn't hardly wanna go in the first place. Once they let us in the building, seem quiet as a airport at four a.m. in there, Darlene shoes was clippity-clopping down that hallway just as loud. We sparked up again in the ladies' and lost our way to the courtroom, even though the place ain't had so many courtrooms. Darlene hoping she gonna catch Eddie outside and not sitting in the witness box or nothing, testifying 'gainst Delicious—maybe they could have a conversation and she could convince him to drop the charges. She kept seeing brothers she would think was him from far away and then get close and be like Oh, can't be him, he got hands. Just before we gone on in the right courtroom, she seen the security guard go inside and her heart went boom but I said, Darlene, calm the fuck down, they ain't gon drug-test you right here.

Darlene nerves had got stretched to the extreme before going into that courthouse—partly she worried she still gon get charged as a manager of the Delicious operation, but I told her that she ain't have to trip on that 'cause her name ain't showed up on none of the official documents. At least we ain't think so. She had did a smart thing and got herself paid as a caretaker, off the books, not as no partner in that ridiculous company. Couldn't nobody prove that she had ran the business the last few years, and if they tried, it would crumble into a their-word-against-hers kinda thing. I said, You ain't controlled nothing, you just had, I don't know, oversight. All you done was paid the bills and the groundskeepers, ain't let nobody buy the joint, and you done shrunk the farm down to something that kept just you and your bosses eating. They not gonna try to take you down with em. At least Sextus ain't gonna do that.

Besides, from day one she done changed the whole joint. The first morning back from the hospital with Sextus, she unlocked the chicken house, and at roll call she made a announcement to the whole crew that they was free to go.

I'm making some immediate changes, she told em. A certain criminal element made it so that people didn't feel they could leave here. I have informed Mr. Fusilier about that criminal element and we've taken care of it. Everybody filled in the blank that How and Jackie been responsible for the criminality, even though Darlene ain't explained.

To her surprise, motherfuckers ain't just immediately broke out into a run away from that madhouse.

A woman name Jequita went, What about my debt? I owe $942.22.

The debt was bogus, everybody, Darlene announced. Forget the debt. Today we start with a clean slate. From now on, we're going to pay you what *we* owe *you*. We're going to keep careful records. Real ones. You can keep staying in the barracks if you like—we're going to clean them up, too, and move the chickens somewhere else—but you can live wherever you want.

Darlene had em take that wheezing dog and his nasty-ass friend out the yard right then to make a show. Most everybody clapped. A couple folks done broke down weeping. But still ain't nobody runned off. Most people standing there with they mouth open, couldn't believe that shit. And why the fuck would they?

For real? said a man they called Taurus.

Another dude who went by the name Ripley went, Is this some kind of a trap?

For real, Darlene told em. Not a trap.

By sundown though, 'bout half them workers had packed up they shit and got on the road by they lonelies, braving that long walk to the next place in life, or back to they old haunts, without no kinda moneys. Another half be talking 'bout they didn't know where they might could go next but they gonna figure it out the next few days, and then you know that turnt into weeks. Me, I wasn't going nowheres, and the folks who stuck around on account a Scotty done figured that shit out but quick.

Darlene remembered her childhood experience on the farm outside Lafayette. She put that together with her business knowledge from the Mount Hope Grocery, and she start keeping good records of what folks done picked and what they was paid, which still ain't been much but it meant the world to a lotta them motherfuckers. They would come up and praise her ass like she Nelson Mandela or some shit. But Darlene ain't really had her heart set on turning Delicious around. She ain't want to make the goddamn place *profitable,* she just want to make it a honest day's work, to pay motherfuckers for what they done, to push that joint a hair closer to the thing Jackie had told her 'bout in the first place. If the farm goes broke, she thought, so be it.

When we walked into that courtroom, though, it felt like we had got to a wedding late—a bad wedding where the families be hating each other. We had the bad luck to walk in during a lull in the action, so a bunch of heads turnt 180 degrees to look at Darlene. The Fusiliers up front on the left, with they lawyer. Sextus turnt around and gave Darlene that helpless look of his, but she averted her eyes from that shit real fast. Behind them, toward the front, Hammer waving her over. He had quit the company right after Eddie done broke out and got hooked up with a different farm 'bout fifty miles away. Darlene ain't want to sit on the Delicious side. As she raising her hand to greet Hammer and beg off sitting with him at the same time, she seen what she thought could've been a ghost. A woman sitting toward back right, staring and leaning forward, probably tryna absorb every word of that damn trial. She wearing a suit and her hair parted in the middle with a pigtail on either side, a style Darlene recognized immediately. Darlene slid herself into the one empty bench right behind the woman but she had to get her bearings 'cause she ain't know for sure if I was fucking with her.

Michelle, she whispered, real loud.

My girl musta startled Michelle, 'cause she jump-turnt and put her left hand on the back of the bench. Darlene realized at the same moment that this well-dressed woman was Michelle for sure and that her right sleeve ain't had no arm in it; she had pinned the sleeve in half and let it flop around like a damn flag announcing the no-arm.

Amazement filled up her voice. You made it, Darlene said.

Just barely. Could you believe this trial? Can you believe it took three years to nail these sons of bitches?

No, I can't. I mean, I can, but it's not easy. I'm so glad to see you made it out.

Darlene had the impulse to lean over and hug her but ain't do it 'cause maybe it gonna offend a one-arm lady to hug? She had a ton of questions 'bout how Michelle had got free and had lost her arm, but the lost arm distracted her 'cause it reminded her 'bout Eddie, and she start searching the room with her eyes instead of asking. Finally she spot him up front right, sitting next to some proper-looking woman she ain't recognized, and a child she couldn't see too well, but from the way he touch the woman shoulder and sat the boy up next to him she got mad 'cause she figured they was a daughter-in-law and a grandchild she ain't never seen or heard of before in her life. It staggered her ass to imagine that she coulda got so separated from Eddie that he ain't never told her about no woman, no wedding, and no baby. I got mad myself. What the goddamn shit!

Darlene covered her eyes with the palm of her hand and get to thinking 'bout everything she ain't never wanna be thinking 'bout. She gripping her face like she gonna pull it off to show somebody else face be under there, maybe the real face she felt she been hiding. Then she took her hand down and looked at me—I guess you could say she looked *inside herself* at me—and I done recognized a expression I dread more than anything. Them big wet eyes said *I'm sorry*, them drooping eyelids said *I'm tired*, and that flat mouth said *I'm determined*. She blaming me for everything that happened and deciding she gonna break up with me. Naturally, I heard this a thousand times before, but that meant I could tell when a motherfucker really mean it.

I freaked the fuck out. Honey, I said—bluffing—give it some time. Like fifteen minutes. You gonna be crawling back on your stomach to get a hit. Slithering for my forgiveness. Let's watch this damn trial, okay? I ain't really wanna watch, but anything be better than a breakup in a courthouse.

Now it did seem real odd to me that them accusations against Delicious ain't had nothing to do with some shit the judge called Certain Irregularities Concerning the Recruitment, Treatment, and Compensation of Laborers, but that go to show how tough it was to take them Delicious motherfuckers down. The prosecution had went on a roundabout strategy instead.

So the lawyer—some motherfucker with saggy cheeks and old-school nerd glasses who be looking like a failed vice president—ain't said nothing 'bout tricking nobody into working for no company, or no jacked-up prices at no store, or no beating the bejeezus outta TT. He talking some shit 'bout how the bad sanitation up at Delicious done polluted the water supply with human waste, saying that Sextus and Jackie and How had lied to the IRS about the company income, and, of course, blaming em for having a interesting relationship with Yours Truly—the kind where they was sometime using me to compensate they workers. Which they still was doing some of. At that point I wanted to get up and leave—behind all the corrupt shit they was perpetrating up in that joint, *I'm* gonna get the blame *again?* And my best girlfriend gonna cut me dead? No, no, Joe! Motherfuckers was about to see a illegal drug go apeshit and burst into tears.

Otherwise, I don't remember much about the trial, I turnt off to it. Once all the rigmarole and legalese got said by the lawyers and the judges and whoever, like a lion saying grace before it eat your ass, and the prosecution side made their dumb remarks, Darlene zoned out thinking 'bout Eddie and changing her life, and I ain't want to face her new state of mind or the character assassination happening on me up at the bench. Judging folks ain't my bag—I guess I could understand why y'all does it, since y'all got bodies people could rape and kill, and possessions motherfuckers could jack, you got to figure out the histories and smack people with the it's-your-faults, but I get tired of that shit real quick. Who cares what happened in the past—for real! Y'all human beings has got enslaved to time, and that's why y'all need me, because just like Darlene y'all need time to stop rushing into the future or chaining your ass to the past. That's why this whole legal-system thing people got going hate me, call me a controlled substance and keep me from making friends with everybody, 'cause I know how to make time go away.

Eventually after all that blah-blah-blah up at the wooden desk, they gave our ass a lunch break. So I said, Darlene, honey, this whole deal so crazy-making, let's go to the ladies' room and kick it for a while. Maybe let's not even come back. Everybody waiting for Sirius to testify on account a he be a Texas celebrity now with his social rhymes, but he had came with a li'l entourage and split early. He wave to Darlene cross the room at one point and she waving back, and he mouthed some shit that look to her like *I'm sorry* but she couldn't tell. She mouthed back *Love your music* but she really only heard one song. Tuck snuck out the courtroom right on Sirius heels, probably desperate to beg him for a gig as a backup singer or some shit.

The top thing on Darlene mind was getting a opportunity to talk to Eddie. She had waved to Sirius, but she ain't feel like talking to him on account a he brought the whole trial on. It's all 'bout Eddie. So she start edging her way to the front, but a mad rush of people come out either side into the middle aisle, and my girl couldn't push through till they got done. She turnt around to go the long way, but two fat white ladies she ain't recognized, dressed in purple and pink, was sitting at the far end, fanning theyself and gossiping, and it ain't look like they gonna go nowheres without a airlift. When Eddie come down through the crowd, he on the far side from her, the woman and child walking closer, and right up next to Darlene be some tall white lawyer guys with big guts and watch chains keeping Eddie from seeing her and her from reaching across and grabbing his arm or even getting his attention. She called out his name and his neck done twisted round, but them lawyers still blocking his view. He kept moving like he ain't heard nothing but a echo from somewheres, but then he stop looking, and she ain't wanna shout, so she ain't said his name again.

Once the crowd thin enough for Darlene to get in the aisle, Eddie almost out the courtroom door. Next thing she know, somebody loud-ass voice up in her face yelling, Oh Lord have mercy, is that Darlene Hardison? And TT bear-hugged her like they was all good friends in the Delicious days, and he ain't ratted her out on the TV. Motherfucker wearing a pinstripe suit that ain't look bad considering all the ways she had seened him look before, but everybody from back then looked like new people to each other 'cause they had a bath, a haircut, and a decent set of threads. Some of em even had new damn teeth, and that made Darlene a li'l jealous.

Darlene told TT how good he look and he goes, It's like the Delicious Cotillion up in here—and he wouldn't let go her forearm until she had to turn around and excuse herself, saying that she ain't talked to Eddie yet and they ain't seened each other in a quite a while. TT put on a face that said *Why you hasn't seen your son?* but she ain't want to explain nothing, so she told him that there be more time to catch up later and she pushed past a couple people to get out the courtroom.

In the hallway I start getting tired of Miss D and I wanted to mess with her, dance her brain around a little, do a little mental foxtrot and shit. It's darker in that hallway than inside the courtroom and her eyes gone screwy and she couldn't tell who was who. She turnt in circles a couple time to get set, but she couldn't see her son nowheres. Then she spot a lady looked like the woman she seen with Eddie, but she ain't see Eddie or the kid they was with, and the woman had her back to Darlene. Darlene grabbed the lady by her upper arm and she spun around; you could tell she made a judgment on Darlene and her missing teeth on account a her face got tight and her shoulders squinched together.

At first Darlene ain't notice that the lady kinda flipped out, 'cause she still on a mission to find Eddie, so she grip on the woman arm even more, probably too tight, and goes, Are you the woman?

The woman yank her whole torso away from Darlene hand and go, What woman? I'm *a* woman, but I don't know if I'm *the* woman. Are you searching for a particular woman?

Darlene did not get to answer 'cause then she saw Eddie coming to em, leading the wobbly boy by the hand with his claw, and her attention gone over there immediately. Eddie looked up from the child face at Darlene and handed him off to the woman, who he called Ruth. The child climbed up on her and she balanced him on her hip.

Ma, Eddie said.

Darlene extended her arms for a hug—she feeling ready to forgive his betrayal and all that hardheadedness, 'cause she recognize how much he like her in a way. But he ain't extended his arms. Then she seen his claws and was like, *Maybe that's why he won't hug me?* She thinking 'bout not hugging, but changed her mind and hugged his non-hug so that at least one motherfucker be hugging somebody.

I thought you might come, he said. You didn't have to.

Oh my chicken-fried goodness, Ruth gasped. Mrs. Hardison! Ruth's attitude went poof and she got all sweet. I am so sorry! she said.

You look a lot different, Ma, Eddie said.

I told Darlene I thought he pretending not to say *worse*.

You mean better or worse? she asked, hoping to laugh off his comment.

Ruth broke up that weird moment by saying, Mrs. Hardison, I'm sorry, I did not recognize you.

Why would you, since we've never met? Darlene shot back

while she still staring at Eddie so there wouldn't be no doubt she blaming his ass for keeping his life a secret from her. I only just heard your name for the first time. Did he even tell you he had a mother?

So Ruth introduce herself as Eddie wife, and Darlene start giving Eddie a bunch of outraged grimaces behind all the shit she never heard from him 'bout Ruth and 'bout they life together. Every new piece of information be dropping like a brick on Darlene big toe. They ain't even get to the boy for a while, and it seem like Eddie start to guess that Darlene ain't gonna have a good reaction to meeting him, so he kinda stepped between Darlene and Ruth, who still got the child in her arms to hide him. But the kid so outgoing and everything that he lean around Eddie arm at one point and goes, I'm Nathaniel! Totally innocent of course 'bout what that name gonna mean to this lady he ain't even know be his grandma.

Soon as Darlene heard that name she grab Eddie by the arm of his suit so hard that it done made a li'l ripping noise and some strings done popped out the shoulder. Her face be quivering, she trying so hard to stomp down the agony she experienced when Nat said Nathaniel. She screamed, Eddie, you—how could you name—! And not tell me! She grabbing his suit jacket anywhere to shake him back and forth.

Eddie said, Ma, I didn't want you to know. The butt-naked honesty of that shit made Darlene close her mouth and flop her hands to her sides.

Ruth put Nat down and changed her stance like she gon have to escort Darlene out the building in a hot minute.

But then Darlene looked at me again, and she caught herself and stepped back from the three of em. She wiped her teary, mucusy face with a sleeve and covered her mouth with her fingers on either side, almost like she praying. Suddenly they was a trinity to her, some sacred folks who had managed to turn they rotten life into something got value, and she blamed herself for failing to do that shit in her own life. And when she understood that they was prepared never to let her into they life, she took a gaspy breath like she 'bout to drown.

It ain't too often that the mother look at the child and get schooled, and that brung on a whole nother tornado of shame to Darlene. She seen how spiderwebby and delicate that connection be between any two people, even when they blood, and how bad she had fucked with it far as Eddie concerned, like it ain't meant nothing to her. For one second she could truly see his side of things, and it be like everything inside her turnt to mud and slid from her head to her foot and she become a monster to her own self. She seen the fear and disgust and judgment in the eyes of her unknown family, this woman and child and the son she ain't really knowed no more, and them feelings done filled up the hole where love and respect and trust oughta gone. By that point, li'l Nat don't understand what the hell he done wrong and he start wailing.

Scotty, Darlene said to me, it's over.

And I knowed her ass wasn't kidding, neither. But I am a badass drug with a reputation for keeping the loyalty of my friends and lovers in a very tight grip, so I laughed at her—a long, nasty, spiteful, smoky laugh—praying that all my ridicule gonna keep her from knowing that without her, I would lose all my strength. She was in my head, too, though, and this time couldn't nobody fool her no more, not even me.

28.

ALMOST HOME

I was experiencing hellacious withdrawal symptoms—after so long, I couldn't function without Scotty, and I used a few more times before I could honestly say I quit. I had no health insurance and I knew I needed to find a free clinic in order to truly detox and finally tear myself free of the drug. It turned out that the nearest place was in Shreveport. When I let Elmunda know that I had decided to get off drugs and move there, she said, Shreveport! as if she had opened her purse and a palmetto bug jumped out. Didn't even congratulate me for kicking my habit. I chose not to argue with her about the merits of Shreveport, since it still meant a lot to me.

At the end of the trial, Sextus had received a fifteen-year sentence for selling drugs and polluting the water supply, and a fine of five thousand dollars for financial restructuring. The court banned him and his family from the agriculture business for life, and the high legal fees required the Fusiliers to sell a large portion of the farm's acreage. I stayed out of the brouhaha to the extent that I could, because I'd finally admitted to myself that my desire for Sextus depended mostly on my perception of his power as well as my need for Scotty. The Fusiliers went through a great deal of infighting and agony as Sextus steeled himself to do hard time and Elmunda and Jed prepared to move to a smaller house with Elmunda's great-aunt in Baton Rouge, closer to where Sextus would be incarcerated. They put the majority of their belongings in storage and cleaned up Summerton, hoping to rent it out for weddings and family reunions. Elmunda wore herself out trying to contact somebody who could make what she kept calling *a computer page* for the home and its grounds.

Though I felt no obligation to assist her, and she put up a confusing amount of resistance to my efforts, I found her a new caretaker before her move to Baton Rouge. When she said that she would miss me, I doubted her sincerity to the point where I had to stifle a laugh. On the other hand, I believed Jed when he said the same thing, and when he wept over his father's upcoming departure, I wept as well, but maybe not for the same reasons. The withdrawal was racking my body with seizures and sweating, I was constantly anxious and paranoid—at one point I had myself convinced that I would actually die within the hour without a hit. Just about anything could make me weep.

I arranged to move my own belongings with a local guy who had a van, and when I left Summerton, I did try to turn around and take a moment to appreciate everything I had experienced there, but the thick kudzu that had grown up around the farm obscured the view. I couldn't see the place at all.

In Shreveport, not many folks have the stamina to go running in the midafternoon even during the spring and fall, and very few—only the extreme types—can tolerate running in the triple-digit heat of midsummer, which could leave the most seasoned athlete dried out like a worm at the side of the road. But it's possible to get in a few sweaty miles during the early-morning and late-evening hours. Once I finally got sober, I instituted a regular exercise routine for myself, one of many good habits I established in the first six months after I left Scotty behind. I also quit smoking, which I found almost more difficult than detoxing from crack cocaine.

But I had always gathered strength from this city, and even though everything else in my life had changed drastically, I still could find, tangled somewhere in its grassy blocks and stooping live oaks, the person I had once known I would be, and traces of the husband I lost. I felt this most strongly whenever I stumbled across a diner that served undercooked grits the way Nat liked, or when I stood on the sidewalk in front of the place we had once lived on Joe Louis Boulevard, where Eddie had been conceived, or if I touched the gas lamp outside the Renaissance Bed & Breakfast (which had not changed at all) and looked up to imagine our shadows still crossing the window frames. One Saturday afternoon, not long after I got to town, I took a walk over to Centenary on what turned out to be graduation day. From the far side of Dixie Road I tearfully watched all the children in their black robes and square graduation hats streaming down the stairs and out of Gold Dome, then snuck into the rapidly emptying building myself. In the foyer, as I peered at all the basketball trophies Centenary had won during Nat's day—especially with his friend Robert Parish—I could've sworn that I felt Nat touch my shoulder. Once I entered the court, I heard Nat's proud, silky voice echo over the shiny floor and up to the spectacular roof that sheltered the bleachers like a space-age quilt.

In comparison to the almost supernatural comforts that

Shreveport gave me, I sometimes thought of my program as bland, but Tony, my sponsor from group, had recently reminded me, and everybody else, that party people think only self-destructive activities are pleasurable and exciting; everything else bores them. The mundane parts of my day had become vital, and so had my acceptance of the past, though the latter sometimes stunned me into silence or tears, and both—the mundane present and the sorrowful past—now had to keep me straight, each one like a rope thrown to me from a boat while I thrashed around in a cold, churning river.

When I moved here, just two months after the trial, I decided on a complete renaissance for myself. No more unhealthy living. I had to emphasize fresh food, exercise, and moderation, like it said in the natural-foods sections in gigantic supermarkets I'd only recently started paying attention to, because my life depended on it. The thought made me imagine wooden grocery-store signs above my head, painted with pictures of celery and beefsteak tomatoes with smiling faces, and the idea made me laugh—another beneficial habit, as Tony and the rest often restated at the six p.m. daily meetings downtown. I started keeping a journal. I didn't need the book anymore either, not with so many new friends living its principles right in front of me. Where had the book gotten me anyway? Delicious, that's where.

Every morning, I rose at five, even if I didn't have the energy—*especially* if I didn't—and cut apples or cantaloupe directly into a particular oversize white porcelain bowl I'd found at a thrift store. The bowl had a pleasing smoothness to it, like a good set of teeth. I'd spoon yogurt over the fruit and sprinkle it with granola, though not too much, since I don't like the way granola sticks in my molars and would rather not spend half the time jogging with my finger stuck in the back of my mouth, trying to dislodge oats. Some days, when I wanted to reward myself,

I'd squirt a little honey over the whole mixture before folding its contents together. I would always think about the people whose hands had touched those apples and that cantaloupe before I ate. Sometimes, at the supermarket, I asked questions about the growers that nobody could answer, and eventually the stock boys started to hide when they saw me coming.

I learned to smile with my mouth closed during job interviews, and in that way I managed to secure a waitressing gig on the other side of Queensborough, at a family place called Quincy's that featured a phenomenal all-you-can-eat barbecue buffet popular with—let's just say, the area's largest men and women. The program required me to take a job as a way of reentering the straight world—it wasn't a job you were supposed to like, just a means to an end, but I happened to enjoy the atmosphere. Morton the Manager, as they called him, was a doughy-faced, empathic gay man who joked around with everyone, the waitresses in particular, and created a warm feeling of community for the staff, a group of smart-mouthed, hardworking women I identified with and admired, even though I often wondered what they said about me behind my back. My acceptance of the job sometimes enabled me to see beyond the present to some latent ambition I had previously expressed only by dating men I considered leaders, and I felt I had something to offer others myself, if only my difficult cautionary tale or the suggestion that if I could survive these experiences, anybody could.

Still, I had life issues to concentrate on before I could think too far ahead. First, I saved up to get my dental implants. Then, after several weeks of rice-and-ketchup suppers, I had put aside enough, if I stretched it, to move out of the program's quarters and rent an upstairs apartment at the Villa del Lago, opposite Cross Lake. The advertising for the place—*Surrounded by beautiful landscaping and all the comforts and luxuries you de-*

sire—looked a lot better than the place itself, but this time I hadn't expected anything much. The brown-and-tan two-story complex resembled a neglected Spanish-style motel from the days when Nat and I first came to Shreveport, but that didn't bother me, considering the kinds of places I'd lived in the recent past. In the courtyard, though, many of the apartments looked out over the small pool, with a good portion of the oblong lake shimmering just beyond it. Mine had a view of one of the wooded interior courtyards, but I could easily visit the pool, with its lake-side view. To me this felt like the kind of place that Jackie had promised they were taking me the night I got in that stupid van.

The Villa del Lago somehow made humility seem elegant. I felt a kinship with the place—we'd both seen better days, I knew, we could use some sprucing up, but something essential and beautiful about our inner construction would never disappear. I didn't much like the clattering racket and loud horns of the freight trains that passed only a few yards away even late at night, but they were part of what made the apartment cheap, and I got used to them. I thought I might start to find them romantic after a while, those resounding whistles floating over the land in the earliest hours of the morning, like the howling of lonely animals.

On the particular morning I'm remembering, once I finished my breakfast, I slid into a pair of shorts and tugged a sports bra over my head, the first one I'd ever bought. I liked how tightly the Lycra blend hugged my upper body. I adjusted the under-seam against my sternum, pulling it forward and making a thwap sound on my skin, then pulled my shorts above my underwear. I swung open my front door to a humid blast of morning air and descended the stairs to cross the parking lot.

As inviting as everybody found the water, Shreveport was a fish-in-the-lake city, not a jog-around-the-lake city, and they hadn't put in a path for running along the shore—you might try

dancing up the wooden ties, football player–style, on the stretch
of railroad that kissed the east side of Cross Lake on its way to
Mount Pleasant or Dallas, but that did not seem realistic. Instead
I crossed Milam Street and made a loop east of the lake, on an
old path partially submerged in dirt and dandelions.

That day I had decided to be ambitious and take a more challenging route farther away from the lake, four miles in total, as
opposed to my usual three. As I passed the local high school, a
hint of dizziness entered my head. That didn't bother me at first.
The beginning of any run always made me short of breath, and
I became conscious of my heart jiggling against my rib cage like
a water balloon. I wiped the sweat off my forehead and spat and
breathed in through my nose and told myself, *Keep going.* My
tongue seemed to swell in my mouth, though, and my left arm
tingled uncomfortably.

I looped around the high school, turned back in the direction
of the lake, and ran toward a bowl-shaped embankment with a
group of trees and a telephone pole. A huge convention of grackles had gathered there, as usual for that time of day, chittering
and squawking in their peculiar way. The tingle in my arm became a throb. With all I have been through, I laughed to myself,
one morning jog is not that much to bear. I gathered strength by
thinking of Eddie and Ruth and little Nathaniel, how they would
someday see me at my best and bring me back into the family.
I was curious to know what my best even looked like! My heart
wobbled and my head felt light as I thought of the joys ahead.
Thanksgivings and Christmases together. Thoughtful gifts, homemade potato salad, loving embraces.

At the same moment I reached the point where Ford Street
parted ways with Route 173 and the sidewalk abruptly ended in a
lawn, a semi barreled around from the left and nearly blindsided
me. The truck sounded its implausibly loud horn, startling not

just me but hundreds of those birds, who collectively fluttered into the orange sky like flecks of charcoal rising from a campfire, as if the deafening noise had broken some invisible force that had bound them to the trees. I leapt back from the street almost involuntarily and jogged in place for a second, regaining my composure. I looked both ways down the street twice before crossing. Shaken, winded, I took a deep breath and found it shallower than I'd expected. *Keep going,* I told myself, *no matter what.* I set my jaw and swallowed the trembling surge that rushed from my chest into my head, inflating the veins in my temples, stealing my breath. My windpipe constricted, and a sharp pain spiraled up my left arm, but I didn't consider stopping. *Can't give up now,* I said to myself. My eyes narrowed as I peered down the street to where the asphalt seemed to come together. *I'm almost there,* I thought. *Almost home.*

Next thing I knew, I was regaining consciousness in a bright green room with a tube in my arm and another in my nose. I heard machines behind my temples, buzzing and chiming. A nurse poured water into a plastic tumbler and asked me if I wanted a glass of water. I nodded, or tried to nod, anyway. As she lifted the glass to my lips, it occurred to me that my life had just gone into overtime.

29.

DAYDREAMING

Eddie heard thirdhand about his mother's heart attack after a friend from her program found Bethella's number and called her. Despite Darlene's six months of sobriety, and her frequent pleas, through Eddie, for amnesty, Bethella still refused to speak to her sister, but she passed the information on to Eddie, who decided to visit. It wasn't that his newly expanded hardware store had begun to make a profit and left him feeling flush enough to spring for a plane ticket, it was that the news had given him a number of unnerving premonitions: that his mother might not survive, that she might not *want* to survive, and that she might die alone. Although he had only the name of the hospital to go on, and though his one phone call to her room had gone unanswered, he flew to Shreveport anyway.

He found his mother sharing a room with a high-school girl also recovering from heart surgery—an athlete, by the looks of the sports-themed decorations around her bed, which sat on the window side of the room, where hazy brightness spilled in through the vertical blinds. The girl or her family had taped greeting cards all over her headboard and pinned many more to the wall; arranged a line of plants on the windowsill, their pots wrapped in colorful foil; left shiny gift bags littering the floor, the chair, the food tray. Above the bed, a banner told her GET WELL MINDY in metallic block letters.

The corner-store daffodils Eddie had brought, their silky white petals supporting orange cups, seemed clownish by comparison. On Darlene's side of the room, the bluish curtain remained half closed, blocking most of the small amount of light her area received, and the only objects in her vicinity were a glass of water on the nightstand and a phone. She had an oxygen tube under her nose, and the monitor beside the bed whirred quietly.

The differences between the two sides of the room suggested to Eddie that his mother had tried, in her usual fashion, to tough it out by herself, doing it her own way without admitting how often her own way went express to Failure. At this late date, it would seem cruel and pointless to harp on her self-destructive patterns; by now even to her they must have felt as obvious as a freight train barreling toward a car stalled on the train tracks. The bare room meant either that Darlene had called no one or that she had, but no one cared. Eddie wasn't sure which was the sadder scenario.

Only when he stepped across the threshold, though, did he feel as if he'd made a mistake. That surprised him, since he'd had so much time to consider his options, his motives, and the possible reactions of his mother.

Her initial response did nothing to reverse his self-consciousness. She lay back in bed, absorbed in a rerun of *Family Feud* on the wall-mounted television, and, when she recognized that Eddie had entered the room, she raised herself slightly with the automatic button by her side and shimmied into an upright position, stiffening her spine. Her body language suggested puzzlement rather than joy.

She glanced at him from beneath lowered eyebrows and said, You couldn't call?

He stopped at her bedside and laid the flowers on a chair. He rested his metal prostheses against the bars at the foot of the bed, making a noise like a service bell. For an instant, the festive atmosphere on Mindy's side of the room caught his eye again. Mindy herself lay on her left side, face toward the window in a patch of sun, peroxide-blond hair brilliantly glistening in the light, snoring like the engine of a small car. His eyes returned to his mother and he focused on the distance between his mechanical pincers and the bare soles of her feet. He could already feel himself becoming angry at the thought that she might turn him away after he had made so much effort to see her, but the glance at the other side of the room had reminded him of Darlene's loneliness, and he thought that she might not decide to send him away for failing to announce his arrival if he could find a way to cure that loneliness without calling any attention to it.

I did, he told her, choosing his words carefully, but no one picked up the phone.

Oh, she said. Well, then. I'm glad you're here, but I didn't want anybody to see me this way. This is not ideal. Without moving, she indicated with her attitude that it would be okay for him to approach and sit beside her, and that while she might not approve of him interrupting the television, which had switched to *Jeopardy!*, they might begin to have an elementary conversation.

Eddie edged his way to the chair by the side of the bed and sat in it at what he determined was a comfortable distance. I heard what happened, he said. You're feeling better. He realized that he'd sat on the flowers, and he raised himself on his haunches enough to move them to the nightstand. A few of the blooms were still intact.

She laughed, and through her laughter asked him not to make her laugh because laughing hurt. If I started feeling worse, I would've died, Eddie. The statement did not strike Eddie as humorous but bitterly true. He felt guilty that he'd destroyed the daffodils. He watched the television and said nothing for a few moments to allow the moment to pass.

Your smile's looking good! he told her.

She brightened up and demonstrated her restored teeth. Why, thank you! she said. You came all the way from Minnesota. Where's the family?

They stayed back. It seemed like the best idea.

Because why? Darlene asked. Are you ashamed to—

No, no. Expenses and everything. Ruth's working, Nat has preschool.

Nat, she said, and when she said the name it sounded to Eddie like she had addressed her husband rather than his son.

She asked when he would let her see young Nat, and while Eddie should've expected to hear the question, he found himself caught off guard a second time.

Obviously, she said, I'm not going to be around forever. I might not be around next week. We're letting too much time go by.

Eddie struggled to find a proper response without lying and once more resorted to silence. There was no way he could try to set guidelines at that point—to do so seemed both premature and overdue, it would be neither useful nor logical. Maybe she had meant to put him on the spot. He could feel it now between them more clearly than ever before in life, an ominous sense of time as an enormous set of gears, each generation interlocking with the ones on either side, all of them forced to react by turning each other in opposite directions.

———

Occasionally speaking over Alex Trebek, they embarked on a rudimentary, halting conversation about the most recent months of their lives. Darlene emphasized her significant time living clean and sober and incorporated many familiar homilies that she credited with getting her through the roughest parts of her recovery and her new life. Fake it till you make it, she said. One day at a time. She returned so frequently to the principles of the program, in practically the same way she had hewn to the precepts of the book, that Eddie couldn't help doubting her. Everything she said reminded him of the book, which made him remember the urine-soaked barracks and the sweltering fields of Delicious Foods. Surely she knew the truth, which was that only time could prove she had conquered all of the terrible patterns, the vicious cycles whose pains he could still feel in his phantom fingers.

Remember Sirius B? Darlene suddenly asked.

Not very well, Eddie said. But you were involved with him, weren't you?

I still daydream about him sometimes, she said.

It seemed like a girlish confession, a chamber of her personality that his mother rarely opened.

He was a very interesting guy, Eddie offered. From what I hear, he's doing well in the music business.

I did a lot of daydreaming back at Delicious, Darlene said. You had to. Especially in the fields on those details. She didn't turn away from the TV.

Eddie allowed her to define what she'd done as daydreaming, choosing not to argue. *Daydreaming,* he thought. *If only.*

Like everybody, she said, she figured out a way to keep her attention focused just enough to accomplish whatever task she'd been assigned, so that her mind could travel in any direction it pleased even if they would not allow her body to follow. She told Eddie that she often found herself disappearing to a strange episode she had shared with Sirius one diamond-clear evening. The sun had tipped over the horizon and turned the land in the west into a velvet silhouette, while off to the east, the sky had become a navy blue felt blanket shot through with pinholes, all of them mysterious—was each one a distant home? A streetlamp? A high, oblivious airplane? Some celestial event?

We knew without having to be told, Darlene said, that we would have to work overtime, into the night. The managers never turned on the work lights until the very last possible moment. How's main purpose in life was to make sure Delicious never went over budget.

Eddie laughed in agreement and said he remembered that.

His mother sought out his hand and looked down when she found his prosthesis instead. An unspoken shame for having momentarily forgotten the past seemed to radiate from her; she skipped over the apparatus, and her fingers made gentle contact with the skin of Eddie's forearm.

It's okay, he said. *Forgiveness never ends,* he thought to himself. *Either it's a bottomless cup or it's nothing. Black—no milk, no sugar.* Come up next month, Ma. I'll take care of the airfare. Immediately he chided himself for having made this offer before clearing it with Ruth.

Really? she said.

Maybe I'll make dinner for you and Ruth and Nat, maybe Bethella will come by.

Let's not go too fast! she exclaimed at Bethella's name.

Darlene locked eyes with her son. Eddie tried not to smile or cry. The longer they held this look, the more it expanded, seeming to contain everything—the events of their past as well as the consequent emotions: pain, joy, betrayal, estrangement, love, hate. Then the moment blew like an overloaded fuse.

She spent a moment trying to remember the subject of their

conversation, then said, Sirius! So me and Sirius, we turned into a couple of black blobs out there that night, squatting to pick straw-berries, turning invisible.

The moon hadn't come up yet. In that sable darkness they found an advantage. Sirius knelt in the dirt behind her to rest, an act that, had How seen it, would've earned him a severe rep-rimand. He had stopped picking anything in favor of shaking the vines in order to make a noise that sounded like work. Darlene stopped too and raised her hand to wipe her brow and take a whiff of the strawberry residue that coated her fingertips, the only plea-sure the job had to offer, and a dubious one at that, given the stickiness that accompanied it. In the midst of his rustling, Sirius quietly begged her to join him, and she inched her way in his di-rection, still squatting, duck-style. By this time, the dusk glowed a striking pink stroke against the black of the distance, and stars revealed themselves like champagne bubbles along the inside of a vast fluted glass. When she arrived at his side, placing her hand on his sweaty back through the cutout sleeve of his shirt, he pointed out various constellations, the centaurs and scorpions in the sky that she had never quite believed in.

He explained to her again the concept of light-years: light trav-eled six trillion miles in one of our years. Somehow that sounded slow to her. She found it disturbing and difficult to fathom when he repeated that the starlight they saw that night had really hap-pened hundreds of years in the past and only reached their eyes that day. It offended her that the past could intrude so literally on the present yet never return. It made her think of everything in her own past that had brought her to Delicious and that she wanted to reverse, and how the light from the stars had come from long before the time she had been with her son, even from before the time when Nat had been alive. Only then could she faintly accept the romance of it; of human beings, all by themselves on a wet rock in an outpost of a universe whose size they couldn't comprehend, staring into the heavens to make primitive pictures in the air based on lights that might not even exist anymore. And one of these days all of it would disappear, at least the way Sirius described it: space would collapse, the planet would get torn apart by a comet, the sun would fry the solar system with a supernova, some catastrophe would obliterate human history and civilization. We'll be lucky, he said, if our bones become somebody else's fossils.

Darlene absorbed all of this information from him but could find no hope in it whatsoever. Why, she asked, if all these small things we do, all this work that gets dumped on us day after day, if all our love and our attachments mean absolutely nothing and everything will eventually get incinerated, why do we bother to do anything? Is there any reason to keep on living? Is that why it's better to smoke our lives away, why oblivion and death seem to call to us continually, like they're summoning us home? How do we do it? How do we go on?

Before Sirius could respond, How turned on the lights, a pair of those bright white spotlights mounted on stands in clusters of six, and unleashed the type of dazzling illumination you might normally find on a Little League field in a suburban town. The two of them must have felt electrocuted. They froze for an instant, then their limbs unclenched, and as if falling out of the cosmos, they reset themselves to the task of foraging in the low plants and vines and dirt to find unbruised, pristine specimens and gently place each berry into one of the small boxes they carried for that purpose.

So I never got to hear his answer to the question, Darlene said. I found my way, but I wanted to know what he thought.

I reckon I heard the answer, Eddie said, and he began to relate how during Sextus's trial, he and Sirius had gone with Michelle and a couple of people on the prosecution team—a lawyer and a young clerk—to a diner a few blocks down the road, the kind that looks like an Airstream trailer, wrapped in aluminum that's been polished and faceted into diamond shapes, flooded inside with that pleasantly unpleasant odor of many years of hot bacon grease. Somewhere in the course of a freewheeling conversation, loosened by the sense that the team no longer had a chance of losing the case and by the solid beams of sun chopping through the space, the clerk turned to Sirius and questioned him about his escape the way someone young and brash would.

The slim kid had on a short-sleeved shirt with a light blue grid pattern, exactly like graph paper. The energy in his body looked like life when he turned his whole torso to ask Sirius, How the hell did you get through all that?

Sirius laughed for a second, and so did Michelle, then a sober expression crept over his mouth and into his eyes. But his answer had already taken too long for the clerk.

I mean, what kept you going? Like, I got snowed in without electricity for a couple of days in a friend's cabin in Colorado, all by myself, and I spent half the time on my knees praying to the Lord until the rescue came through. Wrapped in five blankets, of course.

I went through that phase, Sirius said, nodding. The Lord didn't do shit.

Everybody paused awkwardly at his casual dismissal of the kid's religious faith and stared at Sirius waiting for further elaboration. Michelle stirred sugar into her coffee, her spoon jingling against the mug.

The Lord turned out to be just another story, Sirius continued. After that one, he said, I told myself the story of my family's devastation should I pass, but that was a joke too—their devastation would have lasted about as long as a commercial break.

He changed that into a desire to live for some dream of a future family of his own, he said, or for his music to outlast him, for some legacy that might help him live beyond his life, but those were all stories too. It turned out that all stories betray you when you're down to chasing crickets to get your next meal. A story might help you get through your life, he said, but it doesn't literally keep you alive—if anything, most often people who have power turn their story into a brick wall keeping out somebody else's truth so that they can continue the life they believe themselves to be leading, trying somehow to preserve the idea that they're good people in their small lives, despite their involvement, however indirect, with bigger evils. He said he often thought about the people who were going to eat the strawberries and lemons and watermelons he picked for Delicious, about what those folks would look like, how they might peel the fruit, how the fruit would taste, maybe about the fruit salad they would make, or the pie.

But I'm sure they never thought about me, Sirius said. No, not from behind that brick wall.

After a while out there in the wilderness, Sirius said, the myths and faiths and social everythings stopped meaning anything to him. The survival instinct took over from the day-to-day fairy tales he'd needed when all of them worked for Delicious, and something essential in his brain turned him back into an animal. And there he was, catching fish with his bare hands, navigating by smell, bathing in the rain. Sirius quit asking how he could go on, Eddie told his mother. He had to survive. He had to live. He was free.

ACKNOWLEDGMENTS

For their help, love, and support, the author would like to kiss Brendan Moroney, Ben George, Doug Stewart, Clarinda Mac Low, Kara Walker, Jennifer Egan, Helen Eisenbach, Colleen Werthmann, Timothy Murphy, Alvin Greenberg, John Bowe, Marcelle Clements, Andrew May, Michael Agresta, Brian Parks, Gregory Cash Durham, David Hamilton Thomson, Daniel Clymer, Jen Sudul-Edwards, Joshua Furst, Christopher and Kathleen Moroney, Rosa Saavedra, Laura Germino and the Coalition of Immokalee Workers, Greg Schell, Marla Akin and John McAlpin, Patrick Adams, Carina Guiterman, Fundacíon Valparaíso, the Corporation of Yaddo, the Constance Saltonstall Foundation for the Arts, the MacDowell Colony, the Blue Mountain Center, the Port Townsend Writers' Conference, Ledig House, and his scuzzy former office, ISC 310, at the Pratt Institute.

ABOUT THE AUTHOR

James Hannaham is the author of the novel *God Says No,* which was honored by the American Library Association. He holds an MFA from the Michener Center for Writers at the University of Texas at Austin and lives in Brooklyn, where he teaches creative writing at Pratt Institute.